THE BAY OF HOUNDS

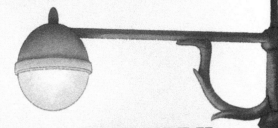

WHISKERS IN THE DARK

THE BAY OF HOUNDS

NICK SMITH

4 Horsemen
Publications, Inc.

Published By: 4 Horsemen Publications, Inc.

4 Horsemen Publications, Inc.
PO Box 417
Sylva, NC 28779
4horsemenpublications.com
info@4horsemenpublications.com

Cover Illustration by Oxford
Cover Typography and Typesetting by Autumn Skye
Edited by Kris Cotter

Library of Congress Control Number: 2024948142

Paperback ISBN-13: 979-8-8232-0724-9
Hardcover ISBN-13: 979-8-8232-0725-6
Audiobook ISBN-13: 979-8-8232-0727-0
Ebook ISBN-13: 979-8-8232-0726-3

"The Isle of Dogs harbors so much friendship, loyalty, and obedience—sometimes too much."

—Julius Kyle

"Cats are not born gamblers; every decision they take in life is a considered, careful, well-judged one. Placing bets on a one-in-a-million chance is not the feline way. The Book of Fingus says as much: 'He who places faith in the gods of the dice loses all hope of salvation. He has no place at Bastet's side.'"

—Bishop Kafel, High Priest of the Church of Bastet

"In case you're wondering, fellas, I'm not on the menu. *Anybody's* menu."

—Sal the catnip addict

"Dogs. What can I say about them that ain't been smelled before?"

—Lugs the soldier

"Keep an eye on me. I never know what I might do."

—Zehra the hermit

"I know what's wrong with you! Your kitten breath."

—Cheveux the barber shop poodle

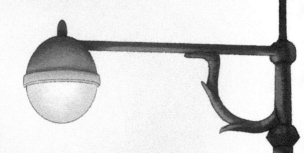

Acknowledgments

Thank you to my Mum for transcribing a portion of this book, to Ros and Sam for their support, and to Erika Lance for her encouragement and enthusiasm.

Catknowledgments

Murder Mittens, a cat who stayed with the author for a while, left the following message for readers:

/';;;;;43\
] QW

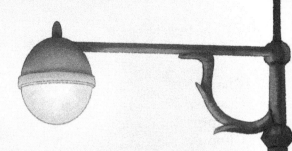

Table of Contents

PART FOUR: RETURN TO BAST

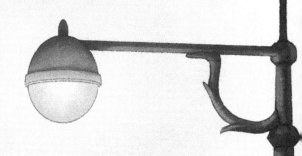

Part One: Cruel Inventions

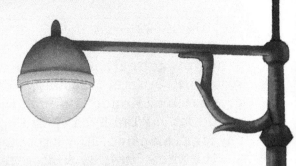

Prologue

We Interrupt
This Broadcast

"This is Scratch, your DJ with the flea spray bringing you all the newest news from Bast, the city run by cats—or is it?

"Mayor Otto Canders, his son Mowbray, and Otto's mom, former mayor Bridget Canders, are all missing and they've been gone for a long time. It's time to suck up the power vacuum and pick a new political figure! Yeah, 'tis the season for an election, the likes of which we ain't seen since my pops was a little kitten. The Canders dynasty stretches waaay back, a pride of lions ruling our city with an iron claw. And hey, maybe it's time to let sleeping lions lie and give us regular cats a chance to run the show.

"Who you gonna choose? Will it be civil servant Woodrow Cormer? Security officer and former prowler Joey Hondo? Or business magnate and all-round fat cat Tad Tybalt? Tad's got the moolah to pay for a campaign, Joey's got the looks, Woodrow's got the know-how. By winter we'll have a winner. Unless that lazy lion Otto comes back with a roar and beats them all. Happy voting!"

—WOTW radio broadcast
By DJ Scratch

1

Got Milk?

All Julius wanted was a pint of milk. He'd stayed up too late, as usual, working on a freelance piece for the local paper, *The Scratching Post*. Better to get it done, he'd reasoned, than go to sleep and extend the agony of writing for another day. He'd finished the article, but now he was paying the price of skipping sleep. And if there was one thing cats needed more than anything else, it was sleep.

Eyes half-open, he dragged his hind paws along the kitchen linoleum, making a slow, yawn-filled trip to the most important appliance in the room. There was no milk in the fridge. A Pyrex dish of strawberries did not appeal to him at that moment, if ever.

"Sal!"

Sal didn't answer. The dopey snowshoe had no trouble sleeping. *Probably on a full stomach of milk,* thought Julius. Someone had drunk it all.

Sergeant Harry Barr was at a sentinel recruitment drive or doing some crack-of-dawn training, which appealed to Julius even less than the berries. The sergeant had left them there, the fit nut. He was known as Lugs to his friends, on account of his long, tufted ears. He was a golden-brown lynx, almost three times as tall as Julius and much heavier, with bigger paws and a stubbier tail. Bred for eating and fighting, Lugs was also a good listener—he couldn't help it, with ears so big. Julius was just a regular house cat, gray and skinny, resigned to Lugs's frequent bursts of energy.

Julius's home was a mess. Old copies of *The Scratching Post* were piled high in the living room in case Julius had to research a story. He also liked to rub his cheeks against the newsprint and inhale its scent, music to his nose. Lugs's free weights and scratch pad took up one corner of the room. Sal Finney didn't have many belongings, but he took up valuable space himself, stretched out over an armchair.

Sal was a snowshoe who was always tripping over his own oversized paws. His body was off-white, with dark brown legs, ears, and tail. His shining blue eyes belied a brainlessness that constantly baffled and amused Julius and Lugs.

Julius's tail flicked in annoyance. While he cared about his friends and enjoyed their company, he also needed freedom and solitude. How was a cat supposed to work in such clutter?

He had to get out of the house, despite the obscenely early hour. Cats were supposed to be crepuscular, after all, at their most active before sunrise and sunset. Just not when they could be having sweet dreams, curled up in a basket.

After a post-work nap, Julius had woken with the dawn light, worrying about the love of his lives, Moira Marti. She was in the far-off city of Carabas, where she'd decided to stay instead of coming home with him. He could take a hint. If space was what she needed, then he'd give her a canyon's worth. Beneath the mature consideration and respect for her feelings was the longing. The longer he was separated from her, the more he cared about her, and the clearer his mental image of her became. He missed her and he wanted her back. In the interim, he cursed himself for letting her go and buried himself in work and newspaper piles.

He contemplated crawling into a bottle of full-fat buffalo milk, getting good and plenty sated on it, and staying there, but that wasn't the answer. He did need a drink, though.

The morning sun was bright in his eyes as Julius left his house. The corner store was a short walk away, down a sketchy street full of catnip addicts and tomcat troublemakers. They'd pick a fight if Julius looked at them funny, so he kept his ears back, his tail down, and his claws out, ready to defend himself.

The neighborhood, where Julius had once felt carefree, had worsened since the mayor had gone missing and the prowlers had gone on strike. No wonder sentinel numbers were up. With narrow career options and an instinct to protect their territory, it was natural for cats to join the army.

Julius sometimes wished he had joined when he was younger; getting paid to scrap sounded like a dream job. He'd seen the flip side, however, in Carabas; the senseless deaths and exhausted soldiers. They didn't get much sleep either, until the end, whether by violence or natural causes. Usually the former. The life of a sentinel was full of danger.

In order to prevent himself from squabbling with his housemates, Julius had vowed to stop and smell the honeysuckle whenever he could, slowing down and enjoying the world around him. It was either that or scratch the fur off his friends. As his eyes grew accustomed to the harsh rays of the sun, Julius stopped and tilted his head upward, listening to the low-pitched hum of the power lines above him, stretched like thick whiskers from one curved utility pole to the next in tidy, perfectly parallel rows. He also listened for other cats, in case one of the locals came to bother him. This was their territory, after all; outside his house, he was fair game.

After his meditative moment, he went to the corner store, a small sanctuary where cats focused on buying essentials, not picking fights. Julius bought a precious pint of milk from the clerk, who was always good for gossip.

"Have you heard the latest?" the clerk asked, a ragdoll with small blue eyes and a large white forehead.

"Probably," said Julius, tired and jaded as ever.

"Woodrow is way ahead in the election," said the clerk. "The polls say he'll win by a landslide."

"Woodrow sure knows how to make a speech," Julius replied, making polite conversation. "Doesn't mean he can back up what he says."

"Oh, I would never vote for him, not for all the sea of tuna."

"Who would you vote for?" asked Julius.

The clerk peered at his customer. Everyone in the neighborhood knew Julius was a freelance reporter. They'd read his stories about lost kittens, food bank heists, and the shocking number of cats accidentally mailed in packages because they liked cardboard boxes so much. Julius assured the clerk that his comments would stay off the record.

"I would vote for Otto in a heartbeat. He's been our mayor for years, and his mother before him. Through the riot and the Bay of Hounds invasion, he was a rock. He made me feel safe. What's more important than that?"

Not getting your head bitten off by a lion, thought Julius. Instead of speaking his mind and offending the clerk, Julius raised his milk in a salute to his wisdom and left the store, watching warily for troll cats mean enough to steal his treat.

Back home, he walked softly, careful not to wake Sal. The snowshoe wasn't the smartest cat he knew, or the most helpful, but he was brave and kind-hearted and far less cynical than Julius. Along with Lugs, who was stronger than the two of them put together, they made a good team. Julius just didn't care to share his milk with them. So he lapped up every ounce, hid the empty bottle behind a bookcase, and washed his whiskers with the back of his paw. *No evidence, no crime,* he told himself as Sal woke up, yawning.

"What's for breakfast?" Sal asked, smacking his chops.

"Strawberries," said Julius, his stomach aching with guilt. "Cold, juicy strawberries."

Bingo had never ridden on a train before. He'd seen plenty, working at the Stick Train Station north of Carabas. Since he was a sheepdog, he was good at fetching luggage and herding passengers. Right now, however, he was taking his first-ever vacation to buy time to deliver a message.

Bingo panted as he watched the trees blur by outside his carriage window. Those trees looked so inviting, but the train was moving way too fast for him to sniff them. He slid the window open and stuck his head out; the wind blew his thick coat back as his ears flapped, tongue lolling. He was exhilarated and scared, trying something so new, so strange to him.

He never would have taken the train if not for Dr. Quincy McGraw, the ginger-furred recluse who lived in a mountain observatory near the station. Not too near—Quincy was a recluse, after all—but close enough for Bingo to lollop up there at least once a week, running errands for the brilliant inventor.

Too filled with trepidation to go himself, Quincy had sent Bingo to Bast with an urgent message. Bingo didn't know what the message was; years of service as a porter had taught him never to open an envelope unless it was addressed to him. This one was not. He had it stowed safely in his backpack, where it would stay until he found its recipient. Come to think of it, he never got letters. One day, he would write one to himself, just so that he could lick the flap of the envelope. That would be his favorite part, he was sure.

Bast had a reputation as a bad place for a dog to go. Bingo was used to cats, as they took the train a lot, but he knew he would be vastly outnumbered in the feline fiefdom. He was a gregarious dog who usually got through life with a smile and a wag of the tail. He hoped he could keep that tail in the big, tough catropolis. Quincy wouldn't send him there, he reasoned, if it was that dangerous. No one would send a dog into danger, at least not without warning him first.

Lugs had tried using the gym on the military base east of the city. It was always so busy, with his superiors taking up more territory than anyone else. Waiting his turn for a treadmill was not his style, so he rarely used the gym.

He had tried a personal trainer, who tempted him with sweetmeats to make him run faster, jump higher, or stretch farther. Lugs spent most of his days being told what to do in the army. It was the last thing he wanted in his spare time. He had fired his personal trainer.

Lugs had even attended civvie exercise classes ("Arch those backs! Flex your paws! Stretch those mouths wide and yawn!"). There was no hierarchy; it was every cat for him or herself, jumping onto equipment, zooming along the indoor running track, gobbling organically raised rodents from the mice chest in the clean, bright lobby. He was gone so often, on military maneuvers, smuggling runs, and adventures with Julius and Sal, that he wasn't getting his money's worth from his membership. So, he had quit the classes.

There was nothing like running around, leaping from platform to platform at the local open-air scrape park. There cats could run freely, dragging their claws along wooden towers and canvas-covered lean-tos, with no prowlers yelling at them to stop. Not that the prowlers were turning up to work at the moment. Bast's finest wanted shorter shifts, higher pay, and free weekly raki massages. It was hard work, prowling around all day. Lugs knew this because he was helping in the prowlers' absence. Larger than most *felis domesticus*, the lynx was able to step in and stop a fight when he found one. He stayed away from the gangs. He did not like to be outnumbered.

So even in peacetime, Lugs stayed occupied. But he itched for battle. He was no longer interested in chasing tail—that urge had been removed from him against his will by a Carabian surgeon called the Vet. All Lugs had left was soldiering, and his friends Julius and Sal.

Even unofficial prowlers had to stay in shape. Lugs sprang for the highest platform, its summit glinting in the rising light. Summer was over, and with it the heat that cats loved to absorb, lazing around or getting hot and bothered. The fall was cooler, rainier, less predictable. Lugs hated the rain and the muddy thoughts that came with it.

From his vantage point on top of the platform, Lugs could see the entire scrape park and the concrete footpaths beyond. A young ocicat struggled to climb a slope, its hind paws scrabbling for purchase on the smooth surface. Lugs wanted to help, but it was better for the cub to fend for himself. That was the way of the cat.

Lugs jumped effortlessly to the ground, landing on fours, ears and tail pointed upright. The ocicat watched in awe as the grizzled lynx strutted away from the park, alert on his patrol of the neighborhood. Lugs hoped that the ocicat felt safe, knowing a sentinel was watching out for him.

Chico Audaz was enjoying a pleasant dream about chasing butterflies when a loud, fur-raising sound woke him up.

He opened his eyes, startled, popping his head out of the sweetgrass basket he used for a bed, looking around. He'd been living underground for months, in a stone cellar with no natural light. He didn't need it; his large pupils helped him see in the darkest conditions. However, he lit a torch when he went to find the source of the sound. He needed as much light as possible to check on his prisoner, to make absolutely sure he was locked up tight. Judging by the roars emanating from his cage, the prisoner was hungry and frustrated.

"What is it this time?" asked Chico, staring bleary-eyed through the bars at Otto. When Mayor Otto, mighty ruler of Bast, had first been captured, Chico's fear and heedfulness had been apparent. Chico was only a lowly jailer, after all, remarkable only for the bright blue eyes associated with his *ojos azules* breed. His sole, simple job was to guard a lion, hundreds of pounds heavier and indubitably smarter. Now, weeks later, Chico was bored.

"It's my blasted tooth," Otto moaned. Although the lion's fur was matted, his eyes retained a devious gleam.

"You went to the dentist," said Chico.

"He didn't pull any teeth! I think he was scared to put his paw in my mouth. Can't fathom why." Otto grinned at Chico, his incisors as sharp as his wit.

"Maybe some soft food would help?"

"Soft food?" Otto bellowed. "I'm a lion, not a new-born kitten! I want a steak, as rare as medical attention is around here."

"I came when I heard you roar…"

"Don't tell me, when you're not imprisoning big cats, you're a practicing orthodontist." Otto glowered at Chico, and his voice dropped an octave. "I am not happy with my smile. I will only be content when my mouth is full of your flesh." Otto roared again, loud and mighty, his fearsome outcry assailing Chico's ears. "I have a cramp in my haunches, too," Otto said softly. "It keeps me awake."

"Me too," said Chico, exhausted by Otto's constant complaints.

"It's because I'm stuck in this cage with no way to exercise. Look at me!" Otto held up his bony tail. "I'm fading to nothing."

"I didn't expect you to be locked up for so long," Chico admitted.

"Oh, really?" Otto shook his unwashed mane from side to side. "It can't be easy being you, Chico."

"No, it's not," Chico said meekly.

"This awful situation will be over very quickly if you unlock my cage."

"So you can eat me."

"I was blowing off steam. I don't really want to devour your flesh."

"I can't let you go." Chico sounded sincerely apologetic. "You saw what Joey Hondo did to—" Chico stopped talking. He didn't want to bring up the death of Otto's favorite son.

"To Mowbray, yes." Otto nodded. "You're in a difficult position. But the longer you leave me here, the worse your situation will become. When I'm found, the whole city will come down on you like a load of dogs."

"They, uh, they're not looking for you," said Chico. He didn't want to anger Otto, but he tried his best to respect his prisoner with honest information. "They're holding an election without you."

Otto slammed against the bars, saliva splashing against Chico's face.

"An election!"

"Yes, Your Honor. They need someone to run Bast."

Otto's face fell. "But... that's me! That's my job. Has Hondo engineered this?"

"He's capitalized on it."

"Of course he has." Otto walked in a circle and slumped down in his cage. "You may go now."

"Your toothache..."

"Is nothing compared to the pain I will cause your superior."

Chico swallowed hard.

"Extinguish the torch on your way out, won't you?" said Otto, dismissing Chico with a wave of his paw.

Chico nodded and backed away from the cage. He had to report his latest encounter to the boss.

Lugs usually spent a couple of hours patrolling his territory, a mile of terraced houses with flaking paint jobs and dirty windows. Sometimes, when a cat needed attention—which was often—the patrol took longer.

An elderly chartreux stood on a curb, tottering a little. Lugs offered her a paw, looked her in the eyes, and smiled his kindest smile. The chartreux was confused and obviously needed help. Lugs led her slowly and carefully across Vendue Street, taking care to move at her pace, checking both ways for trams and wayward pumas. He left her on the opposite curb, where she turned around and faced the road.

Assistance is its own reward, Lugs told himself. *No thanks necessary.* Still, the charteux's lack of gratitude disappointed him. His disenchantment turned to dismay when she turned around and stepped back onto the road, crossing it without him. He wanted to confront her and ask her what she was playing at, but he said nothing; cats are contrary creatures, adept at doing the opposite of what is required.

"I didn't want to go *that* way," said the chartreux with a condescending tone. Lugs remained silent. He was protecting the city, not picking fights with silly old cats.

Lugs continued his patrol, picking up trash and placing it in the dumpster on the corner of Baxter Avenue and Moody Lane. He let go of the lid, and it slammed closed.

"Excuse me," said a voice. Lugs looked around, saw no one, sniffed the air. All he could smell was garbage. He looked down Moody Lane; a valiant chipmunk was digging in a grass verge. As soon as it saw Lugs, it darted away. Lugs set off in the same direction, checking for more rodents.

"Don't go." It was the same voice he'd heard before, louder and more plaintive this time. Lugs went back and checked behind the dumpster.

"Up here. I followed a chipmunk, then it went somewhere I wouldn't follow, then I couldn't go back to where I started following—"

"It's okay. Breathe. I'm a sentinel. I'm trained to help in these kinds of situations."

"Thank goodness," said the Cheshire. "I thought I was the first cat to ever get stuck up a tree."

"You're still special," Lugs assured him. "Not the first, though." The Cheshire was dug deep on a branch, transfixed with vertigo.

"Don't look down at me," Lugs advised. "Look straight ahead."

"I can't! There's.... there's... sky."

"Look at the tree, then. It's not moving, and it's close to you. You'll feel better."

"What part of the tree?"

"The trunk, the trunk," said Lugs, trying to keep his voice calm as he watched the Cheshire slowly shift his weight.

"It's moving." The tree swayed in the breeze, leaves falling as the Cheshire turned around and faced the trunk. "You said it wasn't moving. How can I trust you now?"

"I couldn't see from down here."

"What else can't you see?" the Cheshire yelled. "Lightning bolts?"

Lugs ran out of patience. He climbed the tree at a fantastic pace, fore claws digging deep into the trunk and clipping away bark as he ascended. "Don't move," Lugs snarled as he reached the highest height. "See me? I'm not moving."

"N-no, you're not," said the Cheshire. Eyes wide, tail waving. He was terrified.

"Take your time," said Lugs. "You'll find me. Listen to me and don't forget to breathe."

The Cheshire shook his head. He couldn't budge, and Lugs didn't blame him. The height was tremendous, the tree swayed more with the lynx's weight, and the wind felt ice cold on his fur.

"I can't come to you," said Lugs.

"You'll have to come here, and we'll climb down together. It'll be fine. I said move it!" Lugs's command was so loud that the Cheshire almost lost his grip. "Step lively now! If you don't get your tail over here right now, I'll rip it off and have it for breakfast!"

With a kittenish whine, the Cheshire hurried over to Lugs, who sank his teeth into the smaller cat's scruff and dragged him back down the tree, using the branches like rungs on a ladder. Placing him on the ground, Lugs gulped down a clump of fur and said, "That wasn't so hard, was it?"

"No. Thank you." The terrified cat retreated onto Baxter Avenue, not daring to turn his back on the lynx.

This was a slow morning for Lugs. Helping nervous cats and ungrateful oldsters would have been below his pay grade if he wasn't a volunteer. He missed the sounds of battle and the taste of bloody fur in his nostrils—

He heard a clamor at the end of Moody Lane, not quite the sound of battle, more a scuffle and a hiss, but he would take it. He ran down the lane, ready for action.

Lugs saw five shorthairs surrounding a sheepdog. Their fur bristled, and their tails looked thick enough to brush a chimney. They hissed and spat at the dog, who looked bewildered; his kind, fringe-obscured eyes contrasting with the unwelcoming stares of the cats. They circled the sheepdog, and he took a step forward—big mistake. The cats closed in, and one swiped his claws at the dog's flank. The cats were so focused on the dog, they didn't notice as Lugs got nearer.

The dog sank down, lowered his head, looked up at the cats, and offered them a playful bark. Lugs noticed that his tail was wagging—the dog thought this was a game.

Lugs had seen similar games turn deadly. A dog could bite or stamp on one cat and walk away; five cats were an unstoppable force if they worked together. They could rip this greenhorn to bits if they wanted to.

One of the shorthairs reached out and scratched the dog's nose. The victim yelped. It was a light scratch, a test of vulnerability, but a sore one. The dog looked around charily and stopped wagging his tail. A cat behind him spat, making him turn around; the scratcher took another swipe, this time at his tail. The dog spun back, disoriented.

"Break it up, fellas." When Lugs inserted himself into the melee, the shorthairs were so riled up that they turned on him, leaving the dog to back away. Lugs arched his back, looming above the street cats, cowing them into retreat.

"Enough of this!" Lugs hissed at them. "Why are you picking on this hound? Can't you see he's new?"

"This is our patch," said a shorthair with a torn ear. "Dogs don't come here."

To the street cats, dogs were the eternal enemy, savage and unsavory, contaminated with cruelty, embodying cautionary tales mothers told their kittens to scare them at night. They were so ugly you could hardly look one in the face, so stupid they couldn't even climb—butt sniffers, tail chasers, cat killers, pebble fetchers, barking berserkers, beasts of obsolescence, massive muzzled, omnivorous rug-stainers, flea-bringers, leg biters. Otto had tolerated their presence in the city, encouraged a friendship with the enemy, and according to the media, the dogs had bitten the paws that fed them. The public had the right to say no.

"There's one here now," Lugs reasoned. "Go home, boys. I'll take care of the mutt."

The shorthairs slunk away, muttering among themselves, disappointed that their sport was done. Lugs asked the dog what he was doing on the mean streets of Bast.

"I'm Bingo," said the dog, spelling out his name for Lugs with a singsong lilt. "Thanks for your help! I was asking those cats for directions, and they started hissing and spitting, and before I knew it, they were taking swipes at my nose."

"Where are you from? The Isle of Dogs?"

"Oh, no. I live in Healing, a village right next to Stick Station. That's where I work."

"Up in the mountains?"

"At the foot of the mountains, yes." Bingo puffed out his chest. "I'm a porter."

"I don't see you carrying any bags," said Lugs brusquely.

"I'm off duty. It feels strange, actually, not having anything to fetch." Bingo looked at Lugs expectantly. Lugs picked up a small dead branch and offered it to the dog. Bingo panted at him.

With a sigh, Lugs threw the stick across the park. Bingo lolloped over to it, picked it up in his mouth, and ran back to Lugs, dropping it in front of the lynx.

"Feel better now?" Lugs asked.

"Yap." Bingo crouched in front of Lugs and panted some more. Lugs felt awkward.

"What, uh, directions were you asking for?"

"I need to find this address."

Bingo showed Lugs the envelope. When he read the address, Lugs laughed.

"I think I can help you find it," said Lugs.

Bridget, the lioness's, thick sleep was disturbed by a loud, metallic thump followed by a scraping sound that came from deep beneath her. She opened one eye, slowly took in her surroundings, then opened the other. Her cabin was filled with daylight and everything was in its place, apart from a couple of spilled cushions. She would have to take Pollet to task for those.

"Pollet!" she roared. "Where's my breakfast?" She was thrown from her berth by another scraping judder.

She quickly regained her balance and wobbled her way to a porthole, squinting through the sunlight. She didn't find much, just a calm sea.

"Pollet! For the last time, where are you?" That cat would be her breakfast if he didn't hurry up. Bridget wasn't used to being treated this way. With her stomach growling and the boat still juddering from time to time, Bridget lost her patience. She threw on a robe, thrust her cabin hatch open with a paw, and stuck an imperious nose out into the passageway, which seemed to slope starboard. Light shifted through portholes and open cabins, casting shadows that haunted the passageways.

"Where are you this time?" Pollet was an intelligent tonkinese who made up in brains what he lacked in backbone. He had a habit of disappearing, usually when he was in trouble.

"Got you!" she said with a leonine roar as she checked Pollet's favorite hiding place, a cupboard in the ship's galley. He wasn't there. Bridget tried the upper deck next, prowling from the bow to the stern, where she looked out at the ceaseless open water. The sunlight sparkled on the surface, inviting her to dive into the sea. But with the ship floating aimlessly, she did not want to go for a swim and lose her vessel to the wind and tide.

The entire crew had abandoned her, leaving her stranded on the orders of Joey Hondo. Pollet had stuck around, either through loyalty or fear of what she would do to him if she caught up with him. Bridget suspected the latter.

There were only so many places he could hide. Bridget would find him—she was an expert huntress—and have his hide for her long-awaited breakfast. Then she would take control of the massive cruise ship, navigate her way home, and dine on Joey Hondo's sour flesh.

Tad Tybalt's executive suite was packed with activity: phones ringing, assistants copying leaflets and posters, cats chattering, and advertising gurus guru-ing, all vetted by the industrialist who was running for mayor.

"No generic slogans!" he meowled at his executive assistant and campaign manager, Ramona Pretzel. "I want to stand out from those two oiks I'm running against. Something meaningful and memorable."

"I'm happy to take any suggestions," Ramona huffed. The Persian was feeling overworked and underfed; her fur was unlicked and her tail hung limp. She still managed to look good, though, in a *haute couture* trouser suit that matched her sapphire eyes.

"That do-gooder Woodrow has 'Paws for Peace,' Hondo came up with 'Safety. Security. Sachets,' and what have we got? 'You scratch my back and I'll scratch yours.' It sounds like a mission statement, not a political pick-me-up. How am I supposed to rally Bast's population with that?"

"It sounds corporate because your finest copywriters brainstormed it," Ramona said slowly. "We have time to improve on it. What direction would you like to take?"

"I don't know! A positive direction. Looking to the future. Optimism."

"I'll pass that on," said Ramona.

"To who?"

"To your finest copywriters."

"I need someone fresh. A famous name who knows his or her way around words."

"Swampy McMahon!" The celebrity wrestler had recently published his megahit memoirs.

"He couldn't scratch his name in the sand, that dirty finisher." Tad jabbed a paw at a clerk who leaned back on the floor, washing between his legs. "What's that layabout doing?"

The campaign manager looked at the clerk and said, "Taking a tongue break, sir."

"Tell him he's fired, then he can take all the breaks he wants."

"It's a mandatory break, sir. He's just doing what cats ordinarily do."

"Then fire whoever mandated the breaks, then fire the clerk. We don't do ordinary here. We are special." Tad clapped his paws together. "Who was that fellow who made so much noise on the radio?"

"DJ Scratch?" The down-to-earth disk jockey sounded like an outrageous choice for a slogan writer.

"No, no. The one who sparked the riot. He had a way with words. He roused the rabble, for better or worse."

"Do you really want to be associated with Julius Kyle?"

"We don't have to announce his involvement, just pay him. He's a *littérateur*, a soapbox siren, and he's got a heck of a way with words. No one has caught the city's attention more than him in recent memory, unless you count Mayor Otto, and I haven't heard him roar around here recently."

"I've seen his byline in *The Scratching Post*," said Ramona, trying to sound helpful.

"Yes! He can report on my victory." Tad sat back at his desk, then sprung forward. "Send someone to go find him, Ramona."

"Yes, sir."

"Don't expect me to come up with all the ideas," said Tad. "I can't let my business slide because of this election."

As a long-time guest in Julius's house, Sal politely asked to be let out, then he wanted to come back in again. Then he went back out and scratched his way back in. Julius paid him no mind; this was normal behavior for Sal. By the time the snowshoe had settled down on the windowsill, blinking dopey eyes, Julius had almost finished his milk. He looked at the leftover swallow and offered it to his friend.

"You must be thirsty, with all your comings and goings," said Julius.

"I had to check the weather," said Sal, gazing out the window. "But the first time, I forgot."

Julius smiled. The relaxed atmosphere was shattered by Lugs, who arrived home with a dog in tow.

Sal dashed behind the couch and hid. Julius popped out his claws, ready for a fight.

"Lugs, what have I told you about bringing your work home with you?" said Julius nervously.

"Just helping a lost dog find his way," Lugs explained.

Bingo panted over to Julius and offered him a paw. "Mr. Kyle?"

Julius leaned back, gagging at Bingo's dog breath. "That's me," he wheezed.

"He was looking for our address," Lugs explained. "What are the odds?

Julius smiled. "Considering you've been marching all over town looking for trouble, quite high."

"You are famous, Julius," Sal reminded him. "I'm surprised you don't get more visitors."

"Why were you looking for this place, Bingo? Were you looking for me?"

"I have this for you." Bingo struggled to retrieve the envelope from his backpack, which was crammed with snacks, a dirty old bone, a ball with a chunk chewed off, his porter's cap, and his train ticket stub. Bingo held the envelope in his teeth, offering the soggy message to Julius.

"It's hate mail," Lugs scoffed.

"You could use your paws, you know," said Julius, gingerly taking the envelope.

"Habit. I usually keep my forepaws free to carry luggage."

"It's hard to change a habit," Sal said in support. He knew a thing or two about proclivities.

"Who's it from?" asked Lugs.

"Keep your ears on," said Julius, struggling to lift the dampened flap. "Who's it from?" he asked Bingo.

"Doctor Quincy McGraw," said Bingo proudly. "He entrusted me with the delivery of this message."

"That was brave of him," said Lugs. Julius hushed him and pulled a note from the envelope. Julius knew the name from a newspaper article, one he had read over and over because it was written by a former lover. He was reluctant to look at the note. Nothing good could come of it, he was sure. Nevertheless, acknowledging their expectant faces, he read it out to his friends.

Dear Mr. Kyle,

I trust that this letter finds you hale and healthy. I apologize for reaching out to you in this manner; I do not trust the phone lines where I work and reside, and this missive is intended solely for you.

Julius looked at his friends, who listened attentively. He didn't have the heart to send them out of the room, so he kept reading.

Some time ago, the beautiful Camilla Dolentine visited my laboratory, the most charitable and free-spirited cat I have ever met. The conversations we had were some of the most intriguing and uplifting of my lives.

Sal gasped. "Who's Camilla?" he asked. Lugs jabbed him in the ribs.

When my lab was destroyed and my world fell apart, my first instinct was to reach out to Camilla. Imagine how distraught I felt when I heard of her passing during the riot in Bast.

Julius stopped reading for a moment, a lump in his throat. Lugs gave him a sympathetic look. Bingo panted. Julius took a breath and kept going.

She spoke highly of you, Mr. Kyle. I truly believe you were the love of her lives, much to my chagrin, I must admit. Thus it is that I am writing to you and begging for your help. I have always intended my inventions to help the cats and dogs of this land, not harm them. To my great regret, however, my most hazardous gadget has fallen into the wrong paws. This machine will change the balance of power between cats and dogs.

I have asked the rulers of the North for help, but they have ignored my pleas. I have asked the local dogs, but they just bark for no reason. The barking is so loud it hurts my ears. Only Bingo is willing to fetch you, and I am eternally grateful for his loyalty.

Julius smiled at Bingo, who grinned back.

I beseech you to visit me in the mountains (see above for my exact address) and help me to discern where the Bernoulli tube might be, and if possible, find it for me. I would look for it myself, but I fear that I am vulnerable to the miscreants who made off with my device.

I do not expect you to seek me out for my sake, as we have never met in person. I hope that you will help me for the sake of catkind, and I understand that you are not averse to dogs, either. But I believe from my heart to the tip of my tail that you will perform this arduous task for Camilla, to honor her memory and safeguard the kind of future she would have wanted.

Yours sincerely,
Dr. Quincy McGraw.

p.s. and by the by, there will be a reward for retrieval of the Bernoulli tube.

p.p.s. please throw a stick for Bingo. He likes sticks.

Julius wiped a tear from his eye. He didn't want his friends to see him upset. Without Camilla, without Moira, he felt alone, even with Lugs and Sal beside him.

"I'll take you to Quincy," said Bingo. "We can take the train, and he doesn't live far from the station."

"I can see that," said Julius, rereading the doctor's address. "Thank you for bringing this to me."

"I've never been on a train before," said Bingo.

"This will be my second time." Lugs patted him on the head.

"Trains are overrated," said Julius, who associated them with ferocious feral bandits. Nevertheless, the express was the fastest way to get to the mountains up north, and it would pass through Carabas. Moira was in Carabas.

"When do we leave?" asked Sal.

"After I talk to my editor," said Julius. "And find a stick."

2

He Once Roared and Growled Fiercely

"10 more days until Suspicious Package unleashes its new album, featuring the hit single, 'Daddy didn't Raise no Scaredy Cat.' This will be the ninth S.P. album to hit stores this decade. Although the lineup has changed, the beats have not—you always know what you're getting with these guys, no fretting. Their album, entitled *Scratch That*, has got its work cut out to compete with Mimi Mimu's platinum-selling triple disk, *Whiskers in the Dark*. Stay tuned to hear songs from both class acts on this channel, in this hot half hour.

"Speaking of heat, now the weather's cooling down and getting shady there's no need be crazy, no hot mess tantrums or ugly scenes in the club when you've had one sour milk too many, you know those nights I'm talking about."

"Cool as you may be, the election's hotting up and hoooooo the poll numbers are in, and that handsome cat Joey Hondo is leading by an inch or two. But he don't get to decide who runs our world. You do!"

—WOTW radio broadcast
By DJ Scratch

Chico needed a break from guard duty, and he got it when he was summoned to Joey Hondo's surveillance room. From there, Joey was able to keep tabs on the cats who worked for him, via windows, two-way mirrors, and telescopes built into the walls.

Joey was a korat with a silver mark on his heart-shaped head, large ears, and luminous lime-colored eyes. Female cats adored him; the males admired him. All his supporters appreciated the way he had ascended from security guard to mayoral candidate. He puffed on a cigar as he watched the city go about its business. On Beaverbank Place, members of the Wildcat gang lingered, no doubt hatching a plan to vandalize all they could put their paws on. In the city center, worshippers of Bastet streamed into a church, excited to hear the latest passionate sermon from their new bishop, Kafel. His predecessor had met with a nasty accident, falling from a heavenly height to the streets below. Outside City Hall, vociferous protesters meowled at the leopard guards and waved placards: "Where's Our Mayor?" "Enough Lion Around." "Wanted: A New Leader."

The protesters would be dealt with, but Joey wanted them to express their sentiments, rock the boat, and deepen the void left by Otto's absence. Come election day, he would step in and crush any dissent.

"You wanted to see me, Mr. Hondo?"

"See you?" Joey didn't bother to turn around and face his employee. "If I want to see you, I'll check a monitor. No, I sent for you to get an update on your ... friend."

"We're not bonding, sir." Chico fidgeted. "It's not that kind of situation."

Joey looked over his shoulder at Chico. "In many relationships, one cat is in charge, the other does as they are told," he said. "Some partners feel trapped, desperate for their freedom. Others keep the home secure, their loved one safe."

Chico was hesitant to disagree with his boss, but when the korat turned back to the monitors, Chico spoke up. "That ... doesn't sound like a healthy relationship to me, sir."

"I speak from experience," Joey growled. "You are in the early stages of your love affair with Otto. You must woo him. Make him feel safe from the rigors of the outside world."

Chico took a step closer to Joey. "He's a lion who wants to eat me. He's not afraid of anything."

Joey's green eyes glinted in the light of his monitoring devices.

He stubbed out his cigar, got up, and clapped a paw on Chico's shoulder. "Then you will make him afraid. You have already set his son's head on the ground, right in front of him. Put the fear of Bastet into him. Make him tremble in your presence."

"How?" asked Chico, trying to sound confident.

"Take more from him. A lion cannot run or hunt without his paws."

"I can't get close enough to..."

"His kind sleep for up to 21 hours a day. I am sure that you can use his vulnerability to your advantage. I have spent a lifetime doing just that."

Chico nodded and left the surveillance room. He wanted to quit. It was true that Otto was no friend of his, but Chico pitied the caged beast. Following Joey's orders would mean harming a majestic cat; Chico wasn't sure if he could do that.

While Julius and Sal packed for their trip, Lugs spruced himself up with his tongue. Bingo threw the stick in the air, caught it in his mouth, and chewed it, romping around and making a mess of Julius's small, one-story house. One of his newspaper piles had toppled over and someone had bitten a chunk out of a cushion, creating a snowfall of feather-down stuffing.

"Please stop running around," Julius snapped at Bingo. "If you need to burn off energy, go outside."

Bingo stopped bouncing around the house and looked at Julius, panting. "Sorry," he said. "I didn't even know I was doing it."

Julius couldn't stay mad at the grinning, shaggy dog.

"He can't go outside," Lugs said, not for the first time. "Too many cranky cats out there. You can be quiet and incognito, can't you, buddy?"

"Where's that stick I found for you?" Julius asked Bingo, who barked at the front window.

Worried that trouble was approaching, the cats gathered together to take a look outside.

A small pigeon stood on the stoop, a small cylinder attached to its leg. Julius pounced on the bird, holding it tight while Sal removed the cylinder. A tiny scroll was tucked inside.

"More mail for you?" Lugs asked Julius.

"Not this time," said Sal. "It's addressed to Sergeant Barr, whoever that is."

"It's me, you dolt." Lugs took the scroll, peered at it, and slumped onto the couch.

"What's the matter?" asked Sal, his mouth full of pigeon.

Lugs had received bad news from his commander. Although he would continue to be stationed in Bast, he was ordered to refrain from patrolling the city and helping his fellow cats. Judging by the complaints received by Sentinel Headquarters, Lugs's help was either unwarranted or ill-received. Lugs was no longer required to prowl around, offer advice, or get involved in any fights. For a warrior like Lugs, this was a painful order to receive.

"I'll appeal," Lugs grumbled to Julius. "Get my orders reversed."

"And get sent to the Land of Frozen Fur," said Julius. "Give them time. Your leaders will realize how valuable you are."

"At least I'm still based here," Lugs reassured himself. "With you guys."

"Thank Bastet for small mercies," Julius agreed. He asked Bingo, "What do you know about these 'miscreants' Doctor McGraw mentioned?"

"Nothing, really," said Bingo. "I know Quincy was worried. He wouldn't leave his home, even after his lab was trashed. I brought him his mail and a box of mice crispies last week, and he was hiding in his kitchen beside the stove, where it was nice and warm. He said that he was running out of time, and he needed help, and I was the one messenger he could send here. So he did."

"What about Quincy? Is he a good cat?"

"I've been hissed at, spat on, insulted, and even chased by cats," said Bingo. "All because their train was late, I was too slow for them, or they were bored. Quincy's never done anything bad to me. He's the kindest inventor I've ever met."

"How many inventors do you know?" asked Sal, impressed.

"One. Him."

Julius turned to Lugs, who shook his head.

"Leave me out of this!" said Lugs. "I've got a city to protect."

Julius shook his head. "No, you don't. The prowlers won't be on strike forever."

"Yeah, but until then..." Lugs crossed his paws, being stubborn.

"And you have your orders to stand down." Julius sat down on the couch beside his friend and gave him an imploring stare. "Lugsy, I can't do this without you."

"I'm stationed here, Julius. Up and leaving without permission will get me court-martialed. The sentinels don't take kindly to deserters." Lugs stood up.

"Put in for permission, and while they're dithering about it, deciding what to do with you, you can be off having adventures with us. You'll be back here quicker than you can say AWOL."

"I don't know." Lugs scowled. "I can say it pretty fast..."

Julius gestured at Sal. "Look at this wee guy here. Do you really think he'll survive without you watching his back?

"What will you be doing?"

"Watching my own."

"Okay, okay." Lugs let out a sigh. "I'll submit for leave, or a temporary transfer."

"That's the lynx spirit! I knew you wouldn't pass up an opportunity like this."

"I'm not doing it for you, I'm doing it for Sal," said Lugs, but he also agreed because he craved excitement. He was certain he would find it out there in the mountains, where few cats feared to tread.

Moira Marti was homesick, and she didn't mind admitting it to Tarquin Quintroche. They were both focused on running the city of Carabas, nurturing a system where cats and dogs co-existed. The occasional fight was inevitable, and the smaller cats were naturally intimidated by the larger hounds. But it was an experiment worth conducting if their land was ever going to evolve and improve. The different species couldn't spend eternity nipping at each other's tails.

Moira was tired, though. While Tarquin was the nominal ruler of Carabas, she toiled behind the scenes. It wasn't the dogfights or the greedy cats eating up supplies that posed her real problem, however. It was Julius Kyle.

On a journey to Carabas, Julius had tussled with ferals and led them to the city with his scent. The ferals had gathered in strength as they approached, pouring into Carabas and wreaking hairy havoc within its walls. When the sentinels had stepped in to combat the threat, they had made matters worse, terrifying the populace and drinking the local taverns dry. With the ferals defeated, the sentinels ordered elsewhere, and

Julius back in Bast, Moira was duty-bound to clean up the wreckage they'd left behind.

Moira didn't hate Julius; it was in his nature to cause chaos rather than leave the status where its quo should go. On the contrary, she had deep feelings for him. He cared about her, and he'd given her the confidence to work with Tarquin and move to an important position in government. But he was a Bast cat through and through, whereas her place was in Carabas. She could still be homesick; she missed her crooked old neighborhood, nicknamed the Doghouse because it was so down-at-heel. She missed the particular taste of the birds in her backyard and the polluted purple of the Bast skyline. She would go home one day. Right now, she had too much to do.

The Scratching Post was the longest-running newspaper in Bast, with the highest page count and circulation, innumerable scoops, memorable headlines, and the biggest number of headaches for an editor. Roy Fury didn't like the job anymore. He was putting on weight, which scared him because he did not want to end up like his predecessor Morris, morbidly obese and practically glued to his desk.

Being editor of the city's paper of record also meant hearing an endless stream of cockamamie story pitches, like the one Julius was pushing on him now.

"This is a fantastic story!" Julius gushed. "A mysterious inventor making war machines in the mountains... thieves and stolen gadgets... an intrepid trio of Bast cats, venturing into the unknown to save the day. Imagine the readers sniffing at the newsprint like ink addicts, desperate to find out what happens next? And what will that be? We don't have a bloody clue! Aren't you curious to find out?"

Roy replied with a big, fat yawn. "You've gotta stay here," he said firmly. "To cover the election."

Julius sat on Roy's desk and said, "I swear I'll be back in time for the vote."

Roy looked at Julius. He could tell the reporter would not budge until he got his way.

"You better," Roy finally said.

"I'm not on the payroll, remember?"

"I remember." Roy nodded.

"I'm freelance. You can't order me around."

"It's not that. I trust you, and you alone, to meet your deadlines. The other cats are too busy displaying kittenish behavior and playing around the office to get their work done. You understand there's more to life than naps 'n' treats." Roy sank back in his swivel chair. "This is a nightmare, Julius! Getting the paper out every day, filling the pages, finding the news... it ain't good for my blood pressure. The doc says I have hypertension and I should play more golf. He's bonkers! Cats don't play golf!"

"Have you tried a cold, damp cloth between the ears?" asked Julius, mesmerized by Roy's dilated pupils.

"I don't have time for that! This used to be fun, Julius. I was the office jackass."

"Yes, you were."

"Not a care in the world when I was a reporter." Roy dug his claws into a stack of memos and tore them to strips. "Being an editor sucks."

"Be careful what you fish for," said Julius, climbing off the desk, trying to sound supportive. He was secretly glad to see Roy suffer. Roy had caused many deaths during the riot, leading a mob of cats on a mindless rampage against the local dogs. Through his thoughtlessness, Roy had changed Bast forever. Now dogs were not welcome, and only a few of them still lived in the city. Julius missed the melting pot Bast had once been.

"My point is," Roy said, "I ain't gonna do this forever, and I'm gonna need someone to step in for me, at least so I can take a vacation. Or as you call it, an expenses-paid assignment out of the city."

"I appreciate the offer of expenses. I'll take you up on that. But I'm not going to a leisure spot, Roy. I'm going to the North, where it's grim and full of your least favorite species."

"Dogs! Yeah, you're right. You're not going for a picnic. Okay, head on out, but I want regular updates, and don't forget to be back here when, or even better, before, the ballots are cast."

"I'll be here. I'll phone in the stories, though. That way you won't have to read my copy, since hypertension can cause sudden blindness."

"What?"

Julius left the office.

"What did you just say, Julius?" Roy called after him. "I need to know. Julius!"

Otto Canders, king of the concrete jungle, mayor of Bast, supreme lion of the land, could not believe he'd been laid so low by a tooth.

If not for the pain in his mouth, he would not have gone to the dentist for treatment; if not for the visit and the anesthetic he'd inhaled, he would not have been abducted; he would not be a captive now, drained of his power. Brought low, in a cage, starved, with a blasted toothache.

He would not allow a single nuisance tooth to ruin his life.

A single claw sprang from Otto's massive right forepaw. He used it to push at a rotten canine, four inches long and painful to the touch. It had to go. He shook his head with great vigor, dust fluttering from his mane. He rubbed his cheek against the bars of his cage, hoping to alleviate the pain. It didn't work. He rubbed harder, feeling the tooth move horribly in his mouth.

Enough. He was still the emperor of his city and the mightiest of beasts. He could handle an extraction. He used his claw to scratch at his gum and push his tooth, his eyes watering in agony. With both his forepaws, he opened his mouth wide and swiped at the tooth, knocking it free in a spray of blood. He let out a spine-chilling roar, then sank to the ground, lying on his side, weary from the struggle. His gum throbbed and he felt nauseous, but sleep would help.

In his paw, he clutched the tooth, yellow and gory, his only possession in this soul-crushing enclosure.

He had lost his freedom, but he hadn't lost the power of his cunning, which had helped him gain and maintain power for years. He would use that cunning to escape.

Before leaving his home, Julius had nosed his way through old copies of *The Scratching Post* looking for stories about Quincy. He had a vague idea of when the inventor had left Bast; it was big news at the time. In a musty old paper with the front-page headline, "Cats Not Getting Enough Treats," Julius found an article on Quincy with a picture attached. The ginger cat was holding the Prize for Feline Science .

One paragraph stuck in Julius's memory.

Best known for the invention of the spring-mounted claw cleaner and the cheeseless mouse trap, Dr. Quincy McGraw is one of the leading minds of our city. Unfortunately, Bast will no longer benefit from his mental energy, as Dr. McGraw moved north yesterday. Citing lack of both compassionate and financial support, the inventor is seeking solitude—and new funds—in territory near Stick Station.

Julius saw Camilla's byline. He'd read it the day it was printed; he always read her work. The northern territories had been one of her specialties, and she'd followed Quincy's career after he had left Bast. Julius was glad that she had met him in person and made such an impression before she passed. He couldn't be jealous, not now she was gone. But he could be curious. That was *his* specialty.

Pumas were a rare breed in Carabas, the city that bridged Bast in the south and the Isle of Dogs in the north. They were large and angry and eternally hungry.

Toxic, the most dangerous big cat in Carabas, sat in his efficiency, perched on the edge of his couch eating beef hoof pizza. He watched an old movie on his Viewtone TV, one with vapid cats and a jackal-headed villain. He couldn't remember what it was called and didn't care. The movie distracted him from his desperately dull day.

Like many cats in Carabas, big and small, Toxic worked for Tarquin Quintroche. Tarquin ran the city and needed muscle to do it. Toxic didn't mind acting tough; it was in his nature, and he enjoyed roughing up pipsqueaks and dissenters. The hardest part of being tough was using restraint—he had to remind himself not to go too far and gut the little kitties who got in his way.

The second hardest part of his job was Moira.

The Siamese Moira Marti was Tarquin's adjutant, helping run the city with an incredible deftness of touch. Moira had worked her way up from the ghettos of Bast to the corporate heights of Carabas, a path that Toxic admired. He admired Moira, too, although he'd never told her to her face. She would never show affection to a brawny puma like him. She was aware of his presence, and that was enough for him. For now.

In the movie, the jackal guy was menacing a helpless kitten. Toxic liked this bit. He liked scenes full of action and suspense, unlike his life, which was a routine collection of taking orders and carrying them out. At least he didn't have to do any paperwork. Tarquin and Moira didn't trust him to check the right boxes, let alone sign his name at the bottom of the forms.

His pizza done, Toxic got up and paced around his efficiency. He had insisted on getting a full-length mirror hung on one wall, where he admired his reflection: short, powerful legs, strong, thick neck, round, dishy face. How could Moira resist him?

Maybe if he hadn't kidnapped her, she might look at him more favorably. But Tarquin had ordered him to do it, and she seemed to get on with her boss just fine. What did Tarquin have that he didn't, other than wealth, power, and fabulous dress sense? Nothing.

Toxic slumped back down on the couch. The movie concluded with the jackal defeated, chained to a post by the heroes of the story, and left to sweat in the jungle sun. *Why is it always the big cats who are portrayed as villains in these stories?* Toxic wondered. *We have feelings, too.* He found the trope offensive, and that made him want to go and beat up a puppy. He settled for clawing the couch arm instead.

He would find a way to get close to Moira again and impress her. He would show her how special she was to him. One way or another, he would be a part of her life.

———————————

A cat couple sat on a bench waiting for their train out of Bast Central Station, their forepaws touching, one more attentive than the other. A Siamese snoozed with a beanie pulled over its eyes, blocking out the light, ears poking through holes in her hat. Elderly cats waited patiently, nibbling on Swedish fish. Kittens mewed, scampering too close to the platform edge, their parents grabbing them by the scruff of the neck.

Bingo bounded into the station, followed by Julius, Sal, and Lugs. The sheepdog was so excited to ride on the Northern Express. Sal found it hard to believe the dog had ever been on one before.

"Are you sure you've had a train ride?" Sal asked. Lugs rolled his eyes. How else had Bingo got to Bast?

"Oh yes," Bingo said eagerly. "I'm sure."

"Leave the brain trust boys to take care of each other," Julius said, walking Lugs away from Bingo and Sal. Each traveler carried a pack with essential provisions. Julius had his notepads and pencils. Lugs had iron mittens that fit tight on his paws, ready for a fight. Bingo brought his beloved stick and a bone he had found in Julius's backyard. Sal brought his blankie. They were layered up for the cold of the mountains, with overshirts, jackets, and warm, wooly hats. Julius also brought his fedora with the press pass tucked in the band, his *passepartout* on this journey.

"Julius Kyle?"

"Precisely," said Julius, turning to see an elegant feline slinking toward him in a cinnabar-colored Emma Tweed coat and a black lace fascinator.

"Ramona Pretzel," said the Persian, rubbing up against Julius. "I have an unrejectable job offer for you."

"Does it involve a million turtle doves and unlimited nap breaks?"

"Mr. Thaddeus Tybalt of Tybalt Inc. requires your services."

Ramona expected Julius to be impressed—most cats were when they heard Tad's name. Julius disappointed her. They stared at each other, two lost souls making a much-needed connection.

"Lady, he's got a train to catch," said Lugs, shorting the spark between Julius and Ramona.

"Wait a minute, Lugs." Julius introduced his friend to Ramona and asked her why Tad wanted to hire a beat-up old journalist.

"He wants you for your vocabulary," Ramona said demurely. "I hear it's rather ... large."

"It's sizeable," Julius replied, clearing his throat. "Big enough to please all my readers."

"How did you find us?" asked Lugs.

"With difficulty. I visited your home and asked around. A charming store clerk directed me to the newspaper, and from there..."

"They gave you my timetable. That was generous of them."

"To a fault," said Lugs. The train whistle blew. "Come on, Julius. We've got to split."

"I'm sorry, Miss—"

"Call me Ramona."

"I'd like to help, but I have to catch this train." Julius and Lugs made their way across the platform.

"Mr. Tybalt needs a slogan!" Ramona shouted as the train chuffed impatiently.

"How about, 'A rat in every pot'?"

"That's brilliant!" said Ramona. "Succinct, yet memorable. You certainly have a way with words!"

"Thank you!" Julius grinned at Ramona, who was obscured from his view by a cloud of steam.

"She was sweet," Julius said to Lugs.

"If you say so."

Julius and Lugs got onto the train. Sal and Bingo were already on board with the sheepdog sniffing around excitedly.

"I need you to know we're making a stop on our way to the mountains," said Julius.

"Of course we are," said the long-suffering Lugs. "A pit stop at the waystation?"

"Carabas. We can replenish our supplies, get some gear for the mountains..."

"And visit Moira Marti."

Julius nodded. "You saw right through me."

The three cats, accompanied by Bingo, found a spacious carriage to sit in. Bingo immediately stuck his nose out of a window and sniffed the steam that shrouded his ride. Julius looked for Ramona, but she was gone.

"Not everyone will be pleased to see you," Lugs pointed out. "After that thing with the ferals."

"That thing was an accident, and we saved the day, remember? We'll be welcomed with open paws."

"Have you heard anything from Moira or Tarquin?"

"Not a whisker's twitch. They must be swamped with work."

"I'm not going to help them. I have to keep a low profile."

"Not easy with those ears." Julius giggled to himself. Chilly, he closed the window. Bingo opened it again, sticking his whole head out this time.

"If a train passes opposite, you'll lose your brains," Julius chided. Lugs gave him a look. *What brains?*

"If the top brass learns I'm absent without official permission, I'm in very hot water."

"I like a nice bath," Sal chipped in. A glower from Julius shut him up.

"I thought you'd applied for leave?" Julius asked.

"There wasn't time. If I'd waited for the okay from HQ, I'd still be twiddling my paws in Bast. You'd better be right about us getting back in a jiffy."

"Aren't I always?" It was Lugs's turn to glower. "Forget I said that."

The train made good time, and in contrast to Julius's previous trip north, there were no feral attacks to slow them down. Julius and Lugs sat side by side on a seat, looking out the window. Sal slept up on a luggage rack, and Bingo played with his fascinating stick.

"This is where we met," Lugs pointed out, waggling a paw at a two-pronged rock formation. "Could have been in this carriage."

"I don't think so," said Julius.

"If we hadn't bumped into each other, I might still have my ... dignity."

"Those Carabians were going to hurt you, no matter who you were with."

"Yeah, I'm sorry," said Lugs. His tail twitched with yearning. "I didn't mean to put that on you. And there is a bright side. Since I got the snip, I haven't been wasting time and treasure on females. I've been focused on staying fit and looking after our block."

"You've done a damn fine job of it," said Julius, staring out at the passing rocks so he wouldn't have to make eye contact with Lugs. "Thank you."

"My mission is its own reward," said Lugs. "No thanks necessary."

"That's a shame," said Julius. "Because I was going to show my gratitude by buying you lunch." Julius stood up and headed out of the carriage. "Never mind. Coming, Sal? Bingo?"

Lugs was too surprised to say anything as his friends departed. He sat with his mouth open, wishing he'd brought his berries.

Otto's jaws could decimate bone, but they couldn't chew through the chains that secured his cage. He did have his pulled tooth, however, and he used it to pick at his padlock, allowing himself a low chuckle as the lock sprung open. He froze, listening for Chico; once

Otto was out of the cage, he would make short work of the upstart jailer.

The cage door swung outward, and Otto loped into the gloom of the cellar, feeling the cool dirt floor beneath his paws. Unconscious when he was imprisoned, he had no idea where he was. He heard the faint sound of rushing water; he didn't know whether it was the river, a sewer, or a rain shower draining beneath him. He pressed his ear against a cobwebbed wall, listening closely. The flow was constant, more likely to belong to the River Hune than a storm drain.

There were at least two more obstacles to his freedom. One was Chico Audaz, his jailer, hardly lion-size but healthy and motivated to stop his captive from escaping. Well, Otto was more determined. He had a kingdom to save.

The second obstacle was more immediate. There was a gate set into the archway leading out of the cellar, secured on the other side with a larger padlock and a horizontal iron bar. Even if he picked the lock, he would have to find a way to lever the bar upward and push the gate open.

Otto held out his loose tooth and turned his paw sideways, squeezing it through the bars. Usually, large paws were a boon in a city where every swipe was a statement. Here, they posed a problem. He curled his paw around and held his tooth against the padlock. He froze when he thought he heard movement in the darkness beyond. Chico would take his tooth and leave him locked in this cellar; cage or no cage, he was still a prisoner. He used his nose. He couldn't smell the cat, just damp, slimy stone and his own stale body odor.

Otto was not famous for his patience. He took a deep breath in through his nostrils and out through his throbbing mouth, quieting his spirit. He wheedled his tooth-pick into the padlock, then turned it clockwise at an awkward angle until he heard the spring-loaded pins click. This was easier than he had imagined. With a satisfying clatter, the lock opened, and the chains drooped. Once Otto shoved the iron bar clear, he would be free to find Chico and eat the little upstart.

He held his tooth under the bar and pushed the stubborn metal from beneath. The bar wouldn't budge.

Otto got more frustrated than ever. He slammed his shoulder against the gate, the ear-shredding sound of uprooted metal echoing through the cellar. The gate was still in place, but the iron bar was loose. Placing both paws under it, Otto closed his eyes and calmed himself, as his father had taught him to do when he was a cub, so long ago.

In his mind, the world slowed down around him, every mote of dust hanging in the air. He inhaled through his nostrils again, deeper this time.

He was interrupted by a smell.

Chico was coming, fresh cat food on his breath and a trace of marsh dirt on his paws. He'd been on the riverbank, beyond the cellar. Now he had returned to check on Otto.

The lion opened his eyes and saw Chico facing him on the other side of the gate, holding a large bunch of keys temptingly close.

"You might have slipped by me," said Chico, securing the padlock. "If you hadn't made such a racket."

"I am the mayor of this city! I demand to be treated with respect."

"I had no idea," said Chico, feeling brave with the bars between them. "Thank you for the update."

Otto roared, and Chico's fur was blown back from his face. Chico didn't feel brave anymore. He backed away, his tail tucked between his legs. "You-you're a relic," he stammered. "A replaceable object. After the election, we'll charge the rubes to come down here and see you. Tickets purchased in advance. We'll put up a sign that says, 'He once growled and roared fiercely.' Because you only have so many roars left in you. Mr. Mayor."

It was Otto's turn to back off. He gave Chico the worst look he could give—a hungry one. Chico left him in the darkness, the keys to his freedom jangling as the cat walked away.

"I didn't know this was here," said Bingo, sniffing around the pristine white dining car as the train hurtled north toward Carabas.

"Didn't you take this train down to Bast?" asked Julius.

"It seemed shorter, then," Bingo replied. "Less smells." He said the last word with a delighted lilt.

Bingo was the only dog in this section. A few cat passengers watched him nervously, perched on windowsills or eating a spot of lunch, their tails and whiskers twitching as he joined his friends at a small table. The sheepdog seemed oblivious to the stares.

Although Julius was used to fine dining, he was impressed with the cream-colored tablecloth and gleaming porcelain saucers before him. There wasn't a single hair on the cloth. *Now these are cats who take pride in their work,* he told himself as he checked a menu.

The servers were not as welcoming as the decor. They were snooty as they brought Bingo water in a chrome bowl. They were rude when Sal asked what the surprise was in the fish surprise (the scorn-ridden answer: extra fish). They were impatient while the diners made their selections.

"I'll try the bug *a l'orange*," said Julius, licking his lips.

"The fish surprise," said Sal, nervous in case he said the wrong thing. "With extra fish."

"I think I'll live a little," said Bingo. "And get the fancy feast."

"That's seven courses," Julius whispered.

"Oh, you're right." Bingo nodded. "That will leave me some room for dessert."

Sal hoped that Bingo would share his rich, seemingly boundless fancy feast, or at least give him a drop of gravy. Sal watched, eyes wide, as a server opened a can of mousse pate, held it upside down, and let the delectable lump of meat plop onto a plate. When Sal leaned in to inhale the meaty aroma, Bingo growled at him, and he backed off.

Julius was reminiscing about his Purrlitzer Prize-winning old flame, Camilla. He couldn't help it. This was the train she'd taken to the North after dumping him, after they'd spent years working together at *The Scratching Post*, after he'd given his heart to her—at least, a big part of it. Now she was gone, a victim of the terrible mob he'd stirred up.

Camilla had been smug, vain, supercilious, and beautiful, treating Julius with a ruthless honesty fitting for someone who could see right through all of his writer's folderol. Julius loved Moira and was fascinated by Ramona, but he missed Camilla the most because he would never see her again.

What kind of relationship did she enjoy with Quincy? he wondered. *How did they make such a close connection in such a short time?*

"Well, that was a surprise," said Sal, licking his paws clean.

"What was?" Julius asked, his reverie broken.

"There was extra fish in my fish surprise."

"Sal..." Julius looked at Sal, then Bingo, who was trying to eat his plate. He slumped on his cushion in defeat.

They had a long way to go. First, the train would stop at Waystation, a ward in the southernmost part of Carabas, where they could pick up supplies. Bingo, especially, was going to need lots of food. Next, they would visit downtown Carabas and Julius would call on Moira. Finally, they would ride up to Stick Station and walk from there to Quincy's home and workplace. Julius wasn't sure what he would find there, but at the very least, he could meet the inventor and satisfy his curiosity. What harm could there possibly be in that?

––––––––––––––––––

Doctor Quincy McGraw had always been focused. When he started a book, he read it from cover to cover without a break. Showing acumen for the fiddle as a kitten, he'd practiced until his paws were sore. Studying for his doctorate had been a doddle, and he always saw an experiment through to its conclusion. His powers of concentration were a boon when he was in his laboratory, but not in social situations. He found it difficult to switch from one conversation to another.

Fortunately for Quincy, social situations were a rarity in the mountains north of Carabas, and that was how he liked it. All he wanted was to design and build his inventions, useful tools for cats and dogs. But he kept getting interrupted. That was one reason why he lived alone, with no neighbors in sight. The other: he was not welcome in Bast, receiving no funding from his feline peers and jealous attempts to oust him from his tenured position at the University of Pussylvania. So he'd left to develop his projects in secret, with more support from the Isle of Dogs than he'd ever received down south.

His lab was a mess. Trashed by burglars, he was leaving it in pieces until he finished his latest invention, his greatest priority. Housekeeping was much lower down on his list of to-dos. He knew where all his tools were, vaguely, and he knew what was missing—the Bernoulli tube. He did not want to build another, not until the original was recovered. Why create another temptation for the thieves?

In the meantime, Quincy was constructing an extendable pincer for some wealthy cat clients. At least he could count on some support from the private sector. This invention, which he dubbed the paw claw, was for chubby cats who didn't want to expend effort stooping down when they dropped their food. The pincer telescoped out of a plastic stick to reach the floor. Quincy had the components laid out on a coffee table; all he needed to do was assemble them and then have the paw claw shipped to Bast.

Since his lab was a wreck, he used his living room to complete the project. His couch was cluttered with blueprints and notepads, leaving just enough room for him to perch on one cushion. A framed picture of his beloved sister, Carlotta, had pride of place on a mantlepiece, looking down at him with pride. Quincy missed his sister, who lived in the coastal town of Bubastis. She didn't have any trouble socializing in that tourist spot. Sometimes he envied her outgoing nature.

Quincy was attaching the pincer to the stick when he heard a clatter from the adjoining lab. *Not again,* he thought, hopping from his cushion and listening intently, his ears swiveling sideways to catch as much information as possible. *Something else to study,* he told himself, intellectualizing the situation. The auditory peculiarities on the recurrence of a break-in.

Gripping the tube in his left paw, he walked softly toward the lab. It sounded as if the interloper was looking for something, or was simply determined to cause damage, swiping objects off of surfaces for no good reason. *Must be a cat,* Quincy deduced.

"Who is there?" he called out, a tremble in his voice. "Be warned, I have a paw claw and I am quite willing to use it!"

That sounded silly, even to him. The trespasser had no idea what a paw claw was, and his threat was ignored; the clattering continued. The first burglary had taken place while Quincy was sleeping; this time, he had two choices—fight or flight—and he had no intention of leaving a stranger to run rampant in his workspace.

Pushing his glasses up his nose, Quincy barged into the lab, stick held high. He saw a shadow first, cast by the intruder, knocking over a drawing board with one flailing paw. Quincy saw slavering teeth, a swinging light catching a glint in the beast's eye, a short, ugly muzzle, and a stub of a tail. It was a Boerboel, twice as tall as Quincy and 20 times as heavy, a mass of muscle. Quincy wanted to go back to the relative safety of his living room, but it was too late. The monstrous Boerboel had seen him.

"You," the dog rumbled. "Cavem needs you."

"I am available for hire," Quincy said. "Did Greffin send you?"

The dog, whose name Quincy assumed was Cavem, didn't answer. He took a step toward Quincy, a glass beaker cracking under a hind paw. Cavem dog didn't feel a thing.

"You cannot come in here and destroy my life's work! Have you no sense of personal territory?"

"Need plans," said Cavem in a voice that sounded like he was chewing on gravel. *He probably is,* thought Quincy.

"Blueprints? For what?"

"For tube."

"The Bernoulli tube that you stole?"

Cavem grunted an affirmative.

"The blueprints were taken. Don't you have them? Didn't you know what you had? Without those..." *You can't operate my invention,* Quincy realized. *When he figures that out, this dog is going to rip my head off.*

"Need plans."

"They are gone!" Quincy hissed, keeping a workbench between himself and Cavem. "You probably ate them, you dumb—"

Cavem gave him a blank stare.

"You did, didn't you?" Quincy mewed. "You ate them!"

The dog clamped his jaws down on the bench, yanking it aside.

"Need you."

Quincy ran. He reached his kitchen before the Boerboel caught up with him. Quincy jumped onto a counter, reached up, and pawed open a cupboard. He tossed snacks at Cavem.

"A big boy like you likes to eat, right?"

"Eat you," said the dog.

Ramona Pretzel turned up her coat lapels and bowed her head, hoping no one would see her as she walked as quickly as she could down Chandoha Avenue, ears cocked, listening for paw steps behind her. She was alone, for now, crunching through fallen leaves, her tail tucked away. He reached a four-story brownstone apartment building, stood on the stoop, glanced from side to side, then entered the foyer. After allowing herself a little breather, she went upstairs to the top floor, ascending quickly and gracefully, as if defying gravity. In the uppermost apartment, she found Woodrow, Tad's fiercest political rival.

"I don't like coming here this late," Ramona said quietly.

"The streets are quiet," said Woodrow. He sat on a window seat, the red neon lights of the city giving him a diabolic aura. "Less chance of someone seeing you."

"More chance one of Tad's security goons will pop out of the shadows and pounce on me."

"Do Tad's ... goons make a habit of this?" Woodrow asked.

"They do. In my head, at least."

Ramona joined Woodrow at the window, and they both looked down onto the street. It was empty for the time being.

"How goes the campaign?" Woodrow asked quietly.

"Hectic, but surprisingly slow." Ramona sighed. "Mr. Tybalt hasn't even decided on a slogan yet! He's got to be personally involved in everything, then he complains that his employees—myself included—aren't doing enough."

"The price of power," said Woodrow. "Once tasted, it is hard to relinquish control. Do you have any dirt for me, Ramona?"

"Not yet. Give me time."

"Time is the one mouse we can't afford to hunt," said Woodrow.

"I said give me time. I'll show that cat I'm more than a secretary."

"You certainly will. When you get home, you'll find an extra kettle of fish stored in your icebox."

"I'm not doing this to feed my belly, Woodrow. I'm doing it for revenge. No one spurns Ramona Pretzel, not even the mighty Thaddeus Gregory Tybalt."

Ramona peered out the window into the dusk. When she saw a shadow pass under a lamppost, she tensed up, her ears angled outward.

"There's someone down there," she whispered. "Watching us."

"I don't see anybody."

"It's a cat... it was a cat. He's gone now."

"You have nothing to worry about."

Ramona turned to Woodrow. "I don't feel comfortable going home right now."

"Stay with me then," Woodrow purred. "For a little while."

Cavem opened his mouth so wide that Quincy could see dirty molars and a string of saliva looped around the dog's tongue. Quincy ducked and scurried into his living room, skidding on the wooden floor. Cavem was right behind him, the Boerboel's V-shaped ears flapping, his rump crashing against the fireplace. The picture of Carlotta teetered on the mantelpiece, and Quincy reached for it, choosing sentiment over self-preservation.

Cavem bit down on Quincy's scruff with surprising mildness, enough to snag him but not hurt him. Quincy struggled free and leaped toward the mantlepiece, desperate to secure the picture.

Cavem swiped an angry paw at the memento, knocking it to the ground and smashing it.

Quincy was incensed. Forgetting his fear, he attacked the huge dog, clawing at the chest and throat. Quincy was no match for Cavem, who clamped a paw down on Quincy's head, stunning him.

Cavem lifted his paw, giving Quincy a chance to collect his senses. The cat looked up at the Boerboel, towering above him.

"See real sister," said Cavem, pointing at the picture with his nose. "With me."

"You know where she is?" Quincy didn't understand how the dog could be connected to Carlotta. As far as he knew, she was safe in Bast. "Is she alright? What have you done to her, you cur?"

The dog nodded. He was, indeed, a cur. "Take you," he said. "No eat."

Was the Boerboel making a joke? Quincy wasn't sure. But if Carlotta was caught up in this mess, it was his responsibility to make sure she was safe. He took his coat and a matching hat from their pegs, found his wallet and his pocket watch, left a scribbled note by the phone, and followed Cavem out into the harsh daylight.

3

Return To Carabas

"Hear ye, hear ye! This town's always been trouble. That's why I like it! Trouble with a capital rub. All you cats with different opinions y'all can't keep to yourselves. You gotta express yourselves, get up on a wall or a roof or a soapbox, and cry to the heavens, 'Listen to me! I'm important! What I believe is important and I'm gonna share it with you, whether you like it or not.' I admire that. I got faith too; faith in you, my listenin' brood.

"Case in point of all this: protests are getting bigger and better outside the mayorless City Hall. Now, those rabble-rousers could wait for election day and vote their feelings. They can't wait for that! They're too hot under their fur and they want to shake their placards at the world and say, 'This ain't right! A city this big needs a leader!'

"That's all well and good, my fair listeners, but what kind of leader? In my humble mind, this ain't the kind of decision you wanna rush. Otto's aide, Woodrow, is doing okay in the interim. Maybe he's the cat for the job. Or the pressure'll be too great, and he won't survive until the election. One thing's for sure—those wacky campaigners outside his door ain't making things any easier for the stuffed shirt civil servant. If he's worth his whiskers, he'll encourage all those messy opinions, listen to them, and incorporate them into the way he runs things... if he wins. Because without our voices, without our single minds, we ain't truly alive, and we ain't *bona fide* citizens worth leading, are we?

"Stay tuned for more news and a new song to assault your auricles, 'Wear Me Out' by The Minks. Enjoy!"

—WOTW radio broadcast
By DJ Scratch

Waystation was a constant draw for casual shoppers and gawping tourists alike. Cats traveled from all points across the continent to buy or sell merchandise, pick up a souvenir, or, most importantly, get a glimpse of a world where cats and dogs worked together without getting in a lather.

Thanks to Roy's generous stipend, Julius and his friends had some serious purchasing to do. Julius bought a new notebook with an ornate leather cover. Lugs carefully selected a mixture of fresh berries. Sal couldn't decide what to buy, got nervous, and handed over most of his share to a stallholder without getting anything in return. Bingo bought a meaty biscuit and shared it with Sal.

All around them, the market teemed with local merchants and an eclectic barrage of visitors from Mertown, families from Bast, hippies from Carabas, and sentinels on leave. Julius noticed how focused the cats from Bast seemed to be, compared to the others. He reminded himself to loosen up, stop, and smell the spices.

Closing his eyes, he breathed in peppermint, thyme, citrus, eucalyptus, and cinnamon, each herb and scent tantalizing his nostrils. He felt relaxed and confident until the sounds around him disturbed his thoughts.

"Stick Station? That's too close to the mountains for my liking." A wizened female caracal was selling a warm, used jacket to Lugs.

"We won't be there long," Lugs assured her. He checked the seams of the jacket, sniffing at it as he tried to discern who had worn it before. It smelled a bit too doggy for his linking. "Long enough to help a cat in need, then return home. It's what I do. A sentinel is duty bound to answer a call for help."

"So you'll be there…"

"For as brief a time as possible," said Lugs, handing the jacket back to the caracal.

"You know what's not there?" she asked him.

"Not entirely," said Julius, joining Lugs with Sal and Bingo.

"Nothing!" the caracal spat. "The mountains are no place for a cat to live, or vegetation to grow. It's 'orrible out there, I tell you. 'Orrible!"

The caracal had good reason to loathe the North. Beyond the inhospitable mountains lay No Cat's Land, a place that had earned its name after many explorers had visited, returning with tales of desolation, if they returned at all. Past No Cat's Land and the body of deep, dark water known as the Bay of Hounds was the city of Alcander on the Isle of Dogs, a province where only a few brave cats lived among the canines. Life expectancy was short for those cats, and inevitably involved loud barking and running. Camilla had visited and covered all the top dog news, mainly *exposés* of their shameful behavior. Julius had no intention of ever going there.

"The cat we're visiting lives out there," said Sal.

"I live in Healing," said Bingo. "Near Stick station."

"Dogs'll put up with anything," the caracal mumbled to herself. "What's the latest on the election? Who's winning?"

"I haven't the foggiest," said Sal.

"As far as I can tell, Woodrow Cormer is in the lead because he's already running the city. Joey Hondo's a close second because he's protective, handsome, and buff. As for Tad Tybalt... he might just be running to promote his business, nobody knows for sure. But the truth will come out."

Before Bingo could offer his uninformed opinion, he saw a biscuit-faced kitten and bolted after it.

"Bingo!" Sal shouted.

"Come back here," said Julius. He and Lugs ran after the dog, telling Sal to stay put.

The caracal stared at Sal, making him uncomfortable. She asked, "You want to buy this jacket or not?"

Julius and Lugs searched a row of market stalls, listening for Bingo's distinctive pants and barks. It was hard to pick out any single sound in the raucous shopping area.

"Any sign of him?" Julius asked.

Lugs shook his head. "Maybe we shouldn't bother."

Julius looked at Lugs, surprised to hear this from the do-gooder.

"We can't rely on that dog," Lugs explained, lowering his voice so only Julius could hear him. "We need more information. Do you even know what McGraw looks like?"

"I know he's a ginger tom," said Julius. "It said so in one of Camilla's articles."

"Did it say he was buff?" asked Lugs.

"It did not." Julius was deadpan.

"And you still want to go to the north?"

"This invention Quincy wrote about... whatever it is... if the wrong dogs get their paws on it, finding Bingo won't be the worst of our problems."

"Your absent-minded, note-writing buddy probably mislaid it."

"You don't know," said Julius, checking behind a stall selling seasonal hams. "Here boy!" he called out. "I've got your favorite stick."

"Over there!" Lugs rushed toward the end of the stalls, where a collection of ornately whittled wood figurines flew in the air. A hairy blur of motion had upset a display tray, sending its contents flying. Lugs caught up with the cause of the upset, an overactive sheepdog who had lost his way.

"I saw a kitten." Bingo smiled. "Its face was the shape of a biscuit."

"You can't go wandering off," Lugs admonished, leading Bingo back to the caracal's stand, where Sal waited patiently. "This isn't Stick Station."

"I'm sorry," said Bongo. "I thought I'd never see you guys again! I lost my way, got muddled up."

"First time for everything, I'm sure," said Lugs, acting the sour puss. The lynx was worried about being away from his post for too long. He didn't really believe in Julius's crusade; he didn't believe Quincy's invention would be found. He cared about his friends, though, and he felt it was his duty to keep them safe. He would stick with them for as long as he could.

Sal beamed as his friends approached. He held up an exciting new find.

"I bought a jacket," Sal said proudly. It was the one Lugs had looked at. It didn't fit, but Sal was happy that he'd got something in return for his money this time. The caracal was happy too.

"You do know your allowance has to last you through Carabas, Bingo's village, and all the way back home again?" Julius asked Sal.

Sal gave Julius a blank look and said, "I'm hungry."

Once Julius and his friends had all the provisions they needed, they went back to the station. A short train ride took them to the business district of Carabas.

Julius led Sal, Lugs, and Bingo from the station to Moira's office. On the way, Bingo marveled at the bustling townsfolk, moving in bigger clowders than the market crowds at the Waystation. Sal pointed out the few landmarks he remembered from his last visit, excited to see so much construction taking place. Bingo noted that the labor was done by cats as well as dogs, sharing tasks and working side by side, quietly and efficiently. No hissing, no barking or biting. He could never dream of leaving Stick Station, but to a working dog like him, Carabas seemed idyllic.

Julius ushered him on, telling him there was nothing to see and nothing to herd. Bingo took one more look at the construction workers, hungry for a final glimpse of a life unlived.

Lugs was sullen, unhappy to be in the town where he'd been immolated but unwilling to leave his friends unprotected. Despite its politically correct trimmings, Carabas could be a very dangerous place, and it was ruled by a cat who had every reason to hate Julius.

The sky looked strangely gray and ominous, as though there was a storm brewing. Tarquin washed with care, watching the clouds roll by his window.

Tarquin Quintroche, governor of Carabas, liked to be aware of everything occurring in Carabas: all the important figures who came and went, the moment that dignitaries arrived at the train station, and the major crimes and good deeds that impacted public morale. When Julius, Lugs, Sal, and Bingo arrived in Carabas, Tarquin knew. He did not appreciate the news.

He was surprised to hear of Julius's arrival. The reporter was a Bast cat, through and through, rarely leaving the catropolis. When he did, he brought trouble with him. When Julius had left Carabas, Tarquin had hoped the choice would be permanent; Tarquin had made it very clear that he was not welcome.

From the governor's point of view, Julius was an obstacle. Carabas had the potential to be a utopian citadel, lawful, diverse, and famed throughout the continent for its tolerance and its ideals. Meddlers like

Julius upset Carabas's strictly enforced status quo, directing attention to the cracks in the idyllic veneer. When Julius had inadvertently led ferals into the city, he had shown that the cats there were not as selfless as they were supposed to be, taking care of themselves before they helped their canine neighbors. He had also shown that Tarquin was a flawed and egotistical leader. Tarquin preferred to see himself as perfect. He hoped that Julius was just passing through, and if not, he would personally drag the reporter to the edge of the city and boot him out: good riddance to ugly rubbish.

Tarquin was even more surprised that Lugs was back, too. The Vet had changed Lugs's life forever. Tarquin supposed that since Lugs had nothing to lose, he felt free to reenter Carabas without further harm coming to him. The governor was a little concerned that Lugs would want revenge, even after months had passed. He would be sure to keep his guards close and his wits closer.

He would meet these visitors from the south on his own terms, and a turf of his choosing. He had the power. But he couldn't ignore them. Inquisitive and emulous, he desperately wanted to know why they were back in his city.

"Brothers and sisters! It is all well and good to share our good word among each other here, in the safety of our church. But what of the poor sinners outside these walls? Do they not deserve our help?"

Bishop Kafel was dressed in ornate cream-colored robes, illuminated by the stained-glass shaft of light that reached his grand wooden pulpit. He addressed his congregation, a mixture of poor and wealthy cats from the central district of the city. He recognized some, including Chico Audaz; others were new, including a couple of munchkins and an inquisitive chaussie. Despite the fresh fur, attendance numbers were dwindling; it was time for the biggest recruitment drive he had ever tried.

Kafel read from the Book of Felidae. "The faithful did spread the word of Bastet, and She was gladdened. They did take the word to the forest wilds and the desolate plains, and She was gladdened. They did—"

"Did they, aye?" The church doors burst open and Joey Hondo, flanked by an entourage of female wirehairs, stalked up the aisle as if it were a high-fashion catwalk. Kafel squinted at the newcomers; he'd never seen them in church before, but he recognized Joey Hondo from his campaigning. The bishop looked down at his book, acting as if nothing had happened.

"They did take the message of Bastet to the highest height and the lowest pit, and She was gladdened."

"Sounds like she was easy to please," said Joey, lounging on a front pew. His entourage chuckled and chirped; the congregation was aghast.

"You are welcome here," Kafel said to Joey without looking up. "As all heathens are. Listen to our ways, and you may learn that ours is the true way."

"True way to waste a morning," said Joey. He turned to look at the congregation. "I could be dozing right now."

Kafel went on reading. "And the word was good and true and brought all cats together, under the fearsome yet gentle paws of Bastet. And the word was warmth."

"Give me a break," Joey played to the crowd. "I can get warmth from a St. Bernard."

Kafel looked up, and his eyes flashed with anger just for a second. "Come here," he commanded.

Joey tapped himself on the chest and looked from side to side. *Who me?*

"Enough of your blasphemous behavior." Kafel raised his voice. "Stand before me."

Head raised in defiance, Joey approached the pulpit. His female followers sat closer together; there was safety in numbers.

"You have heard the holy words of Felidae." Kafel glowered down at Joey. "Do they not move you?"

"I've heard words like warmth. I've heard about a deep hole. Sounds like stuff I'd find on the back of a box of cat snacks."

The congregation gasped when they heard this. A young tom hissed, "Throw him out!"

"No." Kafel held up a paw as he descended from the pulpit. "Take heed of what I say. All are welcome here. The boasters ... and the dissenters." Kafel stood face to face with Joey. The bishop was old and frail; Joey was tall and strong, his tail upright in defiance. The air in the church was thick with tension. Chico stood, ready to run to Joey's aid if he had to.

"I don't feel welcome," said Joey.

Kafel shook his head slowly. He reached up and placed a wizened paw on the top of Joey's head, pressing downward. Although he resisted, Joey felt his body lowering, his knees bending until his belly was flat on the ground.

"Bastet is a kind goddess. A true goddess. But she will not be taken lightly."

Joey struggled to maintain eye contact with Kafel. The bishop watched with a benevolent smile as the mayoral candidate turned onto his back, showing his belly in obedience to Kafel and the altar behind him.

The congregation erupted with excitement, praising their goddess. Caught up in the moment, the entourage joined in, jigging in the aisle. Even the cynical Chico was overcome with the positive emotion in the room, tears dancing in the corner of his eyes.

"I'm sorry," said Joey, picking himself up and addressing the churchgoers. "My behavior was ... totally uncalled for. I've been under so much pressure."

"You understand, son of Bastet?" Kafel asked.

"Yes." Joey bowed before the altar. "Now I understand."

The congregations approached Joey, rubbing their foreheads against him, sniffing him, desperate to be close to this miraculous convert. There was no doubt in their minds that above them in the ether, Bastet was gladdened.

Tarquin smiled when he saw the visitors from Bast on the neutral ground of the towering Friendship Center. Newly refurbished, it was a clean white hive of conference rooms, dining spaces, and perfumed litter trays. Tarquin sat at the head of a long boardroom table, insisting that Julius, Lugs, Sal, and Bingo sit at the opposite end, far away from him.

As usual, Tarquin wore a fine vest that complemented his graying fur. "Here to wreak more mischief?" he asked with open paws.

Julius did not tell him that he was hoping to see Moira, although that was obvious to both parties. Instead, he told Tarquin about his assignment for *The Scratching Post*. He would write about Bingo's village, Healing, and life at the foot of the mountains, a background piece to set up their quest for Quincy McGraw.

"Have you heard of him?" asked Sal, candid as a kitten.

"Oh, yes." Tarquin nodded. "Back when I worked in Bast as a junior under clerk at City Hall, he was lauded as one of our smartest engineers. His surfeit of ideas was his downfall."

"How can too many ideas be bad?" Lugs sneered. He squirmed on his cushion, still angry at Tarquin for sending him to the Vet.

"Bast is a city driven by capitalism," Tarquin said. "Each of Doctor McGraw's inventions served as a product, requiring time to be produced, promoted, and sold to buyers. He created a glut of gadgets that the market could not withstand. He had to go."

"What happened to him?" Julius wanted to know.

"His colleagues were paid to discredit him and his creations. Patents were rejected. Credit declined. Within weeks, he was a pariah; he had no choice but to leave the city and build a new life north of here."

"He must be bitter."

"I know not," said Tarquin. "However, someone you know has taken an interest in our outlying regions. It is good to know who and what is out there—both allies and potential threats."

Moira Marti entered the boardroom. She was a slinky white Siamese in a pinstripe pantsuit, ineffably confident and pleased to see her friends. She rubbed her forehead against Lugs and Sal, had a mutual snif-falong with Bingo, and gave Julius a lingering head rub. Julius's heart melted in the presence of his soulmate.

"Join me at my end of the table, Moira," Tarquin ordered. "We have protocols to follow when it comes to visitors."

"Cobblers," said Moira, ignoring the command. "This is my family."

Tarquin's stiff exterior wilted. "Don't think you can ignore me, just because I'm—"

"You're what?" Lugs asked. "An insufferable pinscherneck?"

"No, Lugs." Julius restrained his friend. "There's another reason why you're not obeying your boss, isn't there, Moira?"

"So astute." Tarquin shook his head. "You are right, Julius. For a change."

"I'm the boss," said Moira, sliding her tail across Julius's chest, then walking over to Tarquin.

"You're running this place?" Julius laughed. "No wonder it's running so smoothly."

"Tarquin's taking a trip, aren't you?" Moira said to the governor. She leaned in close to him, too close for Julius's comfort.

"I'm sure you're not going north," said Lugs. "That would take guts."

Sal breathed in sharply. "Oh, so that means you're going to—"

"Bast." Tarquin bowed his head. "You're looking at the city's next mayor."

Julius and Lugs looked at each other. On paper, Tarquin seemed like the perfect candidate for the new mayor; he had experience running a city, and he had worked closely with Otto in the past. In reality, they knew that he was a coward, an egomaniac, and, worst of all, he had placed cats in danger on more than one occasion.

"Are you famous?" asked Bingo, turning to Sal. "Is he famous?"

Sal shrugged, unsure of the determining factors of fame in this instance.

"I'm excited for you, Your Honor," Julius lied. "When do you leave? The other wannabe mayors are campaigning already, so you'd better get a shift on."

"I am not concerned about Woodrow, Joey, or Tad," said Tarquin with a sad smile. "They will step down if necessary, with my say-so."

"He's going next week," Moira added. "His run will start from here, then ta-da! He'll ride to Bast on a train decorated with ribbons and flags, ready to sweep up all the votes."

"I would vote for you," woofed Bingo, caught up in the excitement.

"Alas, you cannot vote in Bast," said Tarquin. "Yet. I will change all that once I am ensconced in City Hall."

"How can you even see who to vote for?" Moira wondered. "With all that hair?"

"I shake my head, then I can see," Bingo explained. "Until I stop shaking." He demonstrated, making himself dizzy. "I bump into things sometimes," Bingo panted. "It makes the passengers laugh. I like making them laugh."

"There's more to life than entertaining others. You have to take care of yourself, too."

"How?"

"Come with me," Moira said to Tarquin, "I'm going to take this dog to get cleaned up. Just like you're going to clean up in the election."

Tarquin nuzzled Moira, making Julius's fur crawl. Moira made sure he got a good look.

"I, uh, should make sure we have everything for the next leg of our journey," said Julius, leaving the room. "Thanks for the information, Tarquin."

"Any time," Tarquin purred, undoing the top button of his vest. Moira was adept at getting him excited.

"Up and at 'em boys." Moira grinned a cheeky grin. "It's time to get groomed."

———————————

The Friendship Center had its own running track, climbing canvas, and spa, all amenities geared toward the modern needs of dogs and cats who came to Carabas for business. Moira took Lugs, Sal, and Bingo to the spa, where Bingo was amazed to see cats giving dogs tongue scrubs and massages. He found it strange; Lugs found it worse.

"This is unholy," said Lugs as he wrapped a towel around his waist.

"We take care of each other here," said Moira. "There is nothing more sacred. It is the core of all religions, or at least it should be."

"But... These dogs are being pampered!" Lugs spluttered.

"They work hard. They're tired. Surely you can relate to that, soldier boy?"

"It should be the other way around," said Bingo quietly. "Dog fetching and carrying for cats. We like fetching."

"I did hear that a lot," said Sal.

"The cats enjoy being of service to others," Moira explained. "It makes them feel valuable."

"It makes me feel lazy," said Bingo as he got his hair trimmed by a Burmese groomer. He asked the cat, "Are you sure I can't do anything to help?"

"There is," the groomer said, dead serious. "You can sit still. That's it. Stay."

Lugs sank into a hot tub, floating in water mixed with tea tree oil. For the first time since he'd been on patrol in Bast, he felt relaxed.

Sal got his oversized snowshoe paws massaged, giggling at the tickly process. He was also treated to a manicure, getting his claws trimmed and polished so they shone in the clinical light of the spa.

Julius swallowed his pride and came to find Moira, leading her out of the spa and onto the rooftop running track. It was empty that evening, brick-red and breezy, with a gobsmacking view of Carabas below.

"I need your help, Moira."

"You always do." Moira smirked.

Julius turned away. "You'd rather I left you alone?"

"That would require you taking a hint, which you can't."

"I'm a writer, not a mind reader."

"Read this." Moira set off running. Julius understood enough to follow her, keeping pace.

"You haven't sent any letters in weeks," said Moira, carefully controlling her breathing. "No phone calls, no pigeon post."

"Pigeon post doesn't work," Julius panted. "The carriers keep getting eaten."

"Don't tell me you forgot to write. You just said, that's what you do."

"I thought you wanted—" *to be left alone,* Julius thought, slowing down.

"That's the trouble. You always know best. This time you didn't."

"I'm sorry." Julius picked up his pace and rejoined Moira. "How can I fix this?"

"I don't know if you can. With Tarquin leaving, I have to run this town, and that's not fair, J. I've got a good mind to leave my colleagues for a few days and see how they get on without me, which they can't. Be careful on this corner—take it too fast and you'll run off the roof."

"Why don't you?"

"I beg your pardon?"

Julius took Moira's paw. They stopped running together, red dust kicked up, forming a sun-tinged mist around them.

"Why don't you leave for a few days? A week?"

"Hmm?" Moira raised an eyebrow. Julius loved it when she did that, her curiosity kicking in, an attractive glint in her eyes.

"Why don't you come with me to this inventor's place, help me solve the mystery of the missing gizmo? It'll give you a break from this place and..."

"Help me clear my head." For the first time that day, Moira looked surprised. "Once again, you make your selfish needs sound beneficial to others. Bravo."

"That's why I like you so much, Moira. You see right through my furry exterior to the alley cat beneath."

Moira grinned. "I'll come. It will take me a day to clean up my paperwork and delegate some tasks to Rusty."

"You sure you want to leave a dog in charge?" asked Julius.

"I'm sure. This mystery of yours—it's not dangerous, is it?"

Julius hesitated. He didn't want to scare Moira off. But this was Moira, the bravest cat he knew. "Yes."

"Good."

Bingo wasn't sure if he liked his new look. His fringe was high above his eyes now, and his ears felt cold when he stuck his head out the train window. His eyes did too, watering in the wind. He did feel lighter, though, faster and more streamlined. It still felt weird to get pampered, but he supposed he could get used to it.

"If you feel cold," said Julius, "get back in this carriage and close the window."

Bingo's response was to pant and keep poking his head out.

"He's being a dog," Moira told Julius. They sat in the carriage with Sal and Lugs. "This is what dogs do." Raised by dogs, Moira was an undoubted expert, so Julius accepted her wisdom. He was ecstatic to have her with him although he wasn't sure how he had managed to convince her to come up north. Maybe he did have a gift with words, after all.

Lugs polished his metal mittens, admiring their shine. "You've been carrying those around the whole time?" asked Moira. "They look heavy."

"Oh, they are," Lugs replied proudly.

"I hope you don't have to use them," said Julius.

"I hope I do." Lugs bashed the gauntlets together with an uncouth clang. "In the defense of those present, of course."

"Of course," said Moira, a faint smile on her muzzle.

Bingo's colleagues hardly recognized him when he returned to work at Stick Station. He drew out detailed directions for the cats, so they could find Quincy's observatory with ease. The sheepdog turned out to be quite an artist.

"I wanted to stay longer with you folks," Bingo ruffed. "But the station master needs me back. Half the porters have quit, the ones who moved here from the Isle of Dogs. They've gone back home; I don't know why."

"I'll miss you, pooch," said Moira, kissing his big wet nose. Bingo gave her a happy lick.

"Thank you for everything," Julius told Bingo. "I still want to write about your village and your family."

"I don't have one. I'm an orphan," Bingo replied.

"You have a family now," said Sal. "Us."

"We'd write to you, if you could read." Lugs's tone was kind even though his words lacked tact.

"I'd like to see you draw as well as him," Moira snapped. "Goodbye, Bingo!"

The sheepdog frolicked off to help an elderly couple with their bags as the cats made their way up the mountain path to Quincy's observatory. The laboratory was in total disarray, with signs of a burglary as if it was committed by ten fat, clumsy canines. The living area was empty with furniture flipped over and a picture smashed on the floor.

"He's gone," said Julius, after they had thoroughly checked the domicile. "We missed him."

"And no note this time," Lugs confirmed. "You think he was taken?"

Julius nodded. "Keep those mitts of yours close," he said. "Whoever created this chaos must have abducted the doctor. I only hope he's still alive."

"We could go back," Sal suggested quietly. "I mean, we answered Doctor McGraw's call and came all the way here. It's not our fault we can't find him."

"We have to find his machine," Julius told Sal. "Find that, and we'll probably find him too."

The cats searched for notes or plans that would help them figure out what kind of machine had been stolen. Once again, Quincy's prolificity created a problem. There were too many blueprints for them to weed through.

Quincy wasn't at Stick. The station master confirmed that no ginger cats had taken a train, not for months. The inventor was either walking south, in which case he would probably have been spotted from the train—another dead end, according to the railway workers they asked—or was headed through the mountains, north to the Isle of Dogs. That was the direction they had to take, despite Julius's deep misgivings.

"We're going to need a guide," said Moira. They stood on platform one of Stick Station, where Bingo was extremely pleased to see them. They could tell by the blur his tail made as it wagged.

"To take us across terrain that only a shortlist of cats has ever returned alive from?" Lugs frowned. "We need a guide as stubborn as, well, you, Julius."

"What's wrong with Bingo?" asked Sal.

Moira looked at Bingo, who was trying to sniff his own nose.

"Bingo has luggage to carry," Julius said. "Don't distract him."

"He's doing a good job of that himself," quipped Lugs.

Lugs asked Bingo, "Where can we find a mountain guide?"

"Apart from me?"

"Yes." Moira nodded. "Apart from you."

"I only know two, and one of them is me."

"Who's the other one?" asked Sal, desperate to be part of the conversation.

"Old Kelly is ... old. So old. Used to be a ginger tom like Quincy but now his hair's turned pale gray, so I guess he's not a ginger tom anymore. No one knows the mountains like Kelly."

"Where can we find him?" Julius prompted.

"In the mountains, generally," said Bingo. Lugs glared at the dog, who hastily continued. "B-but this time of day he's usually on the roof, catching the warmth of the evening sun."

The cats climbed effortlessly onto the hot tin roof of the station, where Kelly lay flat on his back, paws drooping, enjoying the sunshine on his belly.

"I hate to interrupt him," said Julius.

"You already did," Kelly yawned, his voice dry and rough as sandpaper. "Join me."

Sal, Moira, and Lugs lay down in the golden light, closing their eyes, unable to stop themselves from purring. Julius looked out across the mountains, mapping it in his mind. This was one of those rare opportunities for him to take a breath, too, watching nimbus wisps brushing far-off summits.

He took a deep breath, exhaled, then asked Kelly, "Could you guide us to the Isle of Dogs?"

Kelly jumped up, almost losing his balance on the sloped roof. "Guide you where now? What in tarnation for?"

"We're looking for a friend, or rather, an acquaintance," Moira explained. "Quincy McGraw, you probably know him?"

"Of course I know him. The crackpot inventor. He's probably gone and blowed himself up."

"I don't think so," said Lugs, introducing himself and his friends while holding out a paw to support the wobbly Kelly. "He might have been abducted."

"We have experience in such matters," Julius mumbled.

"One of his weapons is gone, too," Lugs added.

"Weapons?" To Lugs's horror, Kelly staggered to the edge of the roof. "Toys, you mean? Half his Gizmos don't work. Dogs probably took it; they don't know no better." As Kelly leaned toward Moira, she smelled sour milk on his breath. The old cat asked, "Is that why you want to go to the Isle of Dogs?"

"We're following a clue," said Julius.

"Just like in one of his books," Sal gushed. He was Julius's biggest fan. "He writes the Tiger Straight detective mysteries."

"Never heard of 'em," said Kelly, making Julius's whiskers droop. "I like dime store tales of the frontier, myself. You write any of those, mister?"

"I do not," said Julius stuffily. "But this will be an adventure better than you'll find in a book, won't it?"

Kelly looked at Julius, making up his mind with a slow, studious, gritty blink.

Lugs gasped when Kelly jumped off the roof, concerned that his obviously advanced age had made him too frail for a long drop. Kelly landed on all fours and walked toward the mountains, waggling a paw for the others to follow.

"Come on," Kelly croaked. "You've got your guide."

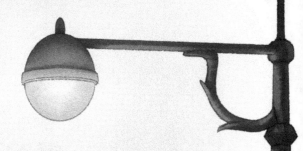

Part Two: The Mountains

4

My Pet Rocks

Beyond Quincy's observatory, at the end of a narrow pass, there was an enormous set of iron gates.

The gates, carved in the shape of two huge paws, swung open onto the land beyond. Julius felt like a mouse, set free in the midst of a tomcat's game, expecting to be trapped again. Nevertheless, the gates stayed open long enough for his group to leave, entering a gray alien world mottled green with sparse patches of grass.

He held a packet of Kitty Mix up to his mouth, ready to gobble the contents. Kelly stopped him, taking the box and stashing it by his side.

"We've a long way to go," Kelly warned. "And we have to ration our vittles."

Vittles? What's the crazy coot talking about? Julius thought. But he needed his guide, and he didn't want the coot to quit, so he kept quiet though his empty belly refused to cooperate.

"Thar be the mountains," said Kelly, pointing a paw at the massive range before them.

"I can see that," Julius snapped. What good was a guide who stated the obvious? "Why have we stopped?"

"This is as far as I go," Kelly cackled. "I don't do mountains."

"What's the big deal?" Lugs huffed.

"Wind. Terrible wind." Kelly shook his head sadly.

"Never mind your personal problems," said Sal. "Why can't we go on?"

Kelly distributed the group's gear, one pack per cat. "Oh, you can. Go ahead, if you don't mind gales that would strip a cat to ribbons like hot claws through rice paper."

"We can handle gales," Julius told him.

"You can venture forth," Kelly continued. "Straight into the clutches of the strange inhabitants that lurk in that shadowy range. Crazed cave dwellers that feast on feline flesh."

"I've handled panicking commuters in the last frenzied minutes of a downtown rush hour," Julius replied, his eyes narrowing. "Troglodytes are nothing compared to a blue-collar Burmese who's late for work, about to throw a hissy fit."

"Even if you get over that range," said Kelly, still deadly serious. "What lies beyond would strike fear into the heart of the boldest Burmese."

"What lies beyond?" asked Sal, his mouth agape.

"That which a cat fears most of all."

"You talk funny," Sal said to Kelly, blinking grit from his eyes.

"You talk nonsense," Kelly shot back.

Julius adjusted his backpack. "We hired you to take us after Doctor McGraw, to track him, and follow him all the way to the Isle of Dogs, if necessary. Yes, the place that would strike fear into the heart of the boldest Bast commuter. You can't take us this short distance, then dump us. Where's your guide pride? What will your neighbors say when they find out you quit your job on the first day?"

"I only quit when I get fired," Sal boasted.

Kelly looked scared. Julius backed off and said, "My editor gave me a generous stipend for this trip. Take us through this range, and I'll split it with you. There's five of us, so you get 20%. What do you say?"

Kelly licked his muzzle in thought. "40%," he said, tilting his head at Sal. "This snowshoe wouldn't know what to do with money if it showered on him."

Sal's mouth dropped open. He knew exactly what to do with money: buy catnip.

"Deal," said Julius. "Lead on."

Kelly took the cats into the range. "If we make good enough time, we'll stop at the foot of Tail Mountain," he said over his shoulder. "I know a good place to shelter there."

"I'm not sure what to do, Mom."

Missy Brighter sat in the Cat's Cradle, a run-down bar on the bank of the River Hune. Right beside her, her mother Desdemona sat on her favorite stool, drinking her favorite brand of sour milk.

"What have I told you about showing your weakness in public?" Desdemona snarled. She couldn't help snarling; she was old and snaggle-toothed, with torn ears and a cranky disposition. She fit right in at the Cat's Cradle; the patrons were ancient, scabby-furred, and drunk on clotted cream. One wrinkly donskoy stretched itself out on an upholstered bench, paws pointed, whiskers adroop in total relaxation; a sad-eyed minuet played on a poorly tuned piano, its little white legs dangling off its stool. Dairy signs adorned the walls, and a chalkboard menu listed lasagna, caramel pilchards, and mouse of the day as its specialties.

"I'm being honest, Mom," Missy whined. Maybe her own pint of milk was making her more truthful than usual. "You told me about that, too."

"Why sincerity has to be the province of us females, I don't know," said Desdemona. "Never met an honest tom in all my lives."

"This is about me," Missy asserted, ordering another round from the barcat. "Not about Dad, or you, for a change. I know we've never been a super-religious family..."

"So, this is about your dad and me," Desdemona cackled, lapping at her new drink. A chubby tabby shoved in between them to order a drink. Desdemona saw him off with one scowl, and he slunk around to the other end of the bar.

"Let me finish," Missy said, with a strength that befitted the leader of the Clute gang. "I don't want to go against Bastet or her believers, just in case she's up there, watching."

"You're agnostic," Desdemona spat. The old cat had lived a long time. She had seen criminal empires rise and fall, some of them her own. She was too cynical for redemption, and she drank her own damnation.

"I'm an opportunist," said Missy. "Like you taught me to be."

Desdemona turned to her daughter. Missy was a younger, more attractive shadow of herself, a fighter and strategist, a stark reminder of her own corruption. "Is this why you came to see me? We don't discuss religion or politics in here."

The bartender showed Missy a sign behind him. "Causes too many catfights," he said, wiping a glass clean with his tail.

"It's not that, it's ... okay." Missy hunched forward on her stool. "We were visited—the gang, I mean—by a priest. Not any old priest."

"You saw a missionary." Desdemona shrugged. "They enter gang territory, bring food and saucers of cream, pray, and try to indoctrinate the unwary. Then they get the snot scratched out of them and they never come back."

"Kind of," said Missy. "No. This Holy Joe wasn't in Clute territory to spread his gospel. He was there to do a deal. And get this... the priest was Bishop Kafel."

This snapped Desdemona out of her ennui. "What was he doing on your patch?"

Missy lowered her voice. "He wants us to work with his brotherhood to keep peace in the city. Look— the prowlers are still on strike, the sentinels are too busy patting each other on the back to make a difference, demonstrators are camping out in front of City Hall, and the mayor has vamoosed. That leaves a vacuum. One that the Clutes couldn't fill alone, but with the Church..."

Desdemona looked at her ambitious daughter. "Your gang is powerful, with an unscratchable rep. Nothing happens in your territory without your say-so. Why risk all that by reaching for more power?"

"It's the city, Mom. The whole city could belong to the Clutes. Imagine what a legacy that would be!"

Desdemona lapped at her milk thoughtfully. "My syndicate got involved with the Church for a while, did you know that?"

Missy shook her head. There was a lot about her mom she didn't know.

"They promised us riches, and extra territory, and all the wetties we could eat. For a while, we had them. Then my lieutenants disappeared, one by one."

"They didn't dare."

"They were untouchable! They were the Church. Not one cat, or a clowder, but an institution. How do you fight that? When my *caporegime* turned up dead in gutters and alleyways, the priests put a good spin on it. Said they were lucky to be in the afterlife now, bathing with Bastet." Desdemona shook her head. She never cried, but at that moment, she looked older than ever. "Despite hitting back the best we could, we knew it was over. The Church took everything. We survived with our tails tucked between our legs." She made sure the barcat was out of earshot. "If you ever tell anyone this, I'll bite your ears off."

"I appreciate you telling me this." Missy was in shock. She knew the Church was corrupt, but this...

This changed nothing.

"You're going to take the deal, aren't you?" Desdemona sighed.

"What happened to you was a long time ago. Kafel makes sense, and he's not dumb enough to challenge a massive gang like mine."

"There's no dumb about it."

"I'll be careful. I have a plan of my own."

"So did we, Beautiful. So did we." Desdemona paid the tab and hopped down from her stool. "If you ever find yourself alone, you know where to find me."

In the same house you've lived most of your life, thought Missy as she watched her mom walk slowly out of the bar. *Bless your old-fashioned ways and warnings. It's time for my generation to seize the power we deserve. If that means breaking bread with a scabby cat in a funny hat, I'll do it. With my claws ready to tear his soul out.*

The northern mountain range reached into the misty distance, its summits capped with snow, its slopes steep or jagged or both. Inured to city living, Julius, Sal, and Moira were cautious and uncomfortable, staying alert as they followed a path around Mount Jaw. Kelly led the way, slowly but surely. Lugs was in his element, enjoying the feel of cool air on his tufts, pointing out rare birds and plants to his friends.

Since the path tapered to a width of two feet, the cats had to move single file and watch their step. The wind blew and the temperature fell as they ascended, winding their way through the range.

The path widened, leading to a ground-level trail strewn with loose stones, which hurt the travelers' paws and slowed them down some more. As they trod on the unsure surface, the cats waved their tails, dark patterns dancing in the shadows around them. The going was poor for hours, and the only respite was caused by Sal, who stopped abruptly. The others were glad to join him for a breather.

"I know this rock," he said with a stare.

"How can you recognize a rock?" Lugs scoffed.

"This one's distinctive."

"Because of its patina?" Lugs replied sarcastically. "It's slate gray. Rock colored."

"No, not the color. It's got extra nobbles on it."

Lugs took a closer look at the offending lump. "I don't see any special nobbles."

Sal gestured at the sides of the rock. "These little lumps. They look like whiskers."

Lugs bent down to take a closer look. "Oh yeah, you're right. They do, don't they?"

"What are you pokin' around for?" Kelly asked, sauntering over to Lugs and Sal. "Ain't got no time for geology."

"We have to keep moving," Julius urged. "Make as much progress as we can before nightfall."

"What's the point of moving if it's in a circle?" asked Sal.

"You don't know what you're talking about," said Kelly. He turned to Julius and said, "Your friend's dumber than a box of dogs."

"You're partly right," said Julius. "He's my friend. He's also survived gang wars, police investigations, riots, and rat attacks. He knows a rock when he sees one."

"Yeah!" Sal jumped in. "I know my rocks."

"Are you sure you know how to get to the Isle of Dogs?" Moira asked Kelly.

"How many times have you been there?" asked Lugs.

"Seldom as possible," said Kelly. "But I been, and I know the way. Your choice—follow me or get lost."

"We'll follow you," said Sal. "You're our guide until I see this rock again. Then you're fired, and we'll find our own way."

Julius looked at Sal with surprise. It was unusual for the snowshoe to be so confrontational; he was usually so happy-go-lucky and eager to please. Julius chalked the attitude down to fatigue and pain. The bigger the paws, the sorer they could be.

Cavem led Quincy up Tail Mountain, named as such by the dogs because it was shaped like a tail jutting out above the rest of the range. The boerboel stopped once or twice to look back and gauge how far he'd come. That was all the rest that Quincy got. Otherwise, they kept climbing; the boerboel breathing hard through his nose.

At the top of the mountain, they looked down to see a windswept plateau pocked with caves and craters. It stretched off into the horizon.

"I'm thirsty," Quincy said.

Cavem ignored Quincy, kept moving along the dusty trail that spread a humble white line down the middle of the gray-brown rock. There were no way stations here, no peddlers, no watering holes.

The wind picked up. Quincy tried to walk so that Cavem's body acted as a breaker, but the gusts came from every direction. As he watched the way the boerboel's fur got ruffled, Quincy wondered for the first time if he was safe. Cavem could not assure protection. He was just a dog, after all, and out on the plateau, the power of the elements seemed infinite.

A heavy gale hit them, and they sought shelter in the coziest-looking cave they could find.

"We could always turn back," Quincy said quietly. "To Healing, at least. Replenish our strength with food and milk. I wouldn't cause a fuss or try to run away."

"Enough." Cavem knew Quincy was lying, but he seemed more concerned with what he'd found in the cave—a few empty tuna tins, a burlap sack, and a couple of battered paperbacks. The boerboel's whiskers twitched. Both cats stayed still, listening for the slightest sound. Then Quincy's eyes widened as a rangy-looking moggy with dirty, unkempt fur dropped down into the cave from a shaft above.

"Bless my soul!" said the angora. "Visitors. So much for solitude! Zehra welcomes you... if your visit is brief."

Quincy and Cavem looked at each other, amazed.

"Bit parky out there, isn't it?" Zehra chattered. The string bean squatted down beside them, offering them some thorny root vegetables that she'd brought down with her. Cavem turned his nose up at the greens. Quincy was so famished that he ate his portion in one gobble.

"Some cat might find a bolt hole like this and want to make it their home," Zehra told them with a sigh. "You're not that type, are you?"

"This is a cave," Cavem said in a superior tone. "Only a wild animal or a crazy hermit would make this their home." He gave Zehra a sniff. The skinny wretch smelled like she hadn't washed herself in weeks. "This is your place, isn't it?"

Zehra burst into movement, teeth bared, claws out. "You won't take it!" she cried. "It's mine. Get your own cave!"

Cavem looked out through the mouth of the shelter. The wind seemed to have dropped a bit.

"We'll go," the boerboel sneered. "If you promise not to tell a soul we were here. Pretend you've been alone for a long time."

That didn't sound so hard to Zehra. "And you won't come back?"

"Scratch my heart and hope to die."

"Your raw meat, ma'am." Pollet offered a slab of bloody steak to Bridget, who was sprawled on a lounger, watching the clouds roll by above her.

"I'm not hungry," Bridget yawned. "Take it away."

"If it's not too much of an imposition, I'd like to remind you that the ship's pantry is getting rather bare," said Pollet, his aquamarine eyes watery with worry. "We cannot waste any food."

"Go fish," said Bridget. "I said I'm not hungry. And what I say is law, at least on this vessel."

"Yes, ma'am."

All attempts to adjust or repair the vessel's controls had met with failure. The crew had tampered with the steering and removed essential parts before abandoning ship, leaving Bridget with only one dinghy. Leaving the ship did not seem like a smart option, so Bridget was making the most of her enforced vacation. The sea was not as endless as it looked; they would reach land eventually.

Pollet turned his back on Bridget, stomach growling.

"You were hiding again, weren't you?" Bridget asked the tonkinese.

"Yes, ma'am." Pollet cringed.

"Where this time? Come on, tell me. You know I'll work it out, eventually."

"On top of the shelving in the supply room."

"What was troubling you this time?"

Pollet faced Bridget. "The water level, ma'am. When we set out, the sea reached up to the portholes on the middle deck. Now those portholes are underwater."

Bridget sat up on her lounger. "The crew took so much from the ship when they left, it should be lighter, not heavier. Does this mean...?"

"I'm terribly afraid so." Pollet's voice trembled. "The Leo is sinking."

As the sun fell, the mountains cast cold shadows on Julius and his friends. They followed the rubbly trail and, thankfully, Sal did not see his pet rock again.

"We need to rest," said Moira. "We've been on the move for hours."

"We have to make the most of the day," Kelly insisted. "You wanna be clambering over these rocks at night?"

Moira shook her head.

"Didn't think so," said Kelly. "Onward!"

As the day drew to an end, Julius and Lugs looked up at the sheer stone faces on either side of them. They had placed their trust in Kelly, and he seemed trustworthy. But their faith was waning. Because the path through the mountains got increasingly narrow, they were in the perfect place for an ambush in a land notorious for ruthless nomads and packs of dogs. Alternately, and more worryingly, Kelly could be leading them astray accidentally. If they got stranded on a mesa with dwindling provisions, or if they were traveling in circles as Sal suspected, their chance of survival was slim.

A raindrop plopped on Sal's head, fouling his mood some more. His ears flattened on his head, and he scowled at Kelly. Dark clouds loomed over the south-ernmost rock face, bringing a shower with it. If there was one thing Sal liked less than traipsing across No Cat's Land, it was rain.

"That's good timing," said Kelly.

"How is it good?" Moira asked him. "If we were in safe, warm beds, with full bellies and dreams of the hunt, that would be a good time for a rainstorm. Otherwise, forget it."

"Follow me." Kelly took them to a large cave mouth where they sheltered, licking the damp from their fur. Lugs looked out and checked the sky for signs that the clouds would pass. The rain obscured his view, so he shrugged and backed into the cave.

"I used to stop here a lot," said Kelly. "It was a resting spot. Too soon to curl up for the night here, though."

"Used to?" Julius asked, brushing moisture from his whiskers.

"Haven't had call to recently," Kelly replied petulantly. "We can cover a lot more ground before it gets dark."

"Not in this weather," said Lugs, standing his ground. Julius investigated the cave mouth. It was deep, dark, and dry. A perfect place for the cats to spend the night. He laid out his provisions, and Lugs did the same.

"We can't stay here," said Kelly.

"Why not?" asked Moira.

"This little shelter goes back farther than you might think. And we might not be the only ones using it as a hidey hole."

"I don't see anything or anyone back here," Lugs sniffed.

"Look up." The cats craned their necks to see a shaft leading upward, a dim light shining through it. Since no water dripped down onto them, they wondered where the light was coming from.

"I'm not going outside," Julius mewed. "I've got soaked once too many times already. By all means, scout ahead if you want to, but we're staying put."

Lugs, Moira, and Sal nodded their agreement. Kelly opened his mouth as if to dicker, then shut it and squatted on the ground beside them.

"How long does this journey usually take?" Moira pressed.

"Depends on a lot of factors," said Kelly. "How many complainin' cats I got with me. The climate. The number of bugs and rodents around to distract them."

"You don't even know," Moira said, desultory and despairing.

"Course I do! We got a few more days, then we'll get to the deep little puddle between the mainland and the Isle. If you don't like this rain, I can't fathom how you're gonna react to that swim."

"There's no ferry?"

"If there was, the dogs wouldn't let you use it. You being of the feline persuasion and all."

Julius narrowed his eyes. "The dogs I've known have been fairly friendly, cooperative...."

"And paid to do a job on your turf." Kelly stared at Julius as if trying to drive sense into him. "This is different. We're entering their domain. They own it and guard it with dogged persistence, giving no quarter to cats. They'll tear you apart like cheap plush toys if they get the chance, without even thinking. Their instinct will take over."

"I believe they're better than that," Julius replied. "They have founded their own city and run it efficiently. They worked alongside cats in Bast—"

"And almost went to war with them," Lugs reminded him.

Kelly nodded, glad to have someone on his side. "Dogs and cats were never meant to coexist. You know the story of Bastet and the Great Dane?"

"Religion bores me," said Moira.

"It confuses me," Sal admitted.

"Everything confuses you, sonny," said Kelly. "Even rocks."

"You confuse me," was the best comeback Sal could muster.

"Tell us the story," said Julius, crossing his forepaws, settling down to listen. The rain poured outside; a veil between the cave and the harsh outside world.

Kelly told his tale.

"There was a time, or so the elders say, when cats feared dogs and did not better them. Many of the dogs were larger, more powerful, and faster to attack; cats did not expend the effort to put the dogs to work.

"When the dogs, led by the Great Dane, became too strong and numerous, the cats sat up and took notice. They knew that something would have to be done.

"The cats encouraged the smaller dogs to take charge. The little ones needed protection, appealing to the protective nature of their bigger cousins. The small dogs were also the loudest, drawing attention with their high-pitched yaps. The big dogs fulfilled their duty and looked after the little dogs. They built warm homes for the shih tzus, the pekingese, and the bichon frisés. When they hunted, they caught extra prey so that the small dogs would not go hungry."

"So, whether the cats had got involved or not," said Julius, "the dogs would have done the right thing, taken care of the weak and helpless."

"Cats were involved, stickin' their noses into everything as we do," Kelly replied. "Before the big dogs knew it, the little ones were bossing them around, establishing a new order. And that's the way it's stayed ever since, right to the present-day rule of Emperor Greffin. The smallest pekingese you ever did see, with the biggest bite."

"I find it hard to believe," Lugs chuckled, "that mastiffs and dobermans would take orders from a hairy tadpole like that."

"The big dogs dream of their glory days." Kelly nodded. "They share tales of the Great Dane. But they are content to rest on this nebulous nostalgia, and they're convinced their prime is behind them."

"Why haven't I ever heard of this Great Dane?" asked Moira.

"It's a dog thing," Kelly patronized.

"I know a thing or two..."

"You're too young! You have to go way back for this myth."

"I bet you know it then," said Lugs.

"Sure do." Kelly cleared his craw. "The Great Dane's muzzle was long and scarred with many battles, his paws large and injurious enough to crush rocks underfoot. His coat was the color of obsidian, with eyes of angry flame. As he exhaled, his breath cooled the air and made it fit for his followers to live. The saliva that dropped from his tongue formed the streams and rivers. And when he ventured north to the Isle of Dogs, he left a shattered trail across the land that formed the pathway through the mountains that still exists today.

"Bastet's eyes were the brightest green. Her fur was sleek and shone with a silver aura. Her claws sliced dark interstices between the stars and her swaying tail made hurricanes. Like all cats after her, she was born to be obeyed. But even the goddess of cats was no match for the Great Dane. So she used her cunning instead.

"'What is that round object in the sky?' she said, poking a paw at the sun. 'Do you think it could be a ball?'

"The Great Dane nodded. This was a possibility.

"'I should like to chase that ball,' said Bastet. 'But it is too far away.'

"'I shall fetch it,' the Great Dane said eagerly. He ran west, toward the sun, disappearing over the horizon, never to be seen again.

"Where did the Great Dane go?" asked Sal.

"He chased the ever-moving ball of fire in the sky," Moira spelled out. Julius liked her maternal tone.

"Oh!" Sal got it. "The sun keeps moving. So he's still running?"

"Some say he settled on the Isle of Dogs," said Kelly. "Ruled there until recent times, when a new leader took his place. Greffin, the emperor and master of all dogkind."

"I can't wait to meet this Greffin," said Julius, sardonic as usual.

"You'll have him lapping out of your paw in no time," Lugs smiled.

"You don't understand," said Kelly. "To get to him, you have to pass through hundreds—thousands—of big dogs, all sworn to protect their monarch. They'll chew you up and slobber on the leftovers. That's why I'm not going onto the island with you."

"I thought it was because you couldn't find it." Sal sounded as guileless as always.

"Oh, it's easy to find," Kelly replied. "You can smell it before you see it. It's not easy to get to, at least not without a guide."

Julius found it difficult to relax. They seemed to be on the main path to the Isle of Dogs. If Quincy were taking the same path, they could catch up with him at any moment. It was possible that he'd stopped in this very cave, on his way farther north. While his friends rested, Julius sniffed around some more. There was a fresh scent in a corner of the cave, but he couldn't be sure that it was Quincy's.

A cat sprang down on Moira from the ceiling. She yowled in surprise, throwing her attacker across the cave. Kelly ran out into the darkness. Julius hissed at the wild-eyed cat; it was Zehra, the scrawny angora who had shooed Cavem and Quincy out of her cave. She had descended from her small shaft, taking them completely by surprise.

Sal kept himself as low to the ground as possible, his eyes squeezed tight shut as if he were wishing himself invisible. Lugs pounced on Zehra, wrapping his forepaws around the strange cat and digging his claws in. Lugs was pushed away, his attack drawing blood and tiny chunks of flesh. He swiped at the angora, knocking her out of the cave. The cat stood in the rain, rangy, missing a couple of teeth, face tense with fury. Her hazel eyes grew wider as she realized she was outside, vulnerable in the open.

Julius wanted to know who this cat was and what she wanted. One look at Lugs's face told him he'd have to wait for his interview, if the angora could even talk.

"Hey!" was Julius's conversation starter. "What are you doing here?"

The scruffy longhair stood in the rain, silent.

"You want to stay out there all night? Come inside; talk to us."

"Julius..." Lugs said warily. Julius ignored him.

Slowly, tentatively, the cat reentered the cave. Its fur was dyed an unusual lavender color, violet dark in its current sodden state.

"That's better," said Julius. "Now, tell me. Please. Why did you pounce on my friend?"

"I live here," the angora growled. "Get out of my home."

Sal stood up and collected a few of his supplies before Lugs stopped him. "We're not going anywhere," the sentinel said.

"Okay," said Sal, putting his supplies back down.

"There's nothing here," Julius said to the angora. "How can this be your home?"

"Not where you are. It's not safe." Zehra gestured at the shaft.

"Up there?" asked Julius. "You live in that hole?"

"I live in secret places all through the mountain, under and over," said Zehra. "I have one or two favorite caves, high above this one. This is too exposed."

"I have a proposal," said Moira. "You stay up there…" She fished for a name.

"Zehra," the angora bowed a little.

"You stay up in your warren, Zehra, and we coopie down here for one night only."

"No!" Lugs pulled Moira aside. "She could drop on us at any second. We won't sleep a wink."

"Do you know this cat?" Julius asked Kelly, who returned to the cave looking bedraggled and sorry for himself. Kelly shook his head.

"Nobody sees me," said Zehra. "When they pass by, I hide."

"I will trust you to sleep above us if you'll allow us to shelter here," Julius said calmly. Zehra considered the reasonable suggestion, flinching at Lugs's glare.

"All's well," Zehra said, jumping to snag a stalactite, hoisting her slender body into the shaft. "Leave at first light, mind."

"We'll take turns keeping watch," Julius told Lugs, bumping him with a brotherly shoulder. "I'll be first."

"No, you won't," Lugs grunted. "If I see one strand of that cat's hair, I'll rouse you all, and we'll dispatch her together. And if the rain lets off..."

"We'll sleep," Moira purred. "We're going to need it. Right, Kelly?"

The guide nodded wearily, made himself as comfortable as he could on the dusty, uneven ground, and instantly fell asleep. Sal was already dozing; Moira joined them. Julius stretched out beside Moira and squinted at Lugs, watching him in secret. Lugs was alert, looking up and around, ready to draw more blood. Julius wondered how long Lugs could stay alert like that.

By morning, the rain had stopped. Kelly and Moira scouted ahead while Julius, Sal, and Lugs packed up and said farewell to Zehra.

"Enjoy your peace and quiet," said Sal as he rubbed shoulders with the hermit.

"Thank you for allowing us to stay the night," said Julius.

"Wait, wait," said Zehra.

Julius and his friends stood in the cave mouth, ready to leave. To their surprise, tears rolled down Zehra's face.

"It's not for me, I've decided," she wept. "At least I think I've decided. I'm in two minds, you see. This kind of life always appealed to me—the solitude, the tranquility, the freedom of not having to worry about anyone but myself. I romanticized it. You can see the attraction, can't you? Then once I got here, I found that it wasn't quite as romantic as I'd imagined. There's a downside. The solitude, the deathly quiet, the self-absorption that comes with being alone for so long—"

"Slow down," said Julius gently.

"How long have you been up here?" Lugs asked.

"Two days. I'm so lonely!" Zehra moaned, burying her face in Julius's chest.

"We all get lonesome now and again," Sal ventured.

Zehra pulled herself away from Julius and snapped at Sal, "Have you ever sat in a cave for forty-eight hours with nothing but rocks for company? That beats lonesome into a cocked hat, pal. I've got no friends here."

"You called me pal," Sal pointed out. "That makes me a friend."

"I don't know you."

"I'm Sal Finney," said Sal. "You can call me Pal Finney if that helps."

Julius got impatient. "Do you want to come with us or not?"

"And leave my cave?"

The city cats nodded vigorously.

"You've lost track of time," Julius deduced. "You've been here a lot longer than two days. Fresh air will do you good."

Zehra dried her face with the back of her paws. "What's the weather like out there?"

"Windy." Julius tried to shut Sal up, but it was too late.

"I'm not going out in any wind. It rips through the mountains like a thousand razor blades, slicing through fur and flesh with no mercy. I don't fancy it."

"It's more like a stiff draft, really," said Lugs.

"I wouldn't even brave a breeze. Not out here."

"Is there any way to defend ourselves from these winds?"

"Find yourself a nice dry cave. Not this one, mind. You can find your own."

"But how do you know when the wind's dropped?"

"Oh, the winds never drop. Hardly ever, anyway." Zehra stared at the cave mouth, her eyes wide. "Some hardy fools try to climb to the highest peak—they never return home. The gales drag them away, stronger than any rope, louder than any scream. It's horrible out there."

"Have you ever seen our guide, Kelly, before?" Julius asked.

"Once, maybe. A long time ago. Never on this path. It could be I just didn't see him; I am very good at hiding. And sheltering."

Julius, Sal, and Lugs left the cave with Zehra staying inside, in the dry warmth she knew so well.

―――――――――――

Tracks formed concentric circles around City Hall like a spiraling metal web. Trams passed Woodrow Cormer's ground floor office every six minutes.

Sometimes passengers peered through his window, trying to catch a glimpse of the lawmaker. He would either wave back at his dwindling number of admirers or spend the day ducking to avoid the windows altogether, depending on what mood he was in. As times grew tougher, Woodrow found the nosy passers-by quite a comfort. He didn't like drawing the shades; it made the office too gloomy, even with the lamps on full, and he found himself fighting the urge to claw at the drapes.

He needed a quiet place. The fussy sealpoint padded up to the City Hall mailroom, staying away from the sorting and yabbering of the junior clerks who worked there, and found an empty cardboard box near a trash chute. He curled up in the box and closed the lid, appreciating the smell, the darkness, and the comfort of his surroundings. His work had overwhelmed him since Otto had vanished—before that, even, when Woodrow had done the lion's share of the lion's work. The only silver lining was the promise that he would soon become the new mayor. He was the obvious choice for the citizens of Bast. So why were they protesting outside his building?

Usually, the prowlers would have cleared the dissenters immediately. It was their job to police the city and restore peace when necessary. Either that or a solitary roar from Otto would cow the protesters into obedience. Woodrow did not have that kind of power, or that kind of roar. What was he going to do, mew at them?

He was certain that Joey Hondo was responsible for the prowler strike. As a security veteran, his ties with the cops ran deep. That crafty cat had convinced them to down tools to make the current administration look bad, never mind the innocent victims of crime and emergencies that would suffer in the meantime.

Woodrow admitted to himself that conditions were bad for the prowlers. Yes, they were underpaid, underfed, and overworked. Without food in his or her belly, any cat was within their rights to stop work. Negotiations were non-existent, however, as the prowler chief demanded to speak to Mayor Otto before considering any offers. The ultimatum offended Woodrow. When he was mayor, he would replace the chief and the other ringleaders in the force. As for Joey Hondo... he would end up at the bottom of a trash chute, forgotten by the populace. Woodrow would make sure of that.

Woodrow's box shifted. He tried to sit up, but the box was too restricting. He felt himself lifting into the air, scrabbling for balance. Then he was tilted, and his box slid at a 45-degree angle. Some mail clerk clod had shoved the box down the chute without checking the contents first.

As he tumbled against the side of the box, Woodrow calmed himself. He would not get angry. He would not panic. He would use his considerable intellect to solve this problem.

Or not. His box flew out of the chute with a crash, throwing him from his ride. He landed on top of one of the protesters surrounding City Hall, knocking a placard from her paws. The sign read, "You're Not The Mane Event, Otto!"

"Don't touch me, your dirty wastrel," said Woodrow, pushing himself away from the protester and washing himself anxiously. He was standing in a pile of torn envelopes, woodchip packaging, and used cat litter. The injured party, a hippie with big, naïve eyes, howled at him in a wash of flashbulbs. *Scratching Post* photographer August Mahogan had heard the calamity and got plenty of snaps before Woodrow shielded his face with the placard.

"August!" he called from behind the sign. "You don't need to submit those. This was just an accident. Wasn't it, madam?"

"I think he broke something," the hippie whined, limping over to lean against August. "My name's Safron, with one F," she told the photographer.

A leopard guard ran over to Woodrow, snarling at August and Safron.

"Print those and we'll have something to talk about," Woodrow warned as the sentry led him away. August looked at Safron with a smile.

"Do you need a doctor?" August asked.

"I think I just found one," said Safron, batting her eyelashes. August led her away to the *Post*, where she was happily interviewed for a juicy front-page story.

"Have you read this?" Tarquin asked Rusty Maxwell, the Anatolian shepherd dog who had once led the Carabian police force. Although Tarquin had demoted him, Moira had brought him back into the municipal fold, insisting that they needed a dogsbody on staff. Now Rusty was Tarquin's sounding board, a dog who was unwaveringly honest in his opinions.

"I sniffed it," said Rusty. "Same old cat city circus."

"You think?"

Tarquin reread the headline in disbelief.

BOXING DAY

Mayoral candidate attacks innocent cat with cardboard box

By Roy Fury

Approval ratings dropped today for city adminis- trator Woodrow Cormer, former favorite to replace missing mayor, Otto Canders. According to wit- nesses, Woodrow pounced on local student Safron Cloud, yelling expletives at her.

"He came out of nowhere," said Cloud, who is studying sociology at the Catanooga Institute of Boarding and Grooming. "I never cared for him, but I didn't expect the rumors to be true. He really

*does hate the common cat. I feel sorry for him;
hate is such a negative emotion."*

*The incident took place behind City Hall. Cormer
was led away by a leopard sentry. Cloud was treated
for emotional trauma and minor scratches at the
City Infirmary.*

*"This is not the kind of leader the city needs," said
rival candidate and business magnate, Thaddeus
Tybalt. "If I had a daughter, which I do not, I would
not want her to fear for her well-being in the presence of this self-appointed tyrant."*

*Candidate Joey Hondo, who worked at City Hall
before joining the mayoral race, also disparaged
Cormer's actions. "I vow to keep Bast safe from
cardboard-carrying lunatics like Woodrow," he
said at an early morning press conference.*

The office of Woodrow Cormer declined to comment.

"Unbelievable," Tarquin muttered, slapping the
paper down on his office desk.

"Why so incredulous?" asked Rusty.

"They didn't reach out to me for comment or even
so much as mention me in the article. I'm paws down
the best mayoral candidate!"

"Do they know you're running?"

Tarquin rolled up the newspaper and waggled it
under Rusty's nose. "Of course they know! But I can
see that I am going to have to speed up my schedule
and get to Bast as soon as possible. Right now, I am
out of sight and out of mind, and that is not good in
an extraordinary election such as this. Has Moira
returned from her walkabout yet?"

"Not yet," said Rusty.

"We need her."

Rusty agreed. Without Moira's diplomatic and organizational skills, supplies were delayed, paperwork was unsigned, and edicts were unuttered. Alone, Tarquin was as useful as a flea collar on a fencepost.

"Send someone to bring her back," Tarquin insisted, tapping the rolled-up paper on his desk. "I don't want this place to go to pot while I'm gone."

"I didn't know you cared so much," said Rusty sardonically.

"I care about the polls," Tarquin sneered. "I was always meant to be mayor. I will be mayor. And the citizens of Bast will revere me."

5

Sushi Conveyor Belt Problem

"Voila!" Tad Tybalt stood in a large, chrome-heavy kitchen, wearing a chef's hat and an apron over his suit. His apron read, "Kiss the cat." Ramona Pretzel, also begrudgingly wearing an apron, watched Tad slide a hot tray from an oven.

"Smells good," Ramona admitted.

"I know you want to try one right way," said Tad. "But let them cool for a minute. They're hot as matchheads."

"I can wait," Ramona pouted. "Are you going to tell me what's cooking?"

"I want you to guess." Tad hopped from one paw to another. "Oh, go on then, try one. Just make sure you blow on it before—"

Ramona popped a baked appetizer in her mouth, impressing Tad with her insouciance.

"Delicious," she admitted. To prove she wasn't pandering to her boss, she ate a second *hors d'œuvre*.

"So, what do you think it is?"

"A rodent," Ramona said, dabbing at her mouth with a dainty paw. "Maybe mouse. Not as sweet."

"Close." Tad giggled, making his tall white hat wobble from side to side. "You're eating a rat."

"Rats're dirty, ugly critters!" Ramona gagged. "Their tails are too chewy. You want to sell these?"

"All kinds of rat-based products." Tad sounded like a kitten with a new toy.

"I foresee consumer resistance here."

Tad moved over to a stove, where flat rat meat sauteed in a pan. Tad lifted the pan and flipped his rat patties in the air. They landed upside down, and he banged the pan back on the stove, shifting it a wee bit to disseminate the heat.

"Nonsense!" Tad bellowed. "Rats were part of our staple diet before our lives got cushy and our tastes more delicate. This is mass market consumption I'm talking about, not some fancy restaurant fare. Coat them in batter and feed them to the hard-ups, provide the hungry multitude with a low-cost, high-protein source of tasty white meat!"

"It looks kinda gray to me."

"The sauce will hide that. Rats don't taste of much anyway. The sauce will bring a tang to the table. What was that stuff we offered with the barbecued bacon rinds?"

"That would be our barbecue sauce, Mr. Tybalt."

"The tastes didn't blend quite right. Pigs've got a distinctive flavor. Whereas with bland rat meat..."

"You need the sauce to give consumers something to remember. And tasteless meat won't clash on the palate. Good thinking, boss. We've got another problem, though."

"Of course we do. Spill it."

"The same supply issues messing up our mice market are also affecting distribution. How do we get these saucy rats to our customers?"

"I've thought of that."

"I was hoping you had." Ramona smiled.

"Listen carefully because we're going to launch this to the press as soon as the schematics are drawn up."

"I'm a good listener."

"Remember the sushi express?"

Ramona licked her lips. "They've still got sections of that running around my part of town. A conveyor belt crisscrossing the city, delivering sushi to every neighborhood. It seemed like such a good idea..."

"But it didn't last."

"Like most government-backed initiatives. It relied on an honor system, but how many cats could let a juicy plate of raw fish slide past them before taking a taste? It got so bad, the strays would time regular deliveries and be waiting to nab the goodies mid-dash. Heck, I was a kitten at the time, and I may have been guilty of a free nibble or two."

"I appreciate your honesty."

"You can't be thinking...?"

"I can be. Loose sushi is out of the question, put a rat in a box, hard to unpack on the move, moving at speed... the infrastructure's there, Ramona. All we need to do is rebuild the missing ramps and monitor each section, at least until the system's up and running properly again."

Ramona wasn't convinced.

"The money we save using rats instead of mice, we spend on the conveyor belt. Cats will welcome the new relaunch with open mouths. Our company will receive a boost, and so will my bid for mayor."

"Our company?" asked Ramona, excited.

"Tybalt Inc. belongs to all of us." Tad grinned. "We're one big profit-generating gestalt."

"Oh." Ramona took off her apron.

"I'll need a speech," said Tad.

"You'll have one." Ramona headed out of the kitchen.

"You like my idea really, don't you?" Tad called after her. "You don't think it's ... half-baked?"

"No," Ramona replied over her shoulder. "It's ready to serve. Excuse me now please boss, I have another meeting to get to."

"Of course." Tad watched Ramona leave the kitchen. He sat by the oven, hoping his scheme would pay off. It had to. He had thousands of mouths to feed.

6

Wind

For most of his life, Julius had taken the easy way out. He'd lived with his mum long past the typical six-month mark, skipped school to avoid tough tests, taken easy assignments when he worked for *The Scratching Post,* and before the riot he had stayed with his sweetheart of yore, Camilla, to save on rent. Affection he could take or leave as the fancy took him, but he never turned down help with the food and utility bills.

There was nothing easy about the northern mountains. The brambled path he took with his friends was littered with jagged rocks that threatened to split his pads. When he looked up, he could see the journey wouldn't get any easier or safer. There was a narrow trail, slippery with dust, not much more than a groove worn through the rocks by passing soldiers and travelers moving single file.

The long way around would be easier on the paws, but it would take much longer to skirt the worst of the mountain range. By the time Julius reached the bay on the other side, Quincy would be long gone.

Best case scenario: he'd get ahead of the abductors, ambush them, and steal Quincy back before the catnappers knew what had happened. At worst, Julius would catch up to his quarry and trail them to their destination.

Small thorn bushes snagged at the cats' legs as they made their way up another slope. Previously, Lugs would be railing against nature, cursing the undergrowth with angry paws. But since his visit to the Vet, he was calmer, less impetuous, as if he was at one with the world. Although Julius was proud of his own prudence and composure, he hoped he would never find himself in such an ambivalent state.

"You sure this is the only path?" asked Sal, short of breath. "It doesn't seem very well used." Julius could have pointed out that an army of dogs had used it less than a year hence, on their way to face off against a legion of cats. He didn't want Sal to slow down as he looked for canine tracks, though, so he skipped the history lesson. He hardly had the air for it anyway—the atmosphere was getting noticeably thinner.

Thanks to Julius's determination, they kept climbing, using their claws to heave themselves up at the steepest points. At night, they found a wide ledge to sleep on, taking turns to keep watch so that a feline dream didn't turn into a real fall. By noon the next day, they were over the first chain of mountains, with a clear look at the drab Kalkan Plains beyond. Julius's keen eyesight caught a glimpse of two figures, one large and dark, one small and ginger-furred.

"It's them!" Julius shouted. He didn't get excited very often, but his sight warranted a loud meow. "Down there, look!"

Cavem and Quincy were much too far away to hear Julius. His friends watched as the boerboel led the staggering tom across an unyielding plateau.

"So that's who we've been chasing," said Lugs. "That's the biggest dog I've ever seen."

Kelly scrunched up his eyes, trying to see what the others saw. He gave up in frustration.

"They're moving slow," Moira noted. "We can catch them up, as long as we don't stop."

"Great," groaned Sal. "The last thing I want to do is stop and have a rest."

"The worst is over, guys," Julius pepped. "Once we get past this stretch, it's downhill all the way."

Julius was wrong. The worst was yet to come.

"I could have stayed in my lab," Quincy grumbled to Cavem as they crossed the high of Kalkan, pockmarked with playas, round hollows caused by rainstorms like the one that had forced Julius's group to seek shelter. Cavem had ignored the rain, shoving Quincy on. "I'm perfectly capable of reconstructing the blueprints you lost, or ate. You could have taken them to your boss."

"No boss," said Cavem, skirting a crater in the arid ground. "All equal."

"Really? That's not what I heard." Cavem stared at Quincy, who kept grousing regardless. "I appreciate you wanting me to meet your, er, equal partner, but this is totally unnecessary. Even you can understand that.

"Journey make you strong," said Cavem. "Toughen up for all the work you will do for us."

This was the longest string of words Quincy had heard from the dog, but they did not impress the inventor. He had expected to demonstrate one machine and go straight home. He had no desire to live on the Isle of Dogs, where no cat lasted long—if they lasted at all.

Cavem slurped from his canteen and passed it to Quincy, who held it upside down. It was empty.

"I can't live on dog slobber," he said waspishly, thrusting the canteen back into Cavem's paws.

With a shrug, Cavem walked over to a puddle of muddy rainwater, used it to fill his canteen, and offered it to the cat.

"Is that how you've been filling...?" Quincy sucked in a breath, turned around, and headed back to the mountains.

"Where go?" Cavem grunted.

"Home. I've got a lot of cleaning up to do, thanks to you." Quincy took the full canteen and Cavem growled low and long enough to make Quincy stop in his tracks. He turned to face the dog.

"You can't just threaten me and drag me halfway across this litter pit. I have a scientific mind. I won the Singapura Prize for Innovation when I was still a kitten." Quincy held up his forepaws. "These are delicate! If you want me to work for you, I don't need conditioning. I need pampering."

Cavem placed the canteen on the edge of a hollow, so deep he could not see the bottom. "Then drink," he said, with the tone of a parent talking to an errant pup.

Quincy looked at the dog, stretched out a paw, and batted the canteen into the hollow.

"No drink," said Quincy, mocking Cavem's monosyllabism.

Cavem stared at Quincy for an uncomfortable minute, then said, "Where go?"

"With you," Quincy relented. "Doesn't mean I like it."

Cavem lumbered onward, Quincy tagging behind. He did not feel tough at all.

In the hollow behind them, two grimy paws reached out of the hole, clawing for daylight.

Julius stumbled down a jagged slope, his scarf wrapped tight around his mouth. Sal and Lugs were right behind him, leaning into a ferocious blast of wind that took their breath away. Lagging behind, dragging his heels, was Kelly, squinting to defend his eyes from flying grit and bright sunlight.

"Which way?" Julius hollered back at him, the wind carrying the sound quickly to his ears. He shook his head, his head hot with exertion.

"I don't know," he mewled back. "Can't we find another nice, cozy cave to shelter in?"

Lugs stopped walking and Kelly bumped into him, an unstoppable force meeting a moving objector. Lugs stretched out an arm and dragged Kelly forward, forcing him to pick up the pace.

"I thought you were sick of caves," the sergeant muttered.

"If we find one that's cozy," Sal chimed in, "I think we should go with it." To him, caves were anything but cozy.

"For the last time, we're not stopping in any caves!" shouted Julius. "I don't want to get stuck in some dark grotto with Bastet-knows-what beasties wriggling around. We've got to get out of these mountains!" He looked at Kelly, who was keeping up thanks to a threatening look from Lugs. "Uh, which way should we be moving?"

"Down there." Kelly pointed to the foot of the slope. "Out of this blessed wind."

"Great," said Sal, tripping on a treacherous stretch of rubble. "Directions from a cat with his eyes closed."

The wind grew stronger, rough enough to drag stray stones and weeds across the ground. The four cats reached the end of the slope and found a precipice overlooking a stark valley with sparse knots of trees and no signs of feline life.

"Which way now, Kelly?" Julius's tone was calm, not accusatory, implying a residual trace of faith in the guide's abilities.

"We keep going down."

"Are you crazy?" Moira pushed Kelly to the ground. "Are you so miserable you want to get us all killed?"

"There's a ledge," Kelly stuttered, showing his belly in deference to the female cat. "It leads to a trail. It's narrow, but if we go single file, we should be okay. We can follow the trail down into the valley and then..."

Julius looked down at the valley; clouds cast vast, shifting shadows on the land. The open space with its room to run and hunt had a certain muted beauty that he'd never seen before.

"This place blows," said Sal, climbing down onto the ledge.

Clinging to the rock face, whiskers quivering, the cats sidled along the ledge toward the skinny path that Kelly had promised. Julius wondered where the guide had got his geographical knowledge from; he obviously didn't come here every day.

"How many times have you taken this route?" he asked the old cat.

"Loads," Kelly replied, fur bristling in the cold. "Always by myself, though. No one ever got this far with me. Not *this* way, anyway." Hearing the comment, his companions stopped sidling for a second to look at him.

"I wonder why," said Lugs, his large frame barely fitting on the ledge.

"I can see the trail." Julius laughed. "We're almost there!"

If only. The cats descended with ginger movements, their chins tilted upward, as graceful as they could be in the buffeting wind. It filled their ears with a deep, loud sound, a constant moan from some white noise wraith's big cousin.

Halfway down, the trail became too narrow for Lugs. He dug his claws into the ledge, trying to gain a purchase, leaning back against the rock face.

"Lugs!" Julius yelled, reaching past Sal to help the lynx. Lugs had an expression of acceptance on his face, one he'd worn countless times in battle. He was ready to die. "Grab him, quick!"

Sal and Moira dropped low and wrapped their forepaws around the sentinel's legs, anchoring him. Julius held Lugs's torso against the rock face. Kelly did nothing, frozen for a moment, then started looking for an alcove to duck into. *At least if we fall,* Julius thought, *we'll land on all fours. We'll be flat as a field mouse flan, but we'll land right.*

"Let go of me, I'm okay," said Lugs gruffly. There wasn't enough room for him to push his friends away from him. Julius released his grip, allowing the lynx to put all his weight on Sal and use him as a stepping stone to a lower, wider stretch of the path.

"They should post up a weight limit," Sal winced. Before he could get up, Kelly also stepped over him.

"Good to see him making himself useful for a change," Lugs said to Julius as if Sal couldn't hear. "Let's get off this blessed mountain."

7

Into the Valley

Bingo always got excited when a train arrived at Stick Station. If he was really lucky, he would meet new cats and make new friends. He liked making friends.

The morning train from Carabas didn't carry many passengers. A few cats disembarked in a hurry, pressing through a wreath of steam to leave the station. Bingo recognized a few commuters on their way to work in Healing or to catch the eastern train to Point Gratiot. They didn't need any help with their bags.

The train sat for a moment, panting heat and smoke. Bingo watched attentively, then ran to the rear carriage, where a big cat got off. It was a puma with jet black fur and glimmering blue eyes, looking around for a porter.

"Here, sir," said Bingo, taking the puma's duffel bag between his teeth. "Where to?"

"You can put that down," the puma growled. "I don't need help with my bags. I need information."

Bingo put the bag down and wagged his tail.

"I'm looking for a Siamese cat. A female called Moira Marti. Have you seen her?"

"Oh, yes." Bingo grinned at the muscular cat, who towered above him. "She's a friend of mine. We rode on the train together. I'd never ridden on a train."

"Where is she?" the puma snarled.

"What's your name?" Bingo jumped up playfully. "Mine's Bingo. B.I.N.G.O. Are you a friend of Moira's? Do you want to be my friend, too?"

"Where did she go?"

"To the mountains," said Bingo. "Looking for Doctor McGraw. He got stolen."

"Did he really?" The puma picked up his duffel bag. "How many are with her?"

"Three. Julius, Sal, Lugs, and Kelly, the guide."

"That's four." The puma frowned.

"I'm great with names, especially friends' names. Numbers, not so much."

The puma peered at Bingo, not sure whether to trust the information he was given. He walked across the platform parallel with the train, Bingo at his heels.

"How much of a head start do they have?"

Bingo looked puzzled.

"You know the train schedules, don't you? Which train was here when they went to the mountains?"

"The Monday morning train," Bingo said quickly.

"Good boy." The puma reached out as if to pat Bingo, then swiped a paw at him, knocking him against the train.

"You'll get more if you tell anyone you saw me," the puma warned. Bingo whimpered his understanding.

"I remember friends' names, that's all."

"Then you won't remember mine, will you?" The puma turned his back on Bingo and left the station. "Toxic. My name is Toxic."

Night fell in the valley. Sal and Kelly flinched at the sound of wild dogs howling in the night, far off but too loud for comfort.

Julius didn't like being cold. He was too old to put up with draughts and surprise shifts in the wind. On breezy nights like this, he'd curl up into a warm coil, his paws tucked into his belly and his tail covering his nose. One eye peeked out from the thick gray bundle of fur, ready to pop open at the slightest sound. Julius was a light sleeper.

"What was that?" Sal mumbled, sitting up on his hind legs.

"I didn't hear nothing," said Lugs, annoyed that his sleep had been disturbed.

"That's 'cause you were too busy snoring." Sal shot a look around a bare tree trunk, trying to make out vague shapes in the darkness.

Moira slept soundly beside Julius, her paws twitching infinitesimally. He was glad to have her so close, but envious of her ability to conk out so quickly and sleep through noise, even after their startling encounter with Zehra.

Julius saw Sal stand up and trudge back the way they had come. He got up and joined the snowshoe.

"Where are you going?" Julius hissed.

"Home. Back to my nice warm airing cupboard and my 'Hungry Kitten' food bowl and my collection of trouting flies."

"You don't have a home, Sal. That's my cupboard you're referring to, and my bowl."

"You have a 'Hungry Kitten' bowl?" Lugs asked, sitting up and staring at them in the darkness.

"I can't vouch for the flies; I don't fish," said Julius. "I'm not all that keen on water. You're going because you're a lightweight who never finished anything in your life."

"You don't know that," Sal said, starting to walk off again. "I've finished lotsa things. Like our friendship, I'm ending that now."

"Whatever you say, Sal." Julius realized that the snowshoe meant every word. He glanced at Kelly and Sarge, both up now, urging them to help him. He loped after Sal, quickly catching up with him.

"I know what you're really after, and you swore off that stuff, remember?"

"I'm sorry about Doctor McGraw and all that. Surely I am." Sal shrugged Julius's paw from his shoulder. "But I've come a long way with you, risked my life even, for some nutty inventor I've never even met. I mean, why are we doing this, J? What's the point?"

Lugs and Kelly wanted to know, too. Julius didn't have an answer.

"Cravings are the last of my concerns right now," Sal continued. "Staying alive is all I care about."

"That's not true." Julius pounced forward to stand in front of his friend, blocking his path. "You care about us. About McGraw. About Mealymouth Sachets. Come on, admit it." Julius thought he was getting through at last. "Without us, what good is a home? A life? You want to be the oldest living loner on the planet?"

"I do," Kelly butted in. The others glared at him. "Sorry, go on with what you were saying."

"Are you saying we're here for some kind of, I dunno, a communal experience?" Sal raised his voice so much that Julius shushed him, not wanting to wake Moira. "Bonding, J., is that what we're doing?"

"We're..." Julius looked down at the ground, unable to face his friends. "We're doing this because I owe it to Camilla. I didn't trust her. I was jealous. She died because of me."

"Didn't she die in the riot?" asked Sal.

"A riot caused or enabled, by me," Julius said bitterly. "This is my way of making it right. She cared about Quincy and this inhospitable world up here. I'm sorry I dragged you all with me."

"We knew the deal," Lugs reassured Julius. "We just didn't know how strongly you felt about this. Did we, Sal?"

"No," said Sal, rubbing any trace of tears from his eyes. "No, we didn't."

"Still leaving?" Julius smiled through his pain. "I won't stop you."

"We'll find Doctor McGraw together," Sal decided. "Tomorrow."

Sal lay down near Moira, closed his eyes, and fell asleep. *He's so good at that,* Julius thought, his heart filled with affection for his eccentric friend. *Must be his special talent.*

Kelly, Julius, and Lugs all settled down as well, with Julius returning to Moira's side.

"I need my sleep," Kelly chattered while Julius and Lugs tried to fall asleep. "Without it, I get crabby, antsy, no fun to be with. Not that I consider myself fun all the time... half-fun, maybe, like happy-go-lucky or something. Not a killjoy. But without my sleep, woah, look out, stay back! I'm Mr. Grumpy Drawers. There was one time—you see, I start picking unnecessary fights with complete strangers, I'm that cranky, all down to sleep deprivation—this one time I was stuck behind a fat guy on a tram, and he was taking ages finding his change, and I just popped out a claw and POINK! Shoved it up his tail! That got him moving, I can tell you. Really shifted him. So that's why I need my sleep. I'm nothing but trouble otherwise."

"Go to sleep then," Julius groaned. Lugs was looking at Kelly's tail, a claw already primed for some poinking of its own.

"I can't," Kelly grumbled. "Sal's snoring keeps waking me up." Sal was dead to the world, haunches flinching mid-dream, silent and cuddly.

"You're the one who snores. Can't you hear yourself?"

"I do not snore. I purr aggressively," Kelly told Lugs with a serious expression, his eyes like two shining saucers in the firelight.

"I don't care whether you do sleep, can't sleep, or want to sleep," Lugs grunted. "Curl yourself up and leave us be, or I'll curl you up myself. And I won't be doing it gently."

With a huff, Kelly sank to the ground, tucked his paws underneath his body, closed his eyes, and fell asleep.

"Finally. I thought he'd never—" Lugs's words were cut short by a resounding snore that was loud enough to wake Sal.

"Wha—what was that?" Sal murmured. Through bleary eyes, he saw Lugs and Julius point at Kelly.

Joey Hondo watched his favorite test subject.

He'd picked five citizens from different sections of the city, different walks of life. He liked to watch a fishmonger, Antonio Cortis, who owned a seafood chain based out of the Crystal District. Antonio had a large tank in his main store, and Joey's eyes would follow the fish back and forth. He found it relaxing.

Joey watched Tippee T., a young chartreux who interned at City Hall, always pushing herself to work hard, carry as many files as possible piled up in her paws, wearing herself out by the end of every week.

Unbeknownst to Chico, Joey watched him too, languishing in the cellar where he guarded Otto, and at home relaxing with his demanding family. It was important to watch Chico with his precious charge. Chico could easily be replaced if he slacked off or went soft on Otto. Joey could not allow that to happen.

Joey sat on his favorite cushion, tilting a mirror so that he could check on his fourth subject. This was Desdemona Brighter, an old cat who fascinated him with her criminal history. These days she lay low, pottering around her house, living on sardines and molasses. Joey still felt that he could learn a lot from her, and when she frequented her favorite bar, the Cat's Cradle, he had her followed by one of his many emissaries.

Joey's final subject was the most unlikely. The most handsome, courageous cat in the city. Joey's system of mirrors allowed him to watch this cat at home and at work, effortlessly completing tasks and balancing multiple projects with confidence and elan. He noted how other cats admired his subject, which to him was quite right.

The subject was mayoral candidate, Joey Hondo.

Joey looked at himself whenever he got the chance, practicing facial expressions for the press, flexing his pecs, rolling on the floor, and flipping back up again like a champion athlete. It wasn't just other cats who admired him; he did too.

Between his Byzantine monitoring system and the spies he hired to keep tabs on his competitors, Joey felt like he understood his city. When he became mayor, he would rule it firmly but justly. To win the race, all he had to do was keep Otto locked away, pose for his voters, and leave his competitors to make fools of themselves.

Toxic the puma, followed Julius's trail to the cave that Zehra called home. She jumped out of the darkness in an attempt to scare him away, realized how large and fierce he was, then retreated with an apologetic shrug. She still found the courage to complain, though.

"A plague, that's what it is! A plague is raining down on me!"

"You're nuts," said Toxic as he stalked into the cave, inhaling the scent of his prey, cornering Zehra.

"A plague of cats invading my home! I did what was asked of me. I delayed those city cats as long as I could. I couldn't hold them any longer."

"What city cats?" asked Toxic, showing Zehra a menacing claw. "Describe them to me?"

"The, uh, the old one was from the village of Healing, fancies himself as a guide, but the others... a skinny gray tabby, a hunky lynx, a snowshoe, and a beautiful white Siamese."

"Moira," Toxic said with longing. "Who told you to stall them?"

"Oh, that was strange. Do you want some tuna?"

"No. Answer my question."

"That's good, because I don't have any to spare. Hermit rations, you understand. A dog made me do it."

"What dog?"

"Big one. Reminds me a bit of you, no offense. A boerboel, if I know my breeds, which I do. And a ginger tom, although he didn't say much. About as happy to be there as a carp at a cat convention."

"Which way did they go?" Toxic sighed.

"Oh, I sent them packing. North, they packed. Following the dog and the ginger. They won't survive out there; no, they won't. Too much wind."

"What makes you think you're safer in here?" asked Toxic, popping the rest of his claws and closing in on Zehra.

Quincy's ears ached from the cold wind. Rain slicked his coat and dribbled into his eyes. Cavem seemed oblivious as they reached the far edge of the plains and entered a stretch of grassland, with no display of excitement or relief, brushing through the foliage at a rapid pace. At the savannah's edge, they saw a wide stretch of water, choppy and unwelcoming.

The dog took a couple of garments from his backpack. "Put this on," he told Quincy in a way that compelled the ginger cat to comply. "Now." It was a musty old cloak cut from coarse cloth, and it smelled strangely familiar.

Cavem put on a larger cloak and pulled a cowl over Quincy's head. Once the cloak was wrapped around him, the cat's identity was fully concealed.

The image clicked in Quincy's mind. These were the kind of cloaks that dogs wore when they wanted to pass unnoticed in the cat city of Bast. They hid their canine form, not because they were scared of the crowds or what would happen if the cats turned on them in unison; most dogs Quincy knew considered all creatures as equal, whether they were cat, dog, or rat. Mainly, they went incognito because they'd got sick of the stares and the hissing and spitting from passers-by. All they wanted to do was go on about their business in peace.

Quincy's cloak even smelled like dog. Despite his limited vocabulary, Cavem had apparently thought of everything. He wondered who Cavem's equal partners were.

Cavem led Quincy along the shoreline. They saw a coal-black terrier untethering a raft.

"Wait!" Cavem called out, keeping his voice as deep as possible. "Two passengers for you."

Quincy didn't say anything. He didn't expect much help from the terrier, all crooked teeth, lopsided eyes, and food around his mouth. Like the hermit, Zehra, he looked half-mad. But then he'd have to be to ferry dogs to the island and back every day, braving the bay in all weathers. Clumps of hair had worn away from his forelimbs, his eyes were weak and bloodshot, his back knotted and permanently aching. He didn't comment on the sudden appearance of the two cloaked figures, the way they moved so quickly and carefully. He took their fare and bade them sit on a small bench bolted to the ferry.

Quincy looked around, trying not to betray a whisker. The raft couldn't hold many passengers—a couple of labradors, a few families who'd planned to spend the day picnicking on the shore but had rolloped in the rain instead. A friendly pup bounded across to him and started to snuffle. Cavem swiped him away while the parents weren't looking. The pup kept away from the newcomers after that.

The smell of the cloaks and dog fur, wet with wake spray, made Quincy feel strangely solemn. The boerboel was very different from the dogs Quincy had dealt with in the past; he was a cruel bully with a narrow mind. But he had one thing in common with those dogs—he also wanted to traverse a city unchallenged. Quincy had no doubt that Cavem would protect him, fight through every block, and tear at every dog he met if he had to. But he didn't understand why.

"Don't you want to tell me why you've dragged you all this way?" Quincy asked. "All this trouble and effort to take me to a place I don't want to go, where I don't belong? I am curious." Cavem answered with a grunt. He didn't need to say anything. Quincy's inquisitive nature urged him on.

The boerboel towered over the terrier, shrouded in dark cloth, casting a shadow over the smaller dog.

"Haven't seen you here before, have I?" the terrier stammered. "I never forget a hem. Where you from?"

"Mountains," Cavem said in his deepest tones. "No more questions."

"I thought I was the curious one," purred Quincy until the boerboel silenced him with a glare.

The terrier turned a crank connected to a long, heavy chain, which stretched across the bay, under the water. He turned it slowly and steadily, moving the ferry toward the Isle of Dogs. Quincy looked nervously at the island; all he could see was a tall chain-link fence with wooden posts, concealing the dog city from prying eyes, locking the inhabitants in.

As the ferry clanked across the bay, the terrier grew suspicious. He kept glancing at Quincy, who sank deeper into his cloak and cowl, barely daring to breathe. Cavem distracted the little dog with an attempt at casual conversation.

"Water deep?" Cavem asked.

"Not here," the terrier gruffed. "But it flows to the sea. Good fishing down there."

Quincy perked up at the mention of fish, but quickly shrank down again.

"Water wet," Cavem said, running out of things to say.

"Uh, yes," the terrier frowned. "Very."

The journey across the bay was painfully slow for Quincy. He looked over the side of the ferry at the agitated water, ready to jump in and swim if he had to. It would not be graceful—he would wriggle and slip and splash—but he would be safe from the dogs.

"Stay put," Cavem told him, as if sensing his readiness to bolt. Quincy looked at the boerboel, then at the terrier, who gave him another distrustful glance. Quincy swallowed hard and closed his eyes like a kitten imagining itself invisible.

When the ferry slowed even more and he felt a clunk, he blinked his eyes open and looked over his shoulder—they had reached the other side. He stayed close to Cavem as the passengers got off the ferry; Cavem gave the terrier a small, dry shank bone.

"Thank you kindly, sir," said the terrier, chomping down on the bone to make sure it was kosher. "Have a good day now."

"We will." Cavem nodded. Quincy walked away from the water, not daring to look back.

Julius was still tired the next morning. His sleep had been broken by Kelly's snores, the remote, mocking cries of hyenas, and the knowledge that Moira was sleeping next to him, so close yet so emotionally distant. He stretched and dragged his claws across the ground, digging faint grooves into the hard, dirt surface. He had never felt so tired and out of his depth; wherever he looked, he saw a wasteland with no buildings, trees, or other signs of life. Like Sal, he longed to return home. He missed his local deli and the corner store with the chatty clerk, the bustling newspaper bullpen, even the smell of wet fur on a crowded tram on a Friday afternoon. But Moira was here, so here was better. He hoped she understood how his devotion was not tempered by his debt to Camilla.

Moira woke up alert and ready to continue the journey. While the others were asleep, Julius took the opportunity to ask her if she would come back to Bast with him once they had found Quincy.

Moira drew close to Julius and looked into his eyes. "It was exciting when we met," she said thoughtfully. "You had so much energy and ... you got me. I didn't have to struggle to communicate with you, not like I did with other toms."

"Thank you," said Julius. "It always feels easier to talk to you, too."

"But."

Julius's ears flattened. Why was there always a but?

"After my brother died," Moira went on, "life wasn't so fun anymore. As for living together... Bastet's bracelets, I like your company, but I need my own territory, my own space to own and roam."

Julius took her forepaws and held them gently. "We'll figure it out together."

"I want to figure it out on my own." Moira pulled away. "We don't have to live all our lives with our tails tucked around each other—"

"Marry me."

"You're not listening. Again." Moira shook her head sadly. "You're just a kitten who's afraid of being alone." She got up and walked off, leaving Julius feeling insulted and confused.

"I do listen," he said. Her terse reply was too distant for him to hear.

"Is it time to go?" asked Sal sleepily.

To his embarrassment, Julius found that Sal had heard the last part of his conversation with Moira.

"I'm sorry, Sal," said Julius. "That comment I made about your addiction... what you're really after... that was uncalled for. You've been clean for months, and I'm proud of you. I think you're doing great."

"I do miss it," Sal admitted. "It was my escape attempt. This terrain would be a heck of a lot more fun if I was rolling around, high on catnip. But I'd be useless to you, and I want to be useful, J. What is a cat's life if it isn't useful?"

Julius smiled and helped Sal pack up his gear for the day. "You've been hanging around me too long," he said. "You're starting to sound like me."

Moira walked away from her friends, away from the mountains, cursing herself for leaving her post in Carabas. Lost in thought, she stared into one of the large, dark hollows that pitted the plains. The city needed her, and she had left it when it needed her most, with Tarquin departing and rebuilding in full swing after Julius had almost caused its downfall. He had led a horde of ferals into Carabas, where they had wrecked everything they had gotten their paws and teeth on.

The wisest course of action would be to return to Carabas and forget all about her ex. But she couldn't. She wanted to be with him, and she had followed her heart instead of her head. *Where's that ever got you?* she asked herself. *In trouble, that's where. Girl, you're never going to learn.*

She looked back at her friends and saw a dark figure in the distance behind them, running toward them.

"Look out!" Moira yeowled, waking Lugs and Kelly. They turned to see Toxic rush past them, slamming into Moira and knocking her to the ground.

"Get off me!" Moira struggled, pushing the puma's heavy weight up, unleashing her claws so they sank into him. Julius, Sal, and Lugs got hold of Toxic and dragged him away from Moira, her claws leaving his hide with a pop.

Toxic swiped at Moira's friends, making them back off. He snarled at Moira with a cry of frustration and paced toward her slowly.

"We're colleagues, Toxic," Moira reminded him. "This is harassment."

Toxic's eyes were red with rage. "I've been sent to get you back, whether you like it or not."

"Not," said Moira. "I'll come back on my own terms. Even though you're my co-worker or no, I'll never forget what you did to me."

"*I* want you back," Toxic said with menace.

Julius moved slowly and silently up behind him; the puma swung around, knocking Julius onto his side, winded. Lugs checked on Julius, hissing angrily at Toxic.

The puma lunged at Moira, but before her friends could help, another cat sprang from the hollow and rammed into Toxic. The city cats were shocked to see Zehra, looking more ragged than ever, standing over Toxic's fallen form.

"Run," said Zehra. "Before this oaf recovers."

Sal and Kelly were already racing away. Lugs and Moira joined them, quickly catching up. Julius stayed with Zehra.

"Where did you...?" Julius asked, breathless.

"Zehra's hideaways go over ... and under," Zehra grinned. "Go!"

Toxic got up, staring at Zehra. She was much smaller than him, but she had caught him completely by surprise.

"I can't just leave you," said Julius.

"Zehra owes you," the angora replied. She stood on the brink of the hollow, tensing up to fight Toxic.

"What do you mean?" Julius flinched as the puma attacked Zehra. She twisted her sinewy body sideways, slashing at Toxic's legs with her dirty claws, snagging him off balance. He fell into the hollow, disappearing into the darkness.

Julius stood on the brink, looking down. He couldn't see the puma. "How far down does this go?" he asked Zehra, who was busy scratching her itchy fur.

"The rains make the tunnels deeper," said Zehra. "They are fathomless."

"Thank you," said Julius, inviting Zehra to join his friends. They had stopped running, taking a breather in a creek bed. Their paws squelched in the drying mud, but the bed gave them a little cover. Kelly especially needed the respite; he was wheezing from the exertion, coughing up a dusty hairball.

Julius watched Moira with concern. She seemed unscathed by Toxic's appearance.

"That puma dragged her all the way from Bast to Carabas," Sal explained to Kelly and Zehra. "He's one bad cat."

"I thought, after he was fixed by the Vet, that I could work with him." Moira sighed. "But vets can be bribed. And I'm sure someone put him up to this."

"Tarquin," Julius growled. "Wait until I get my paws on him."

Moira stopped him. "I'm not returning to Carabas, not yet."

"We'll catch up with Quincy," said Lugs. "If we maintain our pace."

Kelly shook his head. "We're not all soldier boys," he croaked. "You should go on ahead."

"But you're our guide," said Moira.

"Zehra can help guide you," the angora smiled. "Zehra is good at hiding. And tracking."

"Fine," said Lugs. "We'll nap here, then chase after Quincy and the dog at daybreak. Zehra and I will be up front, with Kelly at the rear. How does that sound?"

Zehra laughed, long and hearty. The other cats looked at him.

"Sounds like a plan," said Kelly in a dry tone. He hunkered down in the creek bed and closed his eyes. Sal gathered bracken, and Lugs lit a campfire. Moira slumped into a deep sleep, twitching with bad dreams. Not for the first time, Julius questioned the wisdom of his expedition.

8

Just Keep Swimming

As the sun rose high in the sky and the sleepy felines began to rouse, Zehra jumped up and down, kicking up clouds of cold ash from the fire.

"What's she doing now?" groaned Sal.

"I think she's skipping," Julius said. "What's the hullabaloo Zehra?"

"Come on, you lot! Stop lagging around!" While the other cats dragged their tails and stumbled across the plain, Zehra was bright-eyed and energetic, swiping at butterflies here, stopping abruptly for a furious wash there. She was an intrepid leader, urging her companions to follow her. Lugs, who had stayed on guard most of the night, was too tired to put her in his place.

"What's got into her?" asked Moira, wiping her eyes with the back of her paw.

"She's been alone in the dark for so long," Julius mused. "She's probably excited to be out in the open with company."

"Zehra is excited!" the angora confirmed. "The trail is warm." She pointed out a line of heavy paw prints left by the boerboel.

"What are we going to do when we catch up to this dog?" Sal asked. "He's massive."

"Reason with him," Moira replied.

"All we have to do is make sure Quincy's okay. That he's with the dog of his own volition. Help them find the Bernoulli tube... if they need help."

"This really is a wild duck hunt, isn't it?" Sal complained. "I am so hungry right now..."

Zehra dipped down and used her teeth to pull a dry, rust-colored shoot from the earth. She offered its roots to Sal, who grimaced.

"It's good sustenance," Zehra assured him.

"I'm not that hungry," said Sal, holding up a paw and shaking his head.

"Anyone else want this?" asked Zehra, gnawing on a root. "It's Kalkan valerian."

"I'll take it," Sal said quickly. "If no one else wants it."

Digesting the root, Sal followed the others with a beatific look on his face. He did not complain for the rest of the day.

Tarquin rarely felt excited, but the thought of returning to his home city thrilled him. He had so many cats to visit, so many paws to shake, so many kittens to kiss and heads to rub. Mayor Otto had made him *catus non grata* in Bast, so with the lion gone, it was safe to come back. Carabas needed attention, but that could wait. Toxic would bring Moira back soon, and she would run the show until Tarquin was ready to rule both places. The Quintroche Empire. He liked the sound of that; Papa would be proud.

When his train arrived in Bast Central, Tarquin smoothed down the fur on his head and adjusted his exquisitely silver-stitched vest, making sure all the buttons were fastened. He wanted to look his best for his supporters.

However, when he got off the train, no one was there to greet him. This was obviously a mistake; his campaign team had misread the schedule, or he'd arrived early. He checked his fob watch; no, he was on time.

Cats rushed past him, ignoring him as if they did not recognize him. He visited the ticket booth, found an inscrutable white-furred colorpoint shorthair behind a Perspex window, and said, "Excuse me."

The colorpoint looked up and replied, "Where to?"

"There has been a mistake."

The colorpoint gestured at a phone number taped to the window, labeled CUSTOMER COMPLAINTS.

"That's not what I..." Tarquin struggled to maintain his composure. "There's supposed to be a party."

"I wish," said the colorpoint.

"A party to welcome me! Dignitaries, friends, impassioned voters. Has anyone enquired..."

"No," said the colorpoint, avoiding eye contact with Tarquin. "Where to?"

Tarquin snipped out a claw and said, "You do not understand." He drew himself up to his full height, which wasn't very tall. "I am Tarquin Quintroche, administrator of Carabas, and the front-running mayoral candidate for your city."

"And I'm running late for my train," said a bobcat behind him. The colorpoint cleared his throat, and Tarquin looked around to see a long line of impatient cats.

Tarquin left the booth and walked along the line, greeting everybody, personally introducing himself, and apologizing for holding them up. Although they looked at him nonplussed, he didn't care. Greeting party or not, he had to start somewhere, and a busy train station was as good a place as any. His election campaign had begun.

The Kalkan Plains finally gave way to lush, tall grassland. The cats were delighted, running their noses through the soft emerald blades. Sal stopped to chew on a stalk, stimulated by the actinidine in the valerian.

"Don't get left behind, Sal," Julius told him, waiting for his friend. The others moved on, the grass swishing around them as they walked.

"Nah, nah," Sal drawled. "Hold up. I want to know... how are things going with Moira?"

"How are things? She got attacked by a puma yesterday. How do think things are going?"

Sal flopped onto his back, gazing up at Julius. "I mean, between you and her. Her and you."

Julius helped Sal up. The snowshoe felt like a dead weight. "I can't get through to her, Sal. When you and I were living in her house with her, she was happy, wasn't she?"

"When I was a Wildcat," Sal said, "I tried to be something I wasn't because I wanted the other gang members to like me. There was this one calico called

Scummer who, when I was thinking of what to say, he would say, 'Why the big paws?'" Sal lifted a large hind paw and showed it to Julius. "Get it? A mean joke and a bad one, to boot. No pun intended."

"What's your point?" Julius asked.

"My point is, I put up with the jibes. I wanted to fit in. Moira put up with you because she wanted to better herself. Be on the right side of the tracks."

"I didn't taunt her," said Julius.

"Worse. You ignored her while you were off chasing stories. A cat like that does not deserve to be ignored."

"I know," Julius sighed, leading his dopey friend through the path trampled in the grass by Kelly, Moira, Zehra, and Lugs. "What should I do? I want to be with her."

"I dunno," Sal whispered as he caught up with the others. "But Toxic wanted to be with her, too. Don't be Toxic."

Otto was used to ordering other cats to dig for him.

During his reign, he had reconstructed Bast to a high standard, making it the grandest city known to felinekind. Aqueducts fed clean water from the River Hune to the central district, where Otto presided over Bast in City Hall. Hypocausts warmed the sidewalks in wintertime. The Church helped to keep most citizens decent and honest—not counting the gang members, criminals, casino owners, politicians, and the priests themselves, who saw themselves above such petty ethics.

Quarries in each corner of the city had two purposes; firstly, to provide clay for the countless amounts of kitty litter required by Bast's inhabitants; secondly, to mine for precious minerals, all of which went to Otto's treasury. If Joey Hondo succeeded in usurping Otto's position, that treasure would transfer to the upstart. Otto could not let that happen. So, he dug.

The ground beneath him was hard, but he had time. Time to claw at the surface, making tiny grooves that became larger over his days and weeks of captivity. When Chico came to check on him, Otto blocked the jailer's view of the broken earth. Otto dreamed of digging in his sleep, and recommenced his task as soon as he woke up. It was just one possible escape route, but it gave him hope.

After 23 days of scraping, Otto hit rock bottom. His paws rasped against impenetrable concrete. If he was under the river, as he surmised, then the cellar was part of a tunnel system, built at the time of his ancestor Calvon Canders. Otto let out a roar of frustration, loud enough to rattle the bars of his cage.

There was only one way left to escape. He would have to go through his jailer.

―――――――――――

Julius's group pushed through the grasslands, picking up traces of Quincy and Cavem: more paw prints, small, chewed-up bones, and strands of fur left on thousand-year-old whistling thorns. They were on the right track, getting closer to the Isle of Dogs.

"Water!" Kelly said at last. "I see water. The Bay of Hounds!"

This got everybody's attention. Forgetting any fatigue, the group rushed through a thick clump of grass over a mild incline to see an azure bay.

"Water." Sal shook his dusty head in disbelief. "Well, I'll be ginnocked."

Wild indigos grew close to the bay, creating a pastel fringe of delicate petals echoed in the water. Julius nibbled at a pansy stalk, enjoying the taste of sap on his tongue. He stopped when he saw the mirror image of his own face, fur ruffled, whiskers askew, but still gorgeous, dappled with sunbeams. *It's not easy to be this good-looking so far from home,* he told himself, strutting up and down the bank. "I guess some cats can handle hardship better than others." He directed this comment toward Kelly, whose body half-sagged to the ground.

"Feeling the heat, are you?" Sal asked, watching as the guide shoved his face in the water.

By the time the cats had drank their fill and caught up on their sleep, the moon had risen. "Where do we go now?" Lugs asked, frowning as usual. "We can't go around." The bay was wide, stretching to the east and west as far as the eye could see.

"Back, hopefully," Sal offered, just quiet enough to keep him from getting another lecture.

"It's out there, you know," Julius told his friends, gesturing out across the water with his nose. "The Isle of Dogs."

"So, what's your plan, big brain?" Lugs grumbled. "How do we get to the island (which is a damn fool place to go if you ask me) without getting our paws wet?"

"We don't. Kelly?" Julius looked at the guide, who gave him a gap-toothed smile.

"Ah, yes. I know how to get to the Isle of Dogs. But you're not going to like what I have to say."

"What are you jabbering about?" Lugs hissed.

"I'm going to like it," said Zehra. "I just know it."

"Tell them what kind of cat you are," Julius prompted.

"Well, that's obvious, isn't it?" Zehra laughed. "At least to me it is. I'm a swimming cat!" While her fellow felines stared at her, trying to comprehend, she stripped off her cloak to reveal a grimy old off-white bathing suit. "Don't look so surprised. I haven't been a hermit all my life, you know—even though it feels like it. I like to swim. Anyone for a dip?"

"I'm not going in there." Lugs shook his head, backing away from the water. "Why isn't there a bridge or a boat?"

"Dogs love to swim!" Zehra exclaimed. "They paddle across." She jumped into the bay and splashed around. "Come on, it isn't very deep."

"If my paws don't touch the bed," said Julius, "it's deep."

"It'll be okay," said Moira hopefully.

"I remember a sneak attack where my battalion had to wade through dirty water for days," said Lugs. "It was dreadful, but you should have seen the camaraderie!"

"I can smell it now," said Moira.

"They can suck you under," said Kelly, his voice sounding weaker than usual. "The currents are so strong; they engulf you and drag you toward the sea."

"How would you know?" Sal asked.

"Swam here when I was a kitten. Didn't much care for it."

Sal dipped a paw in and pulled it out with a shiver. Zehra grabbed him and yanked him into the drink.

"It's not so bad, actually, once you're in." Sal smiled, floating on his back with his stomach in the sunshine.

"You're not going to let this niphead better you, are you guys?" shouted Zehra. "Come on in!"

Lugs had to compete with Sal. He jumped into the bay with a yowl, belly-flopping on the glassy surface.

He sank straight down, disappeared for a moment, then bobbed up again, spitting a geyser of water at Zehra. "Ha! Thought you'd get one over on me, eh?"

"I think he just did," muttered Julius, wondering how he'd get through the day without soaking his fur. He hated rivers, streams, rain, and snow in that order. He couldn't stand still all day, though; that was not in his nature. Sal looked like a chubby otter, his ears drooping and his nose jutting out in front of him. But he was swimming.

"You want to catch up with Quincy or not?" asked Zehra. "Follow me, lads." She was already swimming away from the shore. Julius waded in after his friends, still muttering to himself, disgusted by the feeling of water seeping through his fur.

"Yuck," he grimaced before Zehra pulled him underwater, dunking him with glee.

"It's best to get used to it quickly," the swimming cat said, showing the others how to paddle. She was in her element now, a different animal. Julius half-wished they'd left the soggy angora in her alcove.

In this new environment, something peculiar happened. Instead of the usual gripes and banter, the cats shut their mouths, held their breaths, and concentrated on their strokes. The swim became a stoic contest to see who could cross the bay first.

Julius was halfway across when he grew tired. The long journey across the plains, the sleepless night, and his soaking fur all weighed him down. His mouth and nose sank underwater, and he choked on the dark liquid.

"Out of your depth, pal?" Lugs sank his teeth into Julius's nape and hefted him above the surface. "Relax. Get some air in your lungs and float."

Fighting to overcome his panic, Julius coughed his airways clear and let Lugs drag him along. With the lynx's teeth in his neck, he could hardly move anyway. He flashed back to his kittenhood for a moment, recalling the powerless sensation of being carried around, dangling from his mother's mouth in the tenement where he'd grown up.

He didn't want to burden Lugs unnecessarily. As an independent sort, as soon as he felt his strength returning, he demanded that the lynx let him go. Despite his hatred of the water, he allowed himself to relax a little, looking up at the clouds floating in the sky. With the calm surface of the bay reflecting the clouds, it looked as if he was floating on one.

Sal, with a head start, reached the opposite bank first, squatting on dry land and washing himself. Without Julius's dead weight, Lugs was able to move quickly, reaching the island in a breathless, frozen state, annoyed that he was second. He hauled himself up onto the shore and slumped on his side, water dripping from his heavy paws.

Moira and Julius dragged themselves breathlessly onto the bank, while Zehra stayed in the water in case Kelly needed aid. He did. The old cat struggled, his head sinking under water; he didn't have the strength to get all the way across the river. Zehra took him by the scruff and helped him float to safety.

"Are you okay?" Sal asked the guide, who coughed water from his mouth and sat up, dazed.

"You actually care," Kelly cackled. "I knew it. You can't fool a fool who's an old fool."

Sal occupied himself with untangling Kelly's tortured syntax.

60 meters inland, the cats saw the vague outline of the fence running east and west.

"Can you see a gate?" Julius asked his friends. "Kelly, do you know the way in?"

"You know our eyesight isn't that good," Lugs huffed. "Anything more than six meters away is blurry. We're built for close-up hunting, not faraway dreams."

"I can't even see that far," Kelly blurted. The other cats gave him a shocked look. He sounded weaker than ever.

"You've been guiding us," said Moira, awestruck.

"Best nose in the North," Kelly replied. His group didn't believe that now that they were on the Isle of Dogs.

"Do you know where the gate is?" Julius asked slowly.

"Of course I do," Kelly rasped, leading them east along the shore. Lugs bopped Julius with the back of his paw. Sal tilted his head high, proud that he had judged Kelly's character correctly.

After a half hour of walking, Julius staggered to a halt. His friends stopped behind him, peering past him. They saw the ferry, which was close to a jetty where passengers could disembark.

"You lied to us!" Lugs snarled. "How can we trust anything you've said?"

"We could have come over on that thing? Not got ourselves wet at all?" Sal asked no one in particular.

"Not safe," said Kelly.

"We got to swim instead!" Zehra said, trying to improve the mood. "Wasn't it grand?"

Julius was too tired to unleash his claws on Zehra, but the will was there for sure.

"Let's go before we're seen," said Lugs as the ferry landed. The cats stooped low, pressing their bodies to the ground, hearing thick claws clicking on wood. The cats ducked below the jetty as a pair of doberman pinschers panted toward the vessel.

"Watchdogs," Zehra whispered. "Policing the docks. If they find us, they'll chew us up like cheap puppy toys."

"Why?" hissed Sal once the dogs had passed their hiding place. "We haven't done anything."

"We're cats." Lugs squinted. "That's plenty enough."

"You're not scared of a few mangy mutts, are you?" Sal asked too loudly.

The lynx's reply was barely audible. "Yes," he said as they made their way stealthily inland, bellies brushing the ground, moving slowly and cautiously.

They relaxed a little when they reached the high creosoted fence that stretched into the distance on either side of them. No one was watching them, so they stood up straight, dusted themselves off in a frenzy of shaking and scratching, and gave themselves a wash.

Kelly lay down, his nictitating membranes shielding his eyes from the sun. "I need a little rest," he said to himself, his voice small and reticent. Julius looked up at the fence, which seemed insurmountable.

Kelly closed his eyes.

"You should clean yourself up too, buddy." Lugs nudged the guide, who stayed still. "Kelly?"

"He's not breathing," said Moira, rushing over to the old cat. "Why isn't he breathing?"

The cats pawed at Kelly, licked him, meowed at him, but he didn't respond. He was gone, far from his home of Healing, on an island full of dogs.

"Why didn't that old coot tell us he was dying?" asked Sal.

"Pride?" Julius guessed. "He wanted one last hurrah, and he knew we wouldn't take him with us if we knew."

"We wouldn't have got anywhere without him," Lugs said.

"A final, helpful act," Moira suggested.

"No, he was a selfish git," said Sal. "My money's on the last hurrah motive."

"He deserves our respect," said Julius.

Lugs turned on him. "How many more cats are going to die because you love this... ghost of yours? Camilla's gone, and Doctor McGraw, and now so has Kelly."

"We don't know Quincy's dead," Julius countered.

"And how will we find out one way or another? By asking the dogs on that island, the ones who have never helped a cat in their life?"

"I don't know," said Julius. "But this is what Camilla would do."

The cats buried Kelly quickly, in a soft patch of earth near the fence. They didn't want to put him too close to the water in case his grave got washed away. So he would spend his eternal sleep in the shadow of the fence, his grave unmarked and unprotected.

"I want to say something," said Julius, his head bowed.

Lugs glared at him. *Of course, you do.*

"We didn't know Kelly very long. We didn't know much about him. But despite some ... misgivings, we placed our faith in him, and he delivered. He helped us find our new friend Zehra."

Zehra liked this. The hermit nodded at Julius, who looked around. The cats stood still around the grave, ears flat.

"He helped us pick up Quincy's trail. And he got us here—" Julius gestured at the fence. "When we enter this city..."

Lugs gave Julius another harsh look. *Even though we don't know how.*

"We should honor his spirit and his ability to forge ahead, despite the fact that we don't always know what's in front of us."

"Isn't that the truth?" Lugs said out loud.

"We must be brave and optimistic, for his sake and for ours." Julius scratched some dirt onto the grave. "Goodbye, Kelly."

Lugs added to the dirt. "Goodbye, buddy."

Sal followed suit. "Thanks for not taking us in circles."

Moira did the same. "We'll miss you."

Zehra did not join in with the tradition, leaving the grave and encouraging the others to follow her. The farther they were away from the ferry, the better.

Pollet went out on the deck of the Leo to get some fresh air. He was finding it hard to breathe. The surrounding sea calmed him, helping him collect his thoughts.

He had always been loyal to Bridget, and her mother before that. The females of her breed provided the real strength of their dynasty. They were huntresses and power players. He admired them. But that didn't mean he was going to put up with Bridget's nonsense forever on this ship of foolishness, floating across the sea with dwindling food and a cat who wouldn't ration.

They'd checked the engine room together, seeking a loose wire or a jammed switch. The massive diesel-electric motor sat silent, fueled up but refusing to turn the ship's propellers.

"What are you doing?" Bridget had asked as Pollet clambered up the side of the engine, crouching on top.

"Looking for the crankshaft," he had told her. "It must be in here somewhere."

"You have no idea what you are doing, do you?" Bridget had called up to him. "There must be a manual for you to read, somewhere."

"No, ma'am. I've looked everywhere..."

Bridget had turned her back on him. "Then find us an oar or something."

To avoid answering back and potentially losing his head, Pollet had gone up top and got his fill of the sea air. He knew a cooling onshore breeze was nicknamed a cat's-paw. He did not know anything about cruise ship engines. For all his culinary knowledge and his smart vocabulary, he felt useless.

"A boat!"

Pollet jumped onto the railing and perched on top, his paws clutching the chrome, staring out to sea as if staring would bring the object on the horizon closer. He jumped down, ran below deck, fetched Bridget, and brought her topside, showing her what he'd seen. Thank goodness it was still there, looking beautiful in the bright sunlight.

"Look," he said to Bridget. "A boat!"

"Stop jumping around, we're sinking fast enough as it is without you rocking..." Bridget trailed off as she saw what had got Pollet so excited. "Don't just stand there, you nincompoop, attract their attention!"

Pollet hopped back up on the rail, almost losing his balance in his excitement. Bridget threw back her head and let out a mighty roar.

We want to attract them, not scare them off, thought Pollet. But the roar seemed to work. The fishing boat turned about and headed toward the Leo. It was barnacled, with flaking paint on its bow and tears in its sails, but to Pollet, it was still beautiful.

"Help us!" Pollet shrieked. "We're sinking. S.O.S.—Save Our Skins!"

Two mercats piloted the small boat alongside the Leo, and the captain hollered up to Bridget, "Hello there! What are you doing in these waters?"

"He sounds sloppy," Bridget said to Pollet. "Do you think he's alright in the head?"

"I'm sure he's fine," Pollet whispered back. "We're lost," he told the captain. "Can you help us, please?"

"If you want directions," the captain slurred, "check your map."

"We haven't—"

"My good cat," said Bridget, interrupting her steward. "We require passage to Bast. We will brook no delay."

The captain looked at his first mate and laughed. "They want to go to Bast."

"Don't make me climb down there," Bridget chided. The fishing boat bobbed in the water, at the mercy of powerful waves. Pollet stood upright on his rail, ready to jump if necessary. But he didn't want to leave his mistress.

"We've got fishing to do around here," the captain grumbled. "You're welcome to join us, but we need to get on with our work."

"We could help them," Pollet said to Bridget. "Earn our passage."

Bridget looked at him as if he was a dead bug.

"Bast," said Bridget sternly. "Now."

"Lady, you need to wrap up your joyride and get off this shipping lane," said the captain. "Before you cause an accident."

"This is an accident!" Pollet panicked. "We're sinking."

The mercats laughed again, preparing to shove away from the ship. The first mate said, "You'd better get your fat ass down here if you want passage."

"How dare you?" Bridget snorted. "Pollet does not have a fat A."

Pollet looked to the lioness. He had forgotten that she was the former head of the MMA, responsible for the monitoring of morality in advertising. She brooked no foul language, on land or at sea.

"We've got to go," the first mate said to the captain.

"Have you two been drinking?" Bridget asked. Pollet rolled his eyes.

"Ever since we woke up this morning," the captain burped. "The boat's gonna rock anyway, so we figured we should help it along."

Bridget stepped back from the rail. "I cannot travel with itinerant sailors."

"But this is our only—"

"Farewell!" The captain ordered his first mate to steer the boat away. "Enjoy your swim."

Pollet poised, ready for a moment, then responded to an angry look from Bridget and joined her on the deck.

"We're going to drown," said Pollet meekly, watching the fishing vessel sail away.

"It is better to die with dignity," Bridget replied, "than live with riffraff."

Chico had news for Otto, and it wasn't pretty. He couldn't keep it to himself any longer, though. He faced Otto's cage, watching the lion lying on the ground. Lions sure slept a lot, unless the big cat was depressed.

Chico didn't want to wake the mayor, so he waited politely until Otto stirred, opening one eye.

Chico had never seen a lion jump before. He swore that Otto flinched at the sight of the silent jailer standing in front of him.

"I'm sorry. I didn't mean to startle you," said Chico.

"Nothing startles me," said Otto tetchily. "I knew you were there the whole time."

"Of course, of course." Chico shuffled from one hind paw to another.

"What do you want? You're not just standing there for a gawp, are you? Come along, out with it. I have my morning ablutions to attend to."

Chico took a breath. "I've been asked to do something horrible," he said, his ears flat. "I've been asked to harm you. I've been asked to ... chop something off you."

Chico cringed, expecting Otto to go on the offensive. Instead, the mayor took a step forward in his cage, bold as he pleased, showing his dagger teeth with a massive grin.

"By all means," Otto growled. "I could lose a pound or two."

Not really. The imprisonment diet had worked wonders for Otto's figure. He looked lithe and ready to chase his jailer around the cellar as long as it took to catch him.

"I don't think you understand," said Chico. "My boss wants me to chop your paws off. I don't want to do it."

"Yet you are employed to carry out this task." Otto licked his teeth. "You know what I miss? Cigars. I would like to smoke a big, fat stogie before you gnaw on my appendages."

"I wasn't going to bite..." Chico stopped himself. He had never felt such pity for an animal in his life. "I-I'll see what I can do," said Chico, leaving Otto to pace in his cage for possibly the last time.

Not far from City Hall at prowler headquarters, another protest was heating up. No one policed the crowd or cordoned them onto the sidewalk. This time it was the prowlers themselves who waved placards and meowled at the top of their lungs: "More pay for a hairy job! Bad cats need locking up; good cats need feeding up!"

At the forefront of the demonstration was prowler Chief Feargal Cutter, a beefy Bengal veteran of riots, gang wars, and the time the city had almost collapsed during a milk drought. He'd seen it all, he thought; but he had never expected his own cat squad to disturb the peace.

Their picket line was ironclad. They had not seen a single prowler come in or out of headquarters since they'd started their strike. They missed getting fed, but they had each other's company and they knew the sentinels were patrolling the streets in their absence. They didn't like other cats doing their job, but it wasn't forever. Just until they got their salmon ration raised and were assured longer sleep breaks. Even cops needed a nap now and again.

The whole situation had started with a rumor, a mention to one prowler passed to another that spread across the force within a matter of days. The rumor was a vague one of change—a cut in pay and personnel, a heavier workload for the lucky prowlers who remained.

Cutter had seen all this before, too; it was a cycle, and the situation would get back to normal over time, probably with the next tide of civil servants. Cutter cared about his squaddies, but he felt safe in his upper-level position. He wasn't going anywhere until he retired or gave up all his lives in the line of duty.

The rumors got darker, and Cutter's feelings got stronger when he heard the faintest speculation that (gasp) dogs would be incorporated into the department to help police rougher areas of the city. This would not do. Cutter and his fellow cops had no personal beef against dogs, but prowling was a cat's job. Dogs would make a mockery of their profession, sniffing suspects' butts and frightening innocent kittens with their high-strung howling.

Cutter himself had called the strike immediately, urging his prowlers to sheath their claws and leave their beats. There would be no more policing of Bast until they got answers: were the rumors true? If so, how could these wild ideas get quashed before they were implemented? And could he get a raise?

One week later, the sentinels stationed in Bast had received their orders to guard the streets. In the posher parts of town, crime rates shrank to near-zero; in the gang-controlled territories, the Clutes and Wildcats stopped looting their neighboring districts and hunkered down, waiting for the military to lose interest. This was happening faster than anyone could anticipate, as the heavy paws of the sentinels were unsuitable for everyday community outreach. The soldiers had to go; the prowlers had to be reinstated; all they needed was a mayor to give them the green light.

There was no mayor. The strike dragged on.

Chico didn't know where to buy a cigar; he never smoked. Such luxuries were not meant for the likes of him, and he had read somewhere that tobacco was bad for cats.

What he did know—what every cat in Bast knew—was that Otto liked cigars, often appearing in his office window with a panatela in his mouth. It was a signature of his, along with his top hat, his thick mane, and his heart-stopping roar.

Chico went to City Hall, dressed in gray slacks, his oldest T-shirt, and a charcoal overcoat, all chosen to avoid attention. He shoved his way past the citizens protesting the election or supporting it; he wasn't sure which. Since the leopard guards were busy keeping the crowd away from the building, a lone, insignificant cat like Chico was able to slip in behind them. He looked for signs, attempting to remember which floor Otto worked on and which window he usually used to wave to his adoring public.

Otto worked on the top floor, Chico was sure, so he took the stairs at the rear of the building. If someone spotted him, he would say he was a new hire. He looked bewildered enough.

On the top floor, he checked a couple of rooms, seeking out Otto's leonine stench. As he left the second room, he saw a plump young chartreux in a black dress with a scarf around her neck. He tried to duck back into the room before she saw him, but it was too late; she asked him what he was looking for.

"Um, the mayor's office," Chico said, admiring the way the clerk balanced so many folders in her paws.

"You're scratching up the wrong tree if you think it's in there," said the chartreux in a husky voice that sounded like she'd smoked more than Otto.

"Oh, no, I... I was curious." Chico shrugged. "I never get to come up here."

"That explains why I've never seen you, handsome." The chartreux introduced herself, rubbing against Chico's leg. "I'm Tippee T."

"Chico Audaz. What does the T stand for?"

"Tippee," said Tippee perkily. "It's what my mom used to say when she called me for dinner. You know, 'Here, Tippee Tippee!' It stuck."

Chico smiled. This was the cutest thing he'd ever heard in his life.

"So, the mayor's office..."

"Keep going down the hallway until you get to the very end. You can't miss it. It's the largest room on this floor."

"Thank you so much." Chico prepared a story about fetching documents for Woodrow, but he didn't have to use it. Refreshingly, Tippee took him at face value. Once she left him to his devices, he found the mayor's office, checked all the drawers, and dug out a box of cigars. Woodrow wouldn't miss them; as far as Chico knew, the interim administrator didn't smoke or have any vices at all. *He'll probably be our next mayor,* Chico thought. *Whatever games Joey plays won't make that big of a difference.*

Stuffing the small cigar box in his overcoat pocket, Chico headed back to the back of the building, where Tippee was struggling to carry her files downstairs.

"Thank goodness," she breathed. "I thought I'd have to wait here forever for you. I was about ready to give up using these papers as an excuse to talk to you some more."

Chico smiled again, unsure whether Tippee was joking or not. The fur on her forehead curled upward in the sweetest way. Chico took her work from her and followed her downward, taking care to keep the files neat and in order.

A couple of times, Tippee stopped suddenly so that Chico bumped into her.

"I'm sorry," she apologized after the second stop. "New heels. I guess I should be grateful I can afford them." Chico liked the way she dressed, the way her footwear made her as tall as him when they reached the ground floor. The perfect height for a kiss.

A mirror reflected Chico and Tippee's tryst, bouncing off another, a chain of echoed images reaching Joey in his observation room. He watched the couple, incensed. Slamming a paw down on his console, he made his glass monitors shake.

He could not hear what Chico and Tippee were saying, but they were obviously in cahoots. Why else would two of his subjects know each other? He couldn't believe this was a coincidence.

Chico would pay for this skullduggery. But Joey wondered what this meant for his bid for the mayorship. If he couldn't trust Chico, then Otto might not be secure. The lion might come for him, with a hungry belly and a vengeful heart, that very night.

Bishop Kafel was either headstrong or stupid. Or maybe he just had a lot of faith.

A cold wind sighed its icy way through the large, empty warehouse that had once stored litter for the masses. Over decades, the building's roof had fallen into disrepair and collapsed, the end product of lazy construction work.

Now the warehouse was the province of the Clutes, one of the largest, meanest gangs in Bast. They owned the skeletons of old industrial structures through sheer force of fear and reputation. Only ignorant imbecilic non-gang cats dared to set foot in a warehouse like this, unless they were invited for a meet. Kafel had invited himself.

The bishop stood in the center of a recess that had once held great clumps of clay. A pool of light shone down from a hole in what was left of the roof, the shadows of broken rafters framing his frail form.

"You wanted to see me?" Missy appeared in an entranceway, padding softly toward the priest. She was joined by two of her trusted, lethal gang members, Solly and Kierkam, both Siamese. Solly had a habit of clicking two claws together, which his enemies found intimidating. Kierkam, who had lost an ear in a rumble, often reached up and pawed at the stump with a forlorn expression. Missy was surprised that Kafel had no entourage with him, no altar cats, no backup choir.

"I did," said Kafel simply.

Fine, that's how he wants to play it, Missy thought. *Make me do all the talking.*

Kafel stood still and stoic, particles of dust dancing around him. Missy wanted to wipe the peaceful look off his furry face.

"I don't have time to waste," Missy said in an attempt to sound tough for her lieutenants. "Speak your peace and get out of here so I can go wash my whiskers or whatever."

"You know of my great cause," Kafel said quietly, his voice barely louder than a whisper. "To spread the teachings of Bastet and bring order to this chaotic city."

"Hey, we've got order." Missy looked at Solly and Kierkam. "I ordered a Wildcat to be thrown in the river just yesterday, didn't I, boys?"

Solly and Kierkam laughed dutifully, the former clicking his claws faster than usual.

Kafel was unmoved. "I cannot achieve the peace I desire," he said, "without your help."

"You know, Dusty Daddy, a little chaos can be big business." Missy swaggered close to Kafel and licked the tip of his nose. The priest didn't flinch. "Why would I help you? What's in it for the Clutes?"

"Yeah," Kierkam added. "What's in it?"

"Power," Kafel returned. "Control of a considerable part of this city, far larger than you have now. That will mean greater wealth, an increase in your ranks if you so choose, and an overwhelming advantage when it comes to your rivals, the Wildcats."

"Ain't nobody better than the Clutes!" said Solly. "We don't need no more advantage."

"Everybody needs an edge," said Kafel, bowing his head slightly to Missy. "The Church can provide that for you."

Missy blinked at Kafel and slid a paw across his cheek. Again, he did not balk.

Missy asked, "How would we get this power? What edge would you give us?"

Kafel adjusted his holy gold-trimmed cape. "You know how powerful the Church is. So much affluence. So many followers. I propose that we join forces and use our numbers to conquer all that is not ours. Only then can the word of Bastet truly be spoken, and the ears of the city will have to listen."

The Clutes laughed. "That's it? That's your grand plan?" Missy teased. "I didn't think high priests were allowed to be so naïve." She walked around Kafel, as slow as a full-bellied cat measuring a mouse. "My family's had dealings with your kind before. Did you know that, boys?"

Solly and Kierkam shared a look. They didn't know that.

"It didn't end well," said Missy. "The Church broke its promise. You know what we do to cats who break a deal around here?"

Kafel shook his head, not deigning to protest.

"Look under your hind paws," Missy commanded.

Kafel looked down, gave the slightest hint of a shrug.

"What do you see?" asked Solly.

"What do you smell?" asked Kierkam.

"What do you know?" asked Missy.

"I... I do not..." Kafel was none the wiser.

"Get down on all fours, old one," said Missy. "Sniff the floor."

Painstakingly, Bishop Kafel sank onto all four paws and put his nose to the ground.

"Well?" Moira insisted.

"It is fresh," said Kafel, his voice muffled so close to the floor. "Fresh concrete."

"That's right. This pit used to be a lot deeper." Missy looked at her lieutenants again. "There's a lot of cats underneath you. Wildcats. Prowlers. Maybe a priest or two. All buried deep and sealed in tight. We fill in the gaps, the air pockets, with used litter. A sorry way for those cats to go. And all alive when we do 'em."

Solly and Kierkam laughed again, sharing this, their favorite joke.

"One day," Missy raised her forepaws, "the floor's going to be all the way to the ceiling." She snapped her look down to Kafel, who was slowly getting upright. "We just keep adding layers."

"There is no threat greater than the wrath of Bastet," Kafel said with great confidence. "But I appreciate that you take your dealings seriously. I propose that I have a confidential contract drawn up, that you and your closest gang cohorts may read before signing. That will assure the absence of jiggery pokery on either side of our pact."

"You'd have to leave here first to do that." Missy smiled. "What makes you think you'll do that?"

"I beg your pardon?" For the first time, Kafel looked surprised,

"Solly, is the mixer ready?" Missy asked. She knew it was.

"Always." Solly nodded.

"I don't like your deal," said Missy. "Because I don't like you."

Kafel squared his shoulders, his eyes narrowing. A cornered cat was one to be wary of. "You'll like my bodyguard even less, then," he spat, turning to look at a shadowy corner of the warehouse.

The strangest cat the Clutes had ever seen stepped out of the shadows. He was tiny, with black paws, thin stripes on one side of his body, and small spots on the other. He cocked his head, listening for instructions from the bishop.

"If you've got a bodyguard," Kierkam chuckled, "why did you do all that bowing and scraping?"

"To believe in a higher presence is to know humility," Kafel said. "You will come to understand, in time."

"Never."

The black-pawed cat walked up to the Clutes, taking quick, nimble steps on his short legs. Solly clutched his sides with laughter.

"This little kitten can guard your whole body?" Missy sniffed.

"Oh yes. He may look adorable, but deep down, he has a noxious side."

"Sure!" said Solly.

"He will ensure that I leave here safely, won't you, Dineo-Kenosi?"

The small cat replied with a squeaky mew.

Missy turned her back on Kafel and his defender. "Soften these two up," she told her lieutenants. "They've wasted enough of my time."

Kierkam and Solly closed in on Kafel. With a gesture of his paw, he invited Dineo-Kenosi to step in front of him. The little cat did, staring up at the thugs with wide, saucer eyes.

"Aw," said Solly, reaching down to pet Dineo-Kenosi. The bodyguard opened his mouth, showing a set of very sharp teeth. He swiped a paw at Solly and drew blood, claws raking across Solly's arm, making him howl and back off.

Missy spun around in shock. Kierkam charged at Kafel, but was cut off by Dineo-Kenosi, who leaped onto his head.

"Get him off me! Get him off me!" Kierkam cried while Solly nursed his bloody arm.

Missy took advantage of the chaos, closing in on Kafel and popping a claw right under his chin.

"Get off his head," Missy told Dineo-Kenosi. "Or you won't have anyone to guard anymore."

The small cat jumped down, ready to fight Missy. Kierkam felt around his scalp, relieved to find that his one good ear was still intact.

Missy and Kafel stared at one another, gauging the level of their mistrust.

"We do what we say we're going to do here," said Missy quietly. "We don't change facts to fit our beliefs. We don't hide backup in the shadows..." Missy reminded herself that her lieutenants were listening, and she had to be straightforward. "Much. If we're going to work together, I'm going to need the gospel honest truth from you, understand?"

Kafel couldn't nod with the claw to his throat, so he blinked his agreement.

"We don't need no contract, and we don't need psycho cats jumping on our heads. We need your assurance that there will be no more ambushes, and you won't screw us over." She retracted her claw, ready to fend off Dineo-Kenosi if necessary. "What do you say?"

"I swear on the Book of Felidae that I will not 'screw you over.'" Kafel tugged his cap straight as Dineo-Kenosi joined him, while Missy returned to her lieutenants. "I wish solely to join forces with you and steer this city in the correct direction."

"You heard him, boys," Missy purred. "Let's get saved."

Kafel's sandals were tied so tight that they dug into his hind paws. He wore them like this on purpose, to remind him that his role was one of adversity, not pleasure. His struggle to amass wealth and influence was not an easy one, nor should it be; the easy path downward led away from Bastet's glory.

"Those upstarts," Kafel grumbled to Dineo-Kenosi. "They have such short lives, and so much to learn."

"You are the perfect teacher for them, learned one," said the small cat, keeping pace with the elderly bishop as they walked through a dilapidated stretch of the city.

Houses hunched against each other with barely room to breathe. Once-fancy gothic follies had long since been converted into bedsits and flop sites. Some of the smaller cats slept on the street, never moving, uttering a plaintive mew to passers-by. Their only sustenance came from the cathode light of TV sets lining the sidewalk like eerie footlights on an urban stage, advertising wares they could never afford. A Suspicious Package rap classic echoed from an open bedroom window and the silty smells of the River Hune pervaded every nook.

Kafel and Dineo-Kenosi took a narrow, trash-strewn alleyway out of Clute territory.

"I will teach them that this life is fleeting. That a better world awaits them when they breathe their last in this world. Dominion, gang rivalries, and social status all mean nothing under Bastet's gaze. They had best give all their material goods to me, to the Church, for safekeeping."

"They need lessons." Dineo-Kenosi grinned his cute little grin.

Kafel stopped and turned to his bodyguard. "Oh, they shall have their lessons," the bishop said. "Just as my predecessor had his, when you encouraged him off of a roof to his doom." He looked up at the heavens. "I offer no apologies, my goddess. Bishop Parsimone had to learn the hard way that I am your most apposite mouthpiece here in Bast. Only I can spread your word beyond the Church, beyond the city center, into tawdry neighborhoods such as these." He spread out his paws and turned in a slow circle. "In this garbage pile, in this sad cesspit, I will begin my true proselytization. Dineo-Kenosi, bring me that mattress."

The black-pawed cat dragged a muck-sodden mattress over to the bishop, who curled up between two stains and sang a traditional hymn.

"Thank you for the suffering
"The shattering of dreams.
"Thank you for the anguish
"And curdling all the cream."

"We're grateful for our hunger,
"Our bottoms full of worms,
"The itching and the hairballs,
"The ear mites and the germs."

"On all fours we worship you,
"Ears flat down in praise,
"Purring in your honor,
"Faithful all our days."

Dineo-Kenosi joined in, one octave higher.

"Scouring us with peril,
"Our faith you will revive.
"Besetting us with trials,
"You make us feel alive."

"On all fours we worship you,
"Ears flat down in praise,
"Purring in your honor,
"Faithful all our days."

"I did not know you knew all the words," said Kafel happily. "I am impressed."

Dineo-Kenosi nodded.

"No one else is singing." Kafel called loudly to the apartments on either side of the alley. "Why are you not singing?"

A shirtless tom opened his third-story window and yowled, "Shaddap!"

Kafel said to Dineo-Kenosi, "Show him the error of his ways."

The bishop settled down on his mattress and listened for the tom's screams. What he heard was good. This was going to be a long yet fruitful night.

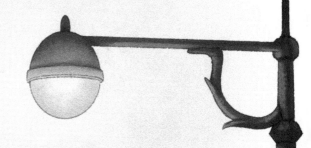

Part Three:
Isle of Dogs

9

The Fence

The sun was setting by the time Julius, Moira, Sal, Lugs, and Zehra found the gate to the dog city. Two mastiff guards, one young and one middle-aged, stood obediently waiting to challenge any visitors.

The cats approached with trepidation; there was no way for them to avoid this encounter. The mastiffs sniffed them, inhaling deep. Lugs kept a close eye on both dogs.

"Keep your nose off my tail!" said Lugs.

"Procedure," said the older dog, whose name was Behemoth. "If you don't like it, you can turn around and hiss off."

"We've come a long way to visit your fair city," said Julius.

"Our fair what?" growled the young mastiff, whose name was Colin.

"We're looking for the Bast Embassy," said Julius in a conciliatory tone. "Could you direct us, please?"

"You gotta pass the sniff test first," said Behemoth.

"How much sniffing do you need to do?" Moira wanted to know.

"A lot," said Colin.

"We know all the odors known to dog."

"If you smell wrong..." Colin said. "If you smell like you've been in the Poison Pool, bring toxins in here; or if you've been around the pitfalls..." The dogs' hackles rose.

"You can't read our minds with your schnoz," said Lugs.

Behemoth peered at him. "This nose of mine can tell when you're sick. It can tell who you've been with. And it can tell when you're desperate. Why are you so desperate to get in here?"

"We're worried about a cat," Moira explained. "An inventor named Quincy McGraw, ginger, so high."

Behemoth shook his head. "No gingers in this city. They stir up trouble. Their bright fur is too easy to spot; when they see them, all the dogs forget their business and chase after them. Anarchy."

Colin backed him up. "We'd know if your friend was in town, unless..."

Behemoth looked at him.

"Unless what?" asked Zehra.

"Unless nothing. You're clean as a cat can be. Move along."

"Thanks!" said Julius, offering his paw to shake, then thinking better of it. "I can't wait to write about this place."

Behemoth and Colin shared a look.

"A writer?" Behemoth asked. "What kind of writer?"

"He writes books," Sal gushed. "And newspaper articles and he has a radio series with his characters in it and sometimes he's on the radio, too."

"Do you have a permit?" Colin asked in a low, authoritative voice.

"I have this," said Julius, pulling his battered hat out of his pack and showing the dogs his press pass.

"You need a permit to report here," Behemoth said. "Orders from our cherished leader, Greffin Hebert himself."

"Well, can we go in and ask him for one?"

"You can apply for one," said Colin. "By mail."

"Oh, I hate mail," Behemoth barked.

Moira tried to slink past the dogs, but they barred her way.

"You already told us we could come in," she said. "I'm not a reporter. I just want to make sure the ginger isn't here."

"We already told you he isn't," Colin replied. "Oy! No trying to sneak past!"

Cowed, Sal returned to his friends.

"Look, Julius is the only journalist here," Moira reasoned. "The last thing the rest of us want to do is write anything. That would be like doing school homework. Why don't you let us through like you were going to? We can sort out the permit, and then Julius can enter as an official correspondent."

Behemoth shook his head and spit dripped from his jowls. "This is highly unprecedented," he growled. "Alright, anyone who finds writing a chore and isn't going to report anything, step through the gates."

Moira, Lugs, and Zehra entered, Moira giving the dogs her best side-eye. Lugs looked back at Julius and said, "We'll be back as soon as we can."

"Take your time," said Julius sourly. "See the sights."

Sal stayed with Julius.

"You should go in, too," Julius told his best friend.

"These dogs are rude," Sal grumbled in earshot of the guards.

"Get used to it," said Julius, dragging the snowshoe away from the gate. "Their idea of manners is wiping their paws on you after they've trampled you."

"Shouldn't we wait for the others to come back?" Sal asked as they traced the fence eastward.

"We'll find them when we get inside," said Julius.

"How do we get in?"

"Not through the gate, obviously. That would take forever. If I wanted to wait for some bureaucrat to do paperwork, I'd go home and put my paws up."

"There is a lot of red tape back home," Sal sighed. "It took forever to get my meds."

When they were out of sight of the guards, Julius poked the chain link with his paw, testing its strength. The fence seemed insurmountably high.

"You're on meds?" Julius asked idly.

"Not anymore," said Sal. "I ran out."

"That explains a lot," Julius mumbled. "Do you mind if I ask what kind?"

"Fluoxetine," Sal mumbled. "The brand name is Peacopuss."

"I thought you were bringing home wetties," said Julius. "Why didn't you tell me?"

"I was embarrassed," said Sal. "And a bit scared. I know how anti-drugs you are."

"I'm not..." Julius slammed a paw against the fence. "I'm sorry, Sal. You can talk to me about stuff like that."

"I am," said Sal.

"Tell me if you feel funny," said Julius tenderly.

"I feel funny."

"I mean, weird."

"I am—"

Julius laughed. "Alright, alright. I'm sure there's fluoxetine in Alcander. Bastet knows there's plenty of, uh, weird dogs around. We'll find another way to get into the city. Did you notice how Moira didn't even say goodbye? She just left me."

"She's very independent."

"I know." Julius smiled and changed the subject. "That younger dog inferred there was another way in, didn't he?"

Sal nodded and suggested, "There's a hole in the fence."

"Or the fence might not reach all the way around the island."

"Why do they even have a fence?" Sal frowned, clawing his way up a few meters, then sliding back down again. "Dogs like to run free, don't they?"

"Security? Why else would they have guards?"

"The guards were facing outward," Sal noted. "What are they keeping out?"

"Us. Cats. With our mendacious thoughts, our fickle vicissitudes—"

"Our big words," said Sal. "No wonder they wouldn't let you in the city, using words like that."

"Look at the crime and dwindling bird population in our own city. And what we did to the dogs there. No wonder they don't trust us."

"We don't trust them either," Sal argued. "They can't control their base instincts."

"I learned to trust one," said Julius. "I want to trust them all. But they have to trust me first."

Moira had never felt so small. She stayed close to her friends, their necks craned up, looking at the haphazard structures around them.

Unlike the gleaming towers of Bast that were sleek and tapered as if they'd been built out of one wraparound skin of steel, these buildings were all higgledy-piggledy. Bricks had been piled on top of one another with little regard for foundation, balance, or architectural aesthetics. They were all afterthoughts, with one floor bolted onto another and extensions built all around them. None of them looked safe.

Most of the homes seemed to lean against each other for support, like houses of crumpled cards. Large chimneys belched smoke and ash into the golden light of the sun, dirtying the view. The windows looked equally grubby, not because the residents didn't keep their homes clean and wash them every week, but because they constantly squooshed their noses against the glass and slobbered on the panes.

Most doggy domiciles were built out of stone; the municipality had tried building them out of wood, but dogs would pull the sticks off and run away with them, so those buildings fell apart.

Nevertheless, the cats were in the dog city of Alcander at last, self-consciously washing themselves, eyes peeled, waiting for a bark to send them into a furball fit. Lugs stood frozen, waiting for one of the passing dogs to pick a fight with him; Zehra grinned nervously.

"What've we got ourselves into?" asked Zehra, wishing she was back in her cave, overwhelmed by the sights, sounds, and especially the smells around her. Lugs shushed her—a loud meow might be enough to get a dog excited, start an undignified chase.

The air was muggy, heat blocked by clouds overhead that threatened to burst at any instant. An occasional drizzle-spit got the dogs excited; unlike cats, they didn't mind getting wet and looked forward to a shift in the weather. A shower would clear the humidity, cool them off, and spice up their dull routine.

If they felt any *ennui*, though, it didn't show. With tongues lolling from their jaws and eyes wide and shiny, the mutts seemed happy to be alive.

"What do we do now?" Moira whispered. "Put up 'lost cat' posters?"

"I was hoping we'd catch up with Quincy and that big dog before we got this far," said Lugs. "Julius's idea was to go to the embassy, get help there."

"Some help they'll be," Moira scoffed. "I hardly ever hear from them. I imagine they spend their days barricaded in their building, not daring to wave a whisker out here. They'll probably point us back south and pat us on the back on the way out."

"So, let's go to the embassy," said Zehra, watching a business-suited border collie cock his leg against a lamppost. "At the very least, we can get food there. Maybe they'll have a basement to hide in, too."

Chico sat in the cellar, munching on mice cakes, daydreaming about Tippee, and worrying about her, too. He found her fascinating although he loved his wife and cubs. Tippee certainly liked him; her passionate kiss told him that much. But he was sure she would lose interest when she found out he didn't work at City Hall, that he was a security guard for a shady politician.

Not that he could ever tell her that since it was a secret. He would come across as a sneaky, moggy instead.

He wanted to be with his family. Wild trysts were for longhairs and storybook characters, not for cats like Chico, and no illicit kiss could compete with the persistent company of a litter of kittens. He would stay away from Tippee T.

"What in the name of all that's sacred is going on?" Joey Hondo burst into the cellar, looking mad as a rabid bulldog.

Chico jumped to attention, dropping his mice cakes. "Sir, I don't understand—"

Joey rarely visited the cellar. Chico was so surprised to see him that he didn't complain when Joey swatted him with the back of his paw, knocking him to the ground.

"This place is a sty," Joey growled. "What have you been doing in here, throwing parties for your floozy?"

"My... my what, sir?"

"That City Hall strumpet. I saw you two together. I know what you've been up to."

Chico could take abuse from his boss, but he did not take kindly to Tippee being insulted. "You've been peeping at us? At me?"

Joey instinctively shook his head.

"Then how do you know what I've been up to? What business is it of yours?"

"I own you."

Of course, Joey was going to keep tabs on him, Chico realized, with his precious prisoner locked up in his care. But that didn't give his boss the right to poke into his private life.

"What were you doing, leaving the mayor unguarded?" asked Joey.

"I'm allowed," said Chico. "I meet with you, I go to church, spend time at home... what's this all about?"

"I asked you a question," Joey snapped. "Tell me why you were consorting with that intern."

"The prisoner requested a cigar. A last treat before I carry out your orders and maim him."

"You told him about my command?"

Chico opened his mouth, but no words came out.

"Take me to him. Now." Chico nervously pulled his keys from his belt and stumbled with Joey to the cavernous main part of the cellar where Otto was caged.

"I went to get a cigar," Chico managed to say. Joey confronted his leonine rival, standing in the cage looking confident and strong, puffing on his panatela. "That cigar."

"Hondo," said Otto gravely. "Thank you for my luxury accommodations."

"Captivity suits you," Joey replied, a faint tremble in his voice. "Judging by the look of you."

Otto had spruced himself up a bit, smoothed back his mane with his claws, and washed himself. It was as if he had expected Joey's visit.

"I thought I'd make an effort," said Otto, blowing smoke through the bars into Joey's face. "Considering I may bleed to death today."

"Oh, pay no mind to Chico's bloodlust. Puny mammals like him often resort to threats of violence."

"While others resort to kidnapping." Otto grinned.

"I can understand your frustration," Joey said coolly. "I would hate to be in your position. But please understand, this is temporary. Just until the mayoral election is over, and then..."

"I am the mayor of this city!" The force of Otto's roar blew Joey's and Chico's ears back. "Nothing you do can change that fact! My citizens respect me, and just because they can't see me does not mean they will not heed me! They'll find me down here and when they do..."

"The prowlers are on strike," Joey smarmed. "The sentinels are sequestered in their barracks. Your citizens are fighting among themselves, not because you have disappeared, but because they can't decide on your replacement." He cocked his head to one side. "They will decide. They will choose me."

"Turn around," Otto rumbled. "So I can blow smoke up your ass too."

If Joey was offended, he didn't show it. He placed his paw on the cage and rattled the bars, making sure they were secure. When Otto got closer, he pulled his paw away quickly.

"I heard you chewing out Chico," said Otto. "He should be rewarded, not chastised. He has managed to keep me under lock and key. There's nothing puny about that."

Joey flashed a secret smile at Chico. The jailer was making friends with his captive, after all.

"Then Chico will remain with you a while longer. Be aware, although his threats of harming you may be idle, he is not. He will remain vigilant, won't you, Chico?"

"You can bet my life on it, sir," said Chico.

"I already have," Joey replied. He addressed Otto, who stubbed his cigar out on the cold metal of the cage. "What do you need other than your freedom? What can I bring you to alleviate your discomfort?"

"I have everything I require. I am fed, and I have company. There's just one thing..." Otto purred, then raised his voice to a monstrous shout. "BRING MY SON BACK! RETURN HIM TO ME, ALIVE AND INTACT, YOU SORRY SPLASH OF DOG PIZZLE! BRING ME—"

Joey left the room, perturbed. Otto's voice echoed across the cellar, angry enough to stop the dust from drifting near him, loud enough to place an ache in Chico's ears for the rest of his miserable day.

As her group traversed Alcander, Moira noticed that most of the dogs she saw were larger breeds, such as bloodhounds, borzois, and red setters. She wondered where the smaller dogs were, remembering Kelly's tale about the lapdogs ruling the roost. She missed the old raconteur.

Although the streets of Alcander were wide, the dogs stayed close together, yapping happily with each other, stopping to sniff anyone passing the other way. Moira stopped flinching every time a dog smelled her; as long as she and her friends kept moving, she felt as safe as she could be surrounded by hounds.

Lugs led the way, taking them farther from the fence into what he assumed was the center of the city. There was no grid system, and the street signs were scent-based, not written; miss a smell, and the cats would miss a turn.

"The embassy's a big place; I know that," said Moira as they entered a residential district and passed a row of metal kennels. "It should be easy to spot."

Three dogs turned to look at her, wagging their tails.

"You mean me?" asked one of them. "My name's Spot."

Moira walked on quickly, remarking to her friends that dogs took everything literally. Lugs was not amused.

"Disgusting," the lynx said under his breath, turning his nose up at the Spots.

"Keep it down," said Moira, worrying that Lugs would attract trouble.

"How can I? It's hard to hold my tongue and my nose at the same time; they don't even cover up their own feces, they don't smoke, they don't drink milk, they think dirty puddle water is a delicacy..."

"Lugs," urged Zehra. The dogs on the street were closing in, curious.

"They think chasing themselves is high-class entertainment, and they're infested with fleas. Makes my fur crawl to be near—"

Lugs was near to a pack of dogs now, too close for his liking. He hissed at a Dalmatian, who growled back. The cats closed ranks, trying to keep moving toward the city center. But their stride slowed more and more as the pack grew larger, with a dozen dogs now eager to see the newcomers.

Lugs couldn't handle the attention. He slashed out a paw at the Dalmatian, who bit back, launching himself into the air and landing on Lugs. The other cats scattered.

"Meet at the embassy!" Moira shouted, pelting down a side street. Zehra leaped onto a fire escape, tightened her muscles, and jumped back down onto the Dalmatian, making the dog yelp with astonishment. Lugs used the moment to free himself, barging past the other dogs, helping Zehra dash with him down the sidewalk and through a mall, dogs gawping at them as they fled. Behind them, they heard the canines baying for their blood. They ducked into a sporting goods store and hid behind a doggy paddle board, catching their breath.

They heard their pursuers run past outside the store, all stamping paws and excited barks. The mall went quiet. They were safe.

"Where's Moira?" Lugs asked after their breather.

"Gone," Zehra said. "I only hope she finds the embassy before those dogs find her."

"Aha!"

Julius ran up to a section of the fence, pushing at the chain link with both forepaws. It gave way, making a space large enough for a boerboel to climb through.

"You found it!" said a relieved Sal.

"They didn't go through the gate, which means they must have something to hide," said Julius. He picked a clump of ginger fur from the opening. "Or the dog did. What have you got us into, Quincy McGraw?"

Curious as ever, Julius took a peek through the hole. He saw a street busy with dogs of all breeds and descriptions, from mangy mutts pushing rag and bone carts to pampered puppies carried on cushions. These were pooches with a purpose, hurrying on their way somewhere, tongues lolling in the breeze formed by their own mad rushing. Julius was hardly surprised that he couldn't see any other species on the street; just dogs, dogs, and more dogs.

"See any dogs?" Sal enquired, trying to scrunch his way in front of Julius to look through the hole.

"Oh, one or two," Julius replied, choosing not to alarm his companions. He was on edge as it was. "I'm going in. Follow me, and no mewing."

10

Dog Water

Reports are coming in of a stray cat causing grid-lock downtown... two Labradors collided on Huger Street while trying to discern the interloper's scent... she has white fur, green eyes, and suspiciously pointy ears. Anyone seeing her is advised to approach, give her a sniff, and try not to bump into anyone in the process.

—Alcander Action Six News Report

Moira ran as fast as she could. Her life depended on it. Beyond the side street was an avenue teeming with potential enemies. But she wasn't one to cower in a dumpster until some mangy forager found her. She stepped boldly out onto the busy sidewalk.

If the pedestrians had been cats, they would doubtless have ignored Moira, pretending she wasn't there or giving her a wide, wary berth. The dogs, however, all wanted to sniff her, their noses nigh-visibly quivering at the arrival of a strange scent. Moira kept moving, heading downtown, trying to avoid the wash of wet nostrils and slobbery tongues, losing the ones who had chased her away from Lugs and Zehra.

At least these hounds seemed friendly. They were all big, shaggy, and cheerful, greeting her with a wag. She returned the hellos with a wag of her own, which the dogs mistook as an invite for more attention. A few swipes of her paws were enough to reeducate them.

"I appreciate the attention, really I do... could you give me some space?" Moira popped out a claw to reinforce the message. She kept moving, too, sidling toward a secluded cut-through called Tully Alley. As soon as she dipped a paw into its shadows, the dogs gave chase, and she had to run again. Even with her aching, tired limbs, she was sure she could outrun them, and the farther she got down the alley, the more distant their barks became. But she hadn't expected a wall, blocking her path, halting her flight long enough for the dogs to catch up.

"What are we supposed to do now?"

Sal looked at Julius, who had helped him through the fence. The dogs here ignored them, busy with their own lives and workday activities.

"Act like dogs," said Julius.

"I could never do that," said Sal with indignation. But he tried all the same, letting his tongue droop out of his mouth until his chin got soggy. "I don't like thith," he lisped.

Julius and Sal moved cautiously into the city, where the dogs seemed less preoccupied and more likely to notice the cats. After some cautious exploring, they found the mall where Lugs and Zehra were holed up.

"Where's Moira?" Julius asked immediately. "You were supposed to take care of her."

"News to me." Zehra shrugged.

Lugs was more worried about himself after his close canine encounter. "She can take care of—"

"Herself, I know," Julius said, agitated. He encouraged his friends to leave the mall, seeking the embassy. As they entered the center of town, the buildings around them got larger, leaning against each other to stay upright. Many of them were kennels and crates piled high, one dog per room, some sleeping, some yipping within.

Dogs are strange, thought Julius. *No wonder cats find it hard to get along with them. What do they want with Quincy?*

There was hair everywhere, snagged on walls, piled on the ground, floating through the air like long, thick snowflakes, making Zehra sneeze.

"I'm thirsty," said Sal, leading his friends to Bowser's, a diner with only a few patrons. Here, they hoped they could eat and drink without causing a stir.

They walked gingerly past a row of food bowls. Chunks of meat were on the floor and on the faces and ears of the diners. Lugs watched one lab walk up to a bowl with only a few scraps in it and chow down.

"How can he do that?" Lugs asked. "I can never eat from a dish unless it's full."

"Quiet, Lugs," Sal hissed. "Don't cause any more trouble."

"I don't even know what currency they use," said Julius.

"Leave that to me." Zehra smiled, digging in her raggedy pockets and triumphantly pulling out a chicken bone. She offered the delicacy to the bartender, a bulldog who introduced himself as Bowser. He didn't seem to mind that his new customers were feline; he was just grateful for the bone.

"Don't choke on it," Zehra warned.

"Wouldn't dream of it," said Bowser, putting the bone in his register. "Saving it for my pups."

The cats sat on stools, tails dangling behind them, relaxing for the first time in the city. They were each given a saucer of water. Lugs lapped at his and gagged.

"What is this?" the lynx asked. Julius tried it too, almost retching from the taste. Sal and Zehra guzzled theirs.

"Dog water," Bowser said proudly.

Lugs almost spat his drink out, wiping his mouth with the side of his paw. Julius swallowed his with a choke.

"Dog water?" Sal asked with a dreamy expression.

"Yeah. It's an environmental measure."

"It is?" Julius heaved.

"We recycle our drool to make this nectar. It's piped from all over the city. We never run dry."

Lugs pushed his saucer away from him. He'd had enough.

"What have you got against dogs?" Sal wondered.

"I'm a sentinel, remember," said Lugs.

"How could we forget?" Julius said saltily.

"I was in the Great Canine Conflict, more years ago than I care to count. I got a lot of scars from that war."

Lugs's friends listened attentively.

"We were positioned on a ridge, ready for action. From the high ground, we saw the army massing; it was a terrible sight for a cat to behold. It bristled with groups of obedient labradors, crack-trained Alsatians, dachshund intelligence operatives, golden retrievers on the supply line, and bloodhound scouts. Rottweilers were at the forefront, bulldogs guarded the flanks, and pomeranians brought up the rear. Rows of teeth and leathery tongues, heaving hides, bright eyes, following orders to their last stenched breath. They were straining to advance, but they waited for the order."

"What happened?" asked Sal.

Lugs lowered his head. "We didn't stand a chance. A small clowder of cats, claws out, standing our ground... we held the line, but it cost us. So yeah, I've seen a bad dog or two. Forgive me for being leery of what I drink here and being particular about the taste."

"Is there no clean water?" Julius asked.

Bowser was more surprised than offended. "There's that spigot over there," he said, gesturing at a rinsing sink next to the counter. Lugs hurried over to it, turned on the tap, and let a thin line of water flow, scooping it up with his tongue. He pulled his head back quickly.

"Ugh!" he said, much too loud for the other cats' comfort. "This is dog water too!"

The diners stared at the cats, their eyes squinting, mouths closed tight.

"I think you'd better leave," said Bowser, "for your own good."

Outside, Julius licked his fur to take away the taste of the foul water. Sal and Zehra lollygagged. Lugs sniffed at the air, sticking his nose against the fence and gateposts. He seemed the most doglike of the four cats.

It's the sentinel training, Julius decided. *It taught him to be obedient, unthinking. Perfect to help get him into a mutt's mindset.* Julius was too cool to chase his own tail, strutting through the city with his trademark catwalk as if he owned the place.

"You'll attract more trouble," Sal complained.

"Not as much as Lugs if he keeps sniffing like a maniac."

"I'm trying to read the signs," the sergeant told him, nose against a particularly pongy post. "Here! It says the embassy is three blocks down on our left." He took one last whiff, then moved on. "Trouble with these street signs is, they dry out so quickly."

The visitors crossed a busy junction, marveling at the rickety buildings that had been slapped together with far more enthusiasm than skill. Compared to Bast's skyscrapers, solid and proud, these structures were dangerous. And they were packed with pups of all shapes and sizes: big ones with thick bushy tails and golden coats, eager eyes staring at the newcomers, fat ones with clumps of hair missing, short ones with stubby legs and squashed-up faces. Worst of all were the tall, skinny ones that shivered in the many draughts.

"Just keep walking," said Lugs out the side of his mouth. Julius and Sal stopped for nothing although they did slow down when they saw a bookstore.

"Think they got any of your mysteries in there?" Sal asked. At a glance, the books on display were simple, *See Spike Run*-level affairs.

"I don't think they sell classic literature," said Julius sarcastically, picking up the pace to stick with Lugs. "The closest they get to reading is a rolled-up newspaper bopped on their nose." He felt they'd be safer if they stuck close together, even though they were desperately outnumbered.

The city bustled with bristling jowls and dribbling noses. Sweaty-pawed strays tramped the streets, begging for scraps from panting commuters. Unlike the solitary denizens of Bast who liked to travel to work individually, the dogs moved in packs, yapping all the latest gossip to each other on their morning walk. They seemed so cheerful, so eager to get to work, that Julius was disconcerted by the sight.

Being social animals, the dogs would stop often to greet fellow citizens or sniff a patch of wall. Urinated slogans and messages were left for them to inhale. Haughty poodles turned their noses up at messy graffiti; packs of puppies were made late to school by the latest wee cartoon.

The Bast Embassy was an architectural history lesson of different layers, extensions, structural changes, botch jobs, whitewashes, fix-ups, and more add-ons. Unlike the busy blocks around it, this building seemed empty.

"Anybody home?" Julius called, leading his friends into the dark, fathomless place.

"Yeah," Lugs bellowed. "Is there anyone here?"

"No," said a small voice from behind a dusty desk.

"Well, we might as well go then," Sal decided.

"Who's there?" Lugs marched up to the desk, placed his forepaws on its blank surface, and leaned over to take a look. "That's strange," he told Julius. "There's no one around."

"So, we're looking for The Invisible Cat?"

"No, Sal, just a really shifty bugger. Oy! C'mon, you mousy nobody!" Lugs pushed the desk to one side, searching the lobby. "We're cats. You know what we do with squeaky little mice."

"Oh, that's different!" A small Cheshire poked his head out from behind a display case. "I thought you were, uh—"

"Dogs?"

"Yes, yes, that's right. I'm, um, Tarenfarthing. Toby Tarenfarthing, Bast's ambassador to, uh, this fair isle."

"*You're* the ambassador?" Julius introduced his friends, rubbing foreheads with the quivering Cheshire, who was relieved but still a bag of nerves.

"How'd you get this dead-end job?" Lugs asked, his words dripped with pity.

"I, uh, was Mayor Otto's chief public relations advisor. Every day he looked the same—flat, thick hair, no nonsense. One day I had the bright idea of advising him to try a new look, to appeal to the younger citizens as it were; curls in his fur, bangs in his mane. He couldn't quite carry it off. His subjects laughed at him; he was displeased. As a result, I got this promotion."

Julius couldn't help smirking. "Are there any other cats here? We haven't seen so much as a whisker."

"Oh, there are a few. Merchants, bohemians, a smattering of feline activists, an anthropologist or two. A large enough community to have its own newspaper. But we try to stay out of sight. Got sick of being chased all the time."

"Where's this kitty paper?"

"The *Tribune*? Oh, it's a rag, really." Julius didn't care. There he could wire Bast, speak to like-minded journalists, find out what they knew about his missing mate—in a population as small as this, tails wouldn't be the only things wagging. If nothing else, he'd be able to send his story home and find out whether there was any news from the Stray Cats Bureau, although he didn't hold out much hope of that.

"Show us where it is," said Lugs none too gently.

"G-go out there?" Once Toby had heard Julius's tale of woe, he agreed. "Very well."

"How come we never heard about the mayor's fab new get-up?" asked Sal as they left the embassy.

"Ah, well, those subjects who saw him... ended up as his holiday banquet. I suppose I was lucky." Toby flinched as a Dalmatian passed them in the street. "Although the longer I'm stuck in this flea-infested dog pile, the less fortunate I feel."

The Cheshire led them to a ramshackle little house on Luath Walk, one window cracked, loose tiles dangling from the rooftop. On the gate was a sign that read, "THE HAIRBALL TRIBUNE: BEWARE OF THE CAT." Julius knew they'd come to the right place.

"Not that much different from your own newspaper office, eh Mr. Kyle?" The ambassador blinked, and Julius nodded politely. At the end of a crazily paved garden path was a small flap that led into the house, too small for a watchdog.

"Should we scratch first or barge our way in?" the Cheshire wondered.

"We thought you'd know," said Julius.

"I don't get out much," Toby admitted.

"It doesn't show." Lugs shoved his way through the flap with the deepest growl he could muster. Inside, he found the last thing he expected to see.

"Don't you ever ask before you come in?" asked a hazel-eyed labrador, shuffling around an aged printing press. His fur was coffee-colored and his chin bristled gray with age. "Mr. Ambassador!" he exclaimed as Toby came in. "Nice to see you out and about for a change."

"Th-this is why I stay in the embassy," the Cheshire said. "Too many surprises. This is Josh Harness, a local celebrity—"

"Aw, shucks," Josh interrupted, not bashful at all.

"I guess, Mr. Kyle, you could say he's your counterpart on the island, albeit a more famous one."

Julius couldn't help feeling indignant. A counterpart? A doggy version of him? Impossible.

"I write books," Josh said modestly. "That's why I'm here. I was supposed to be interviewed by the editor of this here organ, but he never showed."

"Cats keep their own time," Julius told him, eyes narrowed. "We do as we please. We don't care for punctuality."

"Then I'm amazed your little trams run on time." Now the dog was being condescending, whether he knew it or not. Julius decided not to like Josh Harness.

"We're wasting time. Where's a phone? I need to get my story back to Bast."

Harness chuckled. "You should know better'n that. Communications with your city have been down since our two burgs almost went head-to-head last year. We're still on a war pawing. That's the real reason why the cats around here are lying low, ain't that right, Mr. Ambassador?"

"There are multiple, complex, conflicting reasons... and yes, that's the big one."

"There's been a real clampdown since that, uh, war that nearly happened. Y'know we were within a swipe of engaging in a full-on conflict with your species. Well, we started to worry that the mountains weren't enough of a defense against invaders—whatever that might be. Oh, and we were concerned about spies too, especially after the murder of the Carabian ambassador, Fido Frinkel. Hence the media blackouts and spot checks and chips. No one really cares; they go on about their business. They're only miffed if they need to take a leak at two a.m. and they can't because of curfew."

"And cats are still tolerated here?" Zehra asked, looking at Toby.

"As long as they look and act catty. Anyone attempting to pass themselves as a dog is liable to get torn to shreds for suspected espionage. Harsh, I know, but we'd prefer a few innocent furballs to get chomped than for the whole island to be endangered by some fifth column!"

"I didn't know dogs could be so paranoid," said Lugs.

"Just playing safe, pal," said Josh. "Dogs love to play."

"So I can't contact Bast from here either?" asked Julius.

Toby shook his head. "The only way would be to send a courier—and the mail's been erratic at best recently. No one with good sense would cross the mountains this time of year."

"Yeah, they'd have to be really dumb," Lugs growled.

"I did it!" meowed Sal. "I crossed 'em."

"You're braver than me." Josh led the cats back into the street. "I hear there's some nutty cave dwellers up there. No fun to deal with."

Zehra's eyes grew large, but she kept her opinions to herself.

Julius explained to Toby and Josh why they were in Alcander, and who they were looking for. Neither resident had heard anything about the inventor, and big dogs were common on the island, although they said they didn't recollect seeing a boerboel. Moira had to be found too, preferably before curfew.

"It will be dangerous," said Toby, who considered everything outside of the embassy thus. "But you should separate and look for your friends on an individual basis. I can provide maps and Josh here can connect you with tolerant dogs across the city."

"We're all tolerant," said Josh. "Most of us. We get carried away sometimes, that's all."

"The city's so big and strange, though," said Zehra. "So … open. I don't even know where to start."

"You say this Quincy doctor feller is an inventor?" Josh panted. "There's only so many places in Alcander where he can invent. Workshops, technical schools…"

"Give us a shortlist," said Julius. "Please."

"I'll do what I can," said Josh eagerly, reminding Julius of Bingo. Not all dogs were this friendly, as they'd discovered on the street and back home in Bast; Julius hoped that the majority were genial.

Since Moira had had a dog for a stepfather, she was able to cope with the attention. But she missed being on her own turf, where the dogs were always outnumbered by cats. Here she was the rare specimen to be sniffed.

"Yes, I know I'm beautiful. I don't blame you for staring. But do you have to invade my personal space? Even gorgeous creatures need room to breathe, you know."

"Huh?" The dogs looked at each other, panted, then stared at Moira some more. She backed up against the wall, feeling the cold stone pressing against her haunches. She turned the upper half of her body round, grasping the dusty bricks with her forepaws. The dogs lunged at her, and she pulled herself up, kicking at the hounds with her hind legs. It didn't slow them down much. While she scrabbled up the wall, they reached up as high as they could with their slavering jaws, teeth nipping at her bristled fur. She reached the top of the wall with a hiss, balancing on its sliver-thin top, flexing her tail, and moving slowly across the stone.

The doberman lowered his head, took a step back then rammed the wall, ruining Moira's high-wire act. As she fell, she twirled with balletic grace to land on all fours; fortunately, the wall now stood between her and the dogs—what had once barred her escape route now protected her.

"Calm down, boys," she told them, slinking away. The dogs kept charging the wall, smashing their snouts against it as if they suddenly expected it to turn to sausage links.

Moira knew she had to find a safe place to hide and think. A staunch city girl, she wasn't keen on trees; she could climb up one, but there'd be no guarantee she'd be able to get down again. Starvation on an oak branch? That wouldn't be very cool. Every alcove and shadowed nook she'd tried had been sniffed out. She needed somewhere that was full of odors strong enough to obscure her own scent—so she followed her nose, smelling her way from one alleyway to the next, eyes and ears perked for danger.

She could see a wide-open area that led to a tenement row. It would be risky, but she'd try to race across the weed-pocked concrete, then find a shaded place to hide. It would be night soon, and her superior eyesight would help her evade any more hungry dogs as she made for the city limits.

At the edge of the alleyway, a mastiff stepped out of the shadows, stilling her with a deep growl. Behind her, the pack had burst through the wall, some digging a small space in the ground to squeeze through, others chewing through the rusted metal. Moira's instinct was to climb again, but there were no windowsills or drainpipes to clutch, just whitewashed concrete walls.

"Alright boys, you got me. Now what?"

"Now we take you in," said the mastiff. "Get her to the station and don't feel you have to be gentle about it either."

"I'll take the center of town, and the area where you last saw Moira," Julius decided. A map was spread out across the orienting press. Julius ran his paw across it, making a distracting crinkling sound that the cats adored. "Zehra, you cover the warehouses and basements, the dark places."

"Suits me," said Zehra merrily.

"Sal, you'll cover the more upheel districts of town, north and east. You can put those slick snowshoe paws of yours to work."

Sal sagged a little, but nodded.

"Lugs, you'll be in the western quadrant. Josh, tell him what you told me."

"It's the roughest part of Alcander," said Josh. "You'll need to be extra careful. Keep those tufts of yours down and keep a low profile."

"That's my middle name," said Lugs tersely.

"I'll signal you if I hear anything," said Josh. "I have a very loud dog whistle."

"Every hour on the hour, you'll report back here. Okay?" Julius checked with his friends, who acknowledged their understanding. "Toby... you'll stay with Sal, in case he forgets where he's covering. Our base of operations will be the embassy, of course."

Toby exhaled. "Thank Bastet," he said. "I'll be ready with milk and biscuits if you—I mean, when you come back."

11

The Prisoner

The sun shone brighter than ever, smiling its biggest smile. Flowers danced in its light, and the grass stretched up to reach their shining friend. Stretch! Stretch! The grass would take a long time to get to the sky, but that did not stop it from trying. The more it stretched, the greener it got, and the prettier it made the world.

Puppy Happy loved the sunshine. He could run around, visit his friends, have a picnic with them in the meadow near his home. On this bright, sunny day, he went to see Bob Basset. Bob Basset sat in his backyard, looking sad.

"What's the matter, Bob?" Puppy Happy asked, smiling and jumping around.

Bob did not jump around.

"Why are you sad?" asked Puppy Happy.

"I can't find my tail," said Bob in a slow, low voice, his ears drooping low.

Puppy Happy ran around and around his friend, then he skidded to a halt in front of him.

"It's behind you," said Puppy Happy. "Give it a wag."

Bob wagged his tail.

"Oh yeah," said Bob. "I couldn't see it. Thanks Puppy Happy!"

Next, Puppy Happy visited his Uncle Doug, who liked to build things. Sometimes he let Puppy Happy help, just for a little while. Puppy Happy could not stand still for long. He wanted to play!

Today, Uncle Doug was making a boat. But this was not a normal boat to sail in the bay. This boat had a mast, a sail, and portholes, but it also had a very broad keel. Doug and Puppy Happy gave the boat its finishing touch—they painted a name on the side.

"What shall we call it?" Doug asked his nephew.

"Let's call it ... Sunbeam," Puppy Happy said happily.

Uncle Doug liked that name. He gave Puppy Happy a paintbrush, globbed with a generous helping of orange paint. Puppy Happy held the brush in his teeth and painted the word.

"Make sure you don't run out of space," said Doug.

"I won't," said Puppy Happy, his words sounding funny because he had the brush in his mouth. He concentrated hard and spelled out the letters.

S—U—N—B—E—A—N

Doug laughed. "You silly sausage!" he woofed. "Sunbeam is spelled with an M, not an N."

For the first time that day, Puppy Happy was not happy.

Doug saw him looking glum and said, "It's alright. We can fix this with a dab." Doug took the brush and added an extra line to the end of the N. It was a bit messy, but now the name of the boat was Sunbeam.

"Life isn't always perfect," said Doug. "But that makes it more interesting. Now this is the only boat in the world with a wobbly M."

Doug and Puppy Happy both laughed at this. They took the boat to the special place it was built for, the Mudlands, to sail across fields of muck that stretched as far as the eye could see. The sail caught a bellyful of wind, and they traveled over the mud at an incredible speed.

"Yippee!" said Puppy Happy. "This is the fastest, grubbiest sunbeam ever!"

The mud splashed everywhere, and by the time Puppy Happy got home, he needed a bath. He took his own toy boat and steered it through the *bubbles, imagining he was a captain. Soon he was clean and ready for sleep.*

The grass had had its stretch, Bob had found his tail, and Uncle Doug had made a boat that could show him the Mudlands in a way no one else had ever seen them. This had been a long, messy, and very happy day.

-Puppy Happy Plays in the Sun
By Josh Harness

Moira actually felt quite comfy in her cube. She liked boxes, appreciating anything with a ceiling; back in the wilds of the Pride Age, cats had sought such shelter. That meant that no predator could attack them from above. Plus, this metal cube was built to hold a fair-sized dog, so she didn't feel cramped; the place was a palace compared to some of the tight spots she'd found herself in since meeting Julius. But she still yearned to be free, even on the Isle of Dogs.

Like her mate, Julius, Moira was an urbanite, used to plenty of shade and a vending machine around every corner. She hadn't adapted very well to the wastes of No Cat's Land, and after struggling, spitting, and slumping to make her arrest as difficult as possible, she was shattered.

To her shame, the mastiff had put cuffs on her fore-paws. The cuffs constricted her blood flow and made it difficult for her to groom herself. The heat didn't help, and she panted with thirst.

I brought this on myself, Moira thought. *Should've learned from Julius's mistakes. Kept my mouth shut when I was spoken to.* She envied her sleep mat, safe and comfortable back in Bast, lapping up the cool of her state-of-the-art AC system; he was probably enjoying the peace and quiet without her around.

She thought about Julius a lot while she was captive, surprised by how much she missed him. *If I ever survive this, I swear I'll never nag you again, my love.* Oh, she was sure he'd breached the fence by now and was trying everything he could to find her—a tortuous visit to the Hound Council, a humble, heartfelt plea to Emperor Greffin...

Moira would reason with her warder when she saw him, if she didn't die of dehydration before then. She sank to the floor, conserving her last dregs of hope.

A flap swung open and artificial light dazzled Moira's eyes. She blinked, babbling out her story as soon as she sensed a watchdog's presence. "I'mMoiraMartiI'mfromBastIgotlost—"

"Save it for our interrogation," said a gruff boxer, leading her out of her cell. Using his big, snotty nose, he nudged her along a corridor full of identical boxes, filled with yelping, whining inmates. Moira pitied the large ones cooped up in those cubbies with no windows and a meager air supply. She noted that there were no small dogs in the cubicles.

"I think you must be the smallest critter we've had in here for years," the boxer told her. "Least as long as I kin remember."

"You only detain big dogs here, then?"

The boxer chuckled. "What other kinds would we detain? Those little fellers always manage to get themselves out of hock. Can't give 'em so much as a parping ticket that they won't wrangle out of."

"A ... parping ticket?"

"You don't want to know."

"So the big dogs get the short end of the stick?"

The boxer perked up when he heard about a stick. "It's the way things are," he said. "The small dogs make the decisions. Big ones, and average-sized ones like me, are sent to obedience school as soon as we can bark our names. We learn to do what we're told ... by the wee dogs in their fancy digs."

That put an idea in Moira's head that her warden quickly quashed. "Don't go reckoning you'll be let off for your size. You've had the whole city in an uproar and half the watch force out looking for you, causin' mayhem wherever you landed. You're in a lotta trouble. The chief is gonna chew you up, spit you out in teeny tiny pieces, and bury you like a bone."

Released from her cube, Moira still felt safer in the corridor, surrounded by stir-crazy hounds, than she had with Toxic—one of her own kind. She chalked it down to her unusual upbringing.

"In here." The boxer switched back to curt mode as they reached a dark, green-walled room at the end of the corridor. It had one small window and a velvet-lined cushion. Moira was left facing the chief of the watchdogs. He sat upright on the cushion, snaggle-toothed, wrinkle-faced, gammy-eyed, and miniscule. He was a pug.

"I know what you whisker-lickers think of us," said the chief. "We're backward. Dirty and stupid. We talk funny, and we have no manners. You can run fancy rings around us and tweak our ears while you're at it."

"Oh no," said Moira. "I work in Carabas—you must have heard of it—where both species live together quite comfortably. It's an experiment, but one that's working. Oh, and I was raised by a dog. I called him Pa."

"Do you think I've got puppy fat for brains?" the chief yapped. "No cat's ever been raised by a dog, and if they had, I'd have heard about it." He shook his head and a lump of snot dripped from his nose. "You're a nuisance. A contamination. Spreading your lies among honest, hardworking dogs."

"Can I go back to the boxer now?" Moira asked. "I was getting on fine with him."

"We have ways of dealing with cats," the chief snarled.

"Please tell me you're going to send me home with a four-course packed lunch?" said Moira dourly. "Or a massage. I could do with a good back rub from a labradoodle with clipped nails."

The chief stood up suddenly, sending the cushion flying into a corner. "How dare you! No day will come when a dog serves a cat in such a manner!"

Moira, realizing she had gone too far, looked behind her for an escape route. The boxer guarded the exit, staring blankly down the corridor. The chief took a squat step closer to her, ready to give her a castigating bite.

"Look!" Moira turned to the window. "A squirrel!"

"Where?" Forgetting his fury, the chief ran to the window to look out.

The warden was distracted too, craning his neck to see through the glass. "I don't see one," he said, puzzled. The pug pressed his squat face against the window, hopping up and down to get a better view.

Moira took her chance and ran from the interrogation room, down the green corridor, past frenzied dogs barking in their cubes, past two startled watchdogs out of the jail, into the bright sunlight of freedom.

12

A Bit of a Do

"I want to put it on a throne.
"I want to call it on the phone.
"I'm sad to leave it all alone.
"I'm talking about my bone.

"I love to crunch it with my teeth,
"Sniff it with my paws beneath.
"I chew on it until it bends,
"I'll never share it with my friends.

"When I lose it, I'm distraught.
"Tasty replacements can't be bought.
"I want to bury it alone.
"I love my juicy bone."

"The Ballad of Marrow Malone"
By Charlie Barker

If the east part of Alcander was upscale, then Sal
was a prize-winning genius. Which he was not. Lugs

escorted him and Toby to the imaginatively named East Avenue, protecting them but also making sure they got to the right part of town.

As Sal saw a pack of flea-bitten, destitute dogs panting in the shade, he started to worry.

"When'm I gonna get fed?" he asked Toby, who stopped for a moment to anxiously lick a paw.

"If you're expecting fine dining," he told the snowshoe, "You're going to be disappointed. Follow me." He led Sal and Lugs to a wooded area at the end of the avenue, where lumberdogs were taking a meal break. The cats stopped at a dilapidated mobile food kiosk, set up for the workers after a hard shift fetching and carrying wood. Flies buzzed around the kiosk awning; an unidentified carcass hung there, framed on either side by strings of sausages. In a clearing, dogs sat around rough-hewn tables chomping down on slabs of raw meat; in the kiosk, an aproned Alsatian was chopping up more cuts for his patrons.

"Got any chicken?" Sal asked the Alsatian, who looked at him as if he'd asked for a puppy's kidneys on the side.

"Here," he gruffed, unhooking a tatty bird from a row of game behind him and dumping it on the kiosk counter. "Pluck it yourself."

Toby, Sal, and Lugs found a few tree stumps to sit on and dug into the bird, chewing on a piece and removing feathers from their mouths as they went. Toby stopped after every bite or so to run his tongue across his teeth. Sal crunched on the wishbone, swallowing the sharp splinters with an unhappy gulp. Lugs spat feathers on the sawdust-covered ground and tore into his food with gusto.

"No sign of Quincy or Moira here," said Sal said with his mouth full. "Where to next?"

Toby looked at him with disdain. "Perhaps Mr. Kyle was right, and splitting up is our best option. You should try looking for Quincy and Moira here, on the east side of town, while I cover the northern quarter and Lugs tests his luck, in more ways than one, on the west side."

"Trying to get rid of us?" Lugs dangled a lump of fat in front of the Cheshire cat's face. When Toby shook his head, Lugs popped the fat in his mouth and gobbled it down.

"On the contrary," said Toby. "I know you'll be able to take care of yourself if we run into," he glanced around, "trouble. You go on ahead, Lugs. Sal and I can watch each other's backs."

"With respect, Mr. Ambassador," said Lugs with no respect. "You haven't proved yourself a great backwatcher," he had another munch, "yet. I'll stick with you two for a while longer. For your own good."

"Don't you want to find Moira as soon as possible, and the inventor, too?" Sal asked quietly. "Then we can go home."

"I have no home," said Lugs. "Just barracks. Which is where I really should be now."

"Neither did I until Julius took me in. Not a real one. We owe it to him to try our hardest. Find Moira and help Quincy."

"Yeah, help someone we've never met."

Lugs noticed Toby looking at him. The lynx was not making a good impression. "Okay." Lugs stood up. "I'll hit the West Quarter. Meet you back at Josh's newspaper office in an hour and a half. You paying for this?"

"Yes," Toby sighed.

"Good. See ya around." Lugs left, giving the Alsatian a cheeky wink on his way past the kiosk. The Alsatian couldn't chase him—he was leashed to the counter so that he couldn't eat all the prime cuts in one go.

"So, uh, what do you think that was we were eating?" Sal asked Toby as they continued their search.

"Some sort of bland, corn-fed domestic fowl."

"Oh, so it wasn't chicken then," Sal replied. "That would've been embarrassing. Chicken bones give me terrible wind."

The west side of town wasn't what Lugs had expected. It was quiet, an unsettling contrast to the bustle of the City Center. Sick of sticking to the shadows, he walked boldly down a main street, alone and unchallenged.

Every now and then he'd see shutters slam closed or sashes drawn; these residents were hiding or keeping themselves to themselves at the very least. His macho side made him inclined to believe that the dogs were wary of him, but he knew that wasn't really true. He almost missed the friendly demeanor of Josh and some of the other downtownies.

Stores were boarded up or sealed for the afternoon with thick steel panels. As he entered a narrow residential street, the only sign of life was the smoke billowing from the chimney of each house. *So there are definitely dogs living here,* he noted. The lights were off, but everyone was home. So why were the roads empty? There was no Carabas-style martial law that he knew of.

Lugs kept walking, sniffing at strange scents along the way. He reached a small piazza bordered by some fat one-story houses and a few dilapidated shops. A lamppost stood in the middle of the square.

He scowled, stuck his nose near the ornate base, and breathed deeply. It was marked by two strong smells, which surprised the soldier; he'd expected an intermingling of stinks left by every dog on the west side. Instead, only two dogs had marked the territory and everyone else had steered clear. Until now.

As Lugs relieved himself, he noticed that one shop was open—one that he hoped would lead him to some information. Forget dockside taverns or embassies; the best place to dig up dirt was a barber's. There, customers let secrets slip amidst all the small talk, blurting out gossip during blow-dries, shedding informative tidbits along with their hair. The proprietor would be the dog to see.

As Lugs entered the establishment, a tinny little bell rang. As he cocked his massive ears, trying to pinpoint the sound's origin, he saw an Old English Sheepdog getting its fringe trimmed, a retriever getting a blonde dye job, and a line of Afghans waiting for a shampoo and rinse. The hairdressers were tall, elegant Afghans, snipping away in time to the tinkle of the bell Lugs had heard.

"Hurry up now, sneep sneep! We 'ave a new customer!" The tinkler was a coiffed and powdered poodle named Cheveux, who stared at Lugs with great delight. The bell hung around his neck and rang when he shook his own fluffy locks.

The Afghans sniffed at Lugs as he passed, walking slowly through a gauntlet of wet, curious noses to the back of the establishment. "Actually, I'm not here for a haircut," he told the poodle, who looked at him with an amused sparkle in his eyes.

"*Nobody* walks out of here without at least getting their fur trimmed." Cheveux showed him a sign on the window that stated the exact same fact. "And you could do with it more than most. What have you done? Gone for a swim in a moat? Have a seat, we'll have a chat a while."

Since he needed information, Lugs sat on his haunches on a circular cushion. There was a thick plastic lip on the seat that ran round three-quarters of the circle, making him tuck his paws in to get comfortable. When he saw Cheveux pick up a large pair of scissors, he tucked his tail away too.

"Zose leettle tufts on the tips of your ears," said Cheveux, merrily snipping at thin air. "You really need them?"

Lugs gave him a vigorous nod.

"Just keedding," the poodle giggled. "You'll 'ardly know I've been around you." The rest of the customers maintained their scowls. He plucked a wayward strand of fur from Lugs's back; it didn't hurt, so the cat relaxed a bit.

"You seem a tolerant sort," Lugs told the barber.

"A customer's a customer. Keep your 'ead still please." The poodle held the back of Lugs's neck gently between his teeth to hold him still while he worked on the lynx's scraggly shoulders. "You have been in the wars, 'aven't you? Let your fur get all matted."

"I've seen some action," Lugs said gruffly. "Uh, I'm off duty right now."

"We'll feex you up. Got to look good for the ladies, eh?"

"Have you seen any?"

"*Quoi?*"

"Female cats."

"*Non.* Not really my forte. But I know where a *gentilchat* like you will find plenty of lady admirers."

Lugs leaped up and surveyed his fixed do in a wall mirror. The poodle had curled his fur up so that it obscured the tips of his ears, making them look smaller.

"Thank you," Lugs purred. "I feel like a new cat."

13

Matt the Hat

"The polls are in, the. Polls. Are In. I've got all the figures to make your brain bigger, right after this message from our sponsor.

"Fleas getting you down? Buy our new collar, coated with organophosphorus chemicals to put the bite on fleas. Now available with (optional) bell from your itch-free friends at Tybalt Inc.

"Now those poll results for your eager ears. It's lookin' like a landslide for goody Woodrow. 18% of listeners are likely to vote for him. Joey Hondo comes in a hot second place with 16%. 12% of you are buyin' what Tad Tybalt's sellin', while it seems like Tarquin Quintroche has been away too long, with a measly peasly 10%. That leaves 44% abstaining from the poll. I know you cats are lazy

and you don't want to do anythin' but listen to my
show, but I need you stop stainin' your abs and
vote on the day that matters. Do our polls, too."

—**WOTW** radio broadcast
By DJ Scratch

As Tad's campaign picked up speed, he tried every
trick in the political pantheon to improve his already
enviable ratings. He sent his supporters to visit the
homes of suspected floating voters, mewing to be let
in, then asking to go straight back out again, purring
and rubbing up against them until they got their attention. While they were making a memorable nuisance
of themselves, Tad pressed pads with bigwigs, licked
the newborn kittens of the great unwashed and broadcast ultra-sincere messages on Radio Bast. He even
wrangled an appearance on *The Big Wall*, the most
popular open-air variety show in the city.

Cats would flock from all parts of Bast—Downtown,
the Persian Quarter, the Docks, and the Doghouse—to
watch host Matt "The Hat" Bowler do his stuff. The
line-up was just that: a bunch of felines perched on the
wall, ready to sing (badly), push their latest product
(pitifully), or bitch about their long-haired neighbors (sourly). The shows were taped for televisual
prosperity and broadcast throughout the South, but
nothing was comparable with watching The Hat live
in action, alternately mocking or making friendly with
his guests as the fancy took him.

"The gags're cheap as chicks, the band's as loose
as a dog's morals, but the repartee's snappy, and the
chat's always catty. So let the fun commence!" The
Hat followed up his trademark intro with a toothsome
showbiz smile. "Tonight's special guest: a charitable

entrepreneur, meritorious factory boss, dapper cat about town... let me hear you yowl for Tad Tybalt!"

Tad stood up high on his haunches, balanced precariously on the old brick wall, and began to sing—a series of unruly, unmusical meows. But his passion and wild abandon were enough to get the audience rooting for him.

"Nice job Tad," said the Hat as the tycoon hunkered down beside him for a chat, three cameras trained on their every twitch. "Run out of rats yet?"

"Oh no," said Tad, slightly out of breath from his minstreling. "Plenty of those in stock. The food's cooperating and consumers are—well, consuming them." He gave Camera Two a well-rehearsed coy grin. "And it's a pleasure to serve the city. Make everyone happy."

"And fill your pockets with cash." Only Matt the Hat would speak to such a powerful cat that way, even in jest, and the audience loved it. Tad took the hits with good grace. "Save the smarm for your stockholders, buddy. Let's talk politics. You going to be the next mayor?"

"Yeah." The audience roared its approval.

"You going to be the best leader this burg's ever seen?"

"That's right!" Another roar. "Let's face it; I couldn't be any worse than the last one." This comment didn't go down so well. No one wanted to remember Otto.

"Well, Tad, it really seems like you've got what it takes to be our civic boss. Wealth, charisma, and a knack for saying the wrong thing." The audience was laughing again.

"I'm only feline, Matt. But I'll do my best when I become mayor. That's all I can do—my best."

"We believe you," said the Hat, giving Tad a friendly, candidate-endorsing shoulder nudge. "You heard it here first, folks. A mayor who wants to do his best. Who'd have thought they'd ever hear those words? Join us for a heap of freaks and folk heroes after our advertisers try to sell you things, including—get this—a hunger-striking tom so strong-willed he can go *four full hours* without eating. Right here on the fun, fun Wall!"

On the other side of town, Woodrow was making a public appearance of a different kind. The residents of Tradd Street, one of the most expensive areas in Bast, had invited him to one of their club meetings to discuss new guidelines for tours of their district. They found tourists disruptive and rude, but were proud of the antiquity and drawing power of their street. They'd drafted their list of regulations for tour operators and had sent a copy to Woodrow.

"I can't thank you enough for asking me to come here," he told the assemblage, planting his paw on a podium as he always liked to do. "It's a pleasure to be in such honorable company. I'd especially like to thank your treasurer, Mr. Pomeroy, for personally inviting me here." He looked out at the gathering of ancient faces—venerable, incontinent cats rich enough to afford a Tradd address though too old to enjoy it for long. They were inscrutable.

Woodrow continued regardless. "You are aware of the long, consistent tradition of fair and wise decisions that your community is known for." This was a fib—the club members had always lived an isolated existence, pleasing themselves, pandering to Otto's whims when strictly necessary—but Woodrow traded in falsehoods, finding them necessary to keep the city running smoothly. "Now I'd like you to make another wise decision. Endorse me as mayor."

"What about the tourist guidelines?" Pomeroy asked in a slow, fussy drawl. "Tell us what you think of 'em."

"The guidelines are, uh, fair, they're wise, they're what this city needs."

Although the members were too polite to boo Woodrow out of the room, as it became obvious that he hadn't read their precious proposal, they got upset.

"What's that young feller's name?" Pomeroy wondered. "The businesscat who's running against you?"

"Him? Oh, you don't want to know about him. Comes from low stock. Can't be trusted." Woodrow also came from low stock, but he left this piece of information out of his wheedling.

"Out of curiosity, what's his name?"

"Tybalt." Woodrow was uncomfortable now, his paws sweet with sweat. "Thaddeus Tybalt."

"Thank you, Mr. Woodrow. Thanks for coming." Woodrow sat and listened in on the rest of the meeting, a lengthy agenda of mopes and gratuitous backslaps. He'd blown it, and he knew it. One of his first acts as mayor would be to bulldoze the historic houses of Tradd Street to make room for a canning plant. But he didn't tell his hosts that. He'd save that nugget for another time, after his victorious election.

14

Puppy Happy

J **ulius was the first cat to return to the** *Hairball Tribune*. Josh was there, setting the blocks in his printing press, adding scent with his paws to make aromatic messages, and closing the press to make the morning paper. He hung his broadsheets on a string, suspended from one side of the office to the other.

"No sign of Moira," Julius panted, grateful for a saucer of cool, fresh water provided by Josh. "Or Quincy. Seen some huge dogs on the street, but no boerboels."

"They're probably lying low. I'm printing an ad, you know, 'If anyone has any information please call this number,' but our readership is ... limited."

"How do you turn a profit?" asked Julius as Josh showed him how to print a page. There was no way

Julius could match his speed, which came from years of issuing the newspaper.

"I don't," Josh admitted. "My publisher says I should give it up, that it's too much of a time suck, taking me away from—"

"My publisher, Boston Tarjé, complains too. Tells me what I should be doing, instead of encouraging me in what I choose to do. He wants me to go all commercial."

"You're preaching to the abridged, my friend."

"He's incessant. Things making money is more important than creating literature that will stand the test of time. He says, 'Why can't you do a book like *Puppy Happy*?'"

"You don't say," Josh smirked. "*Puppy Happy*. So cute he makes me barf."

"Same," said Julius, pointing a paw at his mouth and making a retching sound.

"Let me show you something," said Josh, digging in a drawer full of tweezers, hardwood wedges, and paperbacks. He pulled a book out with his teeth and passed it to Julius.

"*Puppy Happy Wags His Tail*," said Julius, reading the front cover. "By Josh..." he looked up. "No way."

"Oh, yes."

Julius flipped the paperback over and saw Josh's face next to some very simple blurb.

"That's what pays for this, my labor of love," Josh explains. "Most days, I'm not sure if it's worth it. The inane interview questions. The ubiquitous merchandising. The oh-so-cloying way folks like to bark his name when they see me in the street. I'll give 'em Puppy bloody Happy."

"So, why do you keep doing it?" Julius asked, giving the dog-eared book back to Josh.

"Supply and demand, little kitty. They keep asking for it, so I keep writing it one winsome adventure after another. *Puppy Happy and the Rhyming Reasoners. Puppy Happy meets the King of Cloudland. Puppy Happy Goes to the Mall.* Oh, I tried other stories—I thought the Rockabilly Rotts would be a big hit—but nothing stuck like that bloomin' drippy puppy."

"I felt the same about my character, Tiger Straight, for a long time." Julius sighed. "Then fans like Sal made me realize that Tiger served a purpose. To provide an escape. Reality has a habit of biting you right on the tail."

Josh nodded at these sage words. "You could be home in some cozy nook, writing your next gangbuster mystery novel. What's the real reason you're here, placing yourself and your friends in danger? If it's for an article, your lead is tenuous at the most."

"I'm getting on in years," Julius admitted. "This could be my last adventure. And I'm curious. I want to see more of the world before my limbs get stiff and gray. I don't know what kind of reward I'll get if I retrieve Quincy's invention, the Bernoulli tube, but I imagine it will be sizeable. I do feel like I owe it to Camilla, and this engineer, to come here. But the real reason? I read about Quincy, in Camilla's pieces and other articles in *The Scratching Post*. The way he was persecuted, isolated, made to feel so alone and unwelcome... I've felt that way. After the last riot, when the whole city blamed me and the dogs. He is me. I need to help him, if I can. My friends understand that. I don't have to explain it to them. I just wish ... we hadn't lost Kelly."

"This was his last adventure," Josh said softly. "But not yours. You've got plenty more to come." He hung up the back page of his newspaper, breathing in the inky smell with satisfaction.

"I've heard of the Bernoulli tube."

"You have?" Julius perked up. "Where is it?"

"I know what it is, not where."

"Then you know more than me." Julius encouraged Josh to continue.

"It's a mythical instrument of torture. Makes a terrible noise that unbalances the auditory system; as I'm sure you know, being an educated cat, that we can hear sounds up to 50,000 Hz and we have 18 muscles in our ears—"

"Compared to our 30," Julius interrupted.

"Our ears are bigger. It's not just the noise this machine makes, though. It has a nightmarish suction power, pulling anything that gets too close to it. It strikes terror into the hearts of all dogs. The ultimate weapon."

"I feared as much," said Julius.

"Until now, the Bernoulli tube was a theoretical device. One no dog dared to build. But if Quincy has actually constructed one, and it gets into the paws of a bad dog..."

"We have to find it," said Julius. "Before someone is tempted to use it."

15

The Great Debaters

For once, the city of cats was united. The protesters, prowlers, sentinels, and concerned citizens filled the Alicat gym, a space large enough to accommodate a tight-knit crowd and a raised platform, where Woodrow, Tarquin, Tad, and Joey faced each other for a debate. Each had a podium, but made pains not to hide behind their stand, their notes, or their words.

Woodrow looked nervous. His whiskers twitched, and his ears swiveled, as if he expected to be ambushed at any time. Tarquin was tired, the weight of two cities crushing him and graying his fur, seemingly in real-time in front of the cameras and attentive audience. Tad acted as if he did not need to be at the debate; his new job was secure. Joey Hondo was the most youthful and energetic of the four, quick to answer questions, ready to save Bast with a kindly gesture and a smile.

"I've been doing this for a long time," said Woodrow. "I've seen this city through a riot, a huge dip in unemployment rates, and even that time we almost ran out of milk."

The crowd held a collective breath at this. They could not think of anything worse.

"And whose fault was that employment scare? And the milk drought?" Joey interrupted. "If you were there, you were partly responsible."

"Gentlecats, you will each have your own time in the spotlight," said former wrestler, television celebrity, and newspaper publisher Swampy McMahon, who moderated the debate. He addressed Woodrow. "Mr. Cormer, you would do well to remember that the events you mentioned are sore subjects for many of the cats in this audience. Choose your words carefully."

"I will, thank you, Swampy."

Tarquin and Joey looked at each other. Was Swampy showing favoritism? They paid close attention to the proceedings, ready to use a misstep made by anyone present as a bargaining chip to get their dream job.

The crammed crowd was getting restless. A Siberian got smooshed up against a korat; neither cat liked that, bristling up their fur, taking up more space. A beautifully marked, sokoke looked around with its big, green eyes, trying to get comfortable, and stood on an ocicat's pale gray hind paw. The ocicat hissed and the sokoke backed off.

Swampy kept the show rolling. Once each candidate made an introductory statement, he asked a general question concocted by the sponsors of the night's debate, Barbamint ("For a rougher tongue, use Barbamint toothpaste.").

"Bast is getting as crowded as this gym," said Swampy. This elicited a laugh from the audience. "Should we expand north and if so, who would you move into the suburbs?"

"I would leave it up to the citizens to choose," said Woodrow. "Those who wish to stay where they are, well..." He smiled at the spectators. "We're not going to make your move. Those who are willing to undertake a bold new adventure in a new territory, I admire their pioneering spirit."

"We're talking about the 'burbs, not a wild frontier," said Tarquin. Another laugh. "As de facto mayor of Carabas, we would welcome closer neighbors with open paws. Anyone and everyone is welcome, and those who choose to move will be provided with everything they need to start a new life with fresh floorboards beneath them."

Tad rolled his eyes. "My new Rat in a Box™ window-to-window service is set to deliver food to you, wherever you are in the city," he announced, causing a stir of excitement. "Why would you want to move?"

"This is a mayoral candidate debate," Swampy reminded Tad. "Not a sales launch."

"It is now," said Tad, playing to the crowd. "The citizens need something to flavor up a drawn-out series of vanilla questions from a dull moggy moderator. Rat in a Box™ will be yours to open this weekend, folks."

Swampy scratched his bald head. He expected the politicians to pick on each other. "Joey, do you have an answer to my fascinating query?"

Swampy mugged for the audience. They loved him. Joey had to earn the same level of love.

"I honestly don't know," said Joey. "Since the whole point is moot, for now. Bast's budget should be spent on its citizens first, before any expansion takes place. They've put so much into the city, it's time for them to get something out."

The cats in the audience liked this. Tad and Tarquin responded with big, broad smiles. Woodrow scowled. "It's not that easy..." he mumbled into his microphone.

"Let's move on!" said Swampy. Once he had completed his prescribed list of toothless questions, the audience had its turn. One middle-aged female cat asked, "What are you doing about strays?"

"More shelters are being built," said Woodrow. "There's not much we can do... They come to the city for the clement weather and the generous tourists. I'm sure you've seen them, panhandling for kibble. We're trying to help, though, with temporary housing assistance."

"My neighbor's breath never stinks of fish," said a young bobtail. "There's something off about him. What will you do about it?"

"There are vegetarian cats out there," Tarquin answered. "My administration would promote tolerance and respect for the cats around us."

"I can have him investigated," Joey butted in. "My old mates on the force will take care of that weirdo for you, ma'am." The audience liked this answer.

"What are you doing to stop dogs coming back to Bast, roaming the streets and terrifying my kittens?" asked a father, concerned to the point of belligerence.

"Dogs cause a lot of damage," said Woodrow. "We'll be very careful as dogs are weened back into our community."

"I'm really not sure they did what the papers said." Tarquin shrugged. "When I am mayor, I will launch a full investigation."

The crowd was shocked by the comment, and the broadcast ended soon after.

16

What's Lugs Got to Do With It?

After checking in with his friends at the *Hairball Tribune*, Lugs went back to the barber. There was something about Cheveux that comforted him, made him feel at home.

"*Monsieur Oreilles!*" Cheveux woofed with excitement. "Look *mes amis*, our well-groomed feline customer is back. Tell me, *monsieur*, are you going to bring zee other cats 'ere too?"

"I would like that, but they're—pardon the pun—combing the city for a ginger tom called Quincy. Doctor Quincy McGraw."

"Ah, zee ginger! I remember him well."

Lugs squinted at Cheveux. "You do? You're not having me on?"

"Do you know 'ow many ginger cats we get in 'ere?" Cheveux asked Lugs.

"No idea," said Lugs, terse as usual.

"One! Doctor McGraw was that one! Tressa, fetch the locks." Cheveux sent an Afghan to the back of the barbershop, and the long-haired dog skittishly complied.

"Why did you return so soon?" Cheveux asked Lugs. "It is too soon for a treem." The poodle looked sad. "You are not 'appy with your look?"

"I love it," said Lugs in a monotone. "This is as far as I got in my search, and I wanted to start where I finished, if you know what I mean."

"And you wanted to stop een and say 'ello again." Cheveux smiled.

"I suppose. I don't know." He took a pair of duck feet out of his fatigues and offered them to Cheveux. "Got these from the Bast embassy. Thought you might like them."

The poodle's eyes grew big. "I do!" he yelped. "This is very special to me."

"I'm glad," said Lugs. "You, uh, earned them."

Tressa returned with several locks of ginger fur. "We kept these," said Tressa. "They are so rare. We want to use them for a wig or extensions, isn't that right, *mon coiffeur en chef*?"

"These... these could be Quincy's," said Lugs, examining the evidence. "When was here? Was anyone with him?"

"He was 'ere yesterday, accompanied by *un gros chien* called Cavem." Cheveux raised his eyes skyward. "He was a bully! He wanted us to make Quincy look more doggish."

"Is that possible?" Lugs recalled what Toby Tarenfarthing had said about cats not being allowed to pretend to be dogs.

"*Je ne regret rien,*" said Cheveux. "We used makeup to make his nose look bigger, his eyebrows, bushier, and we gave him some throat spray to make his breath fetid. You know what he said when we were finished?"

"'What have you done to me?'" Lugs suggested.

"He said he did not recognize 'eemself, and we had done a wonderful job. But he did not give us duck's feet."

Cheveux told Lugs that Quincy and Cavem had turned right out of the store. "I do not think they went very far. It was broad daylight, and they did not worry that anyone would see Quincy's brand-new look. Ze best styles take time to ... fall in. You know why you really came in here?"

"I ... forgot to ask about Quincy the first time," said Lugs.

"Fate! It was fate, *mon ami*. Why else would you return? Fate is as unyielding as the blades of my scissors. It will continue to guide you."

"I hope so," said Lugs as he left the barbershop. "I need all the luck, fate, and charity I can get right now."

"Goodbye, *Monsieur Oreilles*! Bring your kitty friends to see us!" Cheveux called after Lugs, who took a right turn and checked each building on the street for signs of Quincy and the boerboel, peeking in windows, asking passing dogs. Eventually, he found a plain brick building, painted white, with no front yard or mailbox. An old sign said, "PHARMACY," but the business that had once been there seemed long gone. The windows were barred, but he caught a glimpse of ginger within, just a flash, but enough to arouse his suspicions.

Making sure no one was watching, he marched to the side of the pharmacy and found another window to snoop through. This one was tinted, its blinds almost closed, but he saw Quincy inside wearing a lab coat with safety goggles on his forehead. The inventor was working at a cluttered bench, looking exhausted.

Jackpot, Lugs thought, checking his surroundings to make sure he was safe. He scratched at the window, one paw, then the other in quick succession, and kept scratching until he caught Quincy's attention. Quincy looked worried and gestured at Lugs to stop scratching.

Lugs pointed at the front of the building, but Quincy shook his head. The ginger cat's concern turned to delight—there was hope of rescue. Lugs looked at the pieces of metal and plastic on Quincy's workbench; he could see two curved sections that, when joined together, would make a tube. He also saw switches and circuitry, lined up like a chef's ingredients. Apparently, this was the recipe for the device Quincy had mentioned in his note; but why was he building another one? Or was he overhauling the old one?

Quincy poked his paw at Lugs and mouthed the words, "Get out of here."

I'm not in yet, thought Lugs, turning to try the back of the pharmacy.

As he turned, he faced the boerboel—looming over the lynx like a No Cat's Land cliff face, staring down at him, spittle-growling... Lugs was a large cat, but he was dwarfed by Cavem. What really concerned the sentinel wasn't the dog's size, but the grin on his lips. For Cavem, it was dinnertime.

Lugs regretted running away from Toxic, the puma. That wasn't his style, and neither was leaving a raggedy old hermit cat to do his fighting for him. This time there was no Zehra to get in the way, no friends to protect. He could do what he had trained to do for most of his adult life. He could take on the enemy.

He bushed up his tail and arched his back, firing his best snake-hiss at the boerboel. He wished Cheveux hadn't prettified him; he didn't expect to intimidate the giant dog, but he posed less of a threat with cropped fur and tweaked ear tufts. He listened for any sign of movement behind him; if more dogs heard him and joined the fray, he would be in big trouble.

He had enough big trouble to worry about already. Cavem snapped at him, and he dodged his head just in time, feeling the dog's hot breath on his cheek. Lugs backed off, taking care not to get himself trapped against the building; inside, Quincy stood at the window, anxiously watching the battle.

Lugs swiped at Cavem with his left forepaw, then his right. Neither blow connected; Cavem's reach was too long. Cavem stomped a paw down on Lugs's back, slamming him to the ground. Lugs was pinned, all breath knocked out of him.

Quincy hammered on the window, begging Cavem to let him go. This distracted Cavem long enough for Lugs to writhe his away out from under the dog's weight, sinking his military-grade claws into the boerboel's ankle.

Cavem let out a bloodcurdling howl, glaring at Lugs as the cat staggered sideways, seeing stars.

Thanks, Quincy, Lugs thought. *How's about coming outside and lending more of a paw?*

Quincy was a prisoner, Lugs was sure, but the idea still amused him. He stood up and sneered at Cavem, enjoying the fight despite the pasting he was taking. He didn't enjoy the feel of Cavem's head butting him against the building. The last place he wanted to be.

Cavem heard a howl from the street. Other dogs were coming. They'd heard Lugs's hisses and Cavem's yelps. Lugs was running out of time,

"I'll come back with help," Lugs told Quincy. He turned to face the boerboel, with teeth that looked bigger and sharper than ever so close to Lugs's face.

"Like the feel of my claws, Ugly?" Lugs asked. "You're gonna get plenty more." Cavem was close enough for Lugs to jump up and swipe at the dog's throat, snagging some fur but drawing no blood.

As Lugs dropped back to the ground, Cavem opened his mouth wide and bit the lynx's shoulder. Lugs meowed in agony, tearing himself loose from the bite, staggering into the street, past nonplussed dogs, past the barbershop, and into the center of town.

Cavem did not give chase.

"I saw him... I caught up with the dude we've been following all this time."

"What did he look like?" Sal frowned at Lugs, who was slumped in a corner of Bowser's, drinking thirstily from a bowl of dog water. He was in too much pain to care about the taste or the smell.

Josh had smoothed things over with the owner of the diner. Both dogs watched, concerned, as Lugs sat bleeding. Zehra licked at his shoulder, Lugs stoically abiding her rough tongue. Julius looked distressed—as far as he was concerned, this was his fault.

"He looked ... just like we expected," Lugs grunted. "Ginger. Weedy. Needs our help. He helped me as much as he could."

"Do you think the boerboel is keeping him captive?"

"That dog was a goliath. Bigger than ten cats on top of each other."

"That's quite a mental image," said Zehra between licks.

"I appreciate the attention, but is your tongue clean?" Lugs asked her. "Where's the last place it's been?"

Zehra put her tongue away. "I lapped up some dog water," she confessed.

"Nothing wrong with my water," Bowser grumbled. "I dribble a lot of it myself."

Josh gave the dog a placatory wave of his paw. "You're a good dog," he told the owner, "letting these cats back in."

"As long as they're enjoying my unmatchable nectar," said Bowser proudly.

"Oh yes. Actually, they want more, don't you fellas?"

The cats nodded although Julius looked paler than usual.

"Great. Drink up kitties! I can always make more juice!"

"The boerboel could have done worse," said Lugs.

"Worse than this dog water?" Julius quipped.

"No, worse than my shoulder. It stopped, though, didn't chase me. Maybe it didn't want the other dogs in the neighborhood asking questions..."

"Or it's under orders to guard your ginger pal," said Bowser, cleaning a glass with his saliva. "He's probably doin' it for the High Short Interest."

"The lapdogs," Josh explained. "As you're well aware by now, they run everything."

"And the regular dogs suffer. Emperor Greffin sits up on his throne, rolling in the choicest meat fat, while we squabble over oddments. It's always been that way."

"There are a few dogs who complain," said Josh. "But not enough to make a difference. Those that howl too much get sent to the Collarseum, where they are leashed, whipped, and forced to fight to the death."

"That could be why Quincy has been brought here," Julius reasoned. "If Greffin is at all concerned about retaining his power, then a weapon like the Bernoulli tube could be the ultimate deterrent against dissent."

"Good job you found Quincy," said Sal. "Now you know for sure that he's here, we just have to re-find him."

"Once that's done," said Josh. "All we need is for your Siamese compatriot, Moira, to turn up at the embassy. Then we're golden retrievers."

"Hardly," said Julius. "We still have to get Quincy away from the boerboel." He faced Lugs and wrapped an Ace bandage around the lynx's wound. "I hope the device you saw is the same one that went missing."

"Yeah." Lugs nodded. "I don't know why he would make a second one... sure one weapon of mass suction is enough?"

Hoping for strength in numbers, Julius, Sal, Zehra, and Josh followed Lugs to the pharmacy. Toby stayed at the embassy, in case Moira turned up.

Seeing no dogs, they crept around the building and found an entrance, secured with a thick wire mesh.

"No movement inside," said Sal, who checked the windows.

"I don't think this place has a basement," said Zehra sadly.

Julius showed his friends a set of massive, muddy paw prints. "I thought you were exaggerating," he said to Lugs.

"You weren't," said Sal, putting one of his snowshoe paws in the deep print. The boerboel's paw was more than twice his size. "You could have been hurt."

"I was." Lugs gritted his teeth. "But I am conditioned to embrace pain. It always subsides."

"I don't know," said Sal. "I have this dewclaw that jabs into my pads sometimes."

Julius pushed at the mesh. Where was the streetwise Moira when he needed her?

"He's not here," said Zehra, raising her voice. "Doctor Quincy McGraw! We're looking for you!"

Seeking peace from his friends' nonsense, Julius scrambled up the side of the pharmacy onto the roof, looking around the west side. In the distance, he saw a grand edifice, far more ornate than any other building he'd seen in Alcander, U-shaped in the center with an east and west wing. Its marble walls shone in the sunlight as if showing off to its shabbier neighbors. Lush green gardens surrounded the structure with carefully aligned fir trees and topiary.

Who would live in a palace like that, he wondered, *with so many poor doggies nearby?*

Getting back to the task at paw, Julius checked the roof for a means of entry. He found a skylight open a crack and squeezed his way into the pharmacy, dropping a considerable distance and landing on all fours next to Quincy's workbench. It was empty, and Quincy was gone. Letting his friends in, they looked around but found nothing except for more mud tracks, some made by Cavem, the rest by Quincy.

"We were so close," said Julius, slamming a paw on the workbench in frustration.

"We *are* close," said Josh. "We'll find our carrot-colored cat in distress. First, we should eat. Who wants to come back to Bowser's with me?"

"Is that all you're interested in?" Julius scowled. "The next nap, the next scrap thrown to you under the table? There should be more. There *is* more. That's what we're fighting for here, a cat's freedom."

"Okay..." Josh held up his forepaws in defense.

"Can't you appreciate the sunlight falling on your face as you lie bathing in its rays? Haven't you ever stayed up late to watch the moon reveal its face to the world, its cheeks pale yet glowing with life? Wrapped your paws around a blade of grass, catching it as it bends with the gentlest breeze? Go ahead. Fill your stomach. Fine. Don't expect me to enjoy it with you."

Josh looked at Julius with a frown. "You sure have some funny ideas about my species, don't you? Just you wait 'til tomorrow. I have something to show you."

17

Meet the Resistance

Emperor Greffin's palace was the largest and most sumptuous building on the Isle of Dogs, befitting a perfectly bred, utterly important dog.

Emily ran through the ornate white building, tongue lolling, massive ears flapping. She was a papillon, a small energetic bundle of energy, well-behaved yet playful. Her ears were spread out like sails, or the wings of a butterfly—hence her classification.

Among other tasks, Emily ran messages across the palace, and right now, she was delivering a doozy to the throne room.

The room had a high ceiling, decorated with intricate silver-leaf molding. Its windows were tall and arched. An immense rug was perfect for scratching and rubbing one's rump on. Large, fat cushions were placed around the room for courtiers and visitors alike. Fittingly, the centerpiece was a throne, broad and low, its seat and arms cushioned with the finest velvet known to dog. Small steps were in place to help Greffin reach his seat of authority.

When Greffin sat on his throne, Emily ensured he was served with a constant supply of sweetmeats, cool, fresh water, and small slices of bread. Greffin did not eat the slices; he buried them in the grounds or other dark, secret places. Many palace staff reported going to bed, finding a lump under the sheets, and pulling them back to find an old, toasted hunk of bread with a garland of crumbs.

Beyond the courtroom, the east and west wings of the building were long and sparse enough for dogs to bound around without fear of breaking an expensive ornament. Large red columns were set into the wall, decorative ionics that doubled as urinals. Behind the throne room was an enormous kitchen, always filled with meaty smells that were vented throughout the palace. The sleeping chambers were furnished with round, soft beds, often chewed or ripped apart when the courtiers forgot themselves—which was often—or tickly with crumbs. Below lurked a dungeon, small and horrifically dingy, reserved for Greffin's least favorite subjects.

Greffin loved to throw parties: costume balls, formal dances, garden games, all incorporating massive amounts of gourmet food. If the guests didn't throw up after one of these parties, it was deemed a failure. The big dogs did the heavy lifting behind the scenes—setting up tents and tables, providing the food, and cleaning up afterward. The little dogs they served were grateful, of course, but the big dogs were not invited to the parties—they were too brutish—and they had to settle for scraps to eat at the end of the night.

Emily enjoyed bringing reports to Greffin. It made her feel important, and she got to watch his large, mesmerizing mahogany eyes grow wider with her news. The reports were not complaints. Greffin kept the city standing with his iron will, peccadilloes notwithstanding.

"Your Majesty!" Emily yipped, out of breath after her run. "There are cats on our island."

"Of course there are cats!" Greffin turned his squat Pekingese nose toward the messenger. He was not on his throne that afternoon; he reclined on a cushioned triclinium, which had tall, intricately carved legs. He snorted as he spoke, mucus dripping from his nostrils. Emily did not bat an eye; such snottiness was expected of a Pekingese.

"New cats," said Emile. "Not the ones we monitor. Different cats, different smells, same old trouble. Upsetting dogkind with their airs."

"This is a most unusual message."

"For an unusual situation. I'm sorry, my liege, but I got hot under the collar when I found out. You can imagine how riled up our citizens have become as a result of their presence, and the cats have reacted ... unpredictably."

"Cats do that. Why are they here?"

"We have been unable to ascertain their purpose, Your Majesty, aside from observing and disrupting the very fabric of our noble society."

Greffin thought for a moment. "Greffin is sorry to see you in such distress," he said. A royal nose blower took a step toward him and directly wiped his nose with a lace handkerchief.

"Who are these cats?"

"Nobody knows," said Emily. "They're elusive."

"Ask the resident cats. They're all thick as thieves. They know their kind. Where were they last spotted? Come on dog, Greffin needs to know."

"I cannot appear ignorant before my sovereign," Emily said with an extra-low bow. "They have been seen everywhere! One was seen in the shopping district, another in the city center, a cat with uncommon tufts on his ears was seen strutting along a garden wall on Marrowbone Way."

"Why haven't these strangers been detained?"

"They haven't done anything wrong, except cause a disturbance. We have always allowed felines on this island, after all. It's good for us to spend time with them, practice self-control. If some of the visitors get their tails bitten off, well, they're warned. Most of them."

"You have to find these newcomers," said Greffin. "They can't be wandering around licking their whiskers all over town, worrying our neighbors. Greffin would meet these ... cats."

"It shall be done, Your Majesty."

Emily backed out of the room, ears sagging. Greffin shifted sideways on his triclinium and closed his eyes, snoring the afternoon away.

The city had started small, not much more than a fishing village built by seafarers looking for a patch of home. They'd always had ambitions, though—to attract more dogs to the island, build a strong economy, make it a go-to destination for service sector businesses, and flea circus operators.

During his lifetime, Marius Digger had seen a construction boom. The green preserves, parks, and rabbit runs were left undeveloped, of course; a dog was nothing without a place to exercise. But in the center of the island, kennels had been piled on top of each other, streets narrowed to make way for office extensions, and beachfront property was hotter than ever.

Marius had misspent his youth playing poker and betting on bite matches, running numbers for a scar-faced bulldog mobster. He'd enjoyed his work, local notoriety, his pick of the ladies, and as many bones as he could wrap his mouth around.

When his boss had been nabbed for racketeering, Marius had taken the fall. He was young; he'd be in the pound and back out in a few years, back to the pit bull's heel.

He'd realized something while he was in the big house, though. He'd made himself useful as always, running errands, sneaking contraband in and out of cages, sniffing out as many badasses as he possibly could. Over the course of a year, he met a series of old lags who had spent most of their natural lives cooped up, never selected for release. Others would leave only to commit another crime, get caught, and end up incarcerated again.

He didn't want to live like that.

So he'd turned Island's Evidence, got his boss and all his friends sent down for twenty, and joined a K9 unit. After years of hard work battling mistrust amongst his colleagues, he'd become a watchdog. One of the best. Well-versed in villainy, he could step into a perp's paw prints with ease. And despite all the criminal activities he witnessed, he was never tempted to return to his old tricks.

When he walked into the Third Precinct to file his regular morning report, he knew something was up. The desk sergeant, a long-suffering labradoodle, waved a clipboard toward the evidence room, indicating that Marius should go there straight away. The captain was there, supervising two sniffers who pored over a small brown cloak.

"Found this near the main gate," the captain gruffed. He was an overweight setter with a mean chop-busting rep. "Give it a whiff."

"Don't mind if I do. And good morning to you too, Cap." Marius buried his nose in the cloak and breathed deep. He withdrew, sneezing. "No wonder these boys are excited," he said, watching the sniffers slather. "I smell a cat."

"See what was on the cloak?" The captain held up a small plastic bag containing a few delicate hairs.

"Ginger. Possibly feline."

"Looks like we got a case of passing here, Marius. Could be harmless, could be a spy. Find the cat, Inspector."

"I haven't had my dish of water and my donut yet."

"None of your backbarking, Marius. There's still the question of that little old granny that you bit, Marius. Still hasn't dropped her complaint."

"Then I'll have to go bite her again, so she does."

"I know you don't mean that. You're a good watchdog. But I can't do you any favors until that incident blows over. And then who knows how long it'll be before you upset another citizen?"

"Aw, c'mon Cap..."

"I know you very well, Marius. You're a blunderer. Jump into situations with ears flappin' and your tongue lollin'."

"I just want to make you proud."

"I know. You can impress me by keeping a low profile for a while. Go find the kitty, don't be noisy about it, and get back here without chewing on any pensioners. I'll settle for that."

"I'll sink my teeth into the case, Cap."

"No more wisecracks. Get out there and get on with it."

Marius talked to the bloodhound detectives who'd brought the cloak in. They'd talked to the ferry dog; he'd said there were two cowled characters who'd kept quiet during the crossing. Smelled fine to him, but his nose was full of river rot. The other cloak hadn't been found yet.

"Any other reports involving cats today?" Marius asked the bloodhounds, whose eyes twinkled when he mentioned the "c" word.

"There was a white cat chased around the old Gristle District," one hound told him. "Some neighbors reported a lot of clattering, overturned trash cans, weird sounds. A unit was sent around. By the time they got there, the party was over, and no one stuck around to talk about it."

That was typical of the Gristle District, a rundown part of the island full of no-goods, old-timers, and rabid-acting curs. Marius sighed; that would have to be his first port of call.

Twice a year, the Hound Council organized a clean-up initiative in the rotten old Gristle District in the west section of the city. Volunteers bustled their way through its dingy alleyways and soiled thoroughfares, sticking close together for fear of getting mugged or bitten for being different. The district attracted trouble—deranged dogs, pups from no-good homes, and criminals all congregated there, up to no good, too many for the watchdogs to monitor.

Marius only visited the district when he had to. The majority of dogs were plain-speaking, straight-thinking, honest, and hard-working. A few hundred bad apples made his job a tough one but kept him employed. His questionable background made it easier for him to anticipate trouble, his bushy schnauzer mustache twitching at the faintest sign of trouble.

As he entered the district, the volunteer cleaners filled the street in a single row, sweeping dirt, and worse, into the gutters and placing litter in canvas sacks. The eager participants would make Marius's task harder, but they were easily identifiable in their glowing yellow harnesses. He passed them with a respectful nod, alert for trouble as he walked down the strip that locals had affectionately nicknamed Mange Street.

At the end of the street was a bar notorious for its violence and vice. Marius took a deep breath and went inside, sidling up to the bar and flashing his dog tag at the bartender.

"Official business," said Marius in a stern tone. "Is there a game going on?"

The bartender shook his head. Marius growled.

"Is there a game?" Marius asked again.

The bartender nodded his head at a beaded curtain. Marius went through without asking for permission, finding four dogs in a back room, playing cards.

"I got four phalanges," said a beagle with large, droopy eyes, a corn cob chew toy jutting from his mouth.

"Read 'em and whine," said a bearded collie, spreading his cards on a red leather table. "Six tibiae. Gimme the pot."

"Speaking of whining," said Marius, "I've got a sad story for all of you."

The card players froze when as Marius appeared, the beads rattling behind him. The beagle's mouth drooped open, and the chew toy fell out onto the table with a squeak.

"This story," Marius went on, "is about a game of bonejack, unsanctioned by the Hound Council. The players thought they could have a little fun, get out of their kennels, get a break from their wives and pups... make some non-taxable profit. Or lose some."

The collie got up to leave; Marius breathed his Dogleg bourbon breath on him, and he sank back onto his seat.

"Then a watchdog turned up, and the boys were in trouble," Marius continued. "And the bad dogs were sad. But there's a twist to this tale!" Marius picked up a stack of cards, shuffled through them. "A happy ending. Because, get this, the boys helped the watchdog out. They told him where he could find the Siamese cat he was looking for." He looked at each of the players. "What do you say, fellas? Want to rewrite this fairy story? Otherwise..." Marius plucked a card from the stack, as if by random, and placed it face up on the table. It was illustrated with a dog's skull. The darkest card to deal.

"I, uh, I seen something," said the beagle. His friends looked at him as if he was a traitor. "In Corgi Park. A flash of white in the trees. Coulda been a bird ... but I don't think so."

"What were you doing there, planning to steal the crown jewels?" The park was right next to Hebert Palace.

"N-no," said the beagle with a vigorous shake of his head. "I went for a walk, Detective. That's all, I swear."

Marius gave him a suspicious lour. "Anyone else got leads?"

The card players shook their heads. They didn't know nothing, they said, and they didn't want any trouble.

"Good luck with your game and may the best dog win," said Marius on his way out. "Next time, let me know when you've got one lined up. I might just join in."

18

On the Beach

To: Roy Fury, Editor, *The Scratching Post*, New Bast Tower, Bast

Apologies for lack of communication STOP Journey through No Cat's Land was arduous STOP But trail of Dr. McGraw warm STOP Sighted by one of my party STOP Story is hotting up STOP Lots of intrigue and disparity here = material for a juicy story STOP Save the front page for when I get back STOP Which will be in time for election, I promise END

From: Julius Kyle, Office of the Hairball Tribune, *Malting Street, Alcander.*

Telegram from Scratching Post reporter Julius Kyle

Josh woke Julius early the next morning by running around the cat's embassy bed, ruffing and yipping. As the honeyed rays of sunrise pained his eyes, Julius's first instinct was to claw Josh's nose and go back to sleep. But he remembered that his host had offered him shelter and protection on the perilous island, so he stood up, stretched, and asked the dog what was going on. Josh wagged his tail at a furious rate and led Julius out of the house.

Apparently, Josh was the only mutt crazy enough to be up at this time because no one else was on the streets as they trotted down the block.

"Slow down, will you?" Julius demanded, annoyed that Josh was making him feel unfit. The dog was barely drawing breath as he moved briskly past a row of whitewashed houses.

"Haven't you ever done any running before?" Josh teased.

"Only when I have to."

"You don't run for fun?"

Julius looked down his nose at Josh. "What a ridiculous notion. I chase mice, and I evade my enemies, rather speedily I must say. Sometimes I hurry to catch a tram if I'm about to miss it. I do not," he breathed out a sharp laugh, "run for fun."

"That's probably why you're so out of shape. I run all the time for no reason other than to feel the wind in my fur."

"You don't say."

"I haven't seen you move this fast since I met you. Unless you count disappearing into my wardrobe, that was pretty swift."

"I heard a strange bark," said Julius. "I got alarmed. If I ran everywhere, I wouldn't be able to see anything! To observe the world around me! I'd be too busy keeping the bugs out of my mug. If I did that where I come from, everyone would think I was crazy."

"Crazy is getting so unfit through inactivity that you can't even flee the watchdogs without losing all your breath. Let's keep moving before a stray dog crops up and spots you."

"Where are we off to, anyway?"

"My favorite place." After a few more blocks, they took a sandy path between two detached bungalows, Julius shaking gritty grains from his paws as he walked. The path led to a row of dunes, speckled with reeds and bulrushes. There, the sand was softer and deeper, slowing them down. They left a trail of rounded paw print dents behind them.

"I asked you to slow down!" Julius stopped in his tracks as his gaze took in a wide-open sea, with not so much as a trawler or buoy to blemish its beauty.

"Something, isn't it?" Josh guffawed as he ran a figure-eight across the beach. Julius sat, tried to wash a paw, and grimaced at the sand on his tongue. But he still enjoyed the fresh sea breeze after spending a night in the cold, gray embassy.

"Bastet's knickerbockers!" Julius exclaimed as the breeze filled his nostrils. "That smell!"

"You know what that is, right?"

"Fish?" Julius said hopefully.

"Shrimp. Squid. Crabs. Lobsters. Cockles and mussels. The whole ocean's full of 'em."

"Fish." Julius couldn't help himself. He drooled like a dog.

"The deeper out you go, the bigger they get."

"Big fish," Julius murmured.

"Doesn't it look inviting?"

Julius looked at his host, imagining some fantastic underwater seafood restaurant with mercat servers and an octopoid sushi chef. He was jarred from his delicious daydream by the clump of sand kicked in his face, accidentally scuffed up by Josh as he yomped into the surf.

Never again. Julius shook his head as he watched the barmy dog splashing in the shallows. *No more water for me.* Even if he had to flap his forelimbs and fly home, he had no intention of taking another dip. He tried to make himself comfortable on the shore and waited for the dog to tire. When Josh did, he shook himself to get dry, showering Julius in salt water. Then the labrador flopped down, his chest rising and falling as he caught his breath.

"Why don't you limber up a little?" Josh asked. "You're all rigid all the time. Even your whiskers're stiff."

"Ever considered that if you relax, you're making yourself vulnerable?"

"To what?" Josh got up to scratch himself under his chin. "There's nothin' around here."

Julius couldn't let his guard down.

"You'll be fine," Josh assured him. "Any rabid stray comes our way, we'll see him approaching a mile off. Go on, flex your paws, close your eyes, lie down for a spell."

"No, thanks."

"Trust me. I've snoozed out here a jillion times." Josh walked around three times, slumped on the beach, and rested his chin on his forelimbs, snuffing grains of sand from his nose. Julius watched him for a moment; the soft ground did look inviting. Once he was satisfied that Josh wouldn't become the victim of a sudden attack from a beach creature, he joined him in repose. "Ain't that more comfy?" the dog asked.

Julius tried to ignore his gritty, scratchy coat. "It would be if you stopped talking," he mumbled sleepily.

The surf lapped at the shore like a tongue with an unquenchable thirst, soothing Julius's ears. He felt the sand under his paws, heard seagulls own the air. For a moment, he was at peace.

His eyes snapped open. "I have to find Moira. She's been gone too long. Then we'll all track down Quincy."

"We have a saying," said Josh. "Chase one tail and you may find another."

"Why do you run the *Hairball Tribune*?" Julius asked Josh. "I was expecting someone more ... catty."

"I get help from your species from time to time, but none of them stay in that part of town for too long. Apart from Toby."

"I get that. Nobody wants to be chased for eternity. But why do you edit a newspaper aimed at moggies?"

"I see it more as a hybrid periodical," Josh panted. "Y'know, bringing species together, one headline at a time."

"That's great. I appreciate you letting me behind the scenes. And showing me this."

"Still believe all we care about is eatin'?" Josh asked, standing up and throwing shade over Julius, who laughed.

"No," said Julius. "I'm anxious about Quincy, and his invention, and Lugs getting hurt... I feel like we're running out of time."

"You've done so much," said Josh. "We all have. But you're right, we must fix this situation before anyone else gets bit. It's time to visit the palace."

Corgi Park was quiet early in the morning, with a few whelps playing as their sleepy parents stuck their noses in the bushes, not paying attention. If Marius ever had pups, he mused, he'd watch them like a doberman.

As Marius stepped through the high, wrought-iron gates of the park entrance, he looked up at the tall oak and pine trees. He didn't expect the cat to still be perched in the trees. All he needed was a clue, a tuft of fluff, some indication that she had been at the park, and where she was going next. Something concrete he could take back to the Cap.

Marius saw a flash of movement in the branches, bounded over to the tree, and placed his forepaws on the trunk. He barked at the top of his lungs, desperate to climb up and grab the cat. The white object moved from one branch to another as if it were teasing him.

"Hey copper!" a high female voice called from the oak. "I think you're barking up the wrong tree." The blur turned to a flutter; the object was a dove, which chose that moment to leave the scene. Up in the oak, Moira clung to a branch like an upright sloth. Taking in her luxurious white fur and her glamorous feline features, Marius desperately wanted to chase her.

"Get down from there," he said, embarrassed by his mistake as well as his feelings.

"I wish I could," she replied. "I'm kinda stuck."

"Come on down now, miss. Nothing to be afraid of. I'm an officer of the law."

"I've been hunted all of yesterday and all of last night!" Moira tightened her grip on the branch. "Why should I... I mean, I trust you, you seem alright from where I'm wobbling. But what's to stop other dogs from getting me if I climb down?"

"This." Marius held up his badge, which glinted in the noonday sun. The cat watched it glimmer. "No one messes with this. Except you, it seems." Having said that, Marius read Moira's distressed expression and wondered if she really was trapped. Either that or she was supremely stubborn.

Criminals had tried it on with him before. One burglar found raiding a twelfth-floor flat had insisted he was trying to conquer his vertigo.

"I am genuinely stuck," said Moira.

"Okay." With a smooth movement, Marius produced the sachet from his pocket. It was Mealymouth brand chicken surprise, a delicacy for cats, a quick snack for dogs. He tore the sachet open and as soon as Moira saw the purple packet open, she started to salivate.

"Smells good, don't it?" Marius smirked. Moira didn't know how she got down from the tree, but she was at his side in a flash, breathing deeply to get the most of the joyful poultry perfume. He held the sachet high, teasing her as she jumped up to try to reach it.

"Don't worry, toots. Even a mutt like me wouldn't eat this in front of you, although it does smell awful good." He gave her the chicken and she snarfed down its contents. "Looks like a dog taught you your table manners. Thought you might be hungry, but you must be starving."

"Thank you," Moira told him, sounding tired and distant. He could tell she was getting ready to bolt.

"I have to take you in," he said, keeping his tone light. "Orders. You can imagine what an uproar you're causing, loose on the streets, getting every tail-chasing dog on the island all riled up? We haven't seen a strange cat around here since a journalist visited us last year. You're a new sight and a new smell. You've messed with the status quo."

"So, you've come to lock me up and restore the balance."

"I don't know what's going to happen to you. At least you'll be safe. I'd put in a good word for you if my word was any good at the moment. It's not. You ready?'"

Moira nodded, looking for a likely escape route. The park gates were the best possibility. She followed Marius for a few steps, then glanced at the gates again.

This time she saw Toxic the puma charging toward her. He looked angry, savage almost, all sharp teeth and fierce brown eyes. He rammed into Marius, knocking the dog onto the grass. The two animals tumbled down a slope, coming to a stop near a "Please Keep On The Grass" sign. Only the puma got up.

Moira was already running for the gates, ignoring the surprised yelps of strolling hounds. She wondered how Toxic had found her. Maybe he had her scent, or maybe she was predictable, even to a brute like him. And she wondered why she hadn't cried out a warning to the detective when she'd seen Toxic—to avoid getting arrested, or because she enjoyed the chase? She hadn't seen any of her friends since they'd got separated. It was only natural for her to want to be with her own kind, even in the puma's form, rather than a dog. Had Lugs's intolerant nature rubbed off on her, despite her upbringing?

She didn't stop to find out. Toxic was hot on her heels, his breath on her back, claws out to gain extra traction on the sod. Moira flew through the park gates, swinging them closed behind her. Toxic hit them with a *clong*. She halted, turning to watch the puma glare at her through the wrought iron bars of the gate—then sink to the ground under Marius's full weight.

"You're nicked, mate," Marius told Toxic, signaling Moira to skedaddle. She did.

Moira knew that if she kept running, eventually she'd reach the embassy. Once her friends had accomplished their task, they could skirt the island together and find a vessel to get them back to the mainland. She couldn't imagine what dogs did to feline stowaways, but they didn't have much choice. With watchdogs looking for her, she hid in the shadows of abandoned storefronts and overgrown lanes, slowly making her way to the rendezvous point. She was tired from running, jumpy, which was out of character for her, and turned around, unsure which route to take to get to safety.

By nightfall, she found herself passing a dockyard cluttered with bright-hued containers and shabby-looking warehouses. She didn't see a soul and heard nothing but the chirping of cicadas. It was a peaceful relief after all the barking and gnashing and chasing.

Josh brought Julius and Lugs to Hebert Palace, while Sal and Zehra continued the search for Quincy, and Toby waited for Moira at the embassy.

"Maybe the ambassador should be here to introduce us," Julius suggested to Josh.

"The less cats, the better," Josh told him. "We don't want anyone getting excited here. That includes you, Mr. Lugs."

Lugs nodded, astounded by his lavish surroundings. The gardens were impressive enough, with their tall trees and impeccably manicured lawns, but they paled in comparison to the marble palace. He saluted the four German shepherds guarding the entrance, admiring their focus; they peered at him distrustfully. Josh nodded to them, and they let him in with the two cats, watching them closely as they walked into a long gallery lined with gold-framed mirrors.

"I wish Sal was here," said Julius. "To see all this."

"He would say the wrong thing," Lugs replied. "You can guarantee it."

"And you won't?"

"I'm on my best behavior," Lugs said sardonically, checking his tufts in a mirror that reached from the floor to the ceiling. "And looking my best!"

Josh pointed out a fresco depicting a Pekingese sitting on a cloud, fed treats by a Great Dane. "The little chap is who we're going to meet," Josh whispered. "He had this commissioned himself. Took five years to complete."

Josh led his friends through several rooms, all occupied by servants who kept the palace clean but also watched the cats carefully. "Don't touch anything," Josh said in the Room of Profusion, where Emperor Greffin displayed his jewels, a collection of silken handkerchiefs, and the Pekingese's favorite chew toys. Next was the Room of Adoration, a dining area with an oval ceiling and an oversized statue of Greffin; the Room of War brimmed with armor, spears, and shields.

The cats finally reached a broad staircase with bronze banisters. "These are not the main stairs," Josh told Lugs and Julius. "We're not allowed to use those."

"These look fancy enough for me," said Lugs, admiring the paintings of a small, sunny island, the exterior of the palace, and the city of Alcander, not to scale, split into its north, south, east, and west quarters with the lines of a huge, gilded bronze compass.

Upstairs, Emily, the papillon, was waiting. She led them into Greffin's throne room, where they encountered a number of digniterriers and courtiers: a dachshund who hiccup-yipped at them, a Brussels griffon with a winged white cape and folded ears, a lhasa apso with a parasol, and a sleepy sheltie. They all lounged on cushions, well-fed and indolent, surrounding Emperor Greffin on his heated throne.

At the height of his bestselling fame, living in a penthouse apartment filled with soft furnishings to claw and a maid to clean his litter tray, Julius had considered himself a properly pampered puss. Now his brief victory lap of luxury seemed like life on Skid Row compared with the lapdogs' setup. Emperor Greffin snorted as he raised his head to peer at Julius, his lower jaw set in a majestic little grin. A red setter stood with his back to the Pekingese potentate, tail wagging furiously to fan him with cool air. The courtiers lolled on their gold-embroidered seats, eating jerky from intricately patterned porcelain. The sounds of their lapping and yapping echoed around the vaulted chamber.

"Look what the dog dragged in," said the sheltie drowsily.

"You are the sporadically celebrated Julius Kyle?" Greffin snuffed, waving the red setter away.

"I have that honor, Your Dogship." Julius stood before the Pekingese and bowed.

"Greffin has followed your adventures," said Greffin. "The juiciest ones, certainly. You saved Carabas from utter destruction."

"I had help," said Julius. "Some of it was provided by sentinels like Lugs, uh, Sergeant Barr, here."

"You also kept your head while a bad cadre of dogs wreaked havoc in Bast." Judging by Greffin's tone, he was skeptical about the dogs' guilt. Julius was not ready to encourage that suspicion with his own insight.

"You are far more celebrated than me," Julius said with appropriate deference. "I don't know how you hold this city together, especially with such ... delicate paws."

"These paws have signed death warrants for many a cat," said Greffin. "They have walked on the distant shores of Blackfriar, across the Wayward Hills. They have embraced fiery Pekinese lovers and received treats from the great and powerful potentates of the land. They are blessed," Greffin growled. "Because they are attached to Greffin."

"Forgive me, Your Wagness. I used an inappropriate term. No one should appreciate the importance of words more than me."

Greffin nodded slowly. "Indeed."

"Why did you want to meet us?" asked Julius, hoping Greffin had read his books.

"Curiosity is not the sole province of your species," Greffin snuffled, laughing at his own joke.

"I hope you're satisfied," Julius said under his breath.

"I beg your pardon?" Emily asked.

Julius continued to address Greffin. "I have a boon to ask of you, Your Wet-noseness. I am searching for a ginger cat... an engineer of some renown, Quincy McGraw."

"Greffin is aware of your purpose here." The emperor shared a look with Emily. "Our loyal dogs are looking for Doctor McGraw also. For a bright-furred oddity in these parts, he is uncommonly hard to find."

"Maybe one of your loyal subjects has found him already and made a meal of him," Lugs quipped.

"They would not dare." Emily set him straight. "Punishments are severe for those few who disobey us. A rolled-up newspaper. Solitary confinement. Electrification."

"Positive reinforcement always works better on me." Julius grinned. "If I may be so bold, you could be a benign force in the city if you chose."

"How so?" Greffin placed his chin on a forepaw, indulging Julius.

"Have you been outside your chintzy little tower recently?" Julius caught a worried glance from Emily, but continued. "Your citizens aren't doing so hot. Some of them are dying of starvation and they're too loyal to their glorious Emperor to complain. Others are fast losing that sense of loyalty. They're riled up and they have a common enemy, alright, but it's not us. It's you."

"If the big dogs are so hungry," Greffin replied, "perhaps we should feed you to them."

Emily coughed for attention and said, "I'm afraid that these minnows would make a very short, unsatisfying snack for a thousand hungry hounds, Your Majesty."

"Who are these most unhappy fellows?" Greffin wanted to know.

Josh, who until that moment had felt compelled to stay silent, spoke up. "Not I," he said. "It's true that some are hungry out there."

"Let them eat sweetmeats," Greffin chuckled.

"I'm sure it is their own fault that their bellies are empty," Josh went on. "Not yours."

"Greffin offers opportunities to every one of his subjects," said Greffin. "He throws each one of them a bone. It is up to them to make the most of their prospects."

"I'm not a crusader like Julius here," said Lugs. "I just need to get back to my post in Bast, Your Highness." He flashed a charming smile. "I don't like being AWOL. It happened by accident. It's taken us longer than we expected to track down this inventor dude. Can you help us find him? Then we'll be out of your fur."

"Since it is out of Greffin's reach, Greffin cannot get you back to your city," said the emperor. "But Greffin can send you out of his. We do not tolerate deserters, Sergeant. You and your fellow felines—apart from Mr. Kyle—will be exiled forthwith."

Lugs was stunned. He turned to Josh in dismay.

"You can't do that!" Julius yowled.

"Hasty commands are rarely the strongest," Emily said, then clamped her mouth shut at a look from Greffin.

"As for you, Julius Kyle, you have obviously been consorting with dissident dogs, and I cannot have such insolence spoken in my throne room."

"You going to exile me too? We're here in good faith, Your Impulsiveness, and I am a representative of the press—"

"You are a troublemaker, Mr. Kyle, wherever you go. Your inappropriate epithets fail to amuse. You seek to unbalance the status quo; it is here for a reason. Topple the natural order here, and pandemonium will ensue. Dogs will get upset and hurt. Do you really want that?'

"No," said Julius, meek for once. "I'll leave. With Quincy and my mate, Moira."

"Exile is too soft a penalty for you," Greffin intoned. "Greffin has a far more fitting punishment for an unwelcome, big-mouthed kitty."

Moira ran into a small dockyard warehouse. No sign on the front, no goods stacked near the entrance. Its sparse contents included a few crates, an old desk with a clipboard attached to one leg, and several water bowls sitting in a patch of moonlight. No workers. No night watchdog. She could rest here, take shelter, at least until the morning shift came in.

Eyeing the rafters, she figured that in a pinch she could climb up a couple of crates and use them as a launching pad to claw her way out of bite's reach. She hoped it wouldn't come to that, but she had to be ready just in case.

The chance to test her theory came sooner than she expected. Light spilled into the warehouse as four large dogs entered, two huskies, a white-furred Great Pyrenees, and another dog who stuck to the shadows, padding quietly to the bowls. Moira sprang into a dark corner, her fur afuzz, digging her claws into a wooden beam, using it to scramble into the rafters.

From her vaunted view, she watched the dogs slurp their water until it was gone. They gathered in a circle in the middle of the warehouse and got down to business.

"What's up with you, Todd?" asked one of the huskies. "You look as if you've forgotten where your bones are buried."

"It's my tail, Aaron," said the other huskie. "It's aching like a jilted lover's heart."

"Your sacrifice is a noble one," one of the Great Pyrenees told Todd. "It will not be in vain."

"You wouldn't say that, Rudy, if you felt like someone took a jackhammer to your tailbone," Todd whined.

"We need someone on the inside," the shadow-dog pointed out. He was a balding sheepdog, hair combed over his back to make it look fuller. "You can let us in when it's time—" He stopped, looked around as if he sensed Moira's presence. "When it's time."

Moira tried not to move a muscle. The dust on the rafters made her want to sneeze, and the timber under her feet felt aged and insecure.

"You don't know what it's like," the sheepdog continued. "They want to keep cool all the time, always yapping at me to come and pamper them. I'm sick of pampering. Makes me want to bite something small and noisy."

As if on cue, the aged rafter gave way, and Moira fell into the cluster of dishes. She landed upright, naturally, but the dogs quickly blocked her escape. She shook the dog water from her paws and tightened her body into a compact bundle, ready to attack the first dog to come near her. There was no way she could deal with all four of them, though—they knew that.

Moira said her final prayers.

19

The Clutes in Cahoots

"What are we doing in here?"
Solly's question was apposite. The Clutes never stepped foot in the center of Bast, let alone the Bastet Chapel. He scratched at his suit, layered with zips and chains; he only wore it at funerals. Kierkam and a dozen other gang members were similarly attired, led by Missy in a Gothic dress of silk and lace, with a scandalous studded choker around her neck.

"We're putting the treat into treaty," Missy said in her best imperious tone. "And we are the treat."

Kafel, dressed in his finest priestly garb, greeted the Clutes with open paws. He stood at the altar, with Dineo-Kenosi and Joey Hondo standing on either side of him, as if performing some warped religious ceremony.

"Welcome to the house of Bastet," said Kafel with a wide smile.

"Kierkam, stop rolling on the carpet," said Missy. "No congregation today, Bishop?"

"You are the ones in need of Bastet's succor," was Kafel's rapid reply.

"We're not into all your religious claptrap," said Missy. She nodded to the altar. "No offense. We're here to kick tail, not waste our time with talk and prayers."

"I am sure there are some faithful among you," Joey suggested. The Clutes groaned and spat on the floor, but a few of them looked at each other diffidently.

"Solly was just asking what we're doing here," said Missy, trying to keep control of the conversation. "I second that. Why are we in your house of boring virtue?"

"In order to gain power, we must remove those who already have it," Kafel explained.

"Not including you, I take it?"

The Clutes cackled at Missy's dig. Dineo-Kenosi growled at her, high-pitched and deceptively unthreatening.

"I get where you're coming from," said Joey, approaching Missy. She glared at him, and he stopped, wary. "Kafel's an evangelist, and you're having trouble trusting him. So did I. But I realized that I couldn't get elected mayor on my own; I needed help. By joining forces, we can own this town. With Kafel's money, your muscle, and my strategic shrewdness, we'll get everything we ever dreamed of."

"I dream about my ear growing back," said Kierkam.

"*Most* of what we dream of," said Joey. "All we need you to do right now is join the demonstration outside City Hall. Those aimless cats are getting nowhere with their placards and chants. Bishop Kafel and I can't endorse the protest, but you guys can stir things up a bit. You like making trouble, don't you?"

The Clutes yowled the affirmative. Missy held up a paw for quiet, and told her gang, "You all understand the long-term benefits of helping Bishop Kafel. But we need to know about the short term." She moved closer to Joey, staring him in the eye. "What do you have for us, right now?"

Joey arched his spine, not enough to be threatening, but enough to make himself look bigger. "Nothing," he said. "You're an honorable bunch, aren't you? You appreciate the value of proving yourselves. Joining the rally will prove to us that you're serious about this alliance."

Missy seemed ready to bat Joey in the face. Instead, she broke into a smile, shook her head, and turned back to her gang.

"Let's go, Clutes," she said. "We've got a mess to make."

"This is a surprise," Aaron grimaced, getting close enough to sniff Moira's forehead. She scratched at him, catching his cheek with her claws. He ignored the cut. "When's the last time you gave yourself a wash, li'l mouser?"

"Six hours ago," Moira admitted with shame. "I've been busy—"

"Evading prowlers and a posse of concerned citizens. We know all about it."

"Made quite an impression, didn't you?" Todd smiled.

"I'll slit the throat of the first one of you comes near me," Moira spat, turning slowly to keep all the dogs in view. "Who wants to die with me?"

"Not me." Todd backed off a couple of paces.

"You're not going to die tonight," the sheepdog soothed. "Unless it's from apoplexy. You need to calm down, kitty." He firmly placed a paw a step closer to Moira. She hissed loudly, spooking herself as the sound echoed around the warehouse.

"We're like you," Aaron explained. "We don't get along too well with the authorities. Never have since we were pups. Now we're going to do something about it."

"Enough Aaron," the wolfhound growled. "She may not be what she seems."

"Oh, come on." Todd rolled his eyes. "She's just a cat."

"*Just* a cat?" The wolfhound turned to Todd. "They may be smaller than us, but cats are some of the most cunning, sophistically built animals in the known world. She can see better than us, maneuver more efficiently, and quite possibly out-think us."

"She can sure out-think Todd," said the sheepdog.

"You flatter me, guys." Moira relaxed somewhat.

"Look how she's spread confusion all across the island simply by turning up," the wolfhound continued. "Imagine how she could disrupt our society if she wasn't just blundering about."

"I've been running for my life." Moira sounded sour. "You're right, though. Maybe I ended up in Alcander for that purpose—to blunder around and distract everybody."

"Distract us from what?" asked Todd.

"I don't know. But I think you're the dogs to help me find out."

Missy stood outside City Hall in her striking black dress, standing still in a sea of cats who marched in a large, ragged circle around the building. Hundreds of citizens protested the lack of a mayor, the lack of a prowler force, and the lack of prosperity in a city they worked so hard to sustain.

Missy assessed the situation. There were no barricades between the cats and City Hall; only the imposing leopard guards with their spears and fearsome glowers kept the crowd out of the building. She turned to Solly and Kierkam.

"I'm bored," said Missy. "Let's nine-liven this party up!"

She reached out to a manx carrying a placard that read, "More Jobs For Poor Mogs."

"You don't need that," Missy said, snatching the sign away and brandishing it high. The manx backed away into the crowd, scared of the sneering gang leader.

As the gang merged with the protesters, they got a similar reaction; these were the kind of cats that vanilla citizens were always warned to stay away from.

"Come on, Clutes," Missy rallied. "We'll give 'em something to protest!" She swung her placard around her, smacking it against any non-Clute who marched too close. The gang members scratched at their neighbors, hugging them, taunting them, robbing them, steering the crowd closer to the City Hall steps. The leopards brandished their spears, ready to spike anyone who got too close to them. They were prepared for moments like this. They were larger than regular cats, lean, with keen senses and weapons training. Their reputation alone was an impediment to any attack on City Hall.

They did not know what to do, though, when the Clutes threw some of the smaller protesters at them. The leopards had to pull back their spears so they didn't impale the flying animals. They held them vertically instead, using them like quarterstaffs, blocking all entry. By then, the crowd was forced up the steps, overwhelming the guards who didn't want to take innocent lives.

"This is more like it!" said Missy, picking a fight with a crusty gray korat. The elegant korat fought back, getting a faceful of claw.

Solly agitated the crowd, telling them to storm the entrance. "There's too many of us!" he leered. "They can't stop us all!"

Kierkam chased a female Savannah up and down the steps, his whiskers stiff with excitement. "Here, pretty, pretty!" he called, loosening his suit and tripping out of his trousers. A baton bopped him on the back of his head, knocking him flat on his stomach.

"Enough!"

By the time Missy noticed that the crowd had thinned, she was trapped. Chief Feargal Cutter stood on the steps, ordering the protesters to desist. "Put down your banners and placards. Go home," he said through a loudhailer. "This has gone too far. I know you don't all want to spend the night in jail. Clear this area immediately."

The demonstrators dropped their signs and stopped struggling. They were surrounded by prowlers in riot gear—Kevlar wrapped around the cops' furry tummies, breaching visors covering their ears and faces. Only the Clutes fought on, scratching and biting their way past the prowlers, running back to their turf.

"Come on, Clutes!" said Missy, trying to make the best of the sour situation. "Party's over! The pooper troopers are here!"

"Always spoiling all the fun!" shouted Kierkam, lobbing a soggy hairball at Chief Cutter.

Some of the gang was left behind, arrested, and charged with incitement to riot, Solly among them.

"Where did you fascists come from?" Solly said to an officer, spitting in his face. "Run out of kittens to drown?"

"Strike's over, punk," the officer replied. "Good timing for these misguided folk. Bad timing for you."

Moira dipped her tongue in Todd's water, ignoring the dying fly swimming in the dish. She told the dogs about her role in Carabas, the note from Quincy, her trek over the mountains with her friends, and her flight through the city of the dogs. The listeners panted and wagged their tails, fascinated by the story.

"From what you've told us, you'd make a fine ambassador for your kind," said Aaron "Maybe heal some of the wounds between our two species. There must have been easier ways to lure you here."

"You think I was lured?" Moira raised an eyebrow. "I hadn't thought of that. Interesting theory. But no, I don't think the boerboel knew Quincy had sent a note."

"What about your friends?" asked Todd. "You think they're still waiting for you at the embassy after all this time?"

"My partner Julius couldn't possibly know I'm here with you. He'll be looking for me, though."

"We only know one dog who's had dealings with cats recently," said the wolfhound. "Are you prepared to meet him?"

"Bring it on."

The high street on the east side of Alcander was getting busier, with a large group of dogs heading uptown. "Where's the fire?" Julius asked, trying to see past the throng as Toby led him down a cracked sidewalk. Toby had been called to the palace entrance, and Julius had been relieved to see him; the Cheshire was a voice of reason in this madhouse of hounds.

Josh had reluctantly taken Lugs back to the newspaper office, along with two rottweilers; these dogs would ensure that the lynx and his friends would get booted out of town *tout suite*. That left Julius to face his fate, guided by Toby. He hoped a hot meal and a nap would take precedence.

"It's the big game," Toby told him, stunned that this know-it-all cat didn't know already. "They've got some big challenger in the stadium, one of your kind. Not that he volunteered, of course—must've angered our leaders."

"What game are they playing?" Julius followed Toby as he pushed his way through the multitude.

"Bite fight. The opponents bite each other almost to death. Gets nasty. I don't usually attend."

"And who did you say the challenger was?" Julius asked.

"Some chunky Bast bruiser. All teeth and claws. A puma."

"Toxic," said Julius under his breath. "How did he survive?"

"Straight through here." Toby allowed Julius to take the lead as they walked down a cool stone passageway. The noisy ruffing and yipping of the crowd was louder there, amplified by the arched route.

As Julius reached the end of the passage, a steel gate slammed down behind him. "Sorry, old bean." Toby shrugged. "I'm only obeying orders. Maintaining peace between our nations, and all that."

"What? Toby, you can't—"

Astounded, Julius turned from the impassive gate to see a crowd surrounding him on all sides, booing and jeering. He was in the Collarseum, his fur already collecting dust, with a canine audience watching his every move.

"Where's the puma?" Julius asked, but Toby was gone. The sun stung his eyes as he looked up to box seats filled with lapdogs. A gate opened on the other side of the stadium, and the dogs began to howl with anticipation.

"Ladies and gentlehounds!" The voice belonged to a mastiff in an announcer's booth. "Now the bout we've all come to see! A quaking, timorous, yet maleficent moggy who dared to dismay our glorious leaders, versus our new champion, the merciless, battle-loving, criminal-crunching Toxic, victorious in all his endeavors!" From the opposite passageway came Toxic, looking bigger than ever, a dark-furred, mean-looking, stud-collared berserker, with teeth bared. "With eyes black as night and sledgehammer paws, Toxic sends chills through the hearts of our cowardly cats!" said the announcer. "Let's hear it for our chomping champ!" The mastiff's last entreaty was redundant. The crowd was already raring for its hero before the fighters had had a chance to size each other up.

"What are we supposed to do?" hissed Julius as he approached his opponent. Toxic said nothing, walking to the left, then the right, kicking up dirt and trying to reach Julius's flank. Julius didn't accommodate, turning so that he always faced his foe.

Julius tried to be friendly. "You're not really going to bite me, are you?" His smile did nothing to erase Toxic's grimace. "I didn't push you down that hole. How did you get out, anyway?"

This line of questioning made Toxic angrier.

"Fine," Julius went on. "Then you might as well pick on someone your own size." Julius gave up his attempts to make peace and puffed up his fur as much as he could, spitting at the puma.

Toxic licked saliva from his face and lunged at Julius, who fell backward and scrabbled at the champ with his claws. The puma rolled off, twisting his sinewy neck to snap at the tabby.

Julius backed toward the gate he'd come through. As Toxic charged after him, he sprang high into the air, leaping over the puma using his head for a springboard, and the big cat crashed into the gate. It shuddered with the impact.

Julius made for the opposite passageway, the crowd complaining all the way. He spared a glance at a jolly pack of lapdogs—the High Short Interest—sitting high in a luxurious booth, shaking their heads and chatting away as if no life and death struggle was taking place for their pleasure.

At the moment Julius reached the alternate exit, another gate slid down to stop his escape. The spectators enjoyed that. They enjoyed Toxic's next attack even more, scarcely fended off with a sideswipe from

Julius. This time, the puma continued his lunges, bringing his nose close enough for Julius to give it a good, fat scratch. This infuriated him. His dark eyes clouded red, the snarls turning to hissing rage, with Julius scampering out of reach.

Despite the contender's acrobatics, the crowd still rooted for its favorite, chanting his name, "Toxic! Toxic!" and thumping their tails on the bleachers. Julius was tiring fast, and he knew one bite could be enough to finish him—one close call brought Toxic's jaws down on a support post, rending a chunk from the wood.

Spewing skelps, the puma ducked low, forelimbs flat on the ground, head tilting up to look at his opponent. Toxic was still confident, Julius realized. Why shouldn't he be? He was undefeated.

"There's a first time for everything," said Julius, kicking a clump of dirt in Toxic's face in a move that didn't win him any fans.

Toxic did not like the dirt in his mouth and nostrils. *It must have been terrible,* thought Julius. *Falling into that hollow, down into the earth, almost suffocating. I wouldn't wish that on anyone. Except...*

Julius kicked more dirt in Toxic's face, blinding him and making him thrash with rage. Julius seized the moment and leaped at the puma, wrapping his paws around the big cat's throat and pushing his claws in as deep as they would. This brought Toxic crashing to the ground, the audience roaring with amazement. Julius scooped as much dirt as he could from the floor and rammed it into Toxic's muzzle, choking him until he lay still.

"I'm sorry, Toxic," said Julius, standing up, wiping the dirt from his paws, his ears ringing from the cheers of the watching cats. "These bloodhounds didn't give me much of a choice. Neither did you."

"Where are you sending us?" Zehra asked Josh, who looked crestfallen as he led his feline friends to a watchdog watercraft. "Somewhere with caves?" the angora added hopefully.

"Somewhere idyllic," Josh promised her. He pointed to a small island. "Just over there."

"We have to stay there?" Lugs scowled.

"Everyone who gets put there, stays. Either by choice or because there's no way off. It's too far to swim back here." Josh gave the cats a farewell bark as the cats set off. "I'm sorry. I wish this could have worked out differently."

Josh turned, unwilling to watch the vessel any longer. It hurt his heart, the way the cats had been treated. No amount of newspapers could fix such savagery.

He could, however, continue the cats' search for Quincy and Moira. He visited the nearest watchdog station, in the hope that he could get help there. The Third Precinct was busy, with several officers forming a line to the evidence room. A kilo of aniseed had been confiscated, and they all wanted a sniff. An Afghan hound in cuffs was giving a breathless statement to an officer. Phones rang and a watchdog band radio crackled in the background.

Josh was surprised to find Julius standing at the front desk, free as a bird in No Cat's Land.

"You're alive!" said Josh excitedly, giving Julius a big, broad lick.

"I'm a living celebrity," Julius corrected him, shaking the slobber off his fur. "They let me go once I won the bite fight in the Collarseum. It's a rule, apparently.

Wish I'd known there were rules before I went in." He took a breath. "Wish I'd known I was going in."

"Well, Mr. Celebrity." Josh smiled. "That's quite a feat you accomplished. I feel like I'm looking at a ghost."

"Why write stories when you can become one?" Julius asked him. "Just kidding. I'd much rather be sitting at a typewriter in a cozy bullpen... or lounging on the beach."

"Can I help you?" A labradoodle desk sergeant arrived and ruffed for their attention. "We can't have strangers standing around here. This is a secure location."

"Oh yes, we need your help, if you're willing to give it," said Josh tactfully.

"We're, uh, looking for someone," said Julius. His voice trembled and he hoped he wouldn't have an experience akin to his dangerous visit to Hebert Palace.

"I know who you are," the watchdog sniffed. "I saw what you did to our champion."

Uh-oh. Julius took a tiny step backward, ready to turn and dash out the door. *Here it comes.*

"He deserved every mouthful." To Julius's astonishment, another watchdog appeared, a schnauzer who smiled and offered a friendly paw. "I caught Toxic and locked him up. The High Short Interest gave him a life sentence in the Collarseum, which, mercifully, wasn't very long. You saved that brute from years of pain and humiliation." Julius was grateful for the compliment. "I'm Detective Marius Digger," said the schnauzer. "This dog behind the desk is Sergeant Spike Muldoon. Is there anything we can do for you?"

"I've lost a Siamese cat called Moira," said Julius. "White fur, a real looker. Surely any cat would stand out in this place?"

"Well, you gotta remember," Muldoon scratched a recurring itch on his left hip. "Us dogs ain't curious as you lot. We'll socialize with anyone, sure, but we don't always pay much attention to who they are or where they're going. Still, let me ask around the station. You stay here."

"I saw her!" said a bloodhound, standing in the aniseed line.

"You did?" Julius asked.

"Yeah," the bloodhound's ears flopped as he nodded. "Outside Corgi Park. Shoulda chased her, but she was too fast for me. Whipped past me and before I realized what she was, it was too late. White, big eyes, smelled like chicken, right?"

"Presumably," said Julius.

The bloodhound took his turn in the evidence room.

"Stick with us and you'll see her again," said Marius with the calm of a seasoned negotiator. "Go ahead, Sergeant."

The labradoodle left Julius, asking a rookie, "What are you doing with that bone? You don't have to carry it around all the time. Give it a rest, just for five minutes."

Josh and Marius shared an awkward silence, broken by Marius.

"I know just the dame you're looking for," he said. "In fact, I met her yesterday in the park."

"You did?" Julius's eyes were bright with joy. "What happened to her? Why did you let Sergeant Muldoon...?"

"He needs the exercise," Marius explained. "Too many bone-nuts and not enough walkies. Besides, I want to know if he can fetch any new info. She ran off, you see, toward the docks."

"The docks? Then we should go there!"

"They're not safe, even for a tough tom like you," Josh said to Julius.

"Was she okay?" Julius asked. "How did she look?"

"Gorgeous," said Marius. "For a cat."

"Did she say anything?"

Julius's barrage of questions was interrupted by a griping growl.

"Get your damn clean paws offa me!" yelled a perp as he was dragged into the station. Two Alsatian officers flanked the pit bull, small but powerful. They'd already put a leather muzzle on him, and he had to talk through gritted teeth. "I wanna see my lawyer."

Julius's eyes darted from side to side, danger all around him, the heady smell of dog sweat overwhelming his senses. But he didn't flee. He needed to find out more about the docks and why they were off-limits to him. He stayed close to Josh and Marius, trying to make himself look as small and inconspicuous as possible until Muldoon returned.

"You're in luck, kitty cat," the labradoodle told him.

"How so?" he purred.

"Look out!" a watchdog barked. "He's loose!"

The pit bull shook his head fiercely, showering his guards in spittle, the broken muzzle falling from his jaws. The perp charged at the Afghan, who sat petrified mid-statement. Marius's charming smile vanished, replaced with a determined expression. He bounded over to the Afghan, defending her from the pit bull's attack and slamming both forepaws down on the criminal, stunning him instantly.

"Happens all the time," said Marius, giving Julius an unspoken lesson in the art of cool. "These berserker bullies come in here, see a few cops, think it's party time. We set 'em straight and send them to Mandelo Island."

Julius stood upright, smoothing down his fur with the back of his paw, trying to match Marius's insouciance. "What was that lucky news you were going to give me before the *fracas*?" Julius asked the desk sergeant.

"Fracass." Marius shook his head, smiling again. "You sure do talk funny. Fracass!"

"Your friend's been seen," said the labradoodle. "Not far from here, either. Hey, Skye!"

A black setter looked up from a heap of paperwork and barked back, "Whassup?"

"Where did you say that strange cat was reported?"

"The docks. Suspect was definitely feline, white fur, looked inherently edible. Coincidentally, another stray moggy was seen sneaking around Bacon Street; by all accounts, a ginger-furred freak—"

"Quincy," said Julius.

"Accompanied by a brick outhouse of a dog," Skye continued. "Fur color of dog, and breed, unkown 'cause the witness was knocked senseless by the big dog before he could observe many details."

"Alright Mr. Kyle," Muldoon shrugged. "Let's pay a li'l visit to the docks, then we'll have a sniff around Bacon Street."

In a small wooden workshop, Quincy slaved away on his machine. Cavem had given him a few panels and circuits from the original; apparently, the dog had not understood its worth or known what to do with it, breaking it to fragments after stealing it. Quincy was long past grieving over his superweapon; now he only felt stress, as Cavem continually pressured him to work.

He stopped for a moment to wash himself, rudding his paw compulsively over his head. He picked up a diagram and stared at it, his eyes fuzzy with a disparity of sleep and sunlight. Cavem had learned from their last hideout; this time there were no windows, the front of the workshop was guarded by another dog, and Cavem stayed inside with Quincy, pushing him, pushing him.

"Work more," said the boerboel, looming over Quincy.

"With what?" Quincy shot back. "I need tools and components."

"We got bones. Not to share."

"Not combonents. Nothing to do with bones. I need machine parts! Metal. Plastic." Quincy slammed the diagram down on the workbench.

"Work more."

"That is not going to happen," said Quincy. "Not without—" He saw Cavem's blank expression. "I'll write you a list! Oh no, you can't read." Quincy opened and closed his mouth like a fish. "Can you memorize a list of requirements?"

"I can memorize playing with my parents when I was a pup," said Cavem.

"That's not ... never mind." Quincy rolled down his sleeves. "Let's go shopping."

A pale gray dusk lit Moira's way as she moved along the docks, flanked by the big dogs. She wanted to ask them why they'd met in the secluded warehouse, but sensed they weren't ready to tell her. Dogs were a funny bunch, exuberant one moment, sleepy the next. Unlike cats, who conserved their energy and didn't overexert themselves, dogs competed to see who could run fastest, jump highest. And they were loyal—thick as thieves—while she was an outsider.

"It's always been the way since the first little dog was born," Todd told her excitedly. "They rule, we obey. They're all so wrapped up in their greedy schemes, always wanting something they don't need. Us larger dogs take out of necessity." His stomach grumbled. "It's our own fault, really. It's as if we needed someone to tell us what to do, to do all the fetching and carrying for. We were happy to help the weaker, smaller dogs at first. Now they're not weak anymore. There's too many rules, too much security, too many taxes, and too many of them. We want what's fair, that's all. We want equality. We'll bite to get it if we have to."

"You seem too friendly to go around biting anyone," Moira said.

"Oh, deep down we all want to bite and chew and destroy," said Aaron. "Not all the time, but the urge is always there. To block that totally would be a mistake. That's why we send our young pups to the chew room if they're getting mischievous—so they can chomp to their heart's content and get it out of their system. We adults have to restrain ourselves and toe the line or we find ourselves up before the High Short Interest. No fun, I can tell you."

"What can these jug-sized judges possibly do to you?"

"Show her, Aaron," said Todd.

Aaron dipped his head down, turned so that Moira could see his ears. She noticed that part of his ear flaps had been removed. "They said it would make me look more attractive," Aaron whined. "All because I ate chops meant for a curly little bolonka. They got one thing right. I'll never take food again if I'm not sure who it belongs to. And I'll never forget."

"Never forget," Todd intoned. "We have had enough of being downtrodden by mutts smaller than our bowel movements! We want equal rights and equal chow! We're hungry and tired, and whining hasn't got us anywhere. Our instincts have been curbed for too long. We are the Dogged Resistance and it's time to bite back."

Shopping with a dog took a long time. In the hardware store, Quincy wanted to go straight to the tools he needed, check them over to ensure they were adequately manufactured, and whisk them to the register. Not so with Cavem, who stopped to sniff each lower shelf in the store, licking a couple of metal supports.

Once Quincy realized their errands would take all day, he put his mind to the urgent subject of escape.

He didn't want to live on the island forever, building weapons for dogs, and working as their slave. He knew that if he did get out of the city, the journey south would be arduous and distressing; he didn't know if his observatory was still habitable. If not, he would have to go to Bast and face the judgment of his peers—those who remembered him, at least. The mountains were fraught with danger, but the sharp tongues of his former colleagues weren't much safer to a cat who lived on his reputation as an engineering maven. They were jealous, he told himself. They wanted to reach his level of success without putting in the work. While they slept as all cats should, he kept toiling away. He would do the same with the Bernoulli tube. Escape or no, he wanted to complete his coveted gadget. Nevertheless, he selected wire cutters along with his typical tools; he could cut through the fence and figure out what to do from the other side.

Cavem wasn't the only dog sniffing around the store. Nine other customers were doing it, all inhaling messages left by previous clientele or enjoying the fresh wood scent of the lumber department. Quincy rolled his eyes and waited patiently for Cavem to have his fill.

"No need all this," said Cavem, balking at the pile of expensive gear Quincy had chosen.

"I require every single tool in this cart," said Quincy. "If you want me to build your apparatus, pay the blessed bill."

The store clerk, a sarabi with pronounced jowls, watched the exchange with embarrassment. Cavem glowered at Quincy and paid for the gear.

"Next, we need the parts for the Bernoulli tube." Quincy lowered his voice as they left the store. "Sorry, it's going to cost you."

Power lines threaded across the street in a tangle of sun-speckled cable. Every few yards Julius saw a post or a hydrant; every time he breathed in he caught different smells, none of them pleasant. He kept stopping and washing himself, to clean his paws of city grime and to retain his own self-scent. He wondered how he would find Moira amidst all the mutts, and how he would find time to communicate with Roy Fury at *The Scratching Post*. Its readers had to know how bad things were here. No creature deserved to live in this kind of squalor.

Chewed-up trash was piled in the gutters. Half-buried moldy bones jutted from the dirt tracks that

passed for roads. A red setter staggered past him, ine-
briated with an overdose of liver juice. A depressed-
looking collie hunched on a flattened cardboard box,
begging for scraps. Julius couldn't meet the eyes of
either of them.

"I thought we were going to Bacon Street?"
Julius asked.

"Pit stop first," said Marius, showing Julius and
Josh a block of kennels.

The kennels towered into the clear blue sky, stack
upon stack of metal and plastic crates, big enough for
a dog to eat, sleep, and turn around in circles. Julius
was so busy looking upward that it took him a moment
to notice a pack of dogs approaching him.

"Hold back now, hold back," said Josh, waving
Marius and Julius behind him. Todd, the huskie,
rushed up to him, furiously wagging his tail.

"Dawg!" Todd barked.

"Dawg!" Josh barked back. The two old friends
sniffed each other, then Todd picked up another scent.
He raised his leathery nose and breathed deep, locking
down the source of the curiosity.

"Great smell, dude. Where'd you find it?" *At least
this animal hasn't started biting anyone,* thought
Julius. *Yet.*

"I got a cat!" Josh said proudly, showing off Julius
to the huskie.

"Dude, me too!" The dogs at the front of the pack
parted to reveal Moira, looking as if she belonged
with them.

Julius ran to her, oblivious to the potential danger
posed by the dogs. The cats embraced and rubbed
their heads together. Josh and the big dogs smelled
each other with caution.

"You missed me then?" Moira smirked.

"Did I ever!" yowled Julius. "I have so much to tell you." He walked past her, his side touching hers, then back again. "I was so worried about you."

"I can..."

"Take care of yourself." Julius nodded. "And I took care of Toxic."

"You arrested him," Moira said to Marius. She asked Todd, "Is this who you wanted me to meet?"

"The detective with a directive, the hound who fills the pound." Todd smiled. "Moira Marti, meet Marius Digger, who watches the watchdogs."

"Pleased to meet you," Moira blinked.

"I'm Josh Harness," said Josh. "I don't bite. Hard."

"This is quite a pit stop," said Julius, staying close to Moira, worried that if he so much as closed his eyes, he'd lose her again. "Did you plan this?"

"No, not at all," said Marius. "Cross my paws and hope to die. I did want you to meet these dogs. Plus, I want to show you my modest abode."

Rusty iron steps and gantries gave the kennel residents access to their units. Each one bore the name of its occupant—Blue, Jervis, Athena, Leif. Julius read the names with a perturbed fascination, concerned for all the dogs living right next to each other, wrinkling his nose against the stench of crowded fur.

"Here's mine," said the detective. He led Julius, Moira, and the big dogs to a mid-level crate with gray and brown trim. The cats squeezed in to stand next to him, cramped and nervous, while the others waited patiently outside.

I thought dogs liked to roam around through plenty of space. Julius didn't voice his thoughts for fear of insulting the detective's home.

Marius tilted his nose at a corkboard on the back wall of his home. It was busy with notes, surveillance, photographs, documents, and news clippings. A red thread connected them all to a picture in the center—a boerboel slavering at the camera in a shameless mugshot.

"His name is Cavem. I've been tracking this bad dog for months," said Marius. "I'm a good tracker. He connects all this skullduggery you've mentioned, and abduction is part of his MO. I reckon he abducted your friend."

"He's not our friend," said Julius.

Moira was focused on a loose dangling thread.

"How about making an arrest?" Julius suggested.

"She's just messing with string," said Marius. Julius playfully batted Moira's paw away from the board.

"I mean this villain of yours," said Julius.

"No can do. He's an enforcer for the High Short Interest."

"They sanction his crimes?" Moira wanted to know.

"I don't think so. If they know anything about them, they let them slide because he's such a good bully. But listen to this—he's been quiet recently. Went to ground."

"Because he went to Healing and catnapped Quincy," said Julius. "You think he's on Bacon Street?"

"If he is," said Marius with a wry grin, "we'll sniff him out."

20

First, there was one rat loose in Bast, scurrying past a bakery, scavenging for cheese. A caracal found it and made quick work of its body, a morsel to pop in a pie.

The following day, two rats were seen, male and female, twitching their noses downtown as if seeing the sights. They were caught in traps and taken to the Chat Affamé restaurant, where they were deboned and served with a garnish of bugs. Thanks to Tad's savvy marketing, cats were used to indulging in richly seasoned rodent; the boxed kind arrived sedated and ready-to-eat, while the street kind were considered wild game.

On the third day, a small group of rats—five at the most—was spotted on Eno Bridge, having climbed up from the river, alternately terrorizing and tantalizing tourists and workers. The rats were eaten or tossed back in the river, where a couple were washed downstream, evaded the keen eyes of the cats, and ran into the gang-controlled bowels of Beaverbank Place.

Subsequent days saw more rats, dozens turning into scores. In the first week, the indolent cats of Bast ignored them. Several of the rodents moved together, talking in unison, as if they shared one mind. These were the rats that could not be ignored. These were the ones who whispered secrets to Tad Tybalt in his sleep. These were the rats with a plan.

———————————

The Leo drifted on, sitting lower in the sea, tilted from side to side by unfriendly waves, scarred by rocks that slowed but did not stop its passage. All food was gone, eaten, ignored, or tossed overboard after it spoiled. Pollet was hiding more and more often.

Bridget heard a new sound, like rushing wind, a noise that worried her with its insistence. She loped aft, reached an exit, and climbed down a flight of iron stairs to the cargo hold. A small puddle of water was seeping into the ship, threatening to dampen the corners of one of her many trunks. Desperate, she dragged it away from the puddle, immediately panting from the exertion. If she peered hard enough, she could see a minuscule crack in the hold wall, with drops of water slowly collecting along its width. The hull had been damaged while colliding with the rocks. She had to seal the breach.

"Pollet!"

Pollet appeared from behind a crate, where he'd hidden and fallen asleep.

"Y-yes, ma'am?" Pollet asked, fastidiously washing his forelimbs.

"There is a leak." Bridget showed the crack to Pollet.

"That's what I've been..." Pollet stopped himself. "There's nothing we can do to stop the ship sinking," he said slowly. "No land in sight. No provisions, not so much as a saltine. It's time to use the life raft."

Pollet led his boss onto the deck and showed her a small yellow dinghy. "You told me to find some oars. This raft comes equipped with two perfectly good ones."

"Where would we oar to?"

"Row, ma'am. The technical term is row."

"There's just one problem, Pollet," said Bridget, examining the raft.

"What's that?" Pollet groaned. *Is it the wrong color?* he wondered in exasperation.

"You. This raft is only large enough for one."

"Oh, I don't know," Pollet said to himself. "At a pinch..."

"I will not share this raft with a common gofer," Bridget sneered. "And since the Leo is my ship, this is my raft. I shall call it ... the Leo II."

"Ingenious, ma'am," said Pollet.

"You shall swim alongside me," said Bridget. "To keep me company."

Bridget sat in the raft as Pollet dropped it from the ship. "Steady, you impoverished poltroon," Bridget roared up to him. "I demand a smooth descent."

Pollet took his time, lowering the raft until it settled on the water. Stepping into a safety ring and holding it around his midriff, he took a deep breath and jumped into the sea, floating beside Bridget, attaching a red rope from the ring to the raft.

"You have to paddle, ma'am," Pollet shouted over the crashing waves.

"I know, you fool," Bridget sniped back. Despite having the strength of a lioness, Bridget could not row the raft in a straight line, especially with the current smashing her against the hull of the ship.

"You shall have to push," said Bridget. Pollet got between the hull and the raft, heaving away with his hind paws until his limbs screamed with the exertion. He managed to swim out to sea, alternately pulling and pushing the raft. But when he turned back the Leo looked as close as ever.

"It's no good, ma'am," he panted. "I'm exhausted."

"Nonsense!" Bridget said, then mellowed when she saw how drained her steward really was. She helped him onto the raft where he lay, sodden with salt water.

"We'll have to go back to the ship, won't we?" Bridget asked quietly.

"Yes." Pollet nodded. "Yes, we will."

Bridget looked out at the sea. Back at the ship, with its steep, smooth hull. "Pollet?"

"Yes, ma'am?"

"How do we do that?"

The long, wide boulevard of Bacon Street was lined with trees, one every six feet or so. A citizen never had to go far to find a cocking spot. The intertwined branches let patches of hot light fall onto Alcander's sole church, dedicated to the glory of the Great Dane. Dew dribbled from the nostrils of stone mastiffs hunched on the building ledges.

A drop spat down onto Julius's fur, making him flinch. He tried to resist curling up in one of the sunlight patches, taking a nap or a breather at least. No. He couldn't do that—not until he found Quincy.

Julius's group decided to explore the street in sections, to cover the whole boulevard before Cavem did another disappearing act.

Josh and Marius scoped out the church; Moira elected to go with Todd and Aaron to check a row of residential properties. Julius was loathe to let her go, but she insisted that she'd stay within hissing distance, and she'd be safe with the big dogs.

Rudy the Great Pyrenees and Rollo, the half-bald sheepdog, headed for the Mudlands on one side of Bacon Street, behind one row of houses. "Be careful back there," Todd warned them. "One wrong step and you'll be sucked under."

"It's okay," Rudy replied with a wag of his tail. "We like mud."

"Doesn't mean it'll like you," Todd called after them.

Julius was left to check an old workshop made out of wood, an unusual material for the Isle of Dogs. A doberman squatted out front, looking alert, licking its chops with hunger.

Stealthily, Julius moved through a hedge to a corner of the workshop. He squeezed through the broken planks, ruing the three-mouse dinner that swelled his belly. Inside, he trod softly through a maze of scrap metal, left as a security device. A dog would have clattered past the cans and sheeting. Julius didn't touch a single piece.

Free of the obstacles, Julius prowled down a wide hallway. At the end, a ginger tom with round spectacles muttered to himself, tired and irritated.

"Doctor Quincy?"

"Doctor Quincy McGraw," said the tom, not looking up from his work. "Who might you be?"

"Julius Kyle," said Julius with an incredible sense of relief. "I was Camilla Dolentine's partner. I got your note, and I came to save you from this ... whatever it is."

Quincy got excited for a moment, then he calmed himself. "Oh, she liked you," said Quincy. "You're a prisoner here now too, eh? Don't waste your time attempting to escape. I tried it, and almost lost my life both times."

"We have to go."

"Where?" Quincy looked up from his workbench, studied Julius's gray, world-weary face.

"Home. Back to your observatory."

"It's still standing?"

"Like a nobbly rock," said Julius.

Quincy hesitated, then picked up his machine. "I have to take this with me."

Julius sighed. "I suppose you do." They couldn't sneak out the way he'd got in, not with Quincy's gizmo.

"How do you get in and out of here?" Julius asked.

"There are front and rear exits," Quincy said deliberately.

"I saw a doberman guarding the front."

"Oh yes, Brian." Quincy shook his head. "He's beastly."

"I'm assuming Beastly Brian won't let us saunter away without stopping us. We'll have to go out the back."

"Into the Mudlands," said Quincy darkly.

"The dogs like rolling in mud," said Julius. "It's time for us to learn how to get through it."

After they were brought to Mandelo Island, the cats walked up a sloping shore of white sand, feeling lost and hopeless. All except Lugs, who said, "We'll be safe here. It's quiet, away from the dogs." He gazed at the water, the thin, lush trees, and the rolling dunes.

"Why aren't they here?" asked Zehra.

"This is paradise," Sal joined in. "If I was a dog, I'd be romping across the dunes... like that one over there." He pointed out a pit bull running over the steepest hill, tongue dangling from its mouth.

"I wonder what it's chasing?" asked Lugs. "Pit bulls never run just for fun."

"I'll ask him," said Sal, hurrying up a steep dune before his friends could stop him. Soon all they could see was a flash of white fur on the crest of the hill.

"If that dog locks his teeth on Sal, then our daft little buddy will become a permanent fixture in his mouth." Lugs walked toward the dune, then broke into a trot, calling for Sal.

"Get back here, you nitwit!" Lugs called out, glad that Zehra was behind him to back him up if necessary. He climbed over the dune, a second, a third, and ran down the other side, right into a pack of pit bulls. His momentum brought him within snarling distance, but to his surprise, the pits did not attack. Sal was with them, spinning them some yarn.

Lugs wanted to interrupt. He couldn't. The pits were a rapt audience for Sal. He told them about his fictional idol, detective Tiger Straight, and the character's latest appearance in the book, *The Cat Who Stole the Cream.*

"He has to solve a mystery because he's a detective, right? He doesn't even have an office. He burned it down. But he still gets a case when a voluptuous femme fatale makes him an offer—"

"Save it for later, hype cat." Lugs's patience was gone. "Julius would be proud of you."

"Aw, thanks."

"What're you cats doing here?" asked a pit with a dark stripe on his head. "You part of a new menu I ain't heard about?"

"More story," said another pit.

"We don't want to get eaten," said Lugs, paws raised to show he carried no condiments. "We've been exiled by Greffin and his goons."

Zehra was on the summit of the third dune now. Whereas Sal and Lugs had charged into potential trouble, Zehra had sense enough to hold back and get the lay of the land. To the west, she saw a simple settlement, built with wood and thick ferns, looking out to the ocean. *Perhaps these pit bulls will be more amenable than the mutts on the Isle of Dogs,* she thought. She'd faced enough lunacy for one lifetime. Seeing Lugs and Sal surrounded by the pits, she disappeared back where she'd come from, hidden by the dunes. A couple of pits saw her, but it was too hot and the slope was too steep for them to give chase.

"Why were you running?" Sal asked the pit with a stripe, who introduced himself as Flash.

"Training," was the response.

"Good. We need your help," Lugs improvised. "The Isle of Dogs needs you. How up are you on the city's sociopolitical status?"

"It's more of a sovereignty really," said one pit.

"Yes, like it's one little country," said Flash.

"I don't need your help with semantics," said Lugs. "I need your help protecting the strong from the weak, the big from the small, the athletes from the effete, the—"

"No."

"What do you mean, no?" Lugs asked, incredulous.

"Sorry," said Flash. "We're not welcome on that island."

"If we go back there alone, we're dog meat," Sal told them. "Literally."

"We're still going back, though," said Lugs.

"You wouldn't let us defenseless cats get torn apart, would you?"

"We have to discuss this," said Flash. He huddled up with a couple of other dogs, Rocky and Daisy.

Flash gave Rocky a playful nip. Rocky gave the same to his sister, Daisy. She yelped.

"Was that harder?" Flash asked.

"How should I know? I'll tell you which was the sorest, probably. Rocky's."

"Then his decision is the one we follow." The three dogs had another intense discussion, then turned back to Lugs and Sal. "If you can find a way off this island, we'll go with you, kitty cats," Flash told them. "But understand, you may not be welcome there by dint of your association with us."

"We're not exactly in high favor." Lugs shrugged.

"But that won't stop us from making our mark and helping the underdogs. We know all about those."

Julius stood on the back deck of the old workshop, looking out across a huge field of bleak, deep mud. When he placed a paw on the surface, he sank, his balance upset. His tail switched as he backed off, pulling his paw free with a slurping shuck. He scowled at his dirty paw; it smelled like sewage.

"I'd rather wrestle a doberman," Julius said to Quincy.

"No, you wouldn't. Either we go now, or I return to my workbench."

Julius squelched through the mud, pulling his paws up as high as he could, then grimacing as they sank deeper with every step. Laden down with his Bernoulli tube, Quincy fared worse. Julius gave one more thought to turning back, dispelled by the sound of dogs barking in the distance.

"What's that about?" Julius wondered.

"They're always barking at something. Maybe a leaf fell off a tree and got them excited." Quincy chuckled to himself as he struggled on.

The barking got closer.

"They're on the other side of the house," said Julius. "Come on! Keep moving!"

Brian, the doberman guard, flanked by two Alsatians, burst out of the back of the building, baying as they saw the two cats. The faster Julius and Quincy ran, the deeper they sank into the mud—it was up to their haunches. The dogs ran after them, slather flying from their teeth.

Quincy reached for Julius. "I'm stuck! I can't move." Quincy turned his body, trying to pull himself free, and let out a shrill cry.

"You have to!"

Quincy had found a paw sticking out of the mud; it belonged to Rudy, who had sunk under with Rollo.

The guard dogs, equally bogged down, slowly moved closer. "Dump the device!" yelled Julius.

After taking one last, sad look at his masterpiece, Quincy went one better than dropping the tube. He threw his invention at the doberman. It fell short, disappearing into the dirt. The move hardly slowed the dogs although they did take time to sniff around it as they passed.

Julius retraced his steps, held Quincy by the cuff of his lab coat, and heaved. His reach was extended—he didn't want to get stuck, too. Little by little, Quincy worked his way free. The howling dogs spurred him on, and he followed Julius's footsteps forward.

Near the other end of the flats, the mud got shallower. Julius and Quincy were able to pick up their pace, desperate to reach firm land. The dogs reached the deep patch where Quincy had got stuck, and they were bogged down, berserk with excitement.

Julius got out of the mud and washed himself, but the taste was terrible.

The chase had worn them out. The cats sat for a moment; they needed to catch their breath before they could move on. Quincy looked at Julius, feeling lucky to be alive and free.

Heavy shadows fell over them. Julius looked up to see Emperor Greffin in a sedan chair, surrounded by mastiffs, Cavem and Emily at his side.

"You have shown great dedication to indolence," Greffin said to Quincy. "Greffin did not have you brought to his province to play around in mud."

"You're responsible for all this?" Quincy spat.

"Greffin also hears," the emperor said, wagging his paw to lower the sedan, "that you have spent more time shopping than working." Cavem gave Quincy a contrite look as Greffin continued. "Tell us, where is our long-promised machine?"

"Promised to you?" Quincy frowned. "I thought the big dogs were going to use it."

"On our behalf, Doctor McGraw. Greffin cannot wait to see it."

"In all its glory," said Julius sourly.

The Alsatians who had chased Quincy and Julius dug in the mud, sending it flying into the air. Greffin's retinue joined in, getting filthy. The pit they dug kept filling up. While Julius watched in disgust, Greffin snorted with glee, happy to see his subjects having fun.

After an hour of wild digging, Brian, the doberman sentry, slipped in, pushed his muzzle into the mud, and pulled the machine out by its strap.

"It's larger than Greffin expected," said Greffin. To him, most objects were larger than life.

"It's a scaled-down prototype, Your Majesty," Quincy explained.

"And it's covered in effluent," Julius added.

Greffin's mood clouded. He had the power to execute the cats on the spot. Julius realized how harsh this regime really was.

"You will build us a new device at full size; no expense will be spared," said Greffin.

Quincy hid his surprise with a nod and a nervous grin. "It will take time, Your Majesty..."

"How long?" asked Emily.

"Four days, at the very least, dependent on how swiftly I can get my paws on materials."

"Emily! Get this cat his materials!"

Emily bowed and flapped off to get the job done.

"I will make the utmost haste," Quincy promised.

"You had better," Greffin snorted. "Otherwise, you will end up like the guards who dissatisfied Greffin today. I am keeping their heads as stuffed and mounted keepsakes." The Pekingese giggled. "In little glass domes."

"I don't want to end up in a dome," said Quincy, worried.

"You won't," said Julius. "If you follow my lead."

"While you wait for your precious materials, get this contraption cleaned up," Greffin ordered his mastiffs. "Greffin wants it shining as brightly as our dreams. Clean yourselves up too; your dirtiness offends your emperor."

The dogs went to the gates and the bay beyond to wash up and romp around in the water. Julius and Quincy cleaned their own fur; between licks, Julius told the inventor about the other cats on the island.

"That's good," Quincy said, "I'm going to need help, er, real help, not the kind that involves dog slobber." Julius found Moira and returned with her to the workshop, where more guards growled at them but let them in the front; the rear exit was boarded up.

"We've come a long way to help you," Moira pointed out.

"I appreciate that, my dear. I really do," Quincy replied. "I actually have all the intrinsic components I need to build a Bernoulli tube ... but I don't want to."

Moira protested, "Those guard dogs will eat you alive if they—"

"I know, I know. I will complete the machine as slowly as possible without drawing Cavem's attention to the fact." He paused. "The lynx who picked a fight with him. Do you know him? Is he intact?"

"Lugs is fine," said Julius.

"Oh, thank Bastet."

"But we're not. This place is a powder keg, and we're curled up right on top of it. We need to go."

"That's all well and good," said Quincy. "But how?"

Tad Tybalt was used to publicity. He'd used marketing as a tool to increase his wealth throughout his career. He knew that press attention would boost share prices, excite consumers, and increase the familiarity of a brand. He didn't enjoy the whirring, snapping cameras that surrounded him as he campaigned, but he needed them. If he was going to win this race like he won everything else that he desired, publicity was a must.

His crew of marketers arranged a series of photo ops, including a ride on a public tram, his appearance on *The Big Wall*, plus a mock-impromptu visit to Eva Rote's dairy. He knew Eva socially, so the trip was pleasant enough, soured only by the presence of her spoiled brat of a son; as a rags-to-riches cat, Tad had no time to spare for silver spoon types.

His last scheduled stop was an orphanage where stray kittens stayed for a few weeks before being released to fend for themselves. The youngsters stared wide-eyed as Tad entered their home with a phalanx of photographers and noisy journalists.

"How do you do, Sir?" asked the director of the orphanage, following a rehearsed script given to her by Tad's publicists.

"I feel better than a dog in dirt, Miss Harrell." Tad beamed at the Abyssinian, patting a newborn on the head. Surprised by the sudden movement, it bowed its head, trying to look as small as possible. To the press, it looked like the kitten was kowtowing to Tad.

"Come and talk to this wee tom," said Miss Harrell quickly. "He's quite a character."

Tad talked to the tom the same way he talked to everyone younger than himself—as if they were an employee. "Got a good thing going here, little one. Keep your chin up and your whiskers clean. I expect great things of you."

"Is it true what they say about you?" asked the kitten.

"Well, I'm sorry to say that not everyone's as honest as me." Tad flashed a smile at the cameras. "But I believe I'm well thought of in most circles. Why? What do they say about me?"

"That you're a fat greedy cat who's only interested in himself," the cub replied with a lack of tact that only the young can muster.

"I guess not. I mean, they're lying." Tad's smile vanished. "Who's this 'they' anyway?"

"Let's move on, shall we?" said Miss Harrell quickly. The entourage shuffled through the orphanage, and Miss Harrell grabbed the cute newborn for Tad to sniff. He'd rehearsed the scenario many times with a roast chicken in place of the kitten; he'd place his nose against it, sniff gently just long enough for the paparazzi to grab their shots, then pass it back to its carer (in rehearsals, his personal chef). This time around, the memory of that chicken filled his senses as he picked up the tiny cat. With that roast poultry smell thick in his nostrils, he began to salivate, closing his eyes and opening his jaws wide.

When he looked up and recovered his senses, the kitten was crying, and the cameras were snapping faster than ever. He tried to soothe the wee bundle, jigging it and telling it to be quiet.

"Calm down now!" he boomed in his most authoritative tone. "No need to make a fuss."

Tad looked around to see how much the reporters were enjoying the moment. As he did so, the newborn scratched him down the side of his face, almost catching his eye. With an unmayorly yelp, he threw the baby across the room. More cameras flashed, catching its mid-air photo-finish flight into Miss Harrell's paws. As the press rushed toward a gobsmacked Tad, the orphans began to wail. Loudest of all was the newborn kitten.

"Don't come back," she told Tad, keeping her bundle out of his reach. "You're not welcome anymore. Never darken our door again."

Tad held a debriefing at his campaign headquarters, glowering at his minions. "I might as well've gone in there with a banner saying, 'I Love Dogs,'" the tycoon complained.

"How's your eye, Sir?" Ramona Pretzel asked in her most obsequious manner.

"How do we prevent this from happening again?"

"We keep you away from kittens, sir," said Tad's number one yes cat, Chuck, flicking his tail at the back of the room. "Or any small furry living creatures, for that matter. Just until after the elections."

"Yeah," said a marketing exec. "You could be photographed next to buildings, trees, anything inanimate. That'd be safe."

"Trees are alive," Ramona pointed out.

"Maybe not trees then. Posts. Signposts—"

"We need to get to the root of this problem," Tad interrupted. "I want the orphanage closed down immediately."

"Very good, Sir." Ramona scratched a note on her memo pad, then turned to the think tank. "Who wants some cream?"

In the engine room of the Leo, Pollet was covered in grease and sweat, holding a screw. *Why is there always one left over?* he asked himself, shrugging and throwing it away.

"That should do it, ma'am," he told Bridget. "I would have got it done faster, but there's only one of me."

"I'm the one who found the ship's manual," Bridget reminded him as she paced up and down the room. "Work is most edifying when it is shared."

"Yes, ma'am," said Pollet, wiping his forepaws on his apron.

"Enough dilly-dallying. We need to get this ship moving again, before we are swallowed up by the brine." Bridget commanded him to push a lever, and the engine grumbled to life, rattling the bowels of the ship. The obedient Pollet kept pushing until the lever wouldn't move any farther.

On the bridge, the lioness put the captain's hat on her head; it looked ridiculous. "Ahead full," she crowed. "Now all we have to do is change course."

"Where to, ma'am?"

"South, Pollet. We need to make an about turn. Set to it." Scrabbling at the wheel, Pollet turned it 180º in the hope that that would suffice.

"Faster, Pollet. I don't know what your friend Woodrow's up to back home, but we need to get back and sort him out as soon as possible. Know what I used to do with my cubs when they stepped out of line?"

"No, ma'am." Pollet was out of breath, still struggling with the wheel. "Didn't know you had any progeny, ma'am—apart from His Honor the Mayor, of course."

"Let's just say my husband, Bastet rest his soul, didn't always care to question the contents of his meatloaf." Bridget sighed as the ship began to turn starboard. "At last. Put your back into it, Pollet."

"I'm not so sure about this, ma'am." Pollet saw a land mass in the far distance. "We're close to the coast. Instead of heading away from it, we could just follow—"

"Keep turning that wheel." Ears flattened, Pollet did as he was told until a jolt sent him flying back across the bridge.

"We've hit something!" he whined, trying to grab the wheel again. Bridget looked out and saw dark shapes cresting the water ahead of them.

"Rocks. And no marker buoys, no lighthouse..." Bridget snatched a map from the navigation desk. She saw an area marked off limits and shook her head in annoyance. "That's not the mainland out there. It's a small island. Mandelo, judging by its exotic flora." The ship had been scraping along a slew of rocks all morning. Now it was snagged on them.

Bridget and Pollet waded out into the water. It was not very deep for the lioness, and Pollet was able to keep his head above the surface. They dragged themselves onto the beach, Bridget scratching her forepaws in the sand, Pollet sobbing with relief.

He was startled by a pack of pit bulls rushing toward him, accompanied by two cats.

"How did you get here?" asked Flash. Pollet pointed breathlessly at the Leo.

"Can we borrow your ship?" Lugs asked.

"It's dama—" Pollet began. Bridget silenced him with a look.

"Absolutely," she purred. "Have at it. I am never setting my paws on water again."

"But ma'am..." Pollet mewed.

"Thank you," said Sal.

Lugs stooped down to check on Bridget and Pollet, making sure they weren't hurt. "Are you sure you don't want to come with us?" he asked. "We're going to the Isle of Dogs."

"I wouldn't share the same sea with these creatures," said Bridget, too quiet for the pit bulls to hear. "After what they did to my city."

"It wasn't them, it was your..." Lugs stood up straight and joined his friends. "Never mind. Enjoy the rest of your vacation!"

"No, no, no, no!"

Greffin was in the palace gardens, playing his favorite game of Ball. He did not engage directly in the sport, preferring to watch a golden retriever run with a large metal sphere in his mouth, dropping it on command while another one attempted to snatch it up. Guard dog spectators woofed and panted as they watched the game.

At half time, Cavem proudly presented Greffin with the cleaned-up prototype of the Bernoulli tube, and he was most displeased.

"My Emperor, this is what Doctor McGraw build all along," Cavem said, upset that he had disappointed his master.

"This is not what Greffin wanted at all."

"My Emperor, this is a weapon—"

"I have no need of such baubles. Emily!"

Emily ran over to Greffin, ears flapping, never far from her liege.

"Remove this offensive object," Greffin said, nose turned up. "Have it scrapped immediately. Why would Greffin need such a cheat when I command an army of dog fighters?"

"Why indeed, Your Highness?" With a tilt of her head, Emily gestured at the retrievers to take the tube. "Although, Doctor McGraw may be able to use the parts to construct something more to your liking."

"A good point, Emily."

Emily panted with contentment, ordering the retrievers to take the tube to Quincy.

"What you think Quincy make?" Cavem growled.

"An instrument! Greffin needs music in his throne room, new music..." Greffin's eyes got bigger. "With new notes, never heard before, to amuse Greffin's ears and surprise his faithful courtiers! That is what Greffin was expecting. Hence the secrecy bringing Quincy here, and hence Greffin's disappointment."

"I sorry I fail," Cavem whimpered.

"That is quite alright, my loyal Cavem," the emperor said in a soothing tone. "You have served Greffin well, and you will always be by his side."

Cavem wagged his tail gratefully.

"Guards, have this boerboel stuffed and mounted. Alive."

Cavem did not consider escape. As the guards led him away, he bowed his head and cursed Quincy for designing his death warrant.

With the prototype tube back in his possession, Quincy turned his attention to Greffin's new desire. "He probably asked for the Bernoulli tube, then forgot," said Julius.

"He has set me an immense challenge," Quincy murmured. "A new musical instrument, with notes that have never been played or heard before. It's a matter of frequency." As the inventor busied himself with a fresh design, Julius could tell that he was in his element. He left Quincy at the workbench, leading Moira to a quiet corner of the workshop where they could talk in relative privacy.

"Are you ready to come home?" Julius asked Moira.

"Ready? There's too much to do here. Have you any idea what's going on in this city?"

"I think I have an inkling." Julius nodded. "I know there's dogs here. Lots of 'em."

"Some of them are planning a major coup, you boob. Those yappy little lap dogs have had it good for so long, they've grown complacent."

"I don't want you getting stuck in the middle of all this any more than you are already," said Julius.

"We must help them, alert them to the danger they're in. A lot of innocent dogs could get caught in the crush otherwise."

I haven't met many dogs I'd call innocent, Julius thought, but he didn't share his insight with Moira.

"If they panic," Moira continued, "retaliate, there will be bloodshed."

"Yeah. Maybe ours."

Moira sighed at Julius's pathetic attempt at humor. "Don't act like everything's okay," she snapped. "You've been swanning around with your writer friend Josh while I've been chased, nipped, threatened, and barked at 'til my ears got sore. What's the worst you've had to deal with? Dog drool in your salmon?"

"I..." Julius looked over at Quincy, who was already scratching ideas on a drawing board. "I just wanted to cheer you up," Julius said. "Act positive. Thought it might help. We can't all behave like it's the end of the world all the time."

"It could be the end for some of these guys." As Moira paused to take a good look at Julius, she came to a realization. "You don't care what happens to them, do you?"

"If I'm so selfish, what'm I doing trekking all the way here, risking drool in my food to rescue Quincy, frantically looking for you when you up and disappeared?"

"He's a cat. We're both cats."

"So?"

"I appreciate what you did for us. But you have to admit it, Julius. You don't care about these folks because of what they are."

Julius's whiskers stiffened. "You know me better than that." He hesitated, at a loss for words for once. "I searched everywhere for you! You know how long I've had to put up with Sal? Too long. Too right you should be appreciative."

"That's not my point."

"These dogs have really got to you, huh?"

"We try," said Josh, entering the workshop. "Sorry to interrupt,"

"How did you get in here?" Julius snapped at him, then regretted his attitude. "I mean, it's good to see you, but we're supposed to be in lockdown until Quincy finishes his..."

"I had help from a friend. And I needed to talk to the three of you. It's time to act."

Lugs and Sal watched Mandelo Island shrink in the distance as they sailed away from their glorious prison. Lugs had mentally prepared himself to be there for a long time; now he missed its peace and beauty.

"I'll miss the coconut milk," said Sal. "At least there's plenty for Zehra."

"She made her choice," Lugs said sadly. "She hopes to find solitude there. Found some caves."

"She can share her solitude with the lioness and the valet," said Sal.

"I wish her luck with that." Lugs turned away from the island and joined Flash at the helm. Most of the pit bulls were on deck, dragging their tongues through the cool sea air.

"Freedom!" Flash yipped, accelerating the ship. "It only took a few bully pits to get us all painted as bad dogs. Sure, we have the strongest bite. Sure, we're stubborn..."

"You're leaving paradise behind," said Lugs. "You had serenity and plenty."

"Lemme finish. We're social animals. We want to be with other dogs, and we can't be."

Julius had thought all dogs got along, not counting the odd scuffle over a bone or a potential mate. He realized that the domain of the dogs was as complex and screwed up as his own society.

Lugs heard a crash from down below, a yelp, rushing water. Lugs and Sal hurried down below to find water roaring into the engine room.

"Stay here and see what you can do?" Lugs doubtfully asked Sal.

"Aye aye, Captain," Sal replied, splashing into the rising brine.

Back on the bridge, Flash struggled, the ship listing sideways.

"Can we make it to the Isle of Dogs?" Lugs asked, his voice desperate.

"Dunno," said Flash with bared teeth. "We pushed the engine so hard to get off those rocks... and this is my first time trying to moor a sinking cruise ship."

"Do tell," Lugs grunted.

Sal shook himself as he came up to the bridge.

"How's it looking down there?" Lugs asked.

"Not good," Sal frowned. "We had to seal off the engine room. Too much wet, not enough dry."

"Land ho!" one of the pit bulls barked, pointing at the Isle of Dogs.

"Come on," Flash said to the ship.

"I just realized," said Lugs. "There are no life rafts on this ship."

The engine spluttered, a death choke that frightened the cats and dogs.

"I pray to the Great Dane that the tide's with us," Flash mumbled.

"You don't know?" shouted Lugs.

The ship's momentum carried closer to the shore.

"It's another beach," Sal remarked. "Are you sure we're going the right way?"

"Yes!" Lugs and Flash yelled at him in unison.

"Sal the navigator." Sal smiled to himself, attempting to take his mind off the danger he was in.

"Brace yourselves!"

The Leo slowed as it reached the beach, nestling in the sand with surprising gentleness.

"We made it!" Flash declared. The cats and dogs howled with relief. They clambered from the ship, local dogs barking at them in alarm.

"Where to now?" asked one of the pit bulls, hurrying across the sand.

"We should have made a plan," Flash cursed.

"I did," said Lugs. "I got the idea from Zehra. We'll hide ourselves deep."

"Deep where?" asked Sal.

"Deep in dog water. We're going to hole up in my favorite diner until it's time to strike."

Ramona burst into Tad's office with the best of news. "Rat in a Box™ is a hit! The conveyor belts are running smoothly all over the city, customers are ordering rodents in droves..." She stopped, realizing that Tad was slumped on his desk, a paw over his face to shield the glare of the sun.

Ramona closed the office blinds and helped her boss onto his cushion. "For a business virtuoso," she said, "you don't look very chipper."

"I need sleep, that's all," said Tad. "I'm so tired, I'm..." He looked closely at Ramona, judging whether to trust her. "I'm hallucinating."

"We all dream of creamy treats," said Ramona, mock-cheerful.

"Auditory hallucinations," Tad moped. "I hear voices in my head."

Ramona was silent, processing the information.

Tad took this beat as a sign to continue. "The rats, they talk to me in the night. Say they want to be eaten. All hail the Ratking!"

"I'll call Doctor Snoddy," said Ramona.

"Don't you dare! They're just dreams. Bad dreams."

"If you say so." Ramona pursed her lips. "But if those rats keep talking to you, ask them how we can plump them up, so we can raise their price."

"I'm sure it's just the strain. Nothing I can't deal with," said Tad. "Breathe a word of this to anyone and I'll have you skinned more than one way, you hear me?"

"Like you hear your squeaky little friends," Ramona mouthed. She left Tad's office and called Woodrow with her latest scuttlebutt.

"Perfect," Woodrow purred. "He can't handle the pressure."

"Seems that way," Ramona whispered into her phone. "Although this is all very sudden."

"You think it's a ruse?"

"No. I don't think pretending to lose his marbles would be a good move. I mean., what if it got out?"

"That would be a shame," said Woodrow.

"What if he's not imagining things?" Ramona gasped. "If the rats are really talking to him... giving him ideas..."

"Preposterous."

"They've invaded before, and almost overwhelmed us. Now they're being delivered to every home... all thanks to one crazy cat."

Bowser was running out of dog water. He'd never seen his diner so full, with Julius and Moira, Lugs and Sal, Toby, Josh, the big dogs, and the pit bulls, all gathered and lapping up their fill of his drinks. The cats chattered with happiness, swapping stories, grateful to be together.

"I'm so sorry we lost each other," Moira said to Lugs. "I tried to get back to you, but it was as if every dog in the city was after me."

"It's alright," said Lugs gruffly.

"They weren't all looking for you," said Josh. "It's just, if they see a loose cat, they get excited."

"So I gathered," said Moira.

"We have the motive and the numbers," said Julius, "to break into the palace anytime we want."

"I can go one better," said Todd. "Greffin has a bunch of servants, right? Doing his bidding, fetching, and carrying. What would you say if I told you some of the bigger dogs in His Master's Court are sick of being beasts of burden?"

Julius smiled. "I would say, 'woof.'"

"They're sympathetic to our cause and willing to let us in," Aaron added. "No window breakage, no unnecessary mess."

"No looting?" asked Flash sadly.

"Of course, there will be looting!" Todd barked. "We'll take everything that's covered in hair—and that means everything. But we also want it on record that we all met with Greffin, and he relinquished his power to us peacefully."

"He might not want to step down," Moira said.

Josh shook his head. "He won't. We can twist his tail and keep our encouragement out of the history books."

Julius didn't like this. "That seems disingenuous," he said. The big dogs laughed at him.

"You would prefer we wreak havoc and paint the palace with blood?" asked Todd. "You would prefer we ignore our years of suffering and servitude, remaining oh-so-happy with our lot?"

"Of course not," Julius scowled. "My point is, foundations are important. Why not build on truthfulness?"

"Because some of the aristos will survive if we do that," said Aaron.

"Er... bloodshed?" Sal reminded him.

"You can't have a coup without killing some chickens," Josh told Julius.

Julius shook his head. "I'm all in," he said. "You know that. But if any of those cute little dogs get killed, I'm out. Worse for you, I'll be on their side."

"We ask nicely to be let into the palace," said Lugs. "Then we ask extra-nice for Greffin to abdicate."

Aaron nodded. "All we need is a distraction."

21

Boxing Day

With the Bast mayoral campaign funds bolstered by profits from the hot-selling rats, Tad was able to buy his way into the citizens' hearts. He promised more jobs and an end to the city's economic problems. He was a cat of the people, Otto had disappeared, and his opponents couldn't measure up to him in size or wealth. But he kept making promises that he didn't even have to make. His supporters didn't really believe that he'd keep every aspect of his word, but they wanted to, and the vows gave them hope. The city would be clean again, bright and strong, and safe, with no more dogs on the streets, no gangs in the slums.

"For as long as you can remember, you've had no choice. For as long as you can recall, the lions have held sway. Before Otto, there was his mother, Bridget, ruling with keen teeth and ruthless claws.

"Now, thanks to fate or accident or even the inevitable course of change, you have a choice. The leonine line that's controlled this great city for so long has gone. In its place, an opportunity to progress and to improve your lot. I am that opportunity. I bring you bold plans for Bast—regeneration, expansion, revivification. What does my opponent bring you? Minor criticisms of my lot in life. Yes, I have wealth. The big house, the servants, the gold-plated grooming kit. Well, I've got news for that Mr. Woodrow. I'm cleaning house with a brand-new broom; I've doubled my maid's wages, and I've sold my grooming gear to help pay for a new wing for the Central Hospital."

Tad raised his forepaws, immersed in cheers and applause from the audience. Before the polls had ever opened, he was certain of victory. That was obvious from his got-the-cream beam.

Woodrow was so annoyed that he spat at his TV set. He deserved to be mayor. He was the one with the experience, the political know-how, and the correct level of deceit. Tad was a jumped-up pussy footed rag trader who'd had a bit of business luck.

Without his advisors and campaign cronies, he'd be nothing.

Even assassins had to eat. Dineo-Kenosi ordered Rat in a Box™ and waited by his window, head resting on his forepaws, gazing out at Bast. A ribbon of conveyor belts crisscrossed the city, passing all the upper-level apartments, high-rise offices, and studio spaces where hipsters could reach and reach out and touch some rat—for a price. Convenience had a considerable cost, one worth paying if a cat wanted to be current or needed to keep a low profile between murders-for-hire.

Dineo looked so sweet, his furry chin tickling his paws. But his wicked side, Kenosi, was always present, ready to drag him onto the wrong path whenever an opportunity arose.

Opportunity knocked—potentially—and the cat span around as a stealthy figure entered his stark apartment. Dineo-Kenosi hunched low, claws out, ready to fight.

Lunch arrived. A small cardboard box shuttled to Dineo-Kenosi, and he reached toward the window, not taking his eyes off the figure. Fumbling for the box, he lost concentration for a half-second—and the figure was on him, placing its paws on his chest and pushing him onto his back. The box tumbled to the floor, still sealed. Dineo-Kenosi turned his head to look at it, then back at the intruder, disguised with a black balaclava. Her bright green eyes, however, were unmistakable. They belonged to the Clute leader, Missy Brighter.

"How did you find me?" Dineo-Kenosi gasped.

"Rat in a Box™ is fast, easy to order, and it won't break your bank account," said Missy. "It also has a database containing the address of every customer, and my mom has a black book full of accountants' pec-cadilloes. So here I am."

Dineo-Kenosi struggled, but Missy had him pinned. He was astonished when, instead of ripping his throat out with her teeth, she licked his nose.

"I'm going to let you up," Missy said. "Maybe we can share your dinner."

Free of Missy's barbed paws, Dineo-Kenosi got up and stumbled to the box. He was a silken-furred, tiny killing machine who was trained to maim and murder—not split a meal with a female.

"I find you fascinating," Missy purred. "You're so ... duplicitous. Soft on the outside, acid within. You must understand Bishop Kafel very well."

So that was it. Missy was here for information, not pleasure. Dineo-Kenosi didn't get licked and tell.

"The strike ended at the wrong time," he said in his high-pitched, cutesy voice. "For you. The prowlers just had time to put on their armor and quell your protest before you got into City Hall. You weren't supposed to go that far."

"Kafel wanted us to go crazy," said Missy, rubbing her forehead against Dineo-Kenosi, who struggled to resist her. She asked, "Who ended the strike?"

"Joy Hondo," the assassin sighed. "Joey has ties to the prowlers, and he negotiated with them on behalf of the authorities. Made him look good for the voters."

"And Joey's working with Kafel." Missy shook her head. "Does that politician even believe in Bastet?"

"Oh no," Dineo-Kenosi said conspiratorially. "His conversion was a ruse, to get more cats to vote for him."

Missy gaped at the small cat. "You have a good personality," she said. "A shame about the company you keep."

The box rattled, and it toppled onto its side. The two cats approached it cautiously, looking at each other to see who would open it.

"Your order," Missy whispered. "You pick it up."

Dineo-Kenosi popped a claw and slit the box open. A rat leaped out, attacking the little cat. Missy moved in fast, biting down on the rodent and snapping its head off.

"They are supposed to be sedated ... or something," Dineo-Kenosi panted. "What happened?"

The cats heard shrieks and cries through the window. They looked out and saw rats jumping from their boxes as they reached their destinations.

"I saw the database," said Missy. "Hundreds of orders a day... thousands of rats. This isn't a blitz campaign, it's an infestation."

22

Coup de Grâce

The revolution was set for the weekend, since more dogs would be off work and available then. A parade was scheduled in Corgi Park, with free entry and a limited amount of free chow. Alongside the parade were speeches, a Ball tournament, and a live musical performance by the Mongrel Charity Band. Dogs would come from all across the city to see the spectacle, which would culminate in a march on the palace. The valor of the revolutionaries would inspire future generations to sing commemorative anthems about the fateful date.

While the dogs ran around the park, Julius, Lugs, Sal, Moira, and Quincy went to the palace entrance and meowed to get in.

"We have to see Emperor Greffin, now!" Julius demanded.

"We can't allow a mob of you in here," said the senior German shepherd guard.

"Fine." Julius looked at Moira with pursed lips, then told the guard, "She'll wait out here."

"No, I won't!" Moira argued.

Julius lowered his voice. "Time is of the essence, honey, and you're the one with an arrest warrant."

"Then hurry." Moira relented. "And hurry back."

"I must insist," said Quincy, who carried a pentagonal keyboard instrument with Lugs's help. "Your Emperor has ordered me to construct this for him. Do you really want to keep him waiting?"

The guard dogs did not. "There's still too many of you," said one of them.

"Can you even count?" Julius asked.

"Of course we can," the dogs said, glancing at each other.

"Okay," Julius folded his paws. "Count both of us."

The senior guard looked at the cats. "One... two..."

"Thank you," said Julius. "That's not too many, is it?"

"I suppose not," said the senior guard, letting the male cats in.

"Much obliged," said Moira, slinking in with them. "They need help carrying that heavy... whatever it is."

In the palace kitchen, a Cheshire chef put down his spoon and picked up a butcher knife. A spit-kitten stopped rotating a roast pig and ran to a delivery entrance, unlocking the wire mesh and admitting Flash and his pit bulls.

Josh demanded entry via the east wing, using the power of the press as his key, bringing Todd's big dogs with him disguised as cub reporters.

Toby turned up at the west wing entrance, too timid and diplomatic to join the attempted coup, but brave enough to distract the guards with his limitless knowledge of regal regulations.

The party in the park got louder, and busier, keeping the watchdogs busy—all except Marius Digger, who was already in the palace dungeon. He had begged Greffin to let him interrogate Cavem before he got stuffed, describing his board spaghettied with red thread.

In the small, fire-lit dungeon, Cavem had an iron collar clamped around his neck. A chain led from the collar to a stone wall. A short, fat basset hound stood nearby holding a halberd that was so long it almost jammed in the ceiling. Although the hound was sure to stay out of range of the chain and Cavem's jaws, the boerboel was morose.

"He could answer my questions a lot better," said Marius, "if you loosened his collar."

The hound shook his head, gripping his halberd tight.

"Fine," said the detective, "I'll do it."

The hound ran to stop him, and Marius head-butted him, knocking him unconscious against the wall. Marius freed Cavem and led him out of the dungeon.

"You've been a very bad dog," said Marius. "But I need your help."

Emperor Greffin waddled around Quincy's machine, yipping at it.

"You truly are a genius," said the Pekingese. "Gather around, my courtiers! See this new marvel."

Quincy had unveiled his keyboard, resting on the triclinium. "It would have been even more marvelous," the ginger cat said. "If I'd been given more time to build it."

"What does it do?" Greffin sniffed the instrument. Strings slanted away from the 49 keys. It was compact, with had no legs, making it portable and aesthetically pleasing despite its hasty construction.

"Why, it makes music, my Emperor!" Julius laughed good-heartedly. "A special kind of music that my readers will love to find out about back home. We can call it…"

"Greffin's spinet," Quincy suggested.

"Play it for Greffin," Greffin snuffled.

"I am no musician, my Emperor," Quincy said.

"I said, play it."

"I'll give it a go," said Lugs. With a sad lack of ceremony, he placed his paws on the keyboard and played a series of notes.

The courtiers were frightened by the instrument's loud, firecracker noises, its disturbing low and high frequencies, and its eardrum-piercing progressions. Greffin clamped his forepaws over his ears, barking, "Make it stop!"

Sal joined Lugs at the keyboard, playing bum notes, the lapdogs running in perturbed circles or dashing out of the room. Moira stopped as many of them as she could, batting them back into the throne room where sheepdogs and border collies corralled them.

Some of them collided with the pit bulls, who had bitten, thumped, and battered their way past Greffin's guards to get to the throne room, resounding with the bay of hounds.

Opposite the pitties, Todd's dogs raced in with the Bernoulli tube, which had felled any German shepherd guards with its powerful suction.

Greffin skittered on the floor, a purple robe dragging on the ground behind him. He almost made it to the stairs when Cavem appeared, a disillusioned look on his face, spit dripping from his teeth. Greffin moved back to his throne, surrounded by angry cats and dogs. His guards waited, panting, wary of the strange machines the rebels had unleashed on them.

The courtiers wouldn't stop yapping. Their noise got on Todd's nerves far worse than Quincy's instrument, which was now silent and covered with a torn-down tapestry.

"We only want what's fair," the huskie told Greffin. "A decent share of the food on the Isle of Dogs, and decent treatment. Nothing else changes. We fight for you, defend you. You make the political decisions. What do you say?"

"You want to run a protection racket," Greffin snapped. "If Greffin does not comply, no protection and something nasty happens. Isn't that right?"

Todd sighed. This wasn't the first time he'd had his words twisted by a Pekingese. "We're your first and last line of defense, my Emperor," he said quietly. "We kept our place because we were too dumb to know better. We're sick of it. This is no racket, it's justice."

Greffin noticed that his papillon aide-de-camp was standing alongside the Dogged Resistance. "*Et tu*, Emily?" the emperor lashed out. "Greffin is astounded that you do not trip on your trickery."

Emily took a couple of steps backward, broad ears drooping.

With a derisive snort, Greffin showed his brand of justice. The snort was a signal for his recouped guards and courtiers to make a move, close in on Todd and his friends, nipping at their legs to cut them down to size. As the rebel dogs fought back and Todd got close to the throne, Greffin stared at the underdogs.

"Remember your obedience training," Greffin bark. "Heel!"

Todd froze on the spot. The rest of the Dogged Resistance hesitated, too conditioned to resist their emperor's mesmerism. Todd threw a pleading look at Julius.

Cats are obedient to no-one. Julius knew what to do.

He took a step toward Greffin, but he found it slow going. There were so many of the little dogs all over him, gnashing at his tail and back. Only one thing kept him moving forward toward the throne—the faint glint of fear in Greffin's dark round eyes.

Julius used his teeth to wrench an attacker off his shoulder. He shook his head to get another pipsqueak off his throat, flinging it at the throne. Some of the guards simply hampered his progress, getting under his paws and making him stumble. It was time for the secret weapon.

Turning to Moira, he shouted, "Throw the newspaper!"

Moira pulled a copy of the *Hairball Tribune* from her coat. When she threw the rolled-up broadsheet into the air, its pages scattered, fluttering to the floor across the throne room. The younger lapdogs rushed to the paper, sniffing at it and, inevitably, using it. With the pups occupied, Julius made a push toward Greffin—close enough to snarl.

"Call off your lackeys, Greffin." Julius winced through his pain. "You've lost."

"Now how can you talk like that to a poor little dog like me?" Greffin's eyes seemed to get larger, his mouth formed a pout and his shoulders rounded in an obsequious, fluffy hunch. "You're a hero, not a bully." He turned to Todd, Aaron, and the other rebel dogs. "It's not too late for you to show Greffin how loyal you can be. With your help, Greffin can make sure that all of his subjects are content. But he can't do that without you."

Greffin looked so cute that, for a moment, Julius softened. Then he remembered his fight with Toxic, and the chase through the Mudlands, and his rage returned.

"Not this time, Greffin." There was a sadness in his voice. Moira and the rebel dogs had fought their way over to the throne, holding the courtiers at bay.

"We don't want to be your subjects anymore," said Josh. Cavem growled in agreement.

The Pekingese bristled and squinted, dropping every essence of cuteness. "That's easily fixed." With surprising savagery, Greffin went for Julius's nose, sinking his teeth deep. Julius closed his eyes and used his forepaws to push Greffin away, knowing the little dog would take part of his muzzle with him. Worth the sacrifice to bring this toy king down.

Greffin fell against his throne, making it teeter and fall on its side. Greffin looked at it sadly, then cast a look around the room. His few remaining faithful guards were subdued or routed.

It was time for the emperor to relinquish his crown.

The box was much larger than usual, barely fitting on the conveyor belt in the Tybalt Inc. warehouse. Gomez, a scrawny chaussie, hefted it over to his testing area, checking the parcel tape, making sure that there were no greasy paw marks on the sides.

"This must be some size o'rat," he told his Abyssinian neighbor Willy, who dragged the box away from the assembly line. "A big, stinky fella."

Willy sniffed at the box, enjoying the smell of cardboard. He rubbed his face against it a couple of times before he remembered where he was. Breathing in the odor of the sealing tape, he nodded. Inside the box was something very smelly, and it wasn't cheese.

"We don't have time to inspect this," Gomez sighed. "We've got a backlog as it is."

"It's our job to inspect dodgy boxes," Willy retorted. "What do you want to do, pass the buck to delivery?"

"Yep." Gomez was already hauling the box toward the exit ramp.

"We'll lose our livers if anyone finds out."

"Who's gonna?" Gomez asked.

Willy pushed past a longhair mopping the floor with its soft locks. "Why don't you wipe that grin off your face while's you're at it?" he grumbled. Willy didn't like longhairs.

The box slid easily down the ramp, which sloped toward a large wooden container. It joined a pile of boxes, but its contents didn't rustle or scratch.

"Look what you've done now!" Jake whined. "It's burst, for Bastet's sake!" Delivery cats prowled round the container, their curiosity overcoming any attempts at nonchalance. A loose rat was fair game, at worst an excuse for a bout of chasing, at best a juicy snack. Forepaws clinging to the container rim, they snuffled at the box's contents—then wrinkled their noses in disgust.

"That's no ordinary rat," said Willy with dread.

"Not the kind we were thinking." Gomez had his face in the container now, staring at seven rats intertwined with matted hair and glue, their twitching paws jutting from a broken box flap. "Most rats are cute and clean. They make good company and great *hors d'oeuvres*." He lifted the cardboard away to show his workmates the Ratking, which looked at them with 14 eyes the color of blood.

"If this is the kind of vile produce that's going out," said Gomez, "looks like this job is short term, lads."

Willy glanced around at the workers now hunched around the rim of the container, looking in. He tore a small box and snatched out a rat with his teeth; at the same moment, the workers all lunged on boxes of their own.

The air was filled with claw-shredded cardboard, fur and saliva. The small rats didn't stand a chance. The Ratking slipped away, though, to find new ears to whisper into. The city had belonged to the cats for long enough; the many-headed creature craved the warmth and shelter of Bast. Once he was in control, with the felines driven from the city by his filthy legion, he would never fear a cat again.

Julius checked his nose in the hall of mirrors. To his relief, it was still on his face.

"You were very brave back there," said Moira. "As usual."

"Just trying to impress you," Julius quipped.

"It worked. All those big dogs around, and you were the one who—"

"What are we going to do with him?" Josh trotted up, followed by Cavem, who carried Greffin in his teeth.

"I'm sure Todd has some ideas..." said Moira.

"I've got one," Cavem grumbled with his jaws full.

"Taxidermy's too good for him," said Lugs, walking down the hall with Sal and Todd.

"We gave him a chance," Todd sighed. "He threw it away."

"So throw him away," Sal suggested. "Onto Mandelo Island. Like he did to us."

Everyone looked at Sal. For once in his lives, he had come up with a good idea.

Bridget paced atop the highest dune on Mandelo Island, Pollet following her with a bowl of water, trying not to spill its contents.

"I ruled the greatest city in the continent," the lioness said. "I was head of an organization that censured the sins of thousands of cats. I was a wife and mother." She stretched her mighty paws toward the blue sky. "I was adored."

"You still are, ma'am," said Pollet.

"You don't count," Bridget scoffed. "You cease to entertain me."

Pollet waited until Bridget's back was turned then pulled a face at her. He looked around at the paradise island with its brightly colored flowers, its plump, plentiful birds, and its undulant dunes.

"Ma'am..."

Bridget turned, squinting at her steward. Pollet put the bowl on his head, upside down, so the water sloshed over his face. He spat some of the water out and stomped his hind paws.

Bridget burst out laughing, losing her balance and rolling down the dune. Pollet felt a thrill, having pleased his mistress. He scampered down the slope to make sure she was alright.

"Are you two getting lonely?" asked Zehra, looking rangier than ever at the foot of the dune. Her head was sticking out of the sand, as if she'd been tunneling under the ground. Bridget and Pollet stared at her, amazed; they had determined that they were the only two cats on the island.

"I—I don't know," Pollet stuttered.

"Who are you?" Bridget demanded to know.

"Because if you are," Zehra said, "it's alright. You'll get used to it. Eventually."

23

Surf's Up

Woodrow woke with a wide yawn, tired and dehydrated. The constant campaigning and paw-pressing had sapped his strength, and he was beginning to see why Otto's family had been at the top of the political food chain for so long. Otto had been a beast with the stamina to withstand news conferences, late-night lobbying, press stress, and smear attacks. Woodrow wasn't cut from the same regal cloth. It wasn't just the best cat who'd win the mayoral race—it would be the one with the most mettle.

He'd been existing on only twelve hours of sleep a day for longer than he wanted to remember. While the public—even his assistants—took naps, he worked on, plotting, preparing.

Woodrow's bedroom attested to his self-dedication. A desk stood next to the cushions that he slept on, its legs clawed to ribbons by his ritual morning scratches. Sometimes he slept under the desk, comforted by the sturdy wood above his head. But today he was more interested in the piles of paper stacked on its surface: letters of endorsement from fellow politicos who hoped to get a promotion once he was mayor. He couldn't promise them anything concrete—that was against electoral law—but he could drop heavy hints. *Back me, and you'll never have to worry about where the next pigeon's coming from. Ever again.*

Most importantly, Woodrow had half of Bast's media elite in his pocket. Swampy McMahon had been a close business associate since Woodrow had facilitated construction of a Wrestling Dome named after the famed sportscat; now he was a secret campaign contributor. Mimi Mimu had sung "He Fills Our Bowls with Shining Milk" in a political ad. *Mewsweek* had placed his face on four different covers, as savior of the city, its dove cots, its green spaces, and low-wage ringworm sufferers, respectively. Thanks to all his contacts, he was known as the cat of the people. It still wasn't enough.

Rubbing his nose, he moved to the window and leaned out to get some fresh air. The sun was high in the sky, but the streets were quiet; the piledrivers that should have been laying foundations for a new hotel opposite his office were silent. He looked down at the brown and black roadway several stories below and blinked.

The brown and black road seemed to be moving. Undulating. Woodrow leaned out farther, peering straight down. He couldn't see the asphalt, only masses of furry, scurrying bodies packed close together. There was no end to them, and no beginning either. Bast was being invaded.

Woodrow picked up the phone, hitting speed dial, his whiskers quivering with surprise. "This is an emergency," he growled. "Yes. I mean it. Life or death." He looked out the window again as if to check that he hadn't dreamed the rats in a fatigued fugue. They were still there. "You know who this is. Get me the PR department."

On the Isle of Dogs, the beach was less inviting this time, wind roiling the sea into foamy tufts and curls, the Leo still run aground. Josh showed Julius a lozenge-shaped length of wood, dragging it to the shoreline.

"What'm I supposed to do with this?" the cat asked.

"Take it out onto the water, paddle out some more until you're deep, then hitch a ride back on a wave."

"I don't do waves," Julius declined.

"Look at that stuff out there, J. See how it froths and shimmers? See the tiny grains of sand glittering, catching the light as they swirl? This is salty stuff, dude. Super buoyant. Great for surfin'."

"You do this for fun?" Julius gave Josh a mock scowl.

"I am called to it by one of the greatest natural forces known to Dog. First time I ever got on a beach, I jumped straight in the sea, couldn't help myself. It was as if we were one and I couldn't be content without a soggy coat. C'mon, we're missing the best waves! Look at that A-frame!"

"It looks awfully wet to me."

"Hey, you think a chilled-out hound like me would put myself in an uncomfortable spot?"

"Constantly."

With the end of his board clamped between his teeth, Josh pulled it into the water. "You've got to give in to your urges sometimes, cat," he yelled as he dropped the board into the roaring water. "Don't fight your urges!"

The only time I let my instinct take over, thought Julius, *is when I take my claws to something. Or someone.*

He recalled a time early in his writing career when he'd been up for anything. All experiences, no matter how obscure or schemie, had doubled as opportunities for him to taste the spice of life. He hadn't been especially observant or impressionable, but he'd had a great time glimpsing different lives and playing the role of a curious passer-by.

He'd worked as a bodyguard for a showcat, holding hefty toms at bay from the rich little pipsqueak. He'd worked as an extra on a movie set; his most prominent part had been as Cat Curled Up on Cushion #1 (non-sleeping). He'd sang with a live karaoke band, sticking to popular hits like "Don't Shed Your Fur Down on Me" and "Careless Whiskers". He'd binge-drank full fat milk with frat cats, taught martial tree scratching to ungrateful impoverished cubs; he'd even tried catnip once or twice (or maybe a few times) just to empathize with addicts, all to try to become a better writer.

At some point, he'd settled down in Bast and found his comfort zone. The times when he chose to stay at home instead of venturing out to seek new experiences grew more frequent until he was a lollygagging homebody—a house cat. The world outside that had once seemed so full of sensual stimuli and creative sparks had become scary.

If this was his last great escapade, then at least he hadn't just satisfied his craving for exploration. He'd helped some cats and dogs along the way.

Did I do alright by you, Camilla?

The Isle of Dog hadn't transformed all that much overnight, but Julius saw signs of a freer, gentler city: dogs of all sizes romped on the beach with no one to rein them in, sections of the fence had already been torn down or chewed though, allowing everyone access to the bay, and the palace was full of visitors, marking it as their own. There were already tongue-in-cheek talks about renaming it the Taj Mahowl.

"Don't tell me you're yellow?" Josh teased, wiggling his eyebrows as he paddled. "You don't wanna know what they do to old yellow types around here."

"It can't be worse than traipsing in that muck," Julius moaned, but he dipped a paw in the drink to show that he wasn't a coward. Quickly, he whipped it back out of the cold sea; now he was a drippy, shivering coward.

Maybe his thick, shaggy coat helped, but Josh didn't seem to mind the cold. Nose down, he had a leash around his neck connected to the beard in case he fell. He didn't. He aimed straight for a barrel, a large wave curling over and surrounding him; he had perfect balance and a big grin on his face as he took a doggy door out of the tube.

Julius mewed his appreciation, but the celebrations were cut short by Toby Tarenfarthing, stumbling through the sand toward him.

"Cats celebrate their victories in different ways to dogs, it seems," said the ambassador. "Congratulations, I hear that you were undiplomatically involved in the coup."

"Don't mention it," Julius blinked.

"Oh, I won't. Neither will anyone else. I don't want you causing another incident."

"Okay," said Julius, already planning a full-page article about his adventures. Scratch that, a series of articles. Maybe a new book.

"Besides, it's time you went home," Toby said, leading Julius up the beach. "Bast is in trouble, and it needs you."

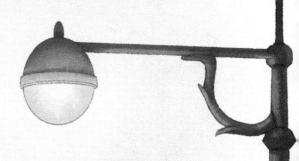

Part Four: Return To Bast

24

Ratking

"Listen up, listen up, cats and kitlens! This is the only voice you want to hear in your ears, DJ Scratch, with a VIV—Very Important Vibe. Before I give you the goods, here's a brief paid message from Tybalt Inc.

"Lost that hiss? Gargle with Victory Venom. For that real snake-like sound! Don't just spit it out, swill it and kill it with venom in your breath.

"Now, back to the ones and twos of the news. If it's Thursday, it must be an emergency here in Cat City, and this time around, rats are popping out of boxes and sewers like this is their favorite vacation spot. My advice: evacuate. City Hall's already making plans for a disaster route. Until that's announced,

it's an all-you-can-eat buffet, baby! Just don't get
bit—this is food that wants to eat *you*."

—**WOTW** radio broadcast
By DJ Scratch

All over Bast, the rats were revolting. They burst
out of their boxes, gnawed through their pretty packaging, and the ones chilling out in freezer cabinets laid
waste to shelf-loads of groceries. Then there were the
ones still in stores who terrorized customers, jumping
from cart to cart, biting kittens, and tripping up clerks.

Rallying them all, running from street to street to
cut loose his blood-curdling battle squeak, was the
Ratking, stirring up as much trouble as he could. By
goading his troops into action, he sparked at least two
house fires, one fright-fueled cardiac arrest, and a panicked mass exodus from a seafood restaurant.

The victims of this well-oiled attack were pan-
ic-stricken and terribly vexed. After all the marketing
hype and hyperbolic comments from Tad, their food
was fighting back. This not only gave them indiges-
tion, but also endangered the lives of their families—
the cats had so many piles of food in their larders that
they were easily overwhelmed by the suicidal snacks.

The prowlers were also out of their depth, flooded
with calls from upset taxpayers. With all their officers
out dealing with the swarming rodents and defending
food supplies, there were few left to protect the station when it was attacked by the Ratking, squirming
around and through their men, chewing up phone
lines and causing chaos.

"We've beaten you before, and we'll beat you again,"
said Chief Cutter, barricading himself in a holding cell.

"Not this time," said the Ratking, seven voices squeaking in unison. "Now we are everywhere. At every window of every home. And the cats of Bast are to blame for their downfall."

Julius and his friends hastily gathered supplies for the return journey to Bast. They would take the ferry this time with the blessing of Alcander's new regime; the walk across No Cat's Land would still be tough, but Moira had already reached out to Carabas to have cats waiting for them there, ready to rush them by train back to their native city.

Sal, Lugs, Moira, and Julius said their goodbyes to the dogs of Alcander. Toby was at the embassy, cleaning it up in readiness for refugees. Julius had told him he didn't think any cats would come this far north.

"It's time to open our doors to the possibility," Toby had told him. "Spread the word. They'll be safe here."

Moira rubbed against the huskies and thanked them for helping her find her way. Lugs was surprised but secretly pleased to spot Cheveux at the city gates, wishing him *au revoir* and giving him a big, heartfelt lick. Emily was there too; the papillon was helping the new regime with a *détente* between the different-sized dogs.

Josh gave Julius a signed copy of *Puppy Happy Hangs Ten*. Quincy wanted to stay on the Isle of Dogs, even though Julius insisted on taking his latest invention.

"I don't know why Greffin commissioned a weapon when he wanted a musical instrument," said Julius.

"He didn't read every request he signed," said Emily with a crafty blink. "The Bernoulli tube was just what we needed, when we needed it."

"I told you we had dogs on the inside," said Todd.

"You don't want to take the weapon?" Emily asked.

"We're going to make music, not war," Julius replied. He hefted the spinet in his paws. "I don't know how to operate this contraption."

"No, you don't," Quincy piped up. "No one does except me."

"You have to come with us," said Julius.

"You do know how to use this," Moira told Julius sweetly.

Julius looked at her, puzzled.

"Oh yeah, of course!" Sal agreed.

Julius didn't get it. He didn't appreciate not grasping something that Sal could.

"Your character," Sal said to Julius. "Your hero, Tiger Straight. He plays an instrument."

"Not like this!" Julius stopped mid-protest. There were few similarities between Tiger's saxophone and Quincy's bizarre but admittedly elegant creation.

"You're still going to have to come with us," Julius said to the inventor.

"Yes," Moira insisted. "Please, Quincy."

"I will," Quincy relented. "The mountains were my home for so long, but Bast... I was born and raised in that cursed catropolis. I will return with you. I will help defend it against the ravagers and then..."

"What will you do, Quincy?" Lugs asked. "Return to your wrecked lab?"

"I don't know what I will do or where I will go. Let's survive the journey home first."

"You're full of great ideas." Sal smirked. "No wonder you're an inventor."

The dogs watched and barked as Julius's party went to the ferry and headed south.

"We should help them," Josh said to the huskies.

"We have too much to do here," said Todd sadly. "Far too much to do."

It would have been a terrible understatement to suggest that the cats had underestimated the rats, their breeding rate, their cunning, and their will to fight. They poured through Bast from depots and citywide conveyor belts, attacking the citizens and eating their cat food. Shivering, nasty pointy teeth chattering, the rats pushed open fridge doors and scamper-scuttled across kitchen linos. Their noses twitched from side to side as their shifty pink eyes picked out open cereal packets and saucers of milk. They swam in gravy boats and attacked tins of albacore. No pantry was safe.

Woodrow assembled a hasty press conference on the steps of City Hall.

"Please stay calm!" Nobody listened to Woodrow. "The armed forces are on their way. There aren't that many rats—"

"But look what they've done, just a few of them," said an anxious tabby. "We need solutions now. No more idle reassurances."

"The prowlers are guarding the municipal grain silos. You won't starve..."

"We already are starving!" said another concerned citizen. "We're always starving. We're cats!"

The conference fell into disarray and Woodrow went back inside the building. The media gnawed on his performance, reporting that his weakness did not a future mayor make.

Quincy was a far better guide than Kelly. He was sure-footed and fast, leading Julius, Sal, Moira, and Lugs through jagged rocks, along narrow mountain paths, and through tunnels dug by long-ago beasts. Sal liked the way his voice carried in the passageways, calling for his dead friend Warren.

"Warren—Warren—Warren. Do you want a pick of pilchard fins—fins—fins?"

"Enough, Sal," Lugs eventually told him. "There are still wild dogs out here. They may hear you."

"Okay—kay—kay!"

Tarquin boarded a train home with no regrets. He would forfeit his bid for mayor and tell the press that he thought it best to focus on Carabian affairs. And if Bast needed help picking up the pieces after the rat attack, he would be gracious enough to lend a paw. Until then, he would be safe. If there was another election, he would be ready.

He looked out of the window as the train slowly chugged out of the platform. He wouldn't miss Bast that much; his experiences there had been disheartening at best. Better to mold Carabas his way, not conform to this age-old termite's nest of trouble.

A few rats ran onto the platform, snatched up by porters and commuters, an unexpected morning snack. More rats appeared, then more, enough to cover the station master and swarm toward the train.

Come on, Tarquin urged. *I've already had my breakfast.*

"Let's get going!" he said out loud.

The train picked up steam, leaving the station and the swarm behind. Tarquin sank back on his seat, letting out a breath of relief. All it would take was a small pack of rats hitching a ride to Carabas to torment his citizens.

Tarquin closed his eyes. That was another problem for another day.

Woodrow frantically scratched through a filing cabinet in his office, his tie loose and his fur askew. "There's a form to fill in for this. I don't know who's in charge of handling crises like this?"

"You are, sir," said Tippee, offering to help Woodrow sort through his documents. She was the only office worker left in City Hall; all other non-essential personnel had gone home to help their families and neighbors battle the rats.

"What about Joey Hondo?" Woodrow asked. "He's adept at municipal security, liaises with the prowlers..."

Tippee pursed her lips. "Since he felt compelled to run against you, Your Provisional Honor, he no longer keeps the city secure."

Woodrow slumped down at his desk. "Who does? Who replaced him?"

"That position has yet to be filled. In the interim, responsibility for the safety of the city falls upon your head."

"Then I shall face the music." Woodrow cleared his throat. "With you at my side."

"Yes sir." Tippee nodded, surprised and apprehensive.

"Contact Chief Cutter at the Thirteenth Precinct. Inform him that we will use Beaverbank Place as a primary evacuation route. His prowlers will cordon off the street and guard us against rats and gang members. The sentinels will sweep the city for intruders."

"I have been unable to reach the precinct," Tippee replied slowly. "The sentinels are backing up the prowlers and helping with our ... pest problems."

"Keep trying." Woodrow wasn't going anywhere without prowler protection. In the meantime, he rooted through his papers, looking for his precious forms.

By the time Julius's group reached the final passage and the ominous gates to the north, the cats were exhausted. They agreed to rest up at Quincy's observatory, where the inventor tidied as much as he could while the others slept, resting their blistered paws. Quincy picked up his sister's picture and placed it carefully on the mantelpiece; judging by her expression, his sister did not approve.

He bustled quickly and efficiently through the lab, doing his best to sweep up glass and wooden shards without waking the others.

Julius joined him, using his tail to help with the sweeping.

"I'm sorry I woke you," Quincy whispered.

"That's okay," Julius replied. "I have a lot on my mind."

"You must be exhausted," said Quincy. "We could have moved faster if we hadn't been hauling the spinet."

"So Lugs kept reminding me."

"Why did you bring it? The sounds it makes aren't all that wonderful."

"But you are!" Quincy was taken aback by the compliment. Julius held the inventor's paws. "You're smart enough to adjust the frequency on that instrument, aren't you?"

Quincy shrugged. "Indubitably."

"Wonderful. I'll go get it; you retool it." Julius hurried out of the lab, calling over his shoulder. "While I compose a rhapsody for rats."

25

The Rats Bite Back

Tad stood in his boardroom, watching the havoc he'd caused on three different news feeds. None of them were blaming him, for now; it was only a matter of time. This was a crisis that was hard to spin. He would find a way.

The rats were in his building, rushing up the stairs, tinging out of elevators, clawing at security. The whole invasion seemed orchestrated, somehow. Rats didn't have that intelligence, though. There was a reason why cats had built their great city, and most rodents lived under it.

Tad had done everything he could to staunch the flow of rodents. His depots were shut down; the conveyor belts stopped. But the rats kept coming. He decided to prepare a statement, *sans* speechwriter, which he would deliver to his supporters. To comfort them, at least.

On the way to his office, he found Ramona running from a large pack of rats. There were so many piled on top of each other that they covered the walls as well as the floor. She stumbled as he reached his office.

"Sir, wait for me!" Ramona called out, picking herself up and batting a rat away from her face.

Tad locked up his office and caught his breath, hearing plaintive howls from outside. Poor Ramona. She would have to be replaced.

Hearing a thumping sound, he looked up. The office air vents buckled and more rats poured out, surrounding him, biting at him. As the rats chewed through his fur into his flesh, it was his turn to scream.

Ramona was upset when she heard Tad's final cries, but that distress quickly turned to delight. The pompous cat deserved it. While the rats were preoccupied with him, she escaped to a supply closet and blocked the entrance with a stationary cabinet. The rats battered against it, desperate to get to her, but the cabinet held firm and there were no vents large enough for them to squeeze through. Ramona was safe, for now.

The rats loved the sewers, tunnels, and cellars of Bast; Otto's place of imprisonment was no exception. When Chico realized that he was being overrun, he dashed to Otto's cage, fumbling with the keys.

"Are you doing this because you need help?" Otto grumbled. "Or is this another mind game?"

"You know I don't play games," said Chico. "That's Joey's bag."

He unlocked the cage, and Otto stepped out. "I have heard the shrieks and pattering rat steps," the mayor said in a deep, ominous voice. "How many?"

"Too many to count, Your Honor."

"At least I can reduce my number of nuisances by one."

Chico was shocked. "Me? I fed you... I'm setting you free."

Otto drew himself to his full height, making Chico shake with fright. The two cats circled each other, Chico preparing to bolt. "No one humiliates me and tells the tale," Otto leered.

Chico had his back to the cage now. He could see rats scurrying toward them, filling the exit.

"I can help you get out of here," said Chico. "I know the way."

"I don't need anyone's help." Otto roared and Chico stumbled backward, falling into the cage. Otto closed it and locked the jailer in, throwing the key into the greasy pile of rats.

"Your freedom is right there." Otto cracked a bloody smile. "Fetch it." He leaped over the rats and out of the cellar, leaving Chico to cower in his cage, closing his eyes, thinking of Tippee.

The Isle of Dogs was already benefiting from Greffin's absence. Life made sense when it was not lived on the whim of a callous lapdog. Todd called a meeting in the palace, sitting on the throne with his tail straight and true.

"Times of crisis call for experienced leadership," Todd told his fellow rebels. "A cool head. I have decided the best course of action in what will no doubt become known as a tumultuous chapter in feline history. Our Bast neighbors need help and by golly, we're going to give it to them. Our army has already been sent kit and kaboodle to the cat city. They'll arrive there by the end of the week and quash the rat rampage. You must agree, there are no finer troops than our dog fighters."

Emily presumed to ask a question. "Isn't this rather heavy-pawed, sending our whole force to deal with these pests?"

"They're more than vermin, remember?" Josh replied. "They've killed or wounded many innocent citizens of Bast. They've kept the prowlers tangled up in grue. It's time we stepped in and got rid of the rats using our sheer superior force."

"How long do you think that will take?" asked Aaron.

"Our military experts project that the conflict will be over in a matter of days," Todd assured him.

Aaron asked him, "Will you go to lead the army in Bast?"

"I cannot join the troops while this government is in its founding throes," Todd answered with a hint of impatience. "The democratic process is too important to be delayed by my absence. And as I said, the conflict will be over by then. But the army does have one of our number at its head. Cavem."

Missy and Kierkam stood back-to-back, eyes wide, claws out, facing an onslaught of rats, rallied by the Ratking.

Missy didn't care who she was allied with at that moment. She was defending her territory with Dineo-Kenosi, a couple of prowlers, and even some members of the rival Wildcat gang. From what she could tell, that gang had been torn apart by the rats; the Clutes were on top. That meant nothing without a territory, so she was determined to defend it to her last breath.

Kafel's alley chapel had grown since his first nocturnal hymn. It was filled with candles, religious icons, and fresh graffiti honoring Bastet. It wasn't the best position to hold in a fight, but Missy and her allies had found themselves there, using dumpsters and mattresses as barricades.

They'd never seen so many rodents. Missy said goodbye to Dineo-Kenosi, feeling completely overwhelmed until the rats parted. A scraggedy old cat waded through the pool of tiny bodies, slicing them up with her claws.

"Mom!"

"Didn't think I'd let you make a last stand without me, did you?"

Desdemona joined her daughter, cutting a swathe through the rats around them. With the help of the veteran fighter, the Clutes would last a little longer.

In his sturdy church, Bishop Kafel raised his forepaws and addressed his congregation.

"We have faced tribulation before. We will face it again. We will survive all these terrible events because the Goddess Bastet watches over us. I have seen it with my inner eye. She knows that we are faithful. She knows that we are willing to sacrifice all we hold dear in her name. We share her word here in Bast; how can we do that if we are gone? For those of you who lack hope, let me remind you of words from the Book of Felidae.

"'The plague of fleas did rain down upon the Four Pawed Ones. For nine days the sky was as night with the blood-gorged bodies of the insects. The tribe did cry with woe and scratch at their garments, sure that the plague would never cease. At the end of the ninth day, the fleas did disappear, and the populace was amazed. Their fury itched with bites and festered with small scratches. They huddled together and washed each other. Lo! Their goddess showed herself in all her green-eyed glory. "Throughout your ordeal," saith Bastet, "you remained faithful to me. You did not falter or seek solace from a darker deity. You proved yourselves worthy of my love." And the sores and scratches were lifted from the bodies of the pious and the tribe rejoiced, singing Basset's praises. No further plagues were visited upon the cats. But woe unto their opposites, the course-haired ones, the barking fools. They shall forevermore be plagued with fleas, with no requite.'"

The congregation listened, rapt, as the bishop read the hallowed passage. He lifted his forepaws high above his head, the gold-embroidered sleeves of his priestly robe catching in the stained-glass light. This flock would do his bidding without question. He had adjured his responsibility to keep them safe; if they were endangered by the rats, their goddess was testing them. If they died, they were sacrificing themselves in Bastet's name.

Kafel closed his eyes and led the congregation in prayer, their utterances drowned out by the sound of the rats scurrying outside. As Kafel completed his prayer and opened his eyes, he noticed that the light was dimming. Nightfall was hours away. Looking up at the stained-glass windows, he saw them darken with small, furry bodies. They pressed against the panes, more rodents behind them, making a ghastly scraping sound against the metal frames. The congregation saw what was going on and crowded close in their pews, muttering and mewing to each other. An old female tortoiseshell looked at Kafel, imploring.

"We are in Bastet's care, my brothers and sisters. All we can do is pray."

As Kafel recited the Invocation of Gratitude, the stained glass cracked. A flattering image of Bishop Constant split in two. The church was pitch black now; a verger lit a candle. The flock held its collective breath, hoping the glass would hold. The windows made a terrible snapping, splintering sound as more bodied pushed against them.

While Kafel and the congregation's attention was focused on the windows, more rats scrabbled at the entrance, squirming their way past the barricade into the church. With all calmness gone, the congregation clamored past Kafel into the vestry.

Kafel turned mid-prayer and said, "Brothers and sisters, fear not. This is all part of Her great plan."

Kafel was ignored, left alone at the altar to face the rodents. They approached the candlelight, beady-eyed and curious. Kafel breathed deep, digging deep to find faith in his own diatribe. He stood firm against the horde, ready to embrace them. After all, they were the goddess's creatures, too.

The rats looked at each other suspiciously; they were used to cats either running from them or fighting them, not standing beatifically before them. As one, they turned to face Kafel, hungry. One rat raised up high on her haunches, nose twitching, eyes shining close to the candle. Opening her jagged mouth, she blew out the flame. Kafel was consumed in the darkness.

Julius hardly recognized his city as he and his friends arrived at Central Station. He'd seen it wrecked in the past—cats were not known for their patience—but not on this scale.

Sal was alarmed as a small clowder of cats staggered past him, bleeding and scruffy, desperate to catch the next train to Carabas. They looked at him as if he was insane, going the wrong way. He needed some nip.

Lugs asked Julius, Moira, Sal, and Quincy to wait while he reported to his unit; he returned shortly afterward, explaining that the sentinels were scattered across Bast, dealing with the rats piecemeal. He would stick with Julius for the time being.

As they left the station, Quincy looked pleased. "If they held onto their engineers," he murmured to himself, "these structures would hold up to disasters. But oh no..."

Julius looked at him judgmentally, as only a cat can do. His city wasn't perfect, but he loved it. "I finished my composition on the train," he told Quincy.

"Of course you did," the inventor replied. "I saw you notating away."

"The machine's ready?"

Quincy nodded. He was looking forward to testing it out.

Julius embraced him. "Then let's spread our music to the masses."

The congregation hunkered in the church vestry, some praying, and some sleeping, exhausted. A kitten let out a high-pitched mew, hungry and scared. His mom shut him up with one glare.

Trembling with nervous energy, the verger crept to the screen and opened his ears wide to listen for danger. All he heard was the creak of a floorboard as he padded out of the vestry, looking around the church, which was now dappled with daylight. The church was empty except for the bishop's robes, torn and unoccupied; whatever the rats hadn't eaten, they'd carried away in triumph.

Bastet did not appear or give the verger a sign, but he liked to think She watched over the churchgoers as they tidied up, sweeping broken glass, picking up candlesticks, and neatly folding Kafel's robes. In time, if Bast survived the rat apocalypse, the garments would be displayed in a glass case behind the altar as a shrine to a great martyr.

The rats had been here before. They had raided the city and tormented even the toughest cats. This time, they were determined to stay. They sniffed around silos and squeezed into schools, chewed on wooden signs, and drooled against restaurant windows. For one week at least, they owned the city.

They were far too numerous for the cats to catch every one of them, too small to dig from every storm drain. The citizens fought over the rodents, unwilling to share their prey, squabbling among themselves instead of working together to staunch the onslaught. In the Crystal District, sparkling with lantern light, they picked different shop doorways to call their own, winning bite-sized victories on every stoop. They were tiring, however, and the rats kept coming.

Joey Hondo set an example of confidence and organization, wading through the sea of vermin with a tomcat swagger, swiping rodents out of the way with his formidable paws, biting the hind of a pack leader as if he was snacking on a marshmallow.

"They've got us cornered!" said Antonio Cortis, the fishmonger who'd lost his wares to the rats. There was nowhere to run; a narrow street behind the citizens was also clogged with beasties.

"No, they don't." Joey shook his head and flashed a grim snarl at Antonio. "Push forward!"

Joey led the residents into the pile of rodents, fighting his way through them, his followers tight in his footsteps. Rats climbed over them, pulling Antonio to the ground, tearing him to shreds. Joey reached up for a lantern and snatched it from its hook, dashing it to the ground. It ignited, sending a pillar of flame and smoke upward. The rats retreated, disappearing under stalls and into dark corners. Joey used the reprieve to lead the cats out of the market and into the central square, where they were greeted by more cats, including Julius's group.

"Joey, are you okay?" asked Moira.

"Fine," said Joey brusquely. "I'm more worried about these citizens than me."

Julius, Lugs, and Quincy had a task to complete. Sal and Moira stayed to help Joey's group take shelter under the Canders' Mewmorial.

"Be careful," Julius said to Moira, giving her a slow blink.

"*You* be careful," Moira replied. "I'll be awesome."

Joey helped three sentinels barricade the shopping district before it met the square. For a moment, the center was quiet. No rats, no squabbling, no histrionics. Joey and Moira were both a calming influence, used to working with high-strung officials and a tantrum-prone mayor. Scared, agitated citizens were a doddle in comparison.

"There's nowhere to go," said a calico in a herringbone jacket.

"We stay right here," Joey asserted. "Until we find out exactly what's going on."

"That's obvious," said Moira. "The rats are winning."

"Yeah," said Sal, looking at Joey with wide eyes. "Rats."

Joey sighed with exasperation. "I mean, we need to know where the vermin is, how many there are, what's being done to stop them. They could just be in this area!"

"Listen," said Moira, her ears cocked. She heard chaos in the distance. "They're causing trouble all over Bast."

"How do we get out of here?" the calico asked.

"We make a stand, here in the center of the city of our birth," Joey proclaimed. "We will eat every rat we set our teeth on; trap every thick, sickly rat we see. The rats have sharp teeth and sharper minds. They will fight back and tear some of our claws. Ask yourselves, would you rather die trembling, an embarrassment to Calvon Canders? Or die fighting and eating and defending Bast?"

The small crowd yowled with approval. They wanted to fight, and they had the perfect bold leader for their crusade.

26

Up to Scratch

"**H**ere's an appropriate dope track. Suspicious Package's 'Ratcatch Fever', with lyrics to die for."

DJ Scratch felt safe in his recording booth, broadcasting, until Julius and Quincy turned up with an ornate machine.

"There's no way I'm letting you back on my show, J. Not after last time. There should be a restraining order on you to keep you away from microphones. You oughtta be banned from broadcasting, period. Who made you the voice of doom in the first place?"

"Ten seconds, Scratch," Julius promised. "Ten seconds and I'll be out of your fur forever."

The DJ crossed his paws. "I don't think so."

"I gave you your big break in radio!" Julius reminded him. "How many times have I plugged your programs in print?"

"How often have you almost cost me my job?"

"We're friends. Friends take risks for each other."

Scratch was adamant. "I only ever let singers get ahold of my mic."

"Since when?"

"New rule, J. Everyone knows it. Where ya bin, on an island?"

Julius glanced at Quincy, then turned back to Scratch. "Okay, I'll sing, whatever, just plug this spinet into your console—that's all I ask."

"Plug a what now? That's even worse. Nobody messes with my playlist."

"You'll dig it. It's a catchy tune."

Scratch stared at Julius as if he'd just been asked to fetch a stick. But he took the disk and placed it on his deck, ready to play.

"You sure I'm gonna like this?"

Quincy was not a cat of violence, but he looked ready to wallop the disk jockey.

"How long have we known each other?" Julius wheedled.

"Too long." The Suspicious Package track was done. DJ Scratch reluctantly cut to commercials.

"Don't want canned, processed food, do you? NO! You want live rats, delivered to your window! Call Rat in a Box™ now to arrange delivery. Brought to you by Tybalt Inc., the company you can trust to make life right."

"Never mind the ads," said Julius. "This is an emergency, a newsflash, whatever you want to call it!"

Scratch hit a large green button with his paw and drawled, "I don't know how many o'you cats're old enough to remember Tiger Straight, but let's just say if you ain't picked up a wild book called *The Cat Who Stole the Cream* by now, you must be a dog. With me now is the author hisself Julius Kyle, creator of Tiger Straight, and he promises not to start no riots today. Ain't that right, J?"

"You know it, Scratch. Listen up everybody, I need your help with this one. If you live by the river, I want you to turn your radios up real loud for the next tune we're going to play."

Scratch gave a cool nod. "That's what I like," he said.

"Everyone else, you got to switch your radios off."

Scratch didn't like this so much.

"Change the channel," Julius continued. "Flip the volume down to zero. Whatever you want—as long as this music can only be heard on the riverbank."

"Why?" Scratch was nonplussed.

"Because if you want your city to be rid of our ... latest batch of tourists, you're all going to have to do what I say."

"You got a plan, right, J?"

"A perfect one, all ready to put into action. But we've all got to work together on this one, folks. I can't do this without you." Julius looked imploringly at the reluctant Scratch. The DJ looked at the record, wondering what he'd do once he lost his job.

"Here we go, cats and kitlins," Scratch told his avid listeners. "The platter that really matters. Do what my book-creatin' friend says, and we'll all be fine. But those of you non-river lovers, please remember to turn your radios back up after a few minutes, won't you?" Quincy plugged the spinet into the DJ's console. Julius turned the pages of a few sheets of scruffy music. Scratch placed his claw on the console and flipped a switch, then grimaced at the sound. It was weird, rhythmic, and catchy.

"You call this music?" Scratch yelled.

"It'll do its job," said Julius. "You wait and see."

"You told me I'd *like* this music. What else did you lie to me about?"

"My plan being perfect." Julius gave a Scratch a "don't hit me" look. "It's foolproof—I'm just not sure if it's Lugs proof."

"Move your tails!" Lugs ordered a team of city workers. With his encouragement, they moved fast, removing bolts and hinges, to shift a system of conveyor belt ramps. They moved the tall, thin metal supports, bolting them back onto the streets leading down to the river. "Make sure there's no gaps... can't let the pests drop through," Lugs reminded them. The workers didn't appreciate this upstart sentinel ordering them about, but they were desperate. From the distant city center, they could hear screeching and howling, an encroaching battle between vengeful rats and outnumbered cats.

"Tighten up that corner!" Lugs looked up at the conveyor belt. It snaked down Polentry Lane, across Tiffin Street, ending on Skyr Terrace.

It wasn't long enough.

"We need more ramp!" said a panicking worker. "We're out of materials."

"We need to make do with what we have," said Lugs calmly. "The scrape park. We have to bring the platforms over here, rig them so they reach the river."

"They're too heavy," the worker whined.

"How many of us are here?"

"20," said the worker. "Oh, wait, 19. Tinker got eaten."

"There's enough of us to drag the platforms." Lugs led the workers to the park. He climbed onto the highest platform and yowled at the workers to listen up. "We have to work fast. I don't know where all these rats came from, but I know where they're going—into our homes and schools, our churches and our hospitals. They are chewing through everything in their path, like a storm of dirty fur, destroying everything they set their teeth to. We can stop them. Dr. McGraw's invention will work, and we will be the ones to send the rodents to a watery grave."

The workers cheered, setting to work dismantling the platforms and gathering ropes to use as harnesses. *En masse*, they dragged the materials across town, not caring if they left grooves in the medians or snagged chunks out of trees. They set up the rest of the conveyor belt. Now, instead of looping around the city, it led to the river. Some rats already nosed along the ramp, inquisitive, led by the tantalizing music played loudly on riverbank radios. But they needed more incentive to fall into the water.

Some of the rodents spilled onto the ground, where the workers shoveled them up in their mouths and crunched down on the squeaking food source. Others ran back to the city center, joining their pack in its mighty incursion.

The prowlers perched on either side of the belt, which increased its speed once a pack of rats heard a hint of the tune. Their mountain, coupled with the movement on the ramp, propelled them into the rushing river.

"Keep shoveling them in!" said Lugs, hoping the cats in the city center were still alive to do their part.

He was relieved to see Sal and Moira running toward him. With the rats scurrying away from the central square toward the river, the cats had gathered all the food they could find, dragging it onto the ramp loader. Joey and his followers had rounded up as much cheese as possible from the local *fromagerie*, dumping it onto the pile. Cats huddled around them, trying to help but getting in the way.

"We need more radios," Moira told them. "To guide the rats onto the conveyor belt." The cats raced to their homes, wading through rodents to get their stereos and soon the riverside was filled with eerie, mesmerizing music.

———

The Ratking, cleverer than most of his brethren, managed to brawl his way to the radio station. Once inside, he scurried through the studios until he found Julius, hunched over the spinet, eyes large, breath held.

"You won't play so well without paws," the Ratking challenged. While one set of teeth snapped at Quincy, making him pull away from his keyboard, another grimaced at Julius and DJ Scratch, daring them to go near the console. "We're immune to your tricks," the Ratking told him. "Too powerful to be misled. We'll feast on you, kitties, and we'll take it slow so you can feel every..."

"Last..." said another mouth.

"Bite!" said a third, lunging for Julius. The large, grubby mass was slow though, giving Julius time to dodge the attack. He had to defend the console, so he popped out his claws and took a dig at the king, sinking his little daggers paw-deep into the matted fur.

They didn't elicit so much as a squeal. Before he could retract his claws, he was pulled off-balance, and the monster was on him, biting at his throat.

Otto chewed and snarled his way to City Hall, where he joined the leopard guards and Chief Cutter at the top of the steps.

"Your Honor!" said Cutter. "You're alive!"

"Of course I'm alive," said Otto. "Who caused this catastrophe?"

"Tad Tybalt," Cutter said tersely.

"He will be dealt with. My cubs?"

"Milo is safe in Carabas, with Tarquin Quintroche," Cutter informed him, swiping rats from the steps with his paw. "No sign of Mowbray, I'm afraid."

"He has been murdered by Joey Hondo."

"That's impossible!" Cutter exclaimed.

"My word is law. And I will be his executioner. Find him for me!"

"Julius, I swear this is the last time I let you in my booth," said DJ Scratch, taking his headphones off his ears and wrapping the cord around the Ratking. Tugging at the cord, he was able to pull the grotesque animal from his friend.

Julius picked up the Ratking in his teeth and threw him against the console, where he gnawed at cables and cut off the broadcast.

"No more show," said Scratch sadly.

Julius crouched down on all fours, nose to nose with one of the Ratking's heads. The cornered animal sprang at Julius, but fell short, snagged in a mess of exposed wires. Risking an exposed belly, Julius reached up and flipped a switch. With a horrible crackle and pop, the Ratking fried and burst into juicy chunks.

Scratch removed the curled-up corpse from his booth, trying not to throw up. Quincy rushed to reconnect the wires, cautioning Julius to turn off the main power supply so he wouldn't go the way of the Ratking.

"We'll get you back on air soon, Scratch," said Julius. "You've got a performance to finish."

"Thank Bastet's belt buckle," said Lugs as Julius's music started up again after several heart-stopping minutes of silence. Moira, Sal, and Joey joined him, fresh from clearing the central square. Lugs had ordered his workers to gather up as many radios as they could find, and the cats turned the volume up on each of them. Lugs winced at the repetitive beats of the rat rhapsody. "This stuff will frighten 'em away, not draw 'em to us."

"I like it," said Sal, bopping his head to the beguiling cadence.

"Stay with us, Sal," said Lugs, placing a firm paw on his shoulder to stop him from going anywhere.

"It will be fine," Moira reassured Lugs. "Julius will get the job done."

"Yeah." Joey nodded. "Like he did in last year's riots. And in Carabas."

"He's not perfect, but I love him," said Moira.

"Maybe that's *why* you love him," Lugs suggested. "Who wants to spend their life measuring up to perfection?"

"Turn it up some more. This is it!" Moira was right. There it was, that irresistible apocalypso beat. Every rat that heard it was driven crazy by the tune, and they couldn't help but head for its loudest source.

In the last stand alley, Missy was amazed to see her rat attackers retreat, heading for the river.

"It's a miracle!" Dineo-Kenosi meowed at the top of his voice.

"No, it ain't," said Desdemona, picking herself up and limping over to her daughter. "Listen." In the distance, the Clutes and their allies could hear the siren music. "They're being drawn to the Hune. Whoever's playing that melody saved our lives."

"They didn't save everyone," said Missy, looking down at a dead prowler. She wasn't going to own half the city as Kafel had promised, but she still possessed her territory, and she could claim the Wildcat patch as well if she wanted. Victory had never felt so bitter.

She held Dineo-Kenosi's paw and felt better.

"I'll tell you what a real miracle would be," said Desdemona. "If the Cat's Cradle is still open."

"You need a drink?" Missy laughed.

"You know me so well," Desdemona said, leading the cats to the bar.

"This is taking too long," Lugs complained. "They're not coming, and this music's doing my head in."

"I thought you military types were used to waiting?"

"Nah. Hurry up and eat. That's our motto. I'm not used to hanging around twiddling my tail to a calypso accompaniment, that's for sure."

"You don't have to wait anymore."

"Huh? What do you—" Lugs shut up. A huge mass of rodents rushed toward them in an awesome rodent stampede. They would have been as single-minded as the Ratking if they'd thought at all. But the music drew them on, a tune they couldn't ignore, heading for the river with the two cats standing directly in their path.

"His plan worked, after all," Lugs conceded. "What do we do now?"

Hurrying down to the water, Lugs's team made sure their boomboxes and portable speakers were cranked to the max. The high-pitched wailing immediately got the remaining rats' attention, diverting them from their destructive path. Dropping everything, they hurried for the water, moving so fast that they couldn't stop themselves when they hit the river.

By the time Julius joined Lugs and the others on the riverbank, most of the rats were gone. Some of them hung on, though, avoiding the moving conveyor belt, biting at any prowler or sentinel who dared to go near them.

"Thank you for helping to keep my friends safe," Julius said to Joey. "And my city. I see not all politicians are self-centered mongrels." Joey was taken aback by the catty compliment.

"Give me a stereo," said Julius. "Make sure it's got plenty of batteries."

A pair of disheveled prowlers escorted Julius to an access ladder. He used it to climb up onto the conveyor belt, moving slowly toward the river. His ears sagged as he balanced on the moving platform, in danger of losing his cool. He took a breath and remembered what Josh had taught him—to limber up, sway with the waves, let his instinct take over.

It was time to let his wild side out.

"Turn up the volume, Julius!" said Lugs. Julius placed his pads on the portable stereo, twisting the volume knob up to the max. The surviving vermin turned to face him, twitching, struggling to ignore his tune. Julius bared his teeth and hissed at the rats, unnerving them.

"It won't work," said Joey Hondo, who climbed onto the belt and stood beside Julius. "These rats are deaf, or too stupid, or too smart to fall for your trap. They were just following their pack for a while."

"Get down from here, Joey," said Julius, his tail weaving. "If they attack us all at once..."

"There's a prowler down there waiting to arrest me," said Joey. "And a lion not far behind him. Your words down there shamed me in ways I can't explain. But this is my city too, Julius. Let me do this."

"We'll do it together."

Julius swung the stereo at the rats. He flinched as it smashed into pieces, knocking a couple of them off the belt. The rest of the rats ran toward Julius and Joey. Julius stood his ground, slicing the rodents open with surgical accuracy. Joey kept running, springing off the edge of the belt, followed by the rats. Julius caught one last sight of Joey sinking into the water, covered in dying rats.

On the ground, Otto loped to the bank of the river, watching Joey sink underwater. His instinct was to jump in and savage the cat, alive or dead, but the current was merciless and the river was still full of rats. He raised his head and emitted the loudest roar he had ever summoned, one that was heard across the district.

The mayor had returned.

27

Catching the Light

"**W**hat do you think of the front-page headline? 'TIME'S UP FOR OTTO' Pithy, ain't it?"

Julius was back in Roy Fury's office, hoping the editor hadn't read his lengthy expense report. Roy had bigger concerns; Chief Cutter had registered a complaint about Otto, saying the lion was more concerned with his vendetta against Joey Hondo than he was about his disaster-stricken city. Officials were suggesting that Otto go look for his mother until a full investigation was carried out. Woodrow, who had resolutely stayed in City Hall throughout the rat crisis, would be mayor in the meantime, abetted by his assistant Tippee T and graciously endorsed by the owner of *The Scratching Post*.

"A city without Otto as mayor would be a whole new ball of wool," Julius said.

"According to your memos, the Isle of Dogs has plenty going for it under new rulership. And your first article... Good reporting there," Roy told him, butting heads with him. "A little *sensitive* for me, but hey, the readers need that old-fashioned touch."

"You were right," said Julius.

"You know it. Sticking around?"

"You're offering me my old job back?" asked Julius in surprise.

"Strictly freelance. No vacations, pensions, or benefits—circulation hasn't picked up that much—but you're our star *du jour*. I'll throw plenty of work your way."

"I see." Julius stood still and silent for a moment, listening to the yack-yack of typewriters in the bullpen, inhaling the faint but distinct smell of the printing presses below them.

"I know you wouldn't wanna be on our payroll anyway," said Roy, interrupting Julius's meditation. "An employee of Swampy McMahon. You don't have to worry about that. Ramona Pretzel, the new head of Tybalt Inc. is buying him out. He's got troubles of his own, what with the rumors of bias during the election campaign. Can't have him owning a paper if he's biased, can we?"

Julius shook his head at the irony.

"All the same," Roy continued, "I wouldn't insult you by offering—"

"Go on. Insult me."

Smiling, Roy clawed a prepared freelance contract from his desk. Julius perused it, noting that his name was already printed on the form. All he had to do was add his personal scent to the paper, rubbing his jowls across the dotted line.

"You got me," he said, looking up at his editor.

"Don't we just?"

Julius handed back the completed form to the smirking tom. "Any preference for my next piece?"

"I hear that Carabas is quite cool this time of year. Nice 'n' dry. Might be worth a look."

"I'll look into it." Julius left the paper without saying goodbye; Roy was a busy kitty.

"Where've they gone?" Prowler Lieutenant Cowl scratched behind his ear and slammed a paw down on a rodent straggler. Not all of the rats had heard Julius's broadcast, continuing their mayhem with squeaky glee. Still, they seemed to sense that their brethren were massing for some reason, and Cowl saw several groups of rats rush down the street as he cleared the Main Library.

"Aw, look at this. They've chewed the *City Prowling Manual*," he told an officer. "No respect for literature." He held up another book. "Swampy McMahon's tell-all autobiography—nibbled. The *Wirehair Chronicles*—whizzed on. Let's start cleaning up this mess. Check with Team Three, try and find out what's doing dockside."

Lugs was back with the sentinels. His sterling service to Bast was taken into account and no questions were asked about his absence. He was grateful to be back with his brothers, following a routine, eating hearty, outdoor-formula dried food. He missed his civilian friends, but he had a duty to perform and a lynx legion oath to uphold.

Cavem had a lot of amends to make. He worked alongside Josh, other big dogs, and the prowlers, cleaning up Bast and even treating the wounded. They did not bring the Bernoulli tube; such a terrifying weapon was not to be used lightly.

Rather than coming with them, the pit bulls stayed in Alcander, assisting the government and proving that their uncouth reputation was ill-earned.

Detective Marius Digger received an Award of Exceptional Merit from the Hound Council, and he was finally able to wind up his red thread and put away his conspiracy board. He continued to keep a close eye on Cavem.

For his part in defeating the rats, Quincy was awarded a key to the city, meaning that he could come and go as he pleased. For the moment, he elected to stay in Bast, sharing his technical knowledge with a new generation of cats, and gaining a host of admirers.

Kafel's church was refurbished, and his robes were displayed behind the altar. His alley chapel became a shrine to the bishop, guarded by Missy and her Clutes. They were now the largest gang in the city, keeping an uneasy peace with the prowlers on the understanding that no flatpaw could enter their territory.

Bast soon returned to normal, with the conveyor belts removed and canines residing in the more tolerant parts of town. Most cats were grateful for their aid and, this time, the dogs were there to stay.

Greffin sat on Mandelo Island, panting in the beach heat, his hindquarters sinking into the sand. The sensitive dogs of Alcander wouldn't leave him stranded forever, he was sure; they wouldn't want his death on their pathetic conscience.

Until they collected him, he would make the most of the warm, picturesque island, rather than complaining about the burning sun and his itchy fur. He had no one to complain to.

He heard paw steps and squinted along the beach. He got up as quickly as his belly would allow, faltering backward in the sand; a lioness was running in his direction, her jaw set, tail flicking behind her.

Greffin turned to flee, falling on his flat face. When he turned onto his back, his muzzle was covered in sand and he spluttered, shaking his head. The lioness stood over him, her eyes keen and unyielding.

There were so many birds and fruits on Mandelo Island, but the lioness craved meat. Although Greffin did not offer much sustenance, Bridget was oh, so hungry.

Julius sat on his back patio, enjoying the faint buzz of city noises, admiring the shooting star that traversed the sky. He reached out, pawing at the light with his paw until it was gone.

"Did you see that?" he asked Moira, who was sprawled on a lounger beside him. They both sipped on sour milk and basked in the pleasure of each other's company. Sal was attending a Catnip Anonymous meeting, so they had their home to themselves for a while.

"No, but you did," Moira replied. "That's good enough for me."

"I love you, you cheeky Siamese," said Julius.

"Ditto, darling," Moira purred. "Although you might get fed up with me now that you're retired."

"About that…"

"You're forming a pop duo with Quincy?" Moira giggled.

"No, this is serious. I've asked you to sacrifice so much for me. Dragged you into danger and all the way back here. It's time I did something for you. How would you feel if we moved to Carabas?"

"You know I have unfinished business there, and I don't dare leave Tarquin to his own devices for too long. Oh! There's one!" Moira said, gesturing at the heavens.

"I didn't see that one," said Julius sadly.

"I tried to catch it." Moira laughed, lightening the mood. "I'll never stop trying."

"Roy's given you an assignment there, hasn't he?"

"You know it." Julius smiled. "What do you say?"

"You'll have to break it to Sal," Moira replied.

"He has plenty of new dog friends. They think he's a hero."

"He is," said Moira. "He'll always be part of our family."

"Family? I like that."

"There will be more," said Moira, patting her stomach.

Julius turned to her, puzzled.

"Shooting stars," she said. "The sky is full of them."

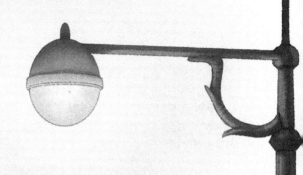

Epilogue

Staying Tuned

"I know you listeners out there been greedy for a fix of me, sending songs from the heart of Cat City. Well, speaking of getting fixed, which I wasn't, you'll be pleased to hear with your furry ears that my set-up is fully repaired and now I can broadcast farther than ever!

"That's right, Carabians, you better listen out for the best auditory experience a cat—or a dog—can have! Our wild waves are hittin' Waystation, Carabas, Ostan, Healing, the Isle of Dogs, and beyond! I hope you like action, 'cause that's what I'll be scratchin'!

"Coming up next, that rat-catching rhapsody that should be hospitalized, its beats are so sick. But before that, I got someone to tell you about. He's a pain in the tail, he's sarcastic but still fantastic, he's the cat you never heard of before but you're hearing about him now. Wherever you are, you can bet he's saved your neck. Pop a claw and scrape this down so you don't forget him. His name is Julius Kyle."

—WOTW radio broadcast
By DJ Scratch

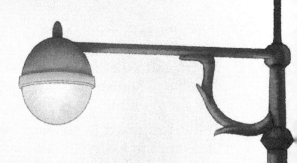

BOOK CLUB QUESTIONS

1. The trek through no cat's land is long and arduous. What vittles would you bring with you to make the journey bearable?

2. Should Moira have stuck with Julius, putting her career on hold?

3. If Julius could be king of Alcander for a day, what cat-friendly advancements do you think he would implement?

4. The Bay of Hounds is a treacherous body of water to swim. Should the cats have risked the ferry instead?

5. How much do you think Lugs's opinion of dogs has changed by the end of the story?

6. Otto is the rightful mayor of Bast. Why should or shouldn't he retake his position?

7. Woodrow presumed his fall through the garbage chute was an accident. If he was pushed, who was responsible?

8. Moira left Rusty Maxwell in partial charge of Carabas when she went off with Julius. Why did she choose him?

9. Julius promised to give a portion of his expense allowance to Kelly. What do you think he did with that allocated amount?

10. Julius wants to settle down, but his thirst for adventure isn't quite quenched yet. What compromise, if any, would you recommend to him?

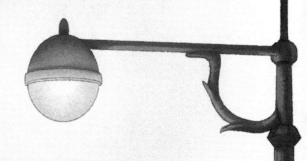

AUTHOR BIO

Nick Smith was born in Bristol, England. His books include *Eat Happy, The Secret Life of Teddy Bears, American Spirit,* and *Cloudwalking.* He is also a feature film director and producer, with 100 movies and TV credits, including the award-winning action movie *Cold Soldiers* and the supernatural adventure *Fears,* which he directed and co-wrote. He lives in New York, where he works as a film professor.

Other works by Nick Smith

Fiction
Milk Treading
Cat City
The Cat Who Stole the Cream

Anthologies
Eat Happy
The Secret Life of Teddy Bears

Poetry
American Spirit
Cloudwalking
Songs for Persephone

Non-fiction
Fletcher Crossman: The Age of Endarkenment
Scriptwriting: The Secrets Unleashed

**Discover more at
4HorsemenPublications.com**

10% off using HORSEMEN10